I0760312

DEON

KINGDOM OF FAIRYTALES
SEASON FOUR

You all know the story of your favorite fairytale, but did you ever wonder what happened after the fairytale ending? Well we know. Not all afters end up happily, sometimes the real adventure starts much later...

Following famous fairytale characters, eighteen years after their happily ever after, the Kingdom of Fairytales offers an edge of the seat thrill ride in an all new and sensational way to read.

Lighting-fast reads you won't be able to put down

Fantasy has never been so epic!

KINGDOM
OF
FAIRYTALES
URBIS PRISON
SHIPLEY
THE VALE
AZREN
BADALAH
KISBU
DESERT
DRACONIS
ZHORE
ELDER
MOSA
ABORIA
URBIS
AZURE
ENCHANTIA
AIRE
SKYLA
EMERALD CITY
OZ
FLORIS
TULIS
THE FORGE
ARCADIA
RENAIS
MELFALL
ATLANTICE
ANTLA
W
E
S

ISBN: 978-1-989997-26-0
Enchanted Quill Press

Contaact the author at www.enchantedquillpress.com
Cover by Enchanted Quilll Press
Interior Formatting by Enchanted Quill Press
Editing by Rose Lipscomb

KING OF DEVOTION

25TH MARCH

The sun made its final leap above the horizon and flooded the garden with thick golden light. A sunbeam dove between the leaves of an apricot tree and touched Lilian's hair with fire, blessing her blonde waves with a sheen that put the stars to shame.

Not that she noticed. The princess of Floris, clad in a dressing gown over her pajamas, was too busy making encouraging noises at one of her pups to worry about her hair. She tossed a felted ball across the grass, and the dog bounded after it for the fifth time, and, for the fifth time, it utterly failed to grasp the concept of bringing the thing back.

Lilian called to the puppy, whose curly white fur had already gotten stained from a romp through one of my flowerbeds, and the dog happily pranced back to her, leaving the ball lying in the dew-soaked grass.

"You're dumb," she said in a baby voice to the puppy. "You're so dumb, and I love you. Yes, I do. Who's the best puppy?"

I suppressed a snort, but not well enough. She glanced up and caught my eye from across the lawn. She burst into laughter that echoed across the grass, the sound as musical as the birdsong that filled the gardens at this hour.

"You're judging me," she called. "I can tell."

"I'm judging your dog," I called back from where I knelt in a bed of violets. "What is this, the third morning in a row?"

"Fourth," she said.

Serving as the palace's head gardener might have made me the luckiest man in the world, but it was watching Lilian on mornings like this that made me the happiest. She retrieved the ball for the dog and threw it again, then ran headlong after it to show the creature what it was supposed to do. The attempt was an unmitigated failure, but the way her dressing gown billowed out behind her as the pup galloped at her heels was a thing of beauty.

Eventually, as she had every morning, she gave up. She clipped the dog's lead back onto its embroidered collar and stopped on her way back to the palace to frown down at me with her hands on her hips. The sky behind her had lightened to a dazzling blue, and I had to squint to make out her face.

"You haven't wished me happy birthday yet."

I smirked up at her. "It's barely past dawn."

"Which means you're late. I was born first thing in the morning."

I offered her my hand. It was grimy with soil, and

hers, when she gave it to me, was covered in grass stains. I kissed the back of her hand. The touch was nothing, and yet it made my heart race.

"Happy birthday, princess," I said.

Her answering smile lit up the garden better than the sun had.

"Thanks for my present."

"You knew it was from me?"

"A mountain of strawberries and strawberry blossoms delivered to my chamber before sunrise?" She laughed. "Who else could have sent that? They were delicious."

"I know. I grew them myself."

Her eyes were so blue they outdid the sky behind them. I was about to lose myself in them when her dog launched itself at me and started licking my face with tactless enthusiasm. I scratched the creature's ear and let it have its way with my cheeks, then handed it up to the princess.

"This is a pretty awful dog."

"The absolute worst," she said. She nuzzled the top of the puppy's head. "Can I come see you after luncheon? I want you to braid flowers into my hair."

I'd done this for her a thousand times since we were children, but today, knowing why she wanted to look her best, the thought of plaiting her beautiful golden waves made my throat close up. I swallowed and smiled up at her.

"Of course."

She offered me another of her heart-wrenching smiles and took off across the lawn, the puppy in her arms wriggling to be let down.

I had just finished transplanting a crate of violets into the flowerbed when a conversation wafted across the rose garden behind me. They weren't bothering to keep their voices down. No one did these days.

"It's no surprise he ended up where he is," Basil said. His musical voice, with its slight whine, put my teeth on edge. I'd always been friendly with Basil, right up until I'd been named Head Gardener. These days, it seemed he'd just as soon spit as look at me.

I understood why he was jealous, but understanding didn't make it feel better.

"As if any of us really had a shot," Chervil grumbled.

He was in his fifties and had been working as a palace gardener for decades, certainly longer than I'd been alive. I understood his resentment, too.

"Kid was in old Hedley's pocket from the minute he started toddling around the kitchen gardens," he added.

Basil scoffed under his breath. "Forget about Hedley's favoritism. If you want to know what happened, you need look no further than the royal family."

Their voices faded out.

The old head gardener, the royal family—it didn't matter who was involved, the one thing everyone agreed on was that I'd gotten my job due to someone playing favorites. After all, I'd been taken in as an infant by King Alder and Queen Rapunzel and raised alongside their daughter, sharing her private tutors and enjoying the privileges that came with the king and queen knowing my name.

It didn't matter that I'd started as a kitchen hand and only become an apprentice gardener after I'd shown a gift for horticulture. It didn't matter that I'd trained that gift day in and day out for thirteen years or that Hedley had worked me harder than anyone else on the staff. No, if the gossips were to be believed, I had this job because I'd wormed my way into the king's good graces, and that was the end of it.

I took a deep breath as I packed up my tools. I had to figure out a way to prove myself and to make sure everyone on my staff felt valued. That was the only way forward. But first, I had to finish this morning's tasks so I could spend the afternoon with Lilian—one last afternoon before I let her go for good.

Lilian threw open the door to one of the garden sheds. "I've been looking everywhere for you!"

I hung my rake on its hook and glanced past her to the sky outside.

Lilian raised an eyebrow at me. "You worked through lunch, didn't you?"

"It's the Spring Flower Festival." I brushed my hair out of my eyes. "I'm moving nonstop, and there's still too much to do."

She held up a small straw pail. The cork of a lemonade bottle peeked out the top. "I had a feeling."

The thoughtfulness of the gesture made my stomach clench. I forced a smile.

"This, right here, is why I'm so supportive of the monarchy," I said. "Thanks, Lils."

"You can eat while I gather flowers," she said.

I sat on a boulder in the shade of a myrtle tree and devoured my sandwich and hard-boiled eggs while I watched her walk thoughtfully along paving-stone paths, picking blooms with care as she went.

The palace of Floris was home to over forty acres of gardens, most of them dedicated to flowers of some kind or another. This particular garden, though, was special. Five years ago, Hedley had given me free rein to design and tend my own quarter-acre patch of land.

He'd suggested I try raising some of the kingdom's prized tulip varieties or plant a kitchen garden full of herbs and vegetables.

But I had known immediately what I wanted to do with the rich earth.

I'd filled it with lavender and daisies and baby's breath, half a dozen different kinds of roses and just as many lilies, three different strains of the Queen's Tulips, and a scattering of other flowers that were both colorful and sturdy enough to survive handling and hours away from their roots. Every bloom that stretched toward the sun of my garden did it in hopes of someday gracing Princess Lilian's beautiful hair.

A kerchief full of blossoms landed on the ground next to me with a soft thump like glimmers of glass.

"Is this enough?" Lilian said.

She knew she'd picked too many; her little smirk made that clear. I shook my head at her and washed down the last bite of my sandwich with a long swig of cold lemonade. It was the cook's special recipe, flavored with mint leaves and orange blossoms. I offered Lilian the bottle and watched as she sipped and closed her eyes in enjoyment.

I loved the way Lilian savored lemonade. If there was beauty or pleasure to be had in a moment, she was the first to find it.

"Sit," I said. "Did you bring your comb?"

She pulled it from a pocket of her gown and settled on a smaller stone in front of me. I ran the golden comb through her hair. The way the strands parted and fell together again reminded me of the way water tumbled from the garden's many fountains. I ran my nail along Lilian's scalp, separating the hair into segments, and she gave a soft sigh of contentment.

My skin tingled at the noise, and I made sure to drag my nails softly across her head for a few moments before I started braiding in earnest.

"How are you feeling?" I said as I tucked a pale pink rose into the plait.

She didn't have to ask what I meant. She fidgeted a little. "I'm all right," she lied.

"Are you nervous?"

"No, of course not."

Another lie. I leaned forward to pick up a spray of lavender. My lips brushed against her hair, and it was everything I could do to stop myself from kissing her.

I'd kissed Lilian before, on the cheek or the hand or the top of the head. They were chaste pecks, the kind of thing that could happen between friends.

They weren't enough, and knowing I could never have what I wanted made it hard to breathe.

"You're not nervous at all?" I said. I let my voice be teasing, let my fingers be light as they twisted the next strand of her hair into place. "Not even a little bit? You're meeting your future husband today."

She laced her fingers together. "Not in the slightest. What is there to be nervous about?"

There were a hundred things, and I wasn't going to be the person to bring them up.

"I'm glad to hear it." I wove a delicate pink poppy into her hair. "If anyone's going to get butterflies today, it'll be the duke. He's not going to know what to do with himself when he sees for himself how pretty you are."

She laughed, and her shoulders tensed. I ran my fingernail along her scalp again as I reached the nape of her neck, and she relaxed.

"You're going to be fine, Lils," I said. "Your parents wouldn't have chosen the duke if they didn't think he was a good man."

"I know." She twisted her hands in her lap.

We'd spent our lives knowing this day would come, and for the last few years, I'd been dreading it. Now that her future husband was on his way to the palace, I had run out of time for wishing things could be different. I arranged a white daisy into her braid, followed by a vivid orange chrysanthemum.

"Oh!" I said as if I'd just remembered something important. "I keep forgetting to tell you. That bird came back—you remember the robin that kept making mischief in the kitchen gardens? He decided the raspberry patch is his personal fortress, and he's being a real jerk about it. Hollis finally had to come get me yesterday so she could prune the bushes without him dive-bombing her."

I spent the rest of the braid recounting the adventures of the bird who had taken the existence of palace gardeners as a personal affront. Slowly, Lilian's anxiety seemed to leak away, and by the time I was finished with her hair, she seemed almost back to her normal cheerful self.

Still, there was a tightness to her face when she turned around to have me check the front of her hair. I tucked a rose behind her ear. Before I could talk myself out of it, I kissed her gently on the forehead.

"I have a gift for you," I said. "Wait here."

When I got back, she was sitting patiently on a stone bench surrounded by roses. She was every bit a lady, her early deportment training visible in her graceful posture and the fold of her hands in her lap. Still, the slight jiggle of her foot revealed her nerves.

I approached, the gift held behind my back.

"Want to guess what it is?"

She gave me a calculating look. “A lizard.”

“I already brought you a lizard this week.” The creature had been tiny and nimble, covered in dark scales dotted with vivid green spots. She had let it run up and down her arms until she’d finally set it free in the succulent bed where I’d found it.

She pursed her lips. “Some kind of fruit, then. Perhaps one of the peaches you’ve been talking nonstop about this year.”

“Floris has a pleasant climate, but it’s not so warm that we’d get peaches this early. Besides, those trees won’t produce for another two years.”

“Then, I give up.”

“Close your eyes and hold out your hand.”

She obeyed, then cracked one eye open to watch me.

“You’re cheating.”

“I don’t know what you’re going to give me.”

“Do you trust me or not?”

She sighed and closed her eyes again. Carefully, I placed the stem of the passiflora bloom between her fingers, and a slight smile crossed her face as she recognized that I’d given her some sort of plant. I arranged the flower so she would get the full effect, and told her to open her eyes.

She did open them, normally at first and then so wide I laughed. She blinked, stared at the flower, and then looked up at me with her mouth slightly open.

“Deon!” she finally exclaimed.

I sat on the bench next to her. “Do you like it?”

“What on earth is it? It’s stunning.”

She twirled the stem between her fingers, and the enormous face of the flower smiled up at her.

The flower’s ten pointed petals ringed a central explosion of curling purple filaments that twisted and spiraled in wiggly coils. The petals beneath were the creamy white of coconut flesh, and yellow stamens glittered with pollen in the flower's center. Lilian raised the flower to sniff it, and her eyes widened at the fragrance—a sweet blending of jasmine blossoms and fresh pineapple.

"It's called a passiflora," I said.

"It's unreal." She looked up at me, blue eyes still huge. "You grew this?"

I shifted on the bench. Despite the strain of the day, excitement bubbled in the pit of my stomach. "It's not a difficult seed to obtain. We grow them elsewhere in the garden, but not like this. Not this big."

"Nor this beautiful. It's bigger than my palm." She held up one of her delicate hands to compare, and the flower covered it almost all the way up her fingers.

"I've always been all right with flowers," I said. In truth, I was more than all right. Hedley had said once that he'd never seen someone with such a green thumb. I didn't want to mention that to Lilian, though. The rest of the gardeners already thought I'd gotten too big for my britches. I didn't need Lilian to share their opinions. "These past few months, though..."

I trailed off. It was difficult to explain how things had changed—not just in the size and beauty of the blooms I had produced, but in the way the plants seemed connected to me somehow as if I'd woken up one day and learned to speak their silent language.

"You *are* the head gardener."

I shook my head. "It's more than that. I feel like I understand them somehow." I furrowed my brow, trying to find the right words to explain it, but I'd always been better with plants than with words. "I got a private garden as part of my promotion, remember?"

She nodded. "Everyone remembers. You didn't talk about anything else for a week."

Maybe that was why the other gardeners were annoyed with me.

"I've been experimenting there," I said, brushing the thoughts of my staff aside. "With flowers, mostly."

Lilian smirked. "I assumed you'd just started growing five thousand kinds of strawberries."

I shook my head at her in mock disapproval, but couldn't help cracking a smile. Lilian never lost an opportunity to tease me about my fondness for strawberries. I'd never told her the only reason I liked them so much was because they were the first plant we'd ever grown together, back when we were children studying simple botany.

"That will be my next project," I said. "Five thousand strawberry varieties, and maybe an apple tree just to mix things up."

"I wouldn't put it past you."

Lilian grinned at me, her smile full of light. We sat in the most expansive and well-tended gardens in all of Floris, and of the thousands of unique blossoms and breathtaking floral displays, she captivated me the most.

My gaze stayed on her smile even as it faded, my attention caught on the rosy curve of her lips and the dainty freckle just above her mouth. The air between us filled with electricity. My heart thudded in my chest. I wanted those lips—wanted to catch them with my own and taste Lilian's sweetness.

Her breath skipped. Her fingertips twitched against the stem of the flower, and she leaned toward me.

I turned abruptly away and stared resolutely across the garden. In the distance, a tree danced in the breeze, and its glossy leaves caught the sunshine and tossed it back in fragile flashes of light.

"You should go in." My voice was strained and throaty. "The duke will be here soon."

Lilian hesitated for a long moment, and then her hand closed over mine. Reflexively, my fingers squeezed hers.

"We have an hour still," she said, and the weight of the words almost crushed me. "Can I see your garden?"

It would be like showing her a piece of my heart. And just like my heart, it was already hers.

My private garden was a long walk from the ones that ringed the palace. We passed through a rose garden, full of vivid pink buds peeking out of their tight casings, then a stand of willows ringing a pond that held ducks and a few elegant swans. Beyond that, was an orchard full of spring blossoms that perfumed the air. Lilian twirled and laughed as pink blossoms fluttered down on our heads like slow-moving rain. I watched her and wished I could save the joy on her face as easily as I could pluck a flower or harvest seeds for next year's planting.

Past the orchard, tucked into a walled-off corner, the stone walls of my garden stood heavy with climbing ivy. I brushed aside a rogue vine hanging over the wooden door. Behind me, Lilian stopped and hung back, as if she suddenly unsure whether she was really allowed.

I gestured her forward.

"You must be very quiet," I said, making my voice low and solemn. "The dandy lions might bite."

She froze, then narrowed her eyes at me and swatted

at my arm. "You think you're funny, don't you?"

"I'm hilarious."

I pulled out the ring of keys that always hung from my belt and found the worn key that had once belonged to Hedley and was now mine. It fitted smoothly into the old lock.

I pushed the door open and nodded at Lilian. She stepped cautiously over the threshold, and I guided her through the doorway with my hand on the small of her back.

Her sharp intake of breath was everything I had hoped for. She turned slowly as she walked down the paving stone path, lips parted in amazement.

I closed the door behind us and leaned up against it. "You like it?"

"Deon," she breathed, and then she didn't seem capable of saying anything more.

The garden was wild, every corner bursting forth in a profusion of leaves and blossoms. Vines swung overhead, draping from the stone walls and tree branches and forming a jungle-like canopy that filtered the light and made it fall on dappled patterns across Lilian's face. The paving stones below were hedged in on every side by moss and succulents—ground covers with opposing needs, that shouldn't be able to survive side-by-side in the same soil. They grew anyway, each patch of living carpet lush with life.

Flowers surrounded us in more colors than I could accurately name. The pinks alone were overwhelming—rose and peach and mauve and salmon and magenta and a soft shade the color of Lilian's favorite dancing slippers. Lilian passed under an arbor that dripped with pale purple wisteria, then stopped to smell a bearded iris the deep garnet of wine. White flutterbys from the nation of Skyla wiggled as Lilian passed them, and every tiny bloom on the compact bush launched itself into the air. The flock of white blossoms shimmered and soared around the garden, darting over vines and between tree branches and eventually settling on a patch of sky-blue poppies like snow on cool blue ice.

Lilian stopped next to a cluster of gilded goldenrod and touched a flower. The tiny metallic blossoms rubbed off on her fingers like gold dust. She turned to me, frowning.

"This shouldn't be blooming yet," she said. "Goldenrods don't come in until autumn."

I pushed myself away from the door, the excitement from before bubbling again in the pit of my stomach. "I know." I stopped next to her and looked down at the sparkling flowers. "It's not the only thing that isn't doing what it should." I nodded toward a young apricot tree, which had been only a sapling when I'd transplanted it here and had, over the course of a year, aged impossibly fast and started to produce jewel-like fruits that seemed to only grow to the peak of ripeness and no more.

Lilian searched my face, but I didn't have answers for her. I wasn't even sure I knew which questions to ask.

"I don't know why it's like this," I said. "Everything I touch decides to thrive. I've been cross-breeding flowers and growing things I've never seen before."

"Hedley taught you well," Lilian said. "Better than I imagined."

She turned again, taking in the literal dancing flames at the heart of the orange dragontree blossoms and the soft white glimmers that pulsed beneath the caps of the near-black moonlight mushrooms. She faced me and stopped, and her hands settled against my chest.

Somehow, my arms ended up twined around her waist.

She looked up at me, eyes as blue as the poppies.

"I'm scared," she said.

The admission hung between us. I brushed my thumb against the small of her back.

"I said I wasn't nervous about meeting the duke," she said. "I lied. I'm nervous. I'm terrified to leave this garden and leave my childhood and leave y—"

The last word died on her lips. One of her hands clenched into a gentle fist against my chest.

"Part of me always thought it would be funny if we ended up together," she continued, more quietly. The corner of her mouth trembled, and I wasn't sure whether a laugh or a cry was trying to escape. "Me with the golden hair, you with the golden eyes. Our children would look like little sunbeams."

She tried to smile.

Everything inside me twisted, my heart retreating into my ribcage, my stomach vaulting up where my heart belonged.

I brushed a strand of the golden hair from her cheek. "That would have been something."

Her back moved under my hand as she took in a deep, shuddering breath. "Deon?"

"Lils?"

She looked at me, her gaze jumping from one of my eyes to the other. She grabbed my shirt in her delicate fists and pulled me down to her. She hesitated when her lips were inches from mine, and the lemonade scent of her breath warmed my mouth.

I closed the gap. Her lips were as soft as I had imagined and sweeter than strawberries. They moved against mine, gently at first and then with a hunger that mirrored my own. She pressed her body closer as she fell deeper into the kiss, everything about her soft and yielding and perfectly formed to fit me.

A thousand years of that embrace would have been too little, and when she pulled away, it was as if the sun had gone behind a cloud. Birds chirped around us, and the flutterby blossoms' petals quivered on the poppies.

"I'm going to marry the duke," Lilian said. "I have a duty to Floris. I'm going to do my duty, and I'm going to try to be a good wife."

Slowly, gently, she ran one fingertip across my bottom lip. The touch tickled and sent an unbearable tingle down my spine. I froze, afraid of the consequences of allowing myself a single inhale.

"But you will always be my first love," Lilian whispered. "And you will always have a home in my heart."

She looked over my face as if trying to memorize it. Then, before I could blink, she turned away and headed back down the garden path. I watched her go, and it was a long time before I dared move again.

26TH MARCH

I stabbed my spade into the soil, breaking up the clumps with far more force than was necessary. Once the dirt was broken up, I used my hands to mix in heaps of rich, fragrant compost.

We had tools for this sort of thing, and it was the kind of work that usually got delegated to the apprentices. After yesterday with Lilian, though, I needed hard physical labor. It would tire me out and make it easier to sleep, hopefully without my dreams replaying that kiss over and over in my mind.

In the meantime, I fixed my thoughts resolutely on the upcoming Spring Flower Festival.

It was an annual event, our chance to show off new plant varieties, trade tricks, and seeds with horticulturists from other nations and compete with breeders and gardeners from all around the world. It was an enormous event and my first-ever as Head Gardener.

The list of things to be completed over the next month overwhelmed me, and I welcomed the chance to run over our to-do list in my mind.

My staff and I needed to harden off the thousands of seedlings we would sell at the festival, cut the blooms the palace florists would arrange into stunning displays, set up the elaborate garden galleries, finalize the schedule of speeches and classes that would be offered throughout the event, and, most importantly, pack up the thousands of tulips and tulip bulbs that were the highlight of the event every year. That was to say nothing of the other tasks that made up each day, from feeding the roses to making sure our youngest garden apprentice, Aspen, was managing to avoid overwatering the greenhouse cacti.

I finished spreading the compost and began planting the host of summer-blooming bulbs that would line this new walkway: fat pink begonias, showy orange cannas, and cheerful yellow lilies with their speckled faces. The path would be beautiful. I took a moment to feel gratitude that, at least, Lilian would be able to see these flowers when they bloomed. She was the heiress to the throne of Floris, after all, which meant the duke would move to the palace after their wedding.

Knowing Lilian would marry another man made every corner of my soul ache. But even though I was losing my love, I wouldn't lose my best friend. Not entirely. She would still be here, and I would still grow flowers for her hair.

It had to be enough.

When the morning chill had been burned off by

the sun, I buried the last bulb and stood to stretch. I tossed my tools atop the compost in my wheelbarrow and wheeled up the path to the palace. Colorful poppies waved at me from either side of the walkway, their petals like ruffled orange silk or striped yellow and white chiffon. And there, up ahead, were the Queen's Tulips.

Floris had gardens to rival any in the world, but when it came to our tulips, there could be no rivalry. Their variety and abundance seemed to grow by the year, and the blooms near the palace were the brightest jewels of them all.

They glittered in the sunshine as I approached, their waxy petals shimmering with gentle iridescence. Queen Rapunzel had bred these tulips shortly after her marriage to King Alder, and she had spent years refining and perfecting the variety until they were beautiful enough to take my breath away. I had never seen a mermaid, but the way the tulip petals sparkled in the light made me think these flowers must look like mermaid scales, or perhaps like gossamer fairy wings or gleaming unicorn horns. They came in a dozen multicolored varieties, but every strain bore the same unearthly sense of magic.

Hedley had told me time and time again that it wasn't magic, just patience and a keen sense for selective breeding. I still didn't believe him. The tulips were enchanting. It was a relief to know that no matter how much work I had to do before the Flower Festival, these dazzling flowers would carry the day.

Except...

My heart pounded as if urging me to pay attention. I stopped walking and set down the wheelbarrow, then approached the tulips nearest the palace. They were sitting in the shade of the castle walls, so perhaps—

But no, it wasn't a trick of the light.

The petals had turned gray.

I knelt and bent across the wide bed of tulips that ringed the base of one of the palace towers. The blooms here had petals of variegated champagne-gold and peach, or at least, they were supposed to. But a few of the flowers, those closest to the palace walls, had turned the same dull, ashy shade as the stone behind them.

I touched one of the petals, very gently. It was soggy, and the normally stiff leaves hung limp. The stem seemed ready to drop with the weight of the bloom—or what had once been the bloom. I couldn't quite call the sad thing atop this plant a *flower.*

Tulips didn't usually suffer from root rot in the ground, at least, not in our gardens. If there was any plant we knew how to keep happy, it was these.

Even so, something had happened—someone must have overwatered, or the shade of the palace had allowed too much moisture to settle into the bulbs. I made a mental note to talk to the tulip specialists about this, although I didn't relish the thought of taking Jonquil to task for neglecting some of his plants.

Unfortunately, that came with the territory of my new job.

"It can't be all be private gardens and losing the woman of my dreams," I muttered to the dying tulips.

They didn't answer.

~

Jonquil received the news as graciously as I'd expected.

"Are you accusing me of something?" He folded

his arms across his chest, his white-blond eyebrows lowering in anger. He was a good decade older than me and a head taller. He narrowed his ice-blue eyes.

I stood my ground. "You're a tulip specialist. Something is wrong with the Queen's Tulips. I'm just letting you know."

"Something is wrong with a handful of the Queen's Tulips, out of thousands," he corrected, voice thick and dismissive. "You think that's worth calling a staff meeting over, *sir?*"

The word dripped with sarcasm. I clenched my jaw and forced my face to stay neutral.

"I just want to be sure that if we're overwatering that area, we stop doing it."

Behind him, the other tulip specialists, Myrtle and Olive, watched us in silence. I'd called all three of them to the bulb storehouse to discuss the issue, but only Jonquil had spoken up so far.

"The festival is coming up," he said. "We have better things to do."

"Then handle this quickly, and you can move on."

We locked gazes, testing strength against strength. He was bigger and older, but I was Head Gardener. Finally, he tore his attention away from me and scoffed.

"Fine," he muttered.

"Thank you. The Queen's Tulips are being entered into several festival competitions. We need to be sure they remain healthy."

Cautiously, Olive raised her hand. She was only a few years older than me and new to the palace. "I think it might be my fault," she said. "I'm usually responsible for that area, and I've been so busy packing up the Cream Puff and Angelique bulbs that I may have been neglectful." She glanced at Jonquil. "I'll look into it."

I shot Jonquil a look as if to say, *was that so hard?* He ignored me and tapped an impatient foot.

"That's all, thank you," I said. "Dismissed."

Jonquil seemed as though he had a few more thoughts to share at the notion of being *dismissed* by me, but he thought better of it when Myrtle gave him a contemptuous look on her way out. He tossed me a dirty glare and strode out the door. Olive watched him go, then shrugged a shoulder. One of her brown braids slipped off her shoulder at the movement.

"Don't know why he's got such a chip on his shoulder," she said. "You'd think he'd just be glad to be working at the palace."

"I've stopped worrying about it," I lied. "We're all stressed about the Flower Festival. Things will cool off once it's over."

She drew her lips toward one corner, her face a comical picture of skepticism. I laughed, and she shook her head and traipsed out of the warehouse and into the bright sunshine.

I turned back to one of the dead flowers I'd placed on one of the worktables in the warehouse before I'd called our meeting. The tulip's bulb was rotten, and the plant gave off a sickly sweet odor I hadn't noticed before amid the breeze and the fragrance of the other blooms.

I had grown wondrous plants in my private garden—plants that shouldn't have been able to exist, at least, not in those growing conditions or this season. And yet everything flourished in a way I couldn't just put down to my long apprenticeship and good judgment. And, I'd heard of people having plant magic before. Some gardeners had an affinity with the earth and with growing things. A magician gardener had first created the dragontree with its flaming blossoms and gentle heat.

Perhaps, I was another such person.

I held a hand over the tulip bulb and tried to push life back into it. I concentrated, forcing all of my attention and focus into the flower and the air between us, straining for any hint of magic or subtle energy. I squeezed my eyes shut and imagined the bloom growing bright and strong again.

I opened my eyes.

Nothing had happened.

Of course, it hadn't. And I had better hope with all the power of my lucky stars that Jonquil would never know I'd tried to *magic* the tulips back to life. If he thought I was an arrogant upstart now, I couldn't even imagine what he'd think of me if he knew I'd thought, for even a second, that I might be the equal of the creator of the dragontree.

I dumped the rotting bulb into a rubbish bin and hurried out of the warehouse. I had things to do, and pretending to be some kind of mighty plant wizard was an even worse waste of time than pining over the princess of Floris.

~

The sweet, dark, taste of the cook's smoked salmon spread across my tongue, and my body welcomed the food. Breakfast felt like a lifetime ago, and this lunch was a late one. Somehow, I'd managed to carry it all the way from the servants' dining hall to my private garden without getting stopped by someone on my staff.

Every moment I had to myself between now and the Flower Festival would be a stolen one. Stolen—and necessary. I needed every spare second to work on my own entry into the festival's biggest contest.

There were dozens of competitions throughout the course of the event, with prizes awarded for things like biggest pumpkin, most beautiful themed garden, and best-tasting orchard fruit. The highlight of them all, though, was the flower contest, and I intended to win.

This was my chance to prove that I deserved my job—to the other gardeners, and to myself.

I layered salmon and cheese onto the next fat slice of bread and tore through the makeshift sandwich as I contemplated the tasks ahead of me. This wasn't just an exercise in selective breeding: My entry into the flower competition required careful pruning, excellent timing, ...and a little magic.

Even an ordinary person like me could purchase water infused with the essence of draconite, as well as fertilizer made from unicorn droppings and decayed lotus leaves. All these little additions were allowed in the flower competition, even encouraged, and I wasn't about to dismiss anything that could give me an edge.

I heaped soil around the base of my flowers and pruned their extra buds with a small pair of silver scissors. I hummed as I worked, playing against the melodies of the songbirds that called my private garden home. Time slipped away, and for a while, I didn't think about the rest of the competition, about Jonquil, about my responsibilities as Head Gardener, or even about Lilian. The world narrowed to the size of my hands as they dug and clipped and arranged.

I was only roused by the peals of the palace bells striking out a cheerful melody. It was six o'clock; the household was being called to take a moment to express thanks. The ritual had been started by Queen Rapunzel shortly after her marriage to the king, and those bells had guided the course of my childhood. I stopped what I was doing, as always, and savored a deep breath.

During our childhoods, Lilian and I had often stopped playing when the bells sounded, long enough to shout our thanks back and forth to one another. We had tossed the words around like a ball: *I'm thankful for lemon tarts! I'm thankful for hummingbirds! I'm thankful for strawberry jam! You're always thankful for strawberry jam, Deon, show a little imagination!*

Now, I touched the thick green stem of the flower before me.

I'm thankful for my job.

I'm grateful for my place at the palace.

I'm grateful for Lilian. Please let him be good to her.

The last bell faded to silence, and I realized the light in the garden was taking on the golden hue of early evening. It wouldn't be true dusk for another couple of hours, but springtime evenings seemed to stretch out in Floris as if the sun itself wanted to linger over the beauty of our gardens.

I put my tools neatly back in the small shed in the corner of my garden, then made my way out and toward the palace. The sweet aroma of jasmine and the subtle beeswax scent of wisteria danced around me as I walked down a paved path under a long arbor.

A few elegant figures came down the path toward me, the women's skirts, the same pale purples and whites of the wisteria overhead. The men were both clothed in rich fabric, the king's a deep emerald silk and the others in ruby and sapphire velvet.

I stepped aside to let them pass, my heart pounding. I bowed as the king approached, then took in the people with him: an older man and woman, both wearing silver circlets, and a handsome man a few years older than me, whose ruby tunic revealed a trim shape and aristocratic posture.

"Your Majesties," I murmured.

I waited for them to pass, but King Alder stopped and nodded at me.

"Deon," he said with a characteristically kind smile.

He was a robust man still, only in his forties, and Queen Rapunzel beside him was radiant. Her bright golden hair was concealed today by an elaborate lace-and-silk headscarf that fluttered prettily down her back, but her face glowed as brightly as ever.

She held out a hand to me. I was supposed to take the hand and bow over it with a delicate air kiss, but the queen had never allowed formalities between us. She squeezed my hand instead in warm greeting.

"Deon," she repeated. She turned to their guests. "Your Graces, this is Mr. Deon Gilding, our head gardener and someone very dear to us all. He's in charge of the palace's preparations for the Spring Flower Festival."

"A momentous task indeed," the older man said.

I didn't need introductions: This could only be Duke Markus, the former Duke of Thornton, and Lilian's future father-in-law.

"I hope I can represent Floris well, Your Grace." I bowed deeply.

"His displays are going to be beautiful," Lilian said.

So far, I had avoided looking at her. Now, I couldn't keep my gaze from flitting toward her face. A single glimpse was enough to reveal a few important facts: she was smiling at me, she was nervous, and she was arm-in-arm with her betrothed.

Her future husband and my future king, Duke Gerritt Remington, nodded politely at me. "If these gardens are any indication, it's little wonder our Spring Flower

Festival is the highlight of every Florian's year. Princess Lilian showed me the hedge maze this morning, and it was nothing short of an experience."

I thanked him with a bow. The hedge maze had been on the palace grounds since before I'd arrived, but I had worked with Hedley a few years back to fill it with surprises: a statue clothed in a gown of climbing ivy here, a cluster of whistling bluebird bells fluttering in the air there, and in the center, a stunning display of Floris's native flowers arranged in an old fountain, the sprays of white bridesbloom and lavender sweetchain tumbling down its layers like water.

Lilian smiled up at Duke Remington. "I've always thought that," she said. "The festival being the highlight of the year, I mean."

It was such a tiny bit of common ground, but watching her find it with someone else made my stomach clench.

I'm grateful for Lilian, I reminded myself. *I want her to be happy.*

I just wished she could be happy with me.

She did, too. The way her gaze caught on my face right after she spoke made our agreement on the subject clear as day. But I was a commoner—not just a commoner, but her servant. The idea of the crown princess of Floris marrying her gardener was laughable.

Having Lilian's love but being unable to act on it felt like I'd been whisked away to the most beautiful scenery on earth and then forced to appreciate it from behind the bars of a cage.

It was a cage I would have to accept. Royalty had to marry within the aristocracy. There had always been rumors that King Alder and Queen Rapunzel had broken that rule, but I had never given the gossip any credit. Queen Rapunzel was every bit the monarch, and King Alder was too honorable to have opposed his parents' wishes and gone against the laws of the land.

Anyway, royal marriages weren't just about laws. Thornton was Floris's strongest duchy, with a militia that put the rest in the land to shame. And the duke's family had wealth that rivaled the king's.

There were a dozen reasons Lilian should marry Duke Remington, and the only argument against it was the wistful look in her eyes.

"I hope the palace plans to display some Thornton roses," Duke Remington said, jerking me from my thoughts. He offered a warm smile. "I am, of course, not impartial, but I think the varieties from my home province are some of the most beautiful in the country."

"No garden would be complete without Thornton reds," I said with a slight bow. "And I wouldn't dream of leaving out some of your cabbage rose cultivars. The salmon blushed is a particular favorite of mine."

The duke's smile widened. "Mine also. Some call the bloom ostentatious, but I'm of the opinion that there is no such thing as *too much* when it comes to roses."

Thorns and stinging nettles, I was at risk of liking the man.

"I was particularly fond of the new raspberry freesia the palace debuted last year," Duchess Annemie said. "The scent was sublime. Will you be showing it again this year?"

"Yes, Your Grace," I said. "We'll also have seeds for sale, as well as freesia oil for perfumes."

Her cool smile broadened a little. "How delightful."

"I'd be happy to send a bottle to your quarters, Madam," I said.

The duchess accepted the offer with grace. Behind her, Lilian mouthed, *thank you,* and I glanced quickly away from her.

They moved on. I made my bows, then turned and marched away, all too aware of the sound of their footsteps receding down the wisteria path.

27TH MARCH

The tension outside the chamber was thick enough I could have cut it with a pair of pruning shears. The other applicants' covert glances had gotten less and less covert every time the Horticulture Council secretary had come out to this hallway to check on me.

The fourth time, my stomach twisted into a knot.

"Any luck?" the man asked kindly.

King Alder and Queen Rapunzel still hadn't arrived for our meeting with the Council—our meeting, which was supposed to be the first of the morning, and the completion of which would allow all these other gardeners and groundskeepers and florists to present their proposals to the group that was the final authority on the Flower Festival.

I shook my head, wishing I could disappear into my seat. It wasn't my fault the monarchs were late, and no one would dare to blame them when they arrived. But I was a boy with dirt under his nails, not a king. The others waiting in this corridor could give me all the filthy looks they liked.

"They must have gotten held up," I said.

I glanced down the line; an older man with an unkempt beard was giving me a distinctly unpleasant glare.

"There's no reason to keep delaying everyone else's meetings," I said. "I'm sure the king and queen won't mind waiting a few moments if you allow these other fine people to have their audiences first."

The secretary frowned, which made his already thin lips get even narrower.

"The Council traditionally uses its audience with the king and queen to inform the rest of its decisions throughout the day," he said.

"I understand that," I said. "But surely, it wouldn't hurt to let one or two people go ahead?"

The secretary hemmed and hawed and finally waved at the next person in line to come forward. There was an audible sigh of relief from a few in the queue.

I understood their frustration. The Flower Festival had us all on edge.

I sank back into my seat and silently prayed to whatever gods might be listening for the king and queen to arrive soon and safely. In the back of my mind, I prayed Lilian would arrive with them, for some unforeseeable reason, but then I took it back and hoped she *wouldn't* show up today because I didn't think I'd be able to get through this meeting with her watching me.

The Horticulture Council was one of the most powerful groups in Floris. Their opinions could make or break the career of any gardener, landscaper, or florist. I had some protection from their whims, thanks to the dumb luck of having been dropped off at the palace instead of an orphanage when I was a baby, but the butterflies in my stomach still performed acrobatic free dives at the thought of presenting to them.

Now that Lilian was to be married, this job was literally all I had. I couldn't be anything less than perfect today.

Murmuring voices drifted through the crack under the heavy door, not loudly enough that I could make out words but enough to convey tone: a quick, anxious pattering on the part of the man who'd just gone in to present, and calm, slow cadences from Council members.

Another person went ahead of me, then another. Each time the door opened and closed, the tension in the pit of my stomach tightened.

Where were the king and queen? It wasn't like them to be late. This was my first-ever meeting with the Horticulture Council, and the first time I would join the monarchs as one of their heads of staff. I was here to provide detailed information about the gardens and our plans for the festival, but King Alder and Queen Rapunzel were to lead the meeting. I couldn't do it without them.

By the time an hour had passed, the Council secretary's demeanor had changed. He pursed his lips at me as he led the next person into the room, skepticism etched on his face. I clenched my hands in my lap.

I was Head Gardener of the palace of Floris, I reminded myself silently. I belonged here, amid these gardeners and breeders from fine estates and universities and the city's Central Greenhouse. I might be young, and I might be new, and the monarchs might be late to our meeting, but I held a title equal to theirs, and my gardens were bigger.

Footsteps sounded at the end of the corridor. A few people whispered among themselves. I glanced up to see King Alder striding toward me, his deep purple tunic and regal bearing making his identity apparent.

Relief flooded my body, and I stood and bowed to the king. The polite smile he returned couldn't hide the lines of tension at the corners of his lips.

"Have a seat, Your Majesty," I said, gesturing at the open chair next to me. "I told the Horticulture Council to go ahead with their other appointments."

He nodded and sat, his posture as straight in the chair as it had been while he was standing. "I apologize for my lateness," he said.

I glanced down the corridor, noting both the absence of the queen and the curious eyes that were now fixed on us from every side.

"Where is—" I started, but the king shook his head at me. The gesture was barely perceptible but held all the force of a royal command.

I fell silent, and we waited our turn.

~

"And that brings our total number of applications to seventeen," King Alder concluded.

He nodded at me, and I pushed the sheaf of papers across the glossy black walnut table to Minister Acacia.

She glanced through the first couple to make sure I'd filled them out correctly, then gave the Head of Council, Minister Rosemary Yarrow, a small nod.

"I've also included my personal application to the Flower Competition," I said.

Minister Acacia raised one eyebrow. "Which division?"

"New Varieties," I said. "It's the last in that pile."

"Noted." She scribbled something in the lined journal in front of her. At the far end of the table, the secretary took detailed notes on an elegant brass typewriter that looked like it might be one of the newer models from the kingdom of The Forge.

Minister Balsam tapped the edge of the table with his pen. He was an intimidating man with silver hair and piercing black eyes, and I fought to stay still when his gaze landed on me.

"We were surprised when the palace appointed someone so young to your position."

I couldn't tell whether the words were a threat or a fact. His solemn face gave little away.

"Mr. Gilding has the full confidence of the palace," King Alder said smoothly. "As my wife often remarks, he was born for the job."

Minister Balsam nodded deeply at the king.

"Her Majesty will, of course, be correct," he said.

"I regret she wasn't able to join us this morning," King Alder said.

The air in the room thickened with curiosity, but it was clear the king wasn't about to give more information, and not even venerable Minister Yarrow seemed willing to ask.

"I think it's always nice to see new blood at the Flower Festival," Minister Blackwood said, offering me a smile that was almost as bright as her wispy auburn hair. “We look forward to seeing the youthful touch. I’m sure you’ll bring to the palace displays.”

“Thank you, ma’am,” I said. “I think you’ll be pleased. Our midnight garden promises to be something special.”

The meeting concluded with a few niceties between the king and Minister Yarrow, whose relationship I knew to be a long one, and then we were back in the corridor with the eyes of everyone in the hall on us again.

The churning in my stomach gave way to a flood of relief, and I enjoyed the sensation in silence as King Alder and I left. We passed through the front doors of the stately Horticulture Building doors and into bright sunlight.

“You did well in there today.” The king smiled at me, but it seemed forced.

“Thank you, Your Majesty.”

“Did you need a ride back to the palace?”

“No, thank you,” I said. “I need to stop by a few specialty florists’ shops.”

He inclined his head at me in farewell. The moment he turned away, his artificial smile disappeared.

I watched him walk down the Horticulture Building steps and toward his waiting carriage. His elegant posture held as much tension as poise, and the rigidity that cloaked his face was unnatural and more than a little disconcerting.

Before I could think it through, I jogged after him.

“Your Majesty?” I said.

He glanced over his shoulder as if he’d already forgotten I was there. I frowned a little.

“Sir,” I said cautiously, “are you all right?”

The mask over his face faltered for a moment, and suddenly, I wasn’t talking to the most powerful man in all of Floris. I was talking to Lilian's father and the compassionate man who'd taken me in when I'd had nowhere to go.

"Is it that obvious?"

I shoved my hands in my pockets and rocked back on my heels a little. "Not obvious. I'm sorry, I shouldn't presume."

He dismissed the remark with a single, economical shake of his head. "You're attuned to the living things around you as ever, Deon," he said. "Forgive me, I hope my preoccupation didn't affect the meeting. I imagine that was a significant event for you."

"It's not that. I just wanted to be sure you're feeling well."

King Alder sighed. "I am. Unfortunately, my wife is not."

I pushed my hands further into my pockets, like that could somehow keep me from fidgeting. "Queen Rapunzel?" I said. "What's wrong?"

My thoughts immediately darted to Lilian. Was she all right? Did she know?

"She's ill." King Alder glanced at the ground and up again. "It's not serious. The palace physician is attending to her, and she'll be quite all right. The timing is just unfortunate with Lilian's wedding approaching and our guests at the palace."

This wasn't the truth, or at least not all of it. I waited, and the king gave me a rueful smile.

"In truth, I just don't like it when she's uncomfortable," he admitted. "I'm fond of that woman. I start climbing the walls when she's doesn't feel well."

A memory flitted through my mind of the time Lilian had caught nettle pox. I had tried to help with the itching by bringing her a salve, but she'd quickly ordered me out of the room and told me, *Stop hovering, Deon, you're making me madder than the blasted spots!*"

I smiled at the king. "I can understand that. We all love Queen Rapunzel. Give her my best wishes for a quick recovery."

"I will," he said. "And Deon? Best not to mention this to anyone else, if you please. I'd hate for everyone to start panicking, what with the wedding so close. Especially to Lilian. I don't want her to worry."

"Of course, Your Majesty," I said.

I bowed, and he climbed into his carriage. The wheels clattered against the cobblestone streets as he drove away.

Water bubbled down the sides of a dozen fountains and splashed into the enormous pool. The evening air was chill and smelled fresh and clean.

I hopped lightly from one stone lily pad to another and paused to nudge Reed's shoulder. He looked up, startled, and his face broke into a grin.

"Shouldn't scare people like that, they might throw you in," he said.

Reed was one of the youngest gardeners and one of the few who still seemed to like me. I crouched next to him and poked the compact bloom of a pearl lotus floating on the pond. The shimmering white petals seemed to sneeze, and a soft cloud of sparkling pollen floated up, carrying a light sugar scent into the air.

"They seem healthier than last time I checked," I said.

"If we're not careful, they'll end up taking over the whole area." He gestured at a soft purple water hyacinth flower fluttering a few feet away. "Don't think those will be happy."

"You'll keep everyone playing nicely," I said. "I managed to hire an extra wagon to transport the water garden elements to the festival, by the way."

"What a hero," a voice drawled behind me. "The head gardener did his job. Round of applause, everybody."

I didn't need to look. The sudden tension in my shoulders identified the newcomer for me.

"I put the seedlings you asked for in the tea garden," Jonquil said, addressing Reed. "And I brought over a bag of compost."

"Thanks."

Reed's gaze darted to me, and he seemed on the verge of saying something, but I shook my head. He was friendly with almost everyone on staff; I didn't need him to ruin his comfortable position.

"Jonquil, don't be an ass," Briar said, coming up behind him.

She could talk like that: She was an attractive, confident young woman, and Jonquil was the kind of man who acted differently around attractive women. I shot her a grateful look, which she ignored.

As far as I could tell, she was as unhappy about my promotion as any of them, but she never let it affect her behavior. I wished some of her professionalism would rub off on Basil or Chervil or any of the others.

Jonquil pressed his lips into a thin line and retreated, his nose in the air ample evidence that his opinion of me hadn't changed, even if he didn't choose to voice it again.

Briar acknowledged me with the briefest of nods, then went to the farthest end of the garden and began checking the water lilies for signs of the beetle infestation we'd only just gotten under control.

"Don't take it personally," Reed said.

He was right, but it was easier said than done. Even here, in one of the most relaxing gardens in all the palace grounds, Jonquil had a way of getting under my skin.

I clapped Reed on the shoulder and walked away. Jonquil's bad attitude didn't have to affect me. I had earned my place here. I'd just had a meeting with the King of Floris and the Horticulture Council. If that wasn't evidence that I was doing all right, nothing was. I was fine. I was better than fine. I was—

"Who stole *your* seedlings?" Lilian asked dryly.

I started, then spun around. I'd walked right past her without noticing, and now she was watching me from a bench with an amused smile.

I ran a hand through my hair. "How long have you been sitting there?"

She rose, her warm pink skirts rippling like poppy petals in the wind.

"The whole time," she said. "From Jonquil leaving the water garden, to you leaving the water garden, to that grumpy look settling all over your face. I can talk to him, you know."

That was just what I needed, for the princess to come to my aid and make it clear to all the gardeners exactly what kind of palace pet I really was.

I shook my head. "I can deal with him."

"I know you can, I'm just not sure you will," she said.

As usual, Lilian had seen more deeply into me than I had planned.

She laced her arm through mine and started walking. I fell into step, matching my strides to her shorter ones.

"Papa said your meeting with the Horticulture Council went well," she said.

She glanced up at me, and my heart skipped a beat at the sight of her blue eyes shaded by the long lashes she'd inherited from her mother.

The king clearly hadn't told her about Queen Rapunzel's illness. That was for the best. Lilian was the kind of person to fret if any of her loved ones so much as stubbed their toe, and she worshipped her mother.

Now, she'd seen my frustration with Jonquil and wanted to cheer me up, so I let myself be cheered.

"It did go well," I admitted. "A few members of the Council seemed unsure about me, but Minister Blackwood was encouraging. And I think our festival displays will impress even stuffy old Minister Balsam."

"You're going to dazzle them."

There was absolute confidence in her voice. I wished I could bottle her faith and dab it on like a flower essence whenever I doubted myself.

"And what about you?" I said. "What have you been up to today?"

She bit her lip as if trying to suppress a smile. "I went boating," she said as if she was sharing a great secret. "Garritt took me out on the lake, and we fed the swans and had a picnic."

"*Garritt* did, huh?" I nudged her shoulder with mine and wiggled my eyebrows at her.

She flushed a pretty pink. "He is my future husband, Deon," she said. "You didn't think I was going to call him Duke right up to the wedding, did you?"

A small, private part of me had hoped she would. But that was a selfish corner of my soul, and I couldn't give in to those impulses. Not when Lilian's happiness was at stake.

"It sounds like you had a wonderful time," I said.

"I did." She flushed again. "Deon? I really like him. He's kind to me, and he seems really eager to do what's right for Floris."

"I'm glad." I squeezed her arm gently with mine. "You deserve the best, Lils. I hope he's everything you ever dreamed of."

~

I walked Lilian through the garden to the private door that opened straight from the rose beds to a flight of hidden stairs that ended in her chambers. The urge to kiss her goodnight gripped me, but I resisted it and gave her a warm smile instead. She disappeared through the wooden door, leaving me alone in the deepening dusk.

There were shortcuts I could take to the servants' chambers, but I didn't want to take them tonight. I could still smell Lilian's magnolia perfume, and I knew I wouldn't sleep so long as her scent clung to me. Instead of cutting between rose bushes or across grassy lawns, I made my way to one of the wide paved paths that connected the gardens. This was a longer walk to my chambers. I needed the time to cool down.

The path meandered through the tea garden and past a showy display of ornamental cabbages, then wove around the enormous blueberry patch the king had commissioned for his wife as a wedding gift. Finally, I broke off to the secluded path that led along the castle walls to one of the servants' doors.

This part of the garden had been created years ago by Hedley, who thought servants' areas should be just as beautiful as those meant for royalty, and I slowed down to breathe in the early night air and enjoy the dazzling display of tulips that surrounded this path. The blooms were closing up for the night, the petals shielding the pollen and keeping it safe and dry.

Most of them were, anyway. A few near the palace walls were still open.

Open, and gray.

I stopped in my tracks and squinted. Dusk often played tricks with my vision. But this was no trick. These blooms were dying.

I cursed under my breath. I didn't have time for a proper round of firehead blight or bulb rot. The Spring Flower Festival required the attention of every gardener, every moment of every day, and disease in these beds would demand the total focus of at least one tulip specialist.

I couldn't begin to imagine whom I'd pull from their festival responsibilities. Jonquil was the best at coaxing unhappy plants back to life, but he'd likely murder me if I tried to put him on this job. Myrtle would probably take on the task but be resentful, and rightly so; she had seniority over the others and shouldn't be stuck at the palace doing damage control when she could be sharing her expertise at the festival. Olive would probably step in with a good attitude, but would it be fair to assign her just because I knew she wouldn't complain?

A frustrated sigh escaped me, and I sank to my knees in front of the tulip beds. The limp flowers indicated bulb rot, but the grayish color usually came from the mold at the heart of firehead blight. It was strange, though. I hadn't seen any of the usual indicators of blight, like stunted shoots or yellow spots. Just these flowers, as dull as if all the life had been siphoned out of them.

No matter what was causing it, I'd need to get the

damaged plants out of the bed so they couldn't continue to spread their disease. I used the clippers attached to my belt to cut the tulip at the base, and my stomach turned at the squelch of the blades cutting through the soggy stem.

I held the dead tulip up to the light of the rising moon.

There was something wrong with these plants. They weren't just diseased; there was something else here, something more. The limp flower in my hand gave off the odor of rot, but it was more than a smell—it was a sense of sickness that echoed in my bones.

It would have to be Jonquil. He understood the tulips better than any of us.

This flower couldn't go in the compost piles, not without putting the whole garden at risk, so I stood with a grimace and headed for the nearest waste bin. I tossed it on top of the other rubbish and hoped I wouldn't end up in the same place when I told Jonquil what he had to do.

28TH MARCH

Exhaustion gripped my bones the next morning when I woke before dawn. I'd always been an early riser; the beauty of the quiet gardens before anyone awoke to enjoy them had always been motivation enough. But the festival had taken its toll, and remembering the new tulip problem I'd have to deal with made getting out of bed difficult.

The fatigue left as soon as I was in the greenhouse with a thousand spring-green seedlings on every side, lit against the pre-dawn darkness by enchanted lamps from Badalah. Lilian and I had agreed a long time ago that baby plants were almost as cute as baby animals, and being surrounded by all this new life made me breathe deeper and move slower.

I thinned the seedlings and misted them with water, turning their trays so the drooping ones would straighten themselves by stretching toward the morning sunlight when it came. I hummed as I worked, while the darkness gave way to the soft pearly gray that hinted at the coming day.

By the time I was back in the servants' dining hall, a mug of coffee and plate of scrambled eggs and toast in front of me, I felt awake, alive, and ready to take on Jonquil and anything else the world chose to throw at me.

And then I opened the newspaper.

It shouldn't have hit me so hard. Lilian had told me they'd gone boating; she'd confessed that she was beginning to like her betrothed. But no words could have prepared me for the smile on her face in the photograph under the headline *PRINCESS, DUKE ENJOYING SPRING FLING BEFORE WEDDING.*

There were three photos, which were three photos too many according to the nausea bubbling in the pit of my stomach. Lilian looked radiant in all of them, with her smile lighting up her whole face. The pictures showed them boating on the lake, walking through the rose gardens I had pruned so carefully just last month, and playing tennis at the city's elite sporting club. Lilian's slim-fitting tennis gown clung to all her curves, and I flushed with sudden jealousy at the thought of Duke Remington touching her while she wore it.

Sticks and stones, I needed to get a grip on myself.

She was happy. She actually liked the man she was about to marry, and from the looks of these pictures, he liked her, too. I should be over the moon for my best friend and thrilled that her life was coming up roses instead of thorns.

And I was. I wanted her happiness.

But stars, I wanted mine, too.

There was no one in all the world I could talk to about this. Lilian had always been my confidant and the holder of all my secrets.

One of the maids ambled slowly into the dining hall, her eyelids still heavy with sleep. She squinted across the room at me.

"Coffee," she demanded.

I poured her a cup and pushed it across the table. She dropped into a seat and stared into the beverage as if it held all her hopes for the future. I bit back a smile and reached for my own drink.

Another sleepy maid followed her, and then a footman with his hair sticking up at odd ends. He was trailed by a stablehand, Pansy, who entered with her hair in two tight braids and her eyes bright.

The stablehands were up before even me most days. I caught Pansy's eye, and we traded grins over the heads of the groggy maids.

"Morning, Deon." She arranged herself on the bench next to me. "Get me some apple juice, would you?"

I poured her a glass while she filled her plate with eggs, toast, and bright red cubes of greenhouse watermelon. She glanced at the paper and gestured at it.

"You done with the current events section?"

I took one last, unwilling look at the pictures of Lilian and the duke.

"It's all yours."

She pored over the pages while I pretended to read an article about a new method of potato cultivation devised by a child prodigy in the next province.

"Princess Lilian seems to be getting along well with

her beau," Pansy said.

The comment was offhand. There was no reason she should know how deeply her words pierced me, and I silently vowed that no one would *ever* know.

I shrugged one shoulder and kept reading as if I didn't find the romantic entanglements of the love of my life very interesting.

"Hard not to get along with a fellow who looks like that," one of the maids, Rose, said with a cheeky grin.

The other maid, Daisy, giggled. The topic seemed to have roused her better than the coffee. "He's awfully handsome, isn't he?"

Pansy pursed her lips to the side. "He rides a beautiful stallion," she said as if this signaled the full measure of a man.

I trained my eyes on the page in front of me and read the same line about seed potatoes three times before the words sank in.

"Seems a nicer man than his father," Rose said. "That's a good omen for the princess, at least."

I glanced up. "Is Duke Markus an unkind man? He seemed decent enough when I met him."

Rose pursed her lips, and she and Daisy exchanged knowing looks.

"He's a bit full of himself," Daisy said. "Not in a way that's justified, if you ask me. King Alder is twice the man the elder duke is in every way, but he doesn't put on airs that are half as grand."

"It's not the airs that trouble me." Rose stirred a heaping spoonful of sugar into her coffee, then another. "Only the way he speaks to his wife..."

She trailed off; her raised eyebrows telling exactly what she thought of that kind of behavior.

I leaned forward. "What do you mean?"

"It's not that he's not permitted to act however he pleases," she said. "I wouldn't presume to know how a retired duke should behave. But I've overheard him talking to the duchess on more than one occasion when I've been tidying up their chambers, and I'd slap any man who spoke to me like that. He's all demands and insults and comments about her waistline. And she's not much better, sniping and moaning back at him. They're a couple of miserable birds biting at each other all day long and no mistake."

Daisy buttered a slice of bread and observed me. "You don't believe her."

"It's not that I don't believe it," I said. "I just—you're sure it was the duke and duchess you overheard?"

"No question," Rose said. "I don't blame you for wondering. They're sweet as apples when they're out and about in front of other people. But behind closed doors?" She whistled.

"Gossip says the younger duke was like that in his youth," Daisy said. "Had a reputation for being a bit of an ass. Fortunately, *he* seems to have grown out of his bad habits."

I imagined Lilian being trapped in a marriage like that one. Seeing her and Duke Remington in the newspaper enjoying themselves had grabbed at my heart and ripped it to shreds, but at least, he didn't seem to have taken after his parents.

It was something to be grateful for.

After breakfast, I headed straight for the walkway from the previous night where the tulips had been dying, but I didn't make it more than ten steps out the door before Reed jogged toward me. His slender, freckled face was pale with worry, making his big dark eyes look twice their normal size.

I stopped in my tracks.

"What's wrong?" I said.

"It's probably nothing."

He shook his head, but it was too late for me to believe that. Something was wrong—terribly wrong. My mind flitted to Lilian, then the festival. Reed fidgeted and twisted his hands together.

"What?" I demanded.

He bit his lip. "You'd better come see."

I knew what I was going to find before we got there, but that didn't stop my stomach from lurching at the sight. Another flower bed near the palace walls—this one full of Queen's Tulips, the flowers that were the pride and joy of Floris—was dotted with the nodding gray heads of diseased plants. The die-off in this bed was worse than I'd seen last night.

Much worse.

"Does Jonquil know?" I said. "The others? The tulip specialists?"

"It's not just the tulips," Reed said.

I followed his gaze. A trellis thick with wisteria lined the walkway nearby. In a few of the clusters, the pale purple of the blossoms had begun to fade toward gray.

"Tulip blight wouldn't affect wisteria."

The words escaped my mouth before I had a chance to think through the implications of such a thing. The questions that could only follow such a statement hung in the air.

"Yeah," Reed said, acknowledging the pregnant silence between us.

I stared at the wisteria, then back at the tulips.

"But yes, the others know," Reed said. "Anyone who's on shift in this part of the gardens, anyway. It's not just these."

Icy cold prickled down my arms in spite of the morning sun. It didn't make sense. No disease that invaded the tulips should impact the wisteria like this. But when I moved closer to inspect the gray blossoms, it was clear that we were dealing, however improbably, with the same illness. The flowers all shared the same flat lack of color, the same sogginess under my fingers, the same sickly-sweet smell of decay.

"Any idea what it is?"

"He hasn't a clue," someone said loudly behind us.

My shoulders tensed at the voice, and I turned to frown at Jonquil.

"This started in the tulip beds," I said. "You should have caught this earlier."

His face flushed red, and the injustice of my words twisted in the pit of my stomach. It wasn't Jonquil's fault. I'd seen the decay, too. I'd never imagined it would spread so fast, or like this.

"Perhaps you should have been keeping a sharper eye on your gardens," Jonquil retorted.

Never mind that I had forty acres to manage, and never mind that I wasn't a tulip specialist. I ground my teeth together to stop myself from saying something I'd regret later.

Always give yourself time before you speak, Hedley had told me a long time ago, back when he'd started quietly training me to fill his boots. *Better to be sure you mean what you say.*

Years later, it was a lesson I still struggled to learn.

"We need to get this quarantined, and fast," I said. "Jonquil, focus on the tulips. See if you can figure out what's gone wrong. Pull in anyone you need to help. Reed, take a few of the apprentices and have them search the whole garden in case this is showing up elsewhere."

"I don't have time for this," Jonquil said.

I hated having thoughts in common with him. The Flower Festival was coming up quickly, and no one on my staff had a second to spare, let alone the full day it would likely take to find and remove every diseased flower in the garden.

"We either make time, or we'll have to spend more of it tomorrow," I said grimly. "With any luck, it won't have gone beyond these beds. Check the walkways along the palace wall, too," I added. "I saw something like this there last night. Meant to talk to you about it this morning."

"Would have been good to know about that before it spread," Jonquil said.

I held up a hand. "There's no way it would have gotten from there to here that quickly. If it's the same blight in both groups of tulips, they're both victim to some outside cause."

Jonquil muttered something under his breath, which I didn't ask him to repeat. I nodded at him to go and was relieved when he slunk away.

He might not like taking orders from me, but the seriousness of this situation wasn't something any of my gardeners could ignore.

"What do you think it is?" Reed said in a low voice once Jonquil had gone.

I shoved my hands into my pockets and stared at the dead gray tulips. They seemed especially bleak, surrounded by the brightly iridescent Queen's Tulips, and the urgency of removing them before the sickness could spread gripped me.

I took a deep breath and tried to get the sudden pounding of my heart under control. "I have no idea."

~

I had never been one for libraries. The dust on the books made me sneeze, and the tiny print on the pages made my eyes ache. I'd been born for sunshine and fresh air, not dim lamplight and this musty scent that tickled the inside of my nose.

I wished I had Lilian here. She adored books of all kinds, and I loved listening to her read aloud. We'd gotten through most of our schooling that way, with Lilian narrating passages in her melodic voice while I weeded herb beds or taught myself to juggle.

Now, of course, the princess of Floris had better things to do than read to her gardener, so I ignored the headache blooming between my eyes and squinted at the page.

Blight is difficult to eradicate once the disease is established in the tulip bed. However, a competent gardener may attempt remedy by any of the following means.

I skimmed the list that followed. All the information was obvious to the point I could have recited it in my sleep. Remove and burn the infected plants. Check bulbs for mold or signs of rot. If planting in raised beds or containers, change out the soil, and if planting in the ground, avoiding putting tulips there for a few years to avoid the spores infecting future plants.

That was all well and good, but this wasn't some common blight. I'd seen firehead blight before, and gray bulb rot, and pythium root rot, and bulb nematode, and breaking virus, and this wasn't *any* of those.

This was something new, and none of these books seemed equipped to identify the problem, let alone deal with it.

Footsteps shuffled along the row of books to my right, then stopped. I looked up from my table, with its mass of stacked tomes, and met King Alder's gaze. I shot to my feet and bowed.

"Your Majesty, my apologies. I didn't see you there."

The king seemed to bite back a smile. A few slender volumes were under his arm, their spines decorated with gold flowers.

"*My* apologies for disturbing you," he said. "I was merely curious as to what had you under such a spell." He nodded at the books. "I didn't expect to find you indoors so close to the festival."

His smile made it clear that this was only a comment, not a chastisement, but my face heated up anyway.

"A good gardener always stays up to date on developments in the field," I said. Thank goodness a few of the books behind me had been published in this decade.

"I've always admired your dedication to your work," King Alder said. "As did Hedley. He told me more than once that your hunger for knowledge of your plants couldn't be matched." He glanced at the towering stack of books, and his eyebrows drew together. "I think he might have understated the case. We *are* prepared for the Flower Festival, aren't we?"

"Everything's well in hand, sir," I said with a slight bow.

I sent a silent prayer to whoever might be listening that it would be true.

The King offered me one of his warm smiles. "I'll leave you to your studies, then."

"Did you find what you were looking for?" I nodded at the books under his arm.

He started as if he'd forgotten he was holding them and glanced down at the floral covers. "I did," he said. He held one up, revealing the elaborately scripted title *The Knight of the Mountain Mists: A Tale of Heroism and Romance.* "The Queen is still abed and beginning to resent her inactivity."

I permitted myself a grin. "Her Majesty has never been one to enjoy sitting still."

The queen was every bit a lady, but always an active one. It was she who had taught Lilian how to shoot a bow, ride horses, and train dogs and birds. I'd rarely seen the queen without something in her hands—a piece of embroidery, the strings of her lute, a hand of playing cards.

"Being trapped in bed must be torture for a woman as lively as your wife if you'll permit me to say so, sir," I said.

"You speak only the truth." The king grimaced, though there was deep affection buried in the expression.

"Is she feeling any better?" I bit my lip. "I realize it's been only a day since we spoke."

"A long day," the king said. "She seems to be brighter this afternoon. The court physician expects a full recovery."

He spoke as if he were reciting someone else's words. I considered pressing him for more, but what good would it do? The king had no reason to share his personal life with his gardener, and I was so full of worry about the blasted tulips that worrying about the queen on top of it was likely to kill me.

"Give her my best wishes," I said.

"I did yesterday," the king said. "She sends her love."

I had never had a mother. But in moments like this, when I was reminded of the queen's kindness to me, I felt a hint of what it might be like to have that kind of sunshine over my life.

I bowed to the king, and he moved away, the books once again firmly under his arm.

I couldn't disappoint him, or the queen. I would find the answer to this problem, no matter what it took.

I turned back to the books. The throbbing in my head returned within moments.

I ignored it.

My soul recoiled the moment I stepped into the greenhouse. Normally this incredible jungle of tropical plants lifted my spirits like nowhere else in the gardens. Today, though, I wasn't met with just the plants.

Jonquil sat with his arms folded at one of the round iron-wrought tables that dotted this large paved clearing. His gaze was trained on me, and there was nothing inviting or forgiving in it. The other gardeners at their various tables were focused on me, too, their faces strained or dismissive or outright angry. The late-afternoon light streaming like gilt through the glass ceiling did nothing to soften their expressions.

This greenhouse, normally used for the queen's luncheons during the colder months, was one of the only garden spaces big and private enough for an all-staff meeting. It was the third I'd held since I'd taken on Hedley's responsibilities almost a year ago and the first to be called to address an emergency.

I swallowed and looked out at them. My heart pounded.

Amid the unfriendly faces, Reed smiled and nodded his support: *You can do it.*

I took a deep breath.

"Thank you all for coming at such short notice," I said. "I know you're busy."

"Get to the point," Jonquil muttered.

I pretended I hadn't heard.

"As most of you probably know, we're experiencing an unusual form of blight in the gardens. We haven't seen it before, and it seems to spread quickly. The tulip specialists and I are trying to identify and eradicate it, but that means we're going to need to redistribute some assignments so we're still ready for the festival on time."

A few groans rose up around the room. Olive's forehead knit in concern. Beneath the dangling leafy tendrils of a variegated pothos, Hollis leaned forward and rested her elbows on the table as she stared intently at me.

"I know it's a lot to ask that anyone take on extra responsibilities right now," I said. "If this situation continues for more than a few days, I plan to ask King Alder for extra holiday time for each of you after the festival is over. For now, we need to band together to deal with this problem and put on the kind of Flower Festival the world expects from us."

Chervil raised his hand. "I heard the disease that's affecting the tulips spread to other plants," he said, spitting the words at me like an accusation. "Is that true?"

My shoulders tensed at the reminder. "It seems to have passed to some nearby wisteria and a few daffodils," I said. "We're wondering if it might be some kind of insect that's causing the issue, although we can't confirm that yet."

Olive clasped her hands on the table in front of her. "What can we do to protect our plants?"

The question hit me like a punch to the gut. I couldn't answer it. Helplessness gripped me, and I fought to rise above its heaviness.

"Keep a sharp eye on your beds." My words rang out clearly, delivered in the voice of someone who knew what he was talking about. Behind them, I hid like a liar. "Let me know immediately if you see anything amiss. The more information we can gather about this issue, the sooner we can handle it."

"That's wishful thinking," Jonquil said without bothering to raise his hand. "For all we know, there's nothing we can do."

It was my worst fear. Hearing it aloud woke something violent inside of me. I fixed him with a sharp glare. "Are you admitting you aren't competent enough to be serving in the court of Floris?"

He shrank back, and I looked out at the rest of them with my head high.

"We are the best this nation has to offer," I said, anger edging my voice like thorns. "Floris is the world's leader in horticulture, and we are the best gardeners in Floris. If we can't beat this thing, it can't be beat. Are you willing to admit defeat?"

They stared at me. A smirk passed over Reed's face, and he grinned when I caught his eye.

"I said, are you willing to admit defeat?" I repeated.

I looked out at them, and finally, after a long, awkward pause, a few people mumbled, "No."

Olive leaned forward and cleared her throat. "I didn't fight my way to the palace gardens just to let a little tulip disease chase me away," she announced. "I'm ready to take on whatever extra work you need."

"I didn't fight my way to the palace gardens to let a teenage upstart give me orders," Chervil muttered, just loudly enough to be heard by everyone. “And yet, here we are.”

Mace raised his hand. I nodded at him.

“No offense intended,” he started. My stomach twisted with dread at whatever was coming next. “But why should we trust that you know how to deal with this problem? I don’t mean to be rude. Clearly, Master Hedley thought you were a good apprentice, or he wouldn’t have left you in charge.” Condescension leaked from his voice. “It’s just that—and you’ll forgive me for saying this, I don’t mean anything by it—it’s just that you’re young, and you perhaps don’t have the experience needed to tackle a problem of this size?”

I let out a long, slow breath before I answered. Reed’s grin had faded, and he looked now like it was taking all his effort not to smack Mace upside the head.

The annoyance on his face gave me strength.

“With all due respect,” I started, unable to keep a slight tinge of sarcasm out of my voice. Reed’s jaw twitched. “I’m not the only person working on this problem. At a rough guess, I’d say that together, we have over three hundred years’ worth of experience in this room. Myrtle alone has been working with tulips for almost forty years now, and Linden wrote the literal book on breeding rot-resistant bulbs. You’re right. I don’t have the experience necessary to solve this problem. We do.”

Reed silently mimed clapping his hands. I made a mental note to buy him a beer later.

Even so, as they all filed out of the greenhouse after the meeting, I couldn’t destroy the echo of Mace’s words in my head. I didn’t have what it took to solve this problem.

But I knew someone who might.

29TH MARCH

The train jerked to a stop. Steam billowed past my window, and the sounds of people gathering their belongings filled the carriage. A woman nearby hoisted her young daughter onto her hip and kissed the top of her head. The little girl was blonde with rosy cheeks and a purple hair bow almost as big as her head. She reminded me of Lilian at that age. I smiled at her, and she grinned shyly back.

I waited until the carriage was mostly empty, then followed the last few stragglers out of the car and onto the platform. People milled about, greeting loved ones and complaining about the journey. Through the crowd, I caught sight of a familiar silver head and salt-and-pepper beard. My heart lifted.

"Hedley!" I called.

I raised a hand, and his gaze landed on me. The crinkles around his smiling eyes deepened, and he stood, immovable as a boulder, as I made my way through the crowd toward him.

His hug was warm and strong as ever, and I let myself squeeze him as hard as I wanted to and hold on for a few extra seconds. When we pulled back, his whole face twinkled with happiness.

"It's good to see you," I said.

"You're a head taller," Hedley said, which wasn't remotely true. "And look at the muscles in those arms. What have they been feeding you, boy?"

"Hard work," I said. "Lots of it."

"Good. Young men need that. Keeps them out of trouble."

He tapped his nose, and I laughed.

We took a leisurely stroll to his house. It was a pleasant walk that exited the train station and wound through the picturesque village of Goldenrod. Red and pink geraniums squatted in window boxes outside shops and the apartments above them, and sweet pea vines crawled up the sides of brick buildings. Away from the pressures and demands of the city, everyone here seemed cheerful, from the baker adjusting her chalk sign to add *SOLD OUT* next to an advertisement for cardamom buns to the street sweeper who whistled as he tidied up the remains of a flowerpot that had spilled all over the sidewalk.

"I ought to move out here," I said after a woman selling flowers handed me a daisy with a wink and a flirtatious "No charge, love."

"Don't let it fool you, small towns can be madness," Hedley said. "Hyacinth is in a proper feud with the lady down the street who keeps stealing our apple blossoms."

I raised an eyebrow. "Why would anyone steal apple blossoms?"

"Well, that's the mystery, isn't it?"

We turned onto a dirt lane that wandered away from the rest of the town. We passed an orchard and a stand of raspberry bushes thick with leaves, and then the bushes gave way to a landscaped front garden that could only have belonged to my mentor. His cottage stood under gently swaying trees, the stone walls covered in climbing roses and the window boxes bursting with petunias.

"And here I thought you'd have less gardening to do," I said.

Hedley boomed out a laugh. We both knew he would garden his way into the grave, and part of me suspected his ghost would find a way to come back every few weeks to tend whatever flowers were planted by his headstone.

"I'll give you a tour, but you'd better come inside first," Hedley said. "Hyacinth was so excited to hear you were coming that she cooked a goose."

"She's a rose among women."

"That's the truth."

Mrs. Hyacinth Hedley greeted me with a shriek and a hug and proceeded to demand to know whether the palace was feeding me and whether I'd managed to get my favorite boots repaired and how I was sleeping now that I had a whole forty acres of garden to worry about. I answered her questions almost as quickly as she could ask them while she piled a plate high with goose and gravy and roasted vegetables.

"That's plenty," I said as she maneuvered a soft roll onto the already-full plate.

"It's not, and there's more where that came from."

I devoured the meal while she looked on in approval. Hedley watched with quiet amusement, and when my second plate was cleaned, his wife finally seemed satisfied to let us go wander the property.

I had missed Hyacinth's cooking ever since she and Hedley had moved away. I'd missed the love that came with it even more.

"She worries about you," Hedley said in a low voice once we were out in the expansive gardens behind the cottage. "How have you been getting on?"

"I'm all right." I considered the words as they came out, weighing them for truth. I wasn't *all right,* not exactly, but perhaps I would be soon.

Hedley saw right through me.

"Everything's not quite as it should be, though, is it?" he said. "Your first solo festival is coming up fast, and yet you're here." He swatted a butter-yellow moth away from his face, and it flitted to a nearby bluebell and slowly beat its wings. "What's the matter?" His face stayed placid, but his hazel eyes sharpened. "Girl troubles?"

He knew how I felt about Lilian. Anyone who'd been paying attention to us over the last eighteen years would, and Hedley paid more attention than most, however quietly.

And no one in the kingdom could be unaware of her upcoming nuptials.

"I'm sure that's part of it," I said.

It was a relief to admit. I'd spent so much time trying to deny my feelings—not to pretend they didn't exist, because that was impossible, but to ignore how much my love for her *mattered.*

"She's marrying someone else," I said. "The world's

ending." I shrugged ruefully. "What can I do? Floris would never accept a gardener as its king, and I have no right to aspire to the position of her husband. It is what it is. I just hope things get easier after the wedding."

"You're a good man, Deon." He clapped me on the shoulder. "Another woman will recognize it, sooner or later."

The thought of ever loving another woman filled me with—I didn't know what it was. Dread. Fear, maybe. Grief.

"This wildflower bed has been coming along better than I expected," Hedley said, smoothly changing the subject and giving me a moment to get the prickling behind my eyes under control. "It seems the scarlet rocket might take it over, but it's facing stiff competition from the winding clover. I'm looking forward to watching them battle it out."

I cleared my throat. "Sounds exciting."

"Gardening always is." He gestured at the path in front of us. "Wait until you see the pond lilies."

After the tour, I sat across from Hedley at his kitchen table and sipped my tea. The sweet chamomile flavor blossomed in my mouth, its fragrance delicate and green.

"I suppose I should bring up what I actually came for before it's time to go home," I said.

Hedley nodded, as tranquil as the surface of the lily-coated pond he had been so proud to show me earlier in the afternoon. Like any good gardener, Hedley knew how to let things unfurl at their own pace.

"I brought it with me," I said.

This piqued his curiosity. "*It?* Have you come up with a new bloom already?"

I glanced at him. "I have, as it happens, but that's

not what I came for."

I collected my small bag from where I'd hung it on the coatrack. Just touching the bag left me with a feeling of contamination that made my fingers recoil from the leather strap. I set it on the table and glanced around.

"Do you have a room that doesn't have plants?"

Hedley's thick silver eyebrows drew together. "Can't say I do."

"It should be all right." I glanced at the philodendrons that curled down from the windowsill and the elegant snake plants in the corners of the room. "I've got it under glass."

"Now, you do have me curious."

I unfastened the bag and took out the bundle inside. The specimen bell jar I'd snagged from the palace apothecary was covered with old newspapers, and Hedley watched with interest as I unrolled the protective layers.

I set the jar on the table between us.

Hedley leaned forward. "What in blazes happened to those?"

"That's what I was hoping you could tell me."

He picked up the spectacles that hung around his neck and put them on, squinting as he did so. He peered down at the blooms: two tulips, a rose, and a bearded iris, each one gray and oozing rot from its wilted petals.

"Stinging nettles, Deon, what have you done to my gardens?" Hedley muttered.

I wrapped my hands around my teacup as if it could provide any kind of comfort in the face of a problem this enormous.

"I don't know what it is," I said. "None of us do. I noticed it a couple of days ago, and already, it's spreading. It affects every plant the same way, first a bit of gray fading at the tips of the petals, and then the whole thing decays like it's got the worst kind of root rot. It's only a matter of time before the king and queen notice."

"What visitors has the palace had lately?" Hedley said sharply.

I startled at the sudden change in his manner. "Just the duke and his entourage," I said.

"The Duke of Thornton?" Hedley shook his head. "No, he wouldn't have what's needed for a thing like this. Nor his parents, pompous upstarts though they are."

"You know the family?"

"I worked at the palace for longer than you've been alive; I know everybody." He squinted again at the flowers. "Who was in their entourage? A witch? A sorcerer? A court magician, perhaps?"

I frowned. "Servants," I said. "Ladies' maids, valets, secretaries, their transport advisor. Fourteen people in all, I think. No one like that."

Hedley picked up the jar and turned it over, muttering to himself. Finally, he set it down and fixed me with his gaze.

"These are cursed," he said.

I raised an eyebrow. "That's a bit extreme."

"No, I'm talking magic."

"That's absurd."

"It's uncommon," he said. "They're different."

He stared at me with pursed lips for a long moment, then blinked and poured us both another cup of tea.

"What's killing these plants isn't natural," he said finally. "I haven't seen a flower like those in over eighteen years, but I can still spot one as well as I can spot a case of blossom rot or leaf curl." He tapped the jar with his knuckle, the glass clinking softly with the impact.

I examined the flowers again. There was plenty odd about this disease, but a *curse?*

"It's not that surprising," Hedley said. He sipped his tea, eying the flowers over the rim of his cup. "The gardens of Floris have always been helped a little by magic, haven't they? Makes sense that sometimes they'd be hurt by it, too."

He didn't seem to be trying to make a joke. I leaned forward. "What do you mean, helped by magic?" I said. "Since when? Was I supposed to be casting spells on the gardens this whole time?"

The thought was horrifying. I didn't have magic. Hedley didn't have magic, as far as I knew. Why would anyone have left me in charge of a magical garden without telling me that it might be prone to curses?

Hedley raised a calming hand. "Don't panic," he ordered.

I took a long, slow breath, and did my best.

"The magic isn't from the likes of you and me," he said. "But it's there anyway, as surely as I'm sitting here. Why do you think the garden is so quick to bloom and so eager to produce the best flowers the kingdoms have to offer? Wisterias don't flower this early in other parts of the world, and yet, I'm sure half the garden pathways are covered with them. And your strawberry patches—I suspect they're producing enough to keep your princess in jams and tarts already, aren't they?"

I knit my eyebrows together. What he was saying was all true, but reaching for *magic* as the explanation seemed like wishful thinking.

"We have a temperate climate," I said. "Spring comes early, and the coast on three sides keeps our summers from ever getting too hot." I'd learned as much from

Lilian's and my tutors. The way we Florians put our climate to such good use was a point of national pride.

"A temperate climate will not cause daffodils and roses to bloom at the same time," Hedley said. "And yet, I'd bet this cottage that both are showing off their full colors at the palace."

I opened my mouth to argue, but he was right. The daffodils were in full bloom, but the roses were unfurling, too. And yet, according to the books I'd read on the subject, daffodils were supposed to bloom in early spring and roses near the beginning of summer.

I'd never given it a second thought. I'd just assumed that Floris's climate was the best, and its flowers were the best, too, so it was no small surprise that we had longer blooming seasons than everyone else.

I set my teacup down and stared at Hedley as the pieces started to fit together in my head.

"You don't want to miss your train," Hedley said. "We'll talk more on the walk there."

The town of Goldenrod was aptly named at this time of day. Evening light streamed from the apricot-and-periwinkle sky, touching the striated clouds with gold and warming the tiled roofs of the shops and houses that lined the main thoroughfare.

"What else can you tell me?" Hedley said as we approached the station.

I'd left the specimen jar on his table, just in case his further examination might reveal anything of note. Now, he seemed hungry for information, but I had little to provide. I didn't know of anyone with magic who'd come to the palace with the duke. I didn't think King

Alder or Queen Rapunzel had met with any magicians or enchanters lately. No one had been using unapproved spells or witch-brewed fertilizer, to my knowledge, and nothing about the palace or gardens seemed different from previous years, aside from Princess Lilian's engagement.

"It started with the tulips," I said, although I was pretty sure I'd already told him this. "The ones right up against the palace walls."

He stepped around a sidewalk display of flowerpots and gardening tools that a shopkeeper was packing up for the day.

"That walkway that leads to one of the servants' entrances?" he said.

I nodded.

"Right flush up against the walls, then," he said. He hemmed and hawed for a moment and drummed his fingers on one of his suspenders. He'd taken to wearing suspenders ever since marrying Hyacinth; there was something old-fashioned and charming about it.

"The disease seems to be spreading out from the palace," I said. "I haven't seen any problems in the orchards or gardens further away, but it looks like it's going to devastate most of the tulip beds near the castle."

Hedley's gait slowed, just slightly. Hyacinth had always accused him of not being able to walk and talk at the same time, and it seemed there was some truth in it. He nearly ran into a small trash bin, then came to a stop and looked at me.

"Spreading from the place, you say?"

"Seems that way."

"Well, I'll be." He frowned and stroked the silvery stubble that frosted his chin. "How is the queen these days?"

The sudden change of subject made me do a double take. He waited.

"She's well enough, I suppose," I said after a moment. "A bit under the weather right now." King Alder's strange behavior of the day before ran through my mind. "I don't think it's serious," I added.

"I'd start there if I were you," Hedley said.

"With the queen? You think *she's* causing the problem?"

The thought was laughable. Ludicrous. Maybe treasonous. Either I knew nothing about the world, or retirement had turned Hedley mad.

But he shook his head. "Queen Rapunzel wouldn't hurt a daisy in those gardens, let alone one of her prized tulips. Even so, you ought to look to her for answers to your problem. The world is a far more interesting place than you give it credit for, and the queen is a far more complicated woman. Not to mention that magnificent hair of hers, which I firmly believe gives life to all around it." He winked. "And now, you'd best get on this train before it leaves without you."

I realized with a jolt that we were already at the station. Steam billowed from where the train sat behind the small office, and the activity on the platform told me I had only a few minutes to get aboard if I didn't want to spend the night in Goldenrod.

Part of me *did* want to spend the night in this relaxed little country town, far from the stress of the festival and the disease that was spreading through my gardens. But I knew what Lilian would say if she saw me shirking my responsibilities, and that was enough to get me moving.

I shook Hedley's hand, and he pulled me in for a

warm hug.

"I'll let you know if I learn anything new about the rot," he promised. "In the meantime, you keep your eyes on the gardens and away from the princess until she's well and married. Honest work will ease a world of heartaches."

He waited as I boarded the train and waved as it pulled away. I waved back from the window of my carriage and watched him standing there until he was only a smudge in the distance.

Hedley's advice to stay away from Lilian and focus on the festival was solid. That didn't mean I was capable of following it. Seeing Hyacinth in the cottage with him had woken a sharp, sweet pain deep in my soul. They were happy together. They'd always been happy, and I figured they always would be.

I remembered when Hedley had first started seeing Hyacinth, back when I was thirteen and had only been apprenticing for a few years. Hedley's mood had changed first. He'd always been a calm, pleasant man, but that summer, he'd seemed downright jovial. I'd caught him lingering in the kitchen a few times before I'd realized he'd come to steal time with Hyacinth rather than the raisin buns or rosemary bread she baked, and I'd noticed that she called him "Sheldon" instead of "Hedley" like everyone else, but it had still taken overhearing the housemaids gossiping about the two of them before I'd put the pieces together and realized she was the reason he'd taken up humming as he worked. When they'd married a few years later, his happiness had only seemed to grow, and the love in their cottage today had been palpable.

I would never have that with Lilian.

A small shelving rack at the front of my train carriage held the usual smattering of dog-eared books and faded magazines, entertainment for passengers who hadn't brought their own. The rack also held a stack of cheap paper and a collection of cheap ink pens, next to a sign that read *Help yourself to paper. Please replace pens after use!* I usually ignored the rack and everything on it, preferring instead to look out the window at the beautiful Florian landscape. Now, my attention snagged on the pens.

Finally, I retrieved one, along with a few sheets of paper, and pulled down the flimsy writing desk set into the wall beside my seat. This carriage was mostly empty and brightly lit with lamps against the fading dusk outside. Aside from the rocking of the train, it was the perfect environment for composing a letter.

I touched the ink to paper and began to write.

Dearest Lilian,

You are *my dearest, and always will be.*

It seems a bold claim to make that any one person in this world could be crowned best, most wonderful, most loved. There are more people across all the kingdoms than I can comprehend, and yet, I can announce with absolute certainty that you are the queen of them all. Whether we were born a perfect match for one another or not, we grew alongside one another like those sweet peas you love so much, twisting and tangling with every shared lesson and inside joke until no gardener in the world would dare to separate us. And yet, we are being separated, as we knew we always would be one day. There are times I don't think I'll survive being torn from you.

I hesitated, my pen above the paper. Outside, the dusk slipped quietly to darkness. Finally, I scribbled out the last sentence.

I'll survive, as will you. We'll continue to grow in our own ways. You will be the most perfect wife for your new husband, and I'll be your gardener.

It doesn't sound like much, does it, being a gardener instead of a husband? But it's everything to me, Lils. If I can't grow old alongside you, I'll do my best to keep you young with all the irises and birds of paradise and fresh strawberries your heart could ever desire. I'll ensure your palace grounds become more delightful with each passing year, and someday, when your children are playing on the lawns as we once did, I'll teach them to plant their first row of tulips and weed their first bed of herbs. And I'll make sure you always, always have roses on your table.

I wish you could choose me, Lils. But since you can't marry your gardener, I'll choose you over and over and over, with every flower I plant and every strawberry I harvest. The gardens will be a testament of my love and will surround you all of your days. How better to

The carriage door opened, and I jumped. A beautiful young woman in a pink gown stood in the doorway, her warm skin framed by glistening black curls. She glanced around the carriage, her gaze skimming over a sleepy elderly man and a teenage girl with her nose in a book.

She stepped lightly into the carriage and closed the door behind her. Reflexively, as if I'd been caught naked, I crumpled the sheet of paper into my fist.

It hurt, acting like everything was fine when I carried the weight of the blight and the festival and Lilian's upcoming marriage on my shoulders. But I would rather carry all that weight alone than ever burden Lilian with it. Sticks and stones, I was a lovesick fool. I shoved the crumpled paper into my pocket and resolved to burn it at the next opportunity.

The woman sank into one of the empty seats opposite me and offered a dazzling smile. She was pretty enough to take my breath away, her cheeks flushed with youth and her dark eyes glittering like onyx.

"May I join you?" she asked politely, even though she'd already done so. "A fellow in the next carriage just lit up his pipe, and I couldn't stand the smell. It seems much nicer in here."

My pen rolled gently from side to side with the rocking of the carriage. I reached out and steadied it. "Of course, there's plenty of room."

Her bright smile widened, and she wrapped her hands delicately around her knees and leaned forward. I realized with a start that she intended to talk to me, perhaps for the whole ride. "Are you going all the way to the capital?"

I relaxed a little at the excitement in her voice. Whatever melancholy place my thoughts had been, this woman's cheery disposition was leagues away.

"A little past it," I said. "I work at the palace. How about you?"

"The capital for me," she said. "I'm going to visit an aunt. I've never seen the city before. Do you really work at the palace?" Her sparkling eyes widened. "That's so exciting! What do you do there? No, let me guess. You're one of the king's grooms."

I ran a hand through my hair and immediately regretted it and wished I had a comb handy.

"Guess again."

"A guard," she said, eyes sparkling. "You protect the

queen from hostile visitors."

I laughed. "How dangerous do you think palace life is, exactly?"

"That's for you to tell me! All right, not a guard." She examined me, her gaze searching my face and traveling down to my hand, resting on the writing table. Her eyebrows flew up as if she'd just spotted something fascinating.

"A gardener!" she said. "You must be."

I pulled my hand back. "There's not *that* much dirt under my nails."

"No, but there's still enough that you couldn't be anything else," she said. "They've got traces of soil, and meanwhile, the rest of you is too tidy. I know a gardener's hands when I see one. My brother grows geraniums, and his hands look just like yours."

I laughed. "You're a good detective. Yes, I'm a gardener." I hesitated, but her wide eyes won out over any inclination I might have had toward modesty. "I'm the head of the palace gardens, as it happens."

She peppered me with questions about what it was like to work at the palace, and I answered as best as I could. She was an enthusiastic listener, and I related stories of visiting royalty and told her what Queen Rapunzel was really like in person.

In a different world, where I'd never met Lilian, a moment like this would have been among the best the world had to offer. Here I sat, relating tales of my glamorous job to a beautiful woman who seemed enchanted by everything I had to say.

It was a perfect moment. I relaxed and tried to enjoy it.

30TH MARCH

I blinked at the guard, unsure if I'd heard him right.

"Her Majesty will not see you," he repeated.

I drew myself up to my full height. He was taller than me, but not by much, and my years working the garden meant I could probably snap him over my knee.

I wasn't going to, of course. But the palace guards were usually more brawn than brain, and a little intimidation could often change their tune.

This one continued to stare impassively down at me.

"Her Majesty has never refused to see me."

"These are Her Majesty's private quarters."

"Her Majesty has never refused me access to her private quarters," I said. Didn't everyone at the palace already know that? Even if I hadn't been Head Gardener, palace gossip had still ensured everyone knew I was the little orphan foundling the king and queen had taken in and educated alongside their own daughter. The other gardeners never let me forget my special treatment at the monarchs' hands.

So why had I picked today to run into the one person on the palace grounds who didn't recognize me? And why had all that special treatment failed on the one day I needed it?

It made no sense. Then again, nothing about my life did these days.

"Tell Her Majesty I'd like to see her at her earliest convenience," I said, voice strained with politeness.

The guard inclined his head, more smug than acquiescent. "Of course."

A dozen sharp retorts sprang to the tip of my tongue. I bit them all back.

Whether or not Hedley was right about the queen having answers for me, his advice about using hard work to get rid of unwanted emotions was decent enough. I marched out to the gardens, startling a few housemaids with the scowl I couldn't seem to wipe from my face, and got to work pulling weeds like each one had personally called Lilian a rude name.

The conversation with the girl on the train had lightened my soul for as long as it had lasted. Coming back to the garden, full as it was with blight and Jonquil and stupid guards that wouldn't let me get anywhere near the woman who might be able to solve it all—the reality of it all had hit me like a thorny branch to the face.

I worked until I didn't feel like punching anyone. And then I worked until I didn't feel like making biting comments to them, either. By the time Reed wandered by my bed, I was able to meet his concerned, "You all right there?" with something close to civility.

"I've got nearly all the horseweed out of this bed," I said. Horseweed was invasive, and none of the gardeners liked dealing with it. Seeing the pile of shoots piled on the grass next to the bed satisfied me in a way nothing else had today.

"No blight here?"

His voice was too casual. I leaned back on my heels.

"None so far. But this bed isn't close to the palace."

"I think we've been able to keep it from spreading," Reed said. "I've got a few apprentices doing nothing but wandering the gardens, pulling out anything that seems diseased and burning it in a little barrel on the spot."

"That was a good idea," I said. "Thank you."

He crouched next to me and began pulling weeds, too. This bed had been neglected longer than it probably should have, since nothing in it was destined for the festival. I could have chosen somewhere more important to work this morning, but no plant in the garden wrestled as hard as horseweed, and I'd needed to fight with something.

"Have you told the king and queen what's going on?" Reed said his voice again too light.

The frustration from this morning flooded back. "I've tried to."

He nodded. "They seem busy. I haven't seen either of Their Majesties for a few days."

So the queen's illness was still under wraps. That had to be a good sign if neither an announcement from the king nor gossip about the court physician's movements had trickled down to the gardens.

But if she wasn't really that ill, why was Her Majesty

avoiding me?

I couldn't keep thinking about it, not unless I wanted to spend the entire day wrangling weeds from unimportant flowerbeds.

"Help me take these to the trash pile?" I nodded at the heap. "Then, we ought to go hunt down some lunch."

"You go ahead," Reed said. "I had a late breakfast. I'll handle the weeds. You get some food."

I stood and looked down at him. His face was bright with the warm smile that usually graced it. Of everyone who worked in the garden, he was one of the only ones I could honestly call a friend.

"You're a good man, Reed," I said. "Your support means a lot."

Reed grinned. "Eh, I'm not that supportive, boss," he said. "Mostly, I'm just glad I didn't get stuck with your job."

I snorted. "You're a wiser man than me. If you ever get news that someone in The Forge has actually built a time machine, do me a favor, and let me know, all right?"

Reed shook his head and waved a dismissive hand at me. "You don't mean that."

I sighed ruefully. "No, I don't."

No matter the frustrations and no matter the challenges, I wouldn't trade this job for the world. Lilian had grown up in this garden, and Hedley had raised it and me together with a love it would take me decades to match. Blight or not, queen's help or none, I would do everything in my power to ensure the garden and the Spring Flower Festival were the best they could be.

~

I passed through the rose gardens near the palace and the tulip gardens that were even closer. The devastation from the blight was clear—so clear it seemed impossible that the king hadn't summoned me to ask about it. Great gaps of soil were visible where flowers should have been, and young apprentices wandered the grounds like ghosts, carrying small metal barrels with smoke coiling from their tops.

Although, to an outsider's eyes, perhaps it just looked like we were preparing for the festival, harvesting beautiful blooms and killing weeds while we were at it. I remembered the apparent devastation of festivals past when whole beds were torn up so their flowers could be sold or displayed at the event. The gardens always recovered beautifully, the new blossoms always more stunning than the ones we'd removed.

If only these missing flowers had gone on one of the festival carts. I didn't know how long we'd be able to keep up the pretense that everything was all right, assuming we were keeping it up at all.

Before I made it to one of the servants' entrances, someone called my name. I turned, and my heart sank like a rock.

Duke Remington was striding toward me, waving like we were old friends.

I took a deep breath and put a smile on.

"Your Grace." I bowed as he approached.

He held out a hand as if we were equals. I hesitated before shaking it. Royal guests weren't usually so polite, not to servants.

"I'm glad I caught you," he said. "Are you busy?"

It didn't matter whether I was busy or not. Duke Remington was a palace guest and my future king. I inclined my head.

"What can I do for you, Your Grace?"

He adjusted his tunic, seeming almost nervous. He was boyishly handsome and charismatic to boot. I wasn't sure if I was glad about that for Lilian's sake or devastated for mine.

"I'd like to ask your advice, actually," he said. "On a personal matter. May we walk?"

He nodded toward the nearest pathway, and I gestured at him to lead the way. We strode in silence for a few moments. Apprentices wandered the gardens around us, and butterflies danced above thick stands of blooming lavender.

"Your staff seems very industrious," he said after a while, taking note of a servant plucking up a wilted gray flower. "Lilian tells me it's always this busy near the festival."

"Have you attended many Flower Festivals?"

"Oh, every year, like any good Florian." He laughed a little, and then his face grew solemn. "Actually, I wanted to talk to you about Lilian."

My heart sank. He knew. He'd noticed the way I looked at her, or she'd let slip something that told him we were more than just a princess and her gardener.

"Sir?"

"I get the impression you and Lilian are good friends," he said. He dared a glance at me, and his demeanor seemed curious rather than upset. "She says you shared tutors growing up."

I nodded, my heart racing. "Their Majesties took me in as an infant. They could have sent me to an orphanage or raised me to be a servant, but for some reason, they decided to give me a gentleman's education instead."

"Lilian said as much," he said. "I wonder what they could have been thinking."

I'd asked myself the same question many times. All these years later, I suspected the correct answer was also the simplest: They were kind people and tried to do their best by everyone who came into their lives. It was no wonder Lilian was such a wonderful woman, as loving as she was talented and as talented as she was beautiful. She'd grown in fertile soil.

"Since you seem to know my beloved better than I do, I was hoping I might ask your advice."

Startled, I glanced over at him. How could a gardener possibly advise a duke about a princess?

"Lilian is a lovely person," he said. "I suppose I don't need to tell you that. She's sweet, intelligent, and everything a man could hope for."

I bit the inside of my cheek. He had no idea how right he was.

"And yet I can't help feeling like she's isn't entirely comfortable around me yet," he continued. "She's always gracious, and I dare to hope she enjoys our time together. But she's so quiet. There's nothing wrong with a lady being reserved, of course," he added quickly. "It can be a charming trait in a girl. But I admit, I hoped she'd open up to me more by now."

I didn't think it would do to stare openly at the duke, so I stared ahead at a patch of bleeding heart bushes instead.

I had known Lilian in a thousand moods. *Reserved* described none of them.

"I like her very much, but I want to get to know her better," the duke said. "I just haven't the foggiest idea how. She seems to like her dogs, so we talk about them sometimes. But surely, she's interested in more than her pups?"

"Flowers," I said.

The duke turned to me, his eyebrows flashing in surprise.

"Pardon me?"

"She loves flowers." I shook my head; the words sounded stupid coming from my mouth. "More than your average Florian, I mean. We all love nature, it's our cultural heritage. But Lilian *loves* flowers. She grows her own, and she's even tried her hand at crossbreeding roses. The results were mixed, but I suspect she'll come up with something splendid someday. She especially loves new, unique flowers. She keeps a collection of rare houseplants in her quarters: dancing mimosas and enchanted butterbells and night-blooming constellatas."

I swallowed, questioning the wisdom of telling the princess's future husband that I knew what her private quarters looked like. But he was asking my advice, and if there was one subject I knew backwards and forwards, it was Lilian and the things she loved.

I was a fool to tell the man anything. However unevenly matched we were for the princess's hand, an ugly churning in the pit of my stomach knew he was the competition.

But there was no competition. I wasn't in the running. I could never marry the crown princess of Floris.

What I could do was make sure her future husband knew how to make her happy.

Lilian deserved to be happy.

"If you want her to open up, I know how to do it," I said. "Follow me."

It was a long walk to my private garden. To the duke's credit, he didn't ask questions or complain about the distance. He just strode along beside me and occasionally pointed out gardens he particularly admired or asked questions about plants he hadn't seen before.

By the time we reached my garden, I had to admit, as infuriating as it was, that I honestly liked the man.

Though not enough to let him into my heart.

"Wait here," I said.

I unlocked the garden and slipped inside. A moment later, I came back out, a bouquet of dazzling pink peonies in my hand. The petals of the flowers shifted and swayed like silk skirts, and a series of low, melodic whistles rose up from the blooms.

The duke's eyes widened.

"They're called pink pirouettes," I said. "They dance in the sunlight, and the sound is from the air whistling between the petals. Lilian's never seen them before."

"Nor have I," the duke said. "Nor anything like them."

He took the bouquet from me and raised it to his ear, listening intently to the music.

"It's like the sound of wooden pipes," he said.

"They're a new variety. The seeds came from a hermit magician I've been writing to for the past few years. Brilliant man. If Lilian doesn't open up to you after she sees these, there's nothing you can do."

The duke lowered the flowers and fixed me with his gaze. He held out a hand.

"Thank you," he said sincerely.

His handshake was firm and full of respect. We walked back to the palace together, the flowers still whistling in the sunshine.

~

Helping the duke win over the woman of my dreams lit a fire underneath me. If I could summon up the strength to do that, I could summon up the strength to do anything.

Maybe even magic.

I'd told Lilian before that I didn't have magic. But if Hedley was to be believed, the gardens did.

After my work was done for the day, I went back to the library and pulled down a variety of tomes, most old and with strange writing on the embossed leather covers. I took them back to my bedroom, along with one of the dreary gray flowers, then lit a lamp and began to read.

If Reed was right, the problem in the gardens was contained. But "contained" wasn't good enough. I had inherited these gardens from the best man I'd ever known, and they were the home of the love of my life. This problem needed to be solved.

So I read, and I read some more. And then, in the middle of an old disorganized spell book, right between a charm to remove freckles and a potion that could ease croup, I found it.

I read the directions three times until I was sure I had them right, and then I took the book and the flower out into the gardens. It was late, not so late that everyone in the palace was asleep but enough that the gardens were empty of everyone but the birds nesting in branches and the rabbits heading home to their burrows. I walked to a wide paved circle where I could set the poisoned flower down without fear of contamination and settled on the ground across from it with my lamp and book and the handful of herbs the spell required.

I laid out the torn herb leaves in the pattern diagrammed in the book. The rosemary leaves glistened in the flickering light, and the lemon balm surrounded me with a sharp citrus odor.

The book's instructions were detailed, and I followed them to the best of my ability. I broke a rose's bloom apart and scattered the petals across the diagrammed herbs. I closed my eyes and tried to raise magical energy within myself. I chanted the magic words and blew out the lamp at the exact moment required.

That should have completed the spell. I sat in silence for a few seconds, then counted slowly to thirty just in case the magic needed time to do its work. Then I re-lit the lamp. My heart pounded, and I held my breath as the little flame flickered back into life, and for a moment, I dared to believe I had what it took to revive my dying garden.

The gray, rotting flower sat limply amid the herbs and petals, staring balefully up at me.

Of course, the spell hadn't done anything because I wasn't a wizard.

Sticks and stones, I had to be desperate if I thought chanting ancient Florian at a blight-damaged flower was going to solve all my problems. I glanced around into the darkness, suddenly convinced that Jonquil or one of the others was out there bearing witness to my idiocy. But the garden was quiet and empty, the only ones privy to my secret the bushes rustling in the nighttime breeze.

I gathered the damaged bloom and all the detritus of my failed spell to throw in one of the burn barrels, then tucked the spell book under my arm. With any luck, I'd be able to get it back on its shelf in the library before anyone realized what I'd been up to.

Part of me wished I could confess the stupidity of my effort to someone.

No, not someone. Lilian. She would laugh—with me,

not at me—and then she'd wrap her arm around my shoulder and tell me that, at least, I'd been willing to try, and wasn't that all any of us could do anyway?

The truth was, though, that Lilian wasn't the one I needed right now. I needed her mother.

Playing at witchcraft in the gardens and searching books for new information on tulip blight was all a grand waste of time, a distraction from the real problem at hand.

I marched into the palace and up the stairs. The corridor outside the queen's chambers was dimly lit with soft lamps, and a guard stood outside the door.

He was my only obstacle. King Alder and Queen Rapunzel didn't bother with much security inside their private apartments, and their only concession to the palace's fussy Head of Security was to permit one guard apiece outside their apartments and Lilian's. I vaguely recognized this guard, which seemed like a good sign. Perhaps he'd realize that Queen Rapunzel would want to see me.

"Good evening," I said, a touch too brightly.

The guard nodded at me, neither friendly nor defensive.

"I was wondering if I might have a word with the queen." I made my smile as warm as I could and tried to sound like this was a request I made every day.

The guard's expression didn't change.

"Her Majesty isn't accepting visitors," he said.

There was finality in his tone. I frowned at him and changed courses.

"Perhaps His Majesty is available, then?" I said. "I won't take a moment."

"His Majesty has retired for the evening."

"I doubt that."

The guard raised one eyebrow at me.

"King Alder doesn't usually go to bed for another hour," I said. Anyone who knew anything about the king knew that. "I just need to speak with him for a minute or two. It's about the gardens. It's urgent."

"King Alder is not to be disturbed," the guard said, as impassive as a brick wall.

I couldn't speak to the combat-readiness of these guards, but if they were ever called upon to frustrate someone to death, it was hard to imagine a defensive force more ready for action.

I clenched my teeth in what was probably a vain effort to keep the irritation from my face.

"I am the head of Their Majesties' gardens," I said. "I would not attempt to disturb Their Majesties at this hour unless it was important."

"Their Majesties are not to be disturbed," the guard said again.

I'd never been the kind of man to solve my problems with my fists. They balled up at my sides anyway.

The guard glanced down, then back up at my eyes. His other eyebrow went up to join the first one.

"Perhaps you'd like to leave a message with me?" he said. His tone was cool and insufferable. I took a deep breath. He was just doing his job, the same as I tried to do mine.

"That would be helpful," I said. "Would you please tell Their Majesties at the earliest opportunity that I require an audience urgently? They know where to find me."

The guard nodded. Something about the nod made me doubt the message would make it anywhere in time to do any good.

Well, fine. If he wasn't going to help me, I knew a

princess who would.

~

Lilian's apartments weren't too far from her parents'. The room that had once served as her nursery, and then a schoolroom, was linked to the king and queen's suites by a door decorated with a colorful painting of Lilian's family tree. I remembered Queen Rapunzel coming through that door every week or two when I was a child, interrupting our lessons to share a fresh lemon tart or unique flower or clever trinket from a foreign guest. Our tutors had always allowed the interruptions—not just tolerated them as any tutor would have when their queen entered the room, but welcomed them as much as Lilian and I did. Queen Rapunzel had that effect on people.

The schoolroom had another door that connected with the corridor outside. There was no guard on this door because it was always kept locked.

Fortunately for me, I had a key. I'd used it to access our schoolroom years ago, and even after the schoolroom had been transformed into a sitting room full of books and embroidery hoops, no one had ever thought to take the key back. Lilian knew I had it, of course, but she seemed to be the only one.

I looked both ways down the corridor, then unlocked the door and slipped inside. The room was dark, but I knew my way around and managed to make my way through the moonlit conservatory and toward the formal parlor at the center of Lilian's apartments. The parlor was where she entertained guests and visited with friends who weren't close enough to be allowed deeper into her space. It seemed like the best place to invite myself for a chat.

I paused outside the glass doors that led from the plant-filled conservatory into the parlor. A gauzy curtain prevented me from seeing too clearly inside, but it was clear the room was occupied. The lights were on, and Lilian's voice sounded from within.

It wouldn't do to interrupt if she had friends visiting. She wouldn't mind if I traipsed in unannounced, but the other ladies of the court would have plenty to say, none of it flattering.

I hesitated and weighed waiting versus sneaking back out and coming to see her in the morning. Then someone else's voice floated through the gauzy curtain, and I froze.

"I've had such a good time with you these past few days," Duke Remington said. His blurry figure shifted on the sofa next to Lilian. "To tell the truth, I was a little worried before I came here. I wasn't sure what to expect."

"Neither was I," Lilian said.

Her voice hit me like a punch to the stomach.

I should leave. I should back away quietly and leave them to this private moment.

I couldn't move.

"I brought you something." Duke Remington sounded almost shy. "I left it in your foyer before the maid showed me in."

"Not another bracelet," Lilian said, only half in earnest. "I can't possibly accept another glittery trinket from you this week. What would people think?"

Duke Remington laughed softly. "Not a trinket," he said. "Something far better."

He stood and left the room, leaving Lilian on the sofa. Her figure was difficult to make out through the curtain, and yet I would have known it anywhere: her regal posture, the glint of her golden hair, the way she fidgeted while she waited as if she would rather be running through the gardens. One of her fluffy white dogs jumped onto the cushion next to her, and she picked it up and cooed at it.

The duke came back a moment later, the telltale bright pink of the flower I had given him in his hand.

Lilian gasped. "They're *beautiful.*" She set the dog on the sofa and stood, drawn toward the flower like a moth toward lamplight. "Stars, are those peonies? They're so bright!" She buried her nose in the bouquet and breathed in. If she had been reserved with Duke Remington before, that was over now. She took the flowers from him—they were in a vase, judging by the pale gold blur beneath the blooms—and rotated it to examine it from every angle. "Heavens, Garritt, where did you get this? I've never seen anything like it. And that fragrance! It's not a Hollingsbrook, is it? I've heard those are especially pretty, but this is superb. And listen! It's like music."

"It's called a pink pirouette," the duke said, his smile audible in his voice. "And you'll find the music isn't its only trick. Place it on your windowsill tonight and look at it tomorrow morning."

"Why?"

The duke leaned in toward her and lowered his voice. "That's for you to find out, princess."

She stared up at him, then laughed. "You're such a tease!"

"Tease a lady? Never."

She put the hand that wasn't holding the flower on her hip. "You are, and I'd scold you for it if this flower weren't *so* lovely. This color is unreal. It's magical, isn't it? It has to be."

"It is," Duke Remington acknowledged. "The flower is as enchanted as you are enchanting." He bowed lightly.

Lilian laughed again. My heart felt like it would tear itself in two at the sound, half of it leaping at the sound of her joy and the other half sinking at the knowledge that I hadn't been the one to make her bubble over like that.

"That's an appalling line," Lilian said in mock sternness. "And I've forgiven you for it already. I'd forgive just about anything for flowers like this. How can I thank you enough?"

Duke Remington hesitated. The silence between them was tangible and crackled with possibilities.

"You might permit me a kiss," he said.

I bolted from the conservatory before I could learn her answer.

31ST MARCH

"This is a right mess and no mistake," Hollis said. She dropped a newspaper in front of me. One corner landed in my coffee cup, and I fished it out and frowned up at her.

"I'm not sure I want to know."

"You have to know," she said, raising her eyebrows. "You're Head Gardener, and I'm sure glad now that Hedley never considered me for the position."

Hollis had never seriously wanted the job. She was a rose specialist and didn't have much interest in anything else. She was one of the few gardeners who didn't seem to want my head on a pike, which was probably why my stomach sank at the way she was scowling at me.

"What's going on?" I said.

But the newspaper was already in my hands, the headline staring me in the face: *DISEASE IN PALACE GARDENS SPREADS TO FARMLAND.* I dove into the article, my sleepy brain working double to make sense of the words swimming in front of me.

The article started off bad and got rapidly worse. By the time I was finished reading, Hollis had already topped off my coffee. The handful of ladies' maids and kitchen hands at the servants' dining table watched me, either waiting to hear the news or my reaction to it.

I set the paper down with slow, measured movements and fixed Hollis with my gaze.

"Who talked to the press?"

She stared back, deadpan. "I'd give you three guesses, but that's two more than you'd need."

I jabbed a finger at the paper lying innocently on the table, with its nausea-inducing paragraphs about blight and damaged spring cabbages and artichokes grown gray with rot.

"Is this accurate?"

"As far as I can tell," Hollis said. "I figured you'd want to send a few of us out to assess the situation. I've cleared my morning."

"Thanks. Take Reed with you."

I could trust Reed. And if things the newspaper had printed were true, I'd need someone I could rely on to give me the news without blabbing it to anyone else.

The sliced ham and fried eggs on my plate had lost their flavor. I shoved a few last bites into my mouth anyway, then escaped the dining room before the other servants had the chance to ask what was going on.

I was going to murder Jonquil, and then I was going to find a sorcerer who could bring him back to life just so I could murder him again.

The moment I stepped outside and into the gardens, I was accosted by a young man holding a notebook. A photographer hovered behind him, holding a camera with a large flashbulb up top.

"Excuse me, I'm looking for a representative of the palace gardens," the man with the notebook said.

I stared at him. "Who let you in here?"

His eyes widened. "The palace gardens are open to the public every Sunday."

"Not this close to the palace walls without a tour group, they're not," I growled. "You're a long way from the public gardens."

"I'm a reporter with The Daily Florian," the young man said, his face too eager. "Are you the head gardener here? The ladies we just spoke to said he looked about like you. What do you have to say about the blight that's been found on the palace grounds? Do you have anything to say about accusations that contamination from the palace gardens has led to crop failures in nearby farms?"

The photographer raised his camera. I put a hand in front of my face just as quickly.

"Put that down, or I'll have you thrown out and charged with threatening the royal family's safety," I snapped.

The photographer lowered the camera and shrugged as if to say I couldn't blame him for trying.

Only I could.

I really, *really* could.

"Who have you been talking to?" I said.

The journalist waved his hand. "Me, I haven't talked to anybody yet," he said. "The Floris Post is the one that broke the story. I'm just trying to get a word from an official palace representative, not some unnamed source." He scoffed, then hit me with a smarmy smile. "This is your chance to set the record straight. Tell the people what you know."

"No comment," I said.

His face fell. "Come on, there's a whole horde of journalists lurking near the main palace doors, and you're going to have to talk to one of them sooner or later. Why not me?"

I gaped at him and took off for the front of the palace with the two men following behind, the journalist still pleading his case.

The mass of people was worse than I'd imagined, at least a two dozen journalists and photographers all crowding one another for space while a couple of harried-looking tour guides aimlessly tried to round them up. The guards standing at the top of the palace steps surveyed the crowd and occasionally glanced at one another, but hadn't decided yet to intervene.

I jogged up to one of the guides. "What happened here?"

She ran a hand through her dark hair. "They said they were coming to meet *you* to talk about the festival," she said. "They had a press pass and everything."

Press passes weren't hard to get, but it was rare that this many people wanted one.

I took a deep breath. "I'll address them," I said. "Tell the guards to make sure these folks leave the palace grounds as soon as I'm done talking. I don't want them going off to get quotes from my staff."

She nodded, and I strode up the palace steps. It took a few minutes for the crowd to settle, but then they all started shouting questions. Flashbulbs went off, their lights mercifully diluted by the bright sunshine overhead.

I held up a hand and waited. Finally, they realized I wasn't going to speak until they all shut up, and the chatter died down.

"It's my understanding that you're all here to ask about the blight that's been found in the palace gardens," I said loudly.

They started shouting again. No wonder Lilian hated speaking to the press if they were always like this. I waited for silence.

"There has been a case of blight on the palace grounds," I finally said. "Every Florian knows disease and pests challenge every garden, and the palace properties are no exception. We're handling the problem quickly and efficiently, as we always do. Claims this blight somehow spread from the palace grounds to nearby farms are entirely unfounded. The palace gardeners rarely leave the grounds this close to the annual Flower Festival, and members of my staff certainly haven't been spending their limited free time in local cabbage patches."

My voice was betraying my irritation. I tried to rein it back.

"I would caution any responsible journalist from accepting claims from unofficial sources. If a case of blight on the palace grounds ever creates a threat to outside gardens and especially our food crops, I guarantee you'll be told immediately both through the palace newsroom and the Horticulture Council. Good day. No questions, please."

~

The queen was nowhere to be seen. The king was busy entertaining the elder duke and duchess, and Lilian, according to palace gossip, was spending the day with Duke Remington on a tour of the Florian Academy of Dance. They were to tour the Academy's facilities and meet its most promising students, then do lunch at the top of the Calendula Tower, and then return to the Academy to attend a preview of the new ballet that would premiere in conjunction with the Flower Festival. It sounded like a delightful way to spend a day, and no doubt, the duke would take every opportunity to kiss Lilian and shower her with jewelry and compliments.

Which left me, alone, to deal with the press and the dying flowers and the staff that had gone rogue under my nose.

The royal family couldn't be unaware of what was happening in the gardens, not now that it had made the news. Why hadn't one of them come to see me? Why didn't they *care?*

I paced along the rows of seedlings and starts in the greenhouse. At least, the blight hadn't touched anything in here. These seedlings were half the reason the festival existed: they included all sorts of rare and beautiful flowers that could only be found in Floris, and people traveled from all over the world to collect plants to carefully take back home. This event made the palace a great deal of money, half of which was always donated to charity. Even if the palace grounds were afflicted by this blight or curse or whatever it was, the event absolutely had to go off as it always did.

A wilted seedling caught my eye. Its leaves were yellow, bits of brown curling at the edges. I pulled the young plant up before I had time to think.

It wasn't blight. This was just the result of too much water, or too little light, or a seed that had never been destined to make it. My heart still pounded at the sight of the now-empty pot.

The Spring Flower Festival had to go well. It had to.

Hollis and Reed returned right before lunch. We grabbed a few sandwiches and apples and retreated to a quiet corner of the gardens where we could talk privately.

"It's not good," Hollis said bluntly from where she sat cross-legged on the grass. She threw a piece of her crust toward a bird, which hopped and tilted its head and pecked at the crumbs. "It's the same blight, no question."

"It's only just appeared here," I said. "No blight spreads that fast. Unless it started in the farms?"

Reed shook his head. "It's appearing at the same frequency there as it is here. Just a few plants at first, getting a little worse every day. A couple of the farmers we talked to said their crops started going gray the same day ours first did."

I chewed my apple. It tasted like wood pulp, and I had to fight not to spit it out.

"Whatever this thing is, it's regional." Hollis sucked a smear of mustard from her finger, then wiped her hand on her stained work trousers. "Has to be spread via spores, or maybe there's something in the water. The farmers say it's moving about as fast as potato blight, though."

She didn't need to elaborate. Potato blight could kill entire crops in a fortnight. If we didn't manage to find and destroy every infected plant, the entire palace gardens could be gone in a month.

I could forget about tending Lilian's gardens and teaching her children how to plant tulips. At this rate, I'd be lucky if I still had a job by then.

Stinging nettles, this garden was dying as fast as my

dreams.

Reed furrowed his eyebrows at me. “You okay?” he said. The slight tilt of his head told me he wasn’t asking about the garden.

I pulled back my shoulders. The kingdom was facing a crisis, the likes of which I’d never seen. It didn’t need me going to pieces over a childhood sweetheart on top of it.

“I want you guys to tell the rest of the staff what you learned,” I said. “And then, we’ve got to figure out a way to stop this thing.”

~

It was the second staff meeting in a week, and this one was going even worse than the first.

“Quiet down!” I shouted over the cacophony of voices.

Nothing happened. My gardeners were angry and scared. Nothing I had said or done had broken through to them.

Hollis whistled loudly enough to make my ears ring. The room lapsed into a shocked silence.

“Thank you,” Hollis said, making it manage to sound like an insult.

Linden, sitting at one of the more distant wrought-iron tables, muttered something under his breath. Chervil crossed his arms and glared at me. Nearby, Olive twisted a strand at the end of her braid.

“So that’s the situation.” I felt like a rabbit in a den of wolves, with every one of them just as likely to tear into me as to listen. I cleared my throat and stood up straighter. “As of now, you know everything I do.”

“More, I should think,” Mace said, not quite under his breath.

I ignored him. "We need to work together. It's going to take every last one of us to solve this."

Myrtle raised her hand, and I nodded at her. "With all due respect, *sir,* you're the boss. If you want us to solve this problem you're going to have to tell us how. A pep talk isn't going to cut it."

I took a measured breath. "I don't know how. And this isn't a pep talk. It's a warning. I've never seen a disease like this, and neither have any of you. Unless you do know, and you're choosing not to come forward."

I glanced over the assembled crowd, searching their faces to see if I'd hit a nerve. No decent person would let an entire garden crumble around their ears just to prove a point, but I wasn't about to risk the palace grounds on the hope that Jonquil or Chervil were decent people. But even they just looked disgruntled.

Olive raised her hand. I gestured at her, grateful.

"We all know this is a serious problem." Her voice was quiet as if she wasn't sure she really wanted to be talking. "But it doesn't seem like any of us know how to fix it. Maybe we need to start thinking creatively."

"And what are we going to accomplish by *thinking creatively?*" Jonquil said in a mocking tone. "What does that mean, exactly? You want to do an interpretive dance about how our gardens are dying?"

"Thank you, Olive," I said loudly. She shrank back into her chair but gave me a slight nod. "As it happens, we're pursuing some unusual possibilities. I spoke to Gardener Hedley about this issue a few days ago, and he's exploring the idea that this blight might be magical in nature."

All through the room, expressions changed, some skeptical and others curious. On the other side of the room, Jonquil snorted.

"Another thing," I said, fixing him with a stare. "This is a sensitive issue. The next person I catch feeding rumors to the press will lose their job."

It was an empty threat. I couldn't lose a tulip specialist with Jonquil's skills, not now. But I held his gaze and tried to look like I meant what I said.

"Censorship," Chervil said loudly. "Yes, just what we need to save the gardens."

"It's not *censorship* to ask that we show a little discretion," Reed snapped.

At the same time, Myrtle threw up her hands. "Well, isn't our head gardener Mr. High and Mighty!"

"This place is going to the dogs," Jonquil said while Basil shook his head, and a few of the younger interns eyed the door like they were looking for an escape route.

"I have the right to fire anyone who fails to reflect—"

I was instantly drowned out by more complaints and accusations. I looked to Hollis for help, but she was now in an intense argument with Basil, and Reed was shouting across the room at Linden.

This meeting, like my life, was a disaster.

I walked out while they were still hollering at each other. The greenhouse door slammed behind me.

An hour later, I sat at the edge of the small lake, the water lapping gently against my ankles. It was cold, and I was glad. The discomfort gave me something to focus on besides the roaring in my head.

I dug my bare toes into the mud. Across the water, a pair of swans floated together, their white wings touched by the blush of early evening.

The gardens were dying. The love of my life was about to marry another man. Everyone on my staff hated me, the queen refused to see me, and the first and last Flower Festival of my career was about to bring shame on the entire country.

Everything was fine. Just fine.

I watched as a duck waddled down to the water and hopped in, its body settling immediately against the surface of the lake. Overhead, thin clouds tinged with pink and purple floated past like streamers. Birds called their evening songs to one another, and the rowboats tied up on the far side of the lake bumped gently against the dock.

I had to find a way to preserve this beauty. Perhaps the solution was to fight my way into Queen Rapunzel's chambers, or tear up every plant in the gardens and start over, or contact a magician powerful enough to prevent the blight or curse or whatever it was from spreading. There were a million possible solutions, each wilder than the last.

I rested my elbows on my knees. A tiny fish came to investigate my foot, and I held still so as not to startle it. I couldn't think. Too many stupid thoughts jostled for space in my brain, like weeds that had overtaken a flowerbed and choked out everything that should have been growing there.

"Deon?"

I jumped. The fish darted away. A duck floating nearby snapped its head straight ahead to look at me with one of its beady black eyes. A hand settled on my shoulder.

"Sorry, I didn't mean to startle you," Lilian said. She sat next to me.

Too late, I reached out a hand to stop her. "It's muddy. Your dress—"

She shrugged. "I'll rinse it out in the sink before my maids can get mad at me."

We sat in silence for a few moments. Lilian kicked off

her slippers and plopped her feet into the water beside mine.

"What are you doing out here?" she said. "The festival's in eleven days. I'd have thought you'd still be working."

What was the use? I didn't know what to do to counteract the blight or to get my staff to stop jumping down my throat every time I opened my mouth. I *wanted* to work. My body itched to be put to use, the more backbreaking, the better. But every task on my list felt pointless.

"Did you see the papers?"

She pursed her lips and looked sideways at me. "I did. It sounded like a whole lot of nothing, journalists trying to drum up an audience with some made-up scandal right before the festival."

Was that what the king and queen thought, too? Was that why neither of them had come to see me?

"The blight's real," I said. "It's worse than they realize."

She stared at me, her blue eyes darker than usual in the rosy light. "What do you mean, worse?"

"I mean worse," I said. "I don't know what it is, and I don't know how to fix it."

She whistled softly. "That's a problem. Have you talked to Hedley? Or the Horticulture Council?"

"Hedley, yes. Horticulture Council, not until I don't have any other options." I thought about mentioning that the queen had barred me from her chambers, but the king had asked that I not mention her illness. I laced my hands around my knees instead. "I don't know what to do."

"Me neither." She stared out at the lake for a long moment. Then she clapped a gentle hand on my knee and turned to me. “Let’s walk,” she said briskly.

It wasn’t like I had any better ideas. I scrambled to my feet and picked up my shoes, and she picked up hers. She laced her free arm through mine as she’d done a thousand times before, and my heart skipped a beat.

Hers must have, too, because she blushed.

“Lils, this is making it harder to stay away from you,” I said, but I didn’t pull away.

We walked without talking for a while, the sun-warmed paving stones comfortable beneath our feet. After a while, we found ourselves standing outside my private garden, though I didn’t recall either of us choosing to go that way.

Lilian took a deep breath as if she was about to say something, and then she clamped her lips shut.

I didn’t ask. I couldn’t ask.

Abruptly, she pulled away from me and strode for several paces, then whirled back around.

“You gave him the flower, didn’t you?”

She stared at me, and I stared back. Slowly, I nodded.

“He asked for my help,” I said. “He said he felt like you were reserved around him. He wanted to get to know you better.”

Her eyebrows furrowed together. “That was kind of him,” she said.

I didn’t know what to say. It *had* been kind of the duke, but I couldn’t praise him to Lilian’s face. Not today.

“Can we go into your garden?”

“Lils.”

I waited for the right words to rise to my lips, words that could explain how I couldn’t let her an inch closer, not without it ripping me apart.

She just looked at me with those wide, beautiful eyes. I relented, the resistance inside me crumbling like mud in the rain. I unlocked the garden with shaking hands, and she followed me inside, her body close enough behind me that I could smell the magnolia scent of her perfume.

She closed the door behind us. I turned.

"Lilian, I can't—"

"I love you."

She looked up at me, her eyebrows drawn together, and her lower lip trembling.

"I do," she said. "I can't help it. I've tried so hard to love the duke, or at least, convince myself that I could love him someday, but I don't. I don't, Deon. I love you."

Tingles ran up my arms, and a lump filled my throat. I blinked back sudden tears.

"Lilian, we can't."

"I know," she said. "And it doesn't change a thing."

She took a step toward me. I felt as immovably rooted as an ancient tree. She rested one of her small hands against my chest, and I knew she had to be able to feel the way my heart pounded at her touch.

"Stars, Deon," she whispered. "What are we going to do?"

Heir of Thorns

1ST APRIL

Ten days.

I had ten days until the Spring Flower Festival, the biggest event to happen annually in the kingdom of Floris, and the best chance we had to shine on the world stage.

And I was sitting here, trying to revive a couple of dying tulips with the judicious application of unicorn manure.

It wouldn't save these flowers, of course, but I hoped it might slow their progression. I'd already applied dragon manure, pixie dust, and phoenix mites to other plants whose petals were tipped with gray. This blight progressed quickly; if any of these interventions had worked, one of these plants should have at least a trace of color left in the next few hours. If any of these worked, I could fill the gardens with dragon manure or basilisk castings or whatever it was, and then maybe the festival could proceed, and the gardens would be saved.

I just needed something to work.

Someone knocked on the greenhouse door. I removed my gloves and covered the diseased plants with their glass covers. The covers were a likely futile attempt to keep the blight from spreading to plants outside this small greenhouse, but I had no evidence they actually helped. Several new patches of blight had appeared in the gardens this morning, all of them further from the palace walls than any we'd seen before.

Olive entered the greenhouse, her hair pulled back with a floral handkerchief.

"Sorry to disturb you, but we've finished packing up the last of the viridian hydrangea starts," she said. "The cart isn't back from the festival, though, and I didn't know where you wanted us to store them in the meantime?"

"They'll have to go inside the palace," I said. "The ballroom's been reserved for our use, so go ahead and stack them in there until the carts arrived."

She turned to go.

"Make sure they're not too close to the orange trees that are already in there," I added. "Just in case."

"I'm not putting anything too close to anything else," she said grimly.

I nodded. It was a good rule of thumb now that everything in the gardens seemed to be poisoning everything else.

The temptation to watch these tulips for signs of spreading gray was strong, but I left the greenhouse and locked the door behind me. This building was small and ordinarily used for propagating houseplants for the palace; now, the place was a hospice for sick plants that had no hope of revival.

I didn't need the tulips in there to come back. I just needed one of them to die a bit more slowly than the others.

Halfway to the palace, where I was supposed to be working on the staffing rosters for the palace's festival booths and displays, I stopped in my tracks. There, across the lawn, amid a colorful party of courtiers in pastel gowns and gold-edged tunics, stood Princess Lilian. She had a croquet mallet in her hands, and her betrothed, Duke Garritt Remington, was helping her improve her swing. His arms were around her, and his lips brushed her cheek as he spoke, and a dozen warring emotions rose up in my chest.

I had kissed Lilian just last night when she'd come to my garden and confessed her enduring love to me. We both knew being together was impossible, and we both found it equally impossible to let go.

One of Lilian's ladies-in-waiting glanced up and caught me staring. I looked away and kept walking briskly toward the palace, but it was too late: she was already on her feet and trotting after me.

"Mr. Gilding!" she called as she approached, and I had no choice but to stop and greet her with a bow.

"Lady Camellia." My smile felt so forced I was worried my face might freeze that way. "What can I do for you?"

She checked behind her shoulder. Lilian was still focused on her croquet game, and no one paid attention to us. Lady Camellia pressed her hands together.

"I was wondering," she started hesitantly. She leaned in and lowered her voice. "I'm sorry; I have to ask. Are the rumors true?"

"Rumors, my lady?"

Playing dumb didn't come naturally to me, and I was almost relieved when she didn't dance around the subject.

"The news in the papers about there being a blight on the palace grounds that's spreading to nearby farms," she said. "I normally wouldn't pay that kind of gossip any mind, but, well..." She glanced pointedly at the grounds around us. Bare patches of soil were visible in almost every bed, evidence of diseased plants that apprentices had pulled up and burned. The garden normally looked a bit disheveled around the Flower Festival, but this was above and beyond anything from years past.

"We are facing a disease that's been affecting some of our flowers," I said, which was the biggest understatement I'd personally ever heard. "There's no reason to think that has anything to do with the issues the farmers are experiencing, though. It's likely that all of our gardens are reacting to quirks of the weather."

The corner of her lip drew down. She was clearly trying to figure out what weather I was talking about, as Floris's spring had been every bit as mild and predictable as usual this year.

"We're doing our best to make sure the festival proceeds uninterrupted," I said. At least, that much was the truth.

Lady Camellia considered this. She seemed to want to say something more but decided against it. "That's good to know," she finally said. "Thank you, Mr. Gilding."

"Of course." I offered another slight bow. "I'm always happy to clear up confusion about our gardens."

She slipped away, back to the carefree game. None

of those courtiers knew the danger our land was in. I silently prayed I'd find a solution in time to keep it that way.

Lady Camellia hadn't been the first one to stop me to ask about the flowers this morning. She had come third, after a stablehand and one of Lady Primrose's maids. It felt like the only people who hadn't come to talk to me about the spreading blight were the king and queen, the two people I needed to see most.

Assuming I could look them in the eye after the way I'd kissed their daughter yesterday, anyway.

There were a million corners in this garden where a person could hide from their thoughts. I went to the most foolproof of them all: My private garden, with its thick stone walls and the lock on the door.

The contagion, whatever it was, hadn't spread to my garden. Not yet. It was still perfect. The vines that swung overhead exploded with profusions of leaves, each one greener than the last, and everything seemed to be in bloom, from the magenta agrostemma to the yellow-striped sun tulips.

The sight of my thriving tulips hit me with a pang. The vast tulip fields surrounding the palace and the Flower Festival grounds were suffering from blight, too, with gray patches creating pockmarks in otherwise colorful fields. The Festival's hot air balloon tours of the region would be marred this year, and there was nothing I could do about it.

At least, I could ensure my entry to the flower breeding competition would be ready. I'd spent years cross-breeding and refining this variety. When it debuted, it would be beautiful and unique enough to hold its own against all the other entries. People came from around the world to enter their plants in the Festival, but someone from Floris usually won. If I could get this bloom to the competition before blight got it, we'd win again.

I hoped so, anyway.

I heaped fresh mulch around the base of the competition flowers in their raised bed, then applied my homemade seaweed-and-banana-peel compost. I'd refined this routine over the years, first with Hedley's help and then on my own.

Hedley hadn't seen my blooms since he'd left the palace. This year's flowers had improved drastically over last year's. I couldn't wait to see his face when he showed up for the flower competition.

Assuming the Flower Festival even happened this year.

Whatever pride I felt over my flowers faded as I considered the upcoming event. It was ten days away. At the rate the blight was progressing, there might not be any point in holding the festival at all. Two weeks ago, it wouldn't have even occurred to me to imagine this kind of devastation. Now, it seemed as if all the plants in the kingdom were dying.

I could forget about the festival. At this rate, we'd be lucky to have food by harvest time.

Frustration made me clumsy. I jerked my elbow toward the compost bucket perched on the edge of the raised bed, and it crashed to the paving stones, sending compost fragments everywhere. I swore and kicked the empty bucket. It rolled across the walkway, rattling loudly.

From the other end of the garden, a cautious voice called out, "Deon?"

Lilian.

My heart leapt, and my stomach dropped, which was

beginning to be a frequent reaction to the sound of her voice. I turned the bucket upright and hurried toward her before she could come find me. My flowers for the competition weren't ready for their debut, especially when they were surrounded by a veritable lake of rotten banana peels.

I hadn't needed to hurry. Lilian was sitting on the rock wall that formed a curving flowerbed along the garden wall, as elegant as ever in her trim, emerald, riding gown. She crossed her ankles and swung her legs, her riding boots gleaming in the sunlight filtering through the web of vines overhead.

"I let myself in," she said. She held out a key. "I stole this from Culpepper's office."

The palace's Head of Security, Clay Culpepper, had skeleton keys for every door on the palace grounds, including my garden's.

"Sorry," Lilian added, while I pretended to scowl at her. She pretended to look ashamed of herself.

"What am I going to do with you, Lils?" I said.

Her face grew serious. "I have an idea about that."

My shoulders tensed. Whatever she was about to say, I wasn't sure I wanted to hear it. As it stood, the choices were to give her up, which was impossible, or to fall more deeply in love with her, which was impossible to avoid.

I sat on the stone wall, too, far enough from Lilian that there was no chance of our legs accidentally brushing against each other.

"I haven't been able to stop thinking about yesterday," she said.

I clenched my jaw and let out a long breath. "I know the feeling."

"You're stuck in a dying garden. I'm stuck in an engagement to a perfectly nice man I don't want to marry." She swung her legs, her ankles still crossed. "So let's say no. To all of it. Let's run away."

I snorted. She bumped my shoulder with hers. Even that touch, unromantic as it was, made my heart pound.

Stars, how was I supposed to stay away from her?

"Where would we go?" I said.

"Badalah. I've always wanted to see their bazaars. Or maybe we could go all the way to Skyla and learn to fly."

"Do they really fly there?"

She shrugged. "That's what people say."

"Well, if people say it, it must be true."

"You're mocking me."

"Absolutely."

"Rude."

"Very."

"I'm serious, Deon." She turned to me, her blue eyes twinkling. "Why not? Let's just run away and get married. My parents will forgive us eventually."

"Your parents will forgive you," I said. "They have no reason to forgive their gardener."

"Papa's never been able to hold a grudge in his life," she said. "And Mother… Well, she'd come around."

The idea shimmered in front of me like a mirage, tempting me like nothing ever had before. We could do it: escape in the middle of the night, find someone across the border to marry us, find work in a foreign garden somewhere, and settle down in a little cottage in a town where no one knew our names. I was a hard worker, and Lilian had a thousand talents. We could make it.

And then Floris would be without its crown princess, and King Alder and Queen Rapunzel would be heartbroken, and the kingdom would lose its chance to ally its princess with the duke of its most powerful province.

Lilian was offering me a one-way ticket to heaven, and I couldn't accept it. Not without harming the whole kingdom.

"You're not making my life any easier," I said.

Lilian gave me a rueful smile. "I'm not trying to make your life easier. I'm trying to make it better. Your life and mine."

"You know I'd run away with you in a heartbeat."

"Then do it."

I glanced over, startled by the intensity of her voice. She stared at me, her eyes large and the same blue as the sky.

"I mean it," she said. "Let's go. I don't want to marry Garritt. You don't want me to marry Garritt. Why are we still sitting here?"

"You'll have to bring that up with your parents." I rested a gentle hand on her knee, and she immediately covered my hand with hers and held it tight. "We can't run off, Lils. We know we can't."

"But what if I want to?"

The petulance in her voice made me smile. Lilian wasn't normally the spoiled type, but she had a way of making the occasional demand that reminded me that she was, in fact, a princess.

I leaned over and kissed the top of her head.

"We don't always get what we want, Your Highness. Welcome to the club."

"It's a stupid club."

"The stupidest."

She sighed and leaned against me, her head on my shoulder, and her fingers twined in mine.

"We have responsibilities, both of us." I sounded like someone else: Someone older, wiser, more sensible than the man who sat here wishing life were different. "You have a kingdom resting on your shoulders. I'm trying to fix the worst case of blight I've ever seen. What will happen to Floris if we leave?"

"Floris can handle its own problems," Lilian muttered against my shoulder, but resignation filled her voice. She wasn't going to flee the kingdom. Neither was I.

No matter how much we wanted to.

"How's your mother doing?" I said. "I haven't seen her in a few days."

She hesitated, no doubt taken aback by what must have seemed to her like a change of conversation. Hedley had suggested that the queen might know something about the blight, but Lilian didn't know that, any more than she knew her mother was ill.

"All right, I suppose," she said. "I haven't seen her lately, either."

I risked a glance at Lilian's face. She didn't seem concerned.

"Oh?"

She shrugged. "Papa said she was feeling under the weather and told me not to disturb her. I'm not surprised. Her ladies-in-waiting have been passing the same cold around for a month; Mama was bound to catch it eventually. I suspect they're trying to avoid getting me sick. No doubt, Garritt would be less than enchanted by a sniffly, red-nosed wife."

Wife. In a matter of months, she would be his wife,

the Princess of Floris, and the Duchess of Thornton. My stomach twisted with pain.

"I hope she gets better soon," I said lightly. "Perhaps, I'll bring some flowers by her chambers."

"She'd love that," Lilian said. "Although you might have to give them to Papa. He insists she's not to be bothered by anyone, and the guards have been perfectly zealous about making sure he's the only person allowed into their rooms." She rolled her eyes. "Apparently, even the kitchen maids have to leave food with the guards instead of bringing it in. Papa makes such a fuss whenever she so much as sneezes."

I smiled. "I like that about him. He loves your mother."

"Yes, enough to drive her up the wall." Lilian laughed. "Unfortunately, her being indisposed means I've had to entertain Garritt's parents more than I planned. They're nice enough people, but there's only so much conversation a person can make about the weather."

"You have a thousand interests," I said. "Surely, they share a few of them."

Lilian grimaced. "Afraid not. The elder duke's main hobby seems to be betting on horse races, and the duchess's passions lie in gowns and needlework. I'm not averse to gowns and needlework, but it's hard to talk about them for more than a few minutes without dying of boredom."

"Maybe you should let Duke Remington handle his parents."

"I'll probably have to." She sighed and gazed up at me. "Stars, Deon, it's good to talk to you. I miss you."

"You see me almost every day."

"That's not what I mean."

I knew. I missed her too. My heart ached with it.

"Walk back to the castle with me, then." I nodded toward a wooden bin where I stored tightly sealed glass jars of nuts and seeds. "We can feed the birds on the way."

Outside my private garden, the world existed in a state of tightly controlled chaos. Apprentices patrolled the palace grounds as they had for the last few days, rooting out diseased plants and burning them on the spot in small, enchanted bins. In theory, removing blight as it appeared would stop the problem from spreading, but I couldn't tell whether it was working. The gray rot kept showing up, and it kept spreading, appearing farther and farther from the palace each day.

Lilian watched one of the apprentices dig out a diseased daylily and toss it into his bin. The fire leapt and devoured the soggy flower with a flash of light, and Lilian's lips tightened into a thin line.

"There's got to be something we can do," she murmured.

The same thought had played over and over in my head since I'd first discovered the blight, the words growing more frantic with each new death in the gardens.

"At least, the birds don't seem to have noticed," I said.

It was a small consolation, but a distracting one. Nesting season had begun, and the robins and sparrows were eager for the seeds we tossed them. They danced and pecked and flew away, only to be replaced by others who had realized what was happening. A couple of doves swooped in to join the feast, and Lilian laughed at their little head bobs.

"Must be nice to be a bird." Lilian tossed another handful of seeds, and an enterprising robin jumped on the fresh offering with a flap of its wings. A tiny chickadee hopped along behind, gathering up the crumbs the other birds had left behind. "They get to choose their own mates and live wherever they want."

"No hands, though," I said. "They have to use their beaks for everything. That's got to be inconvenient."

"I guess that would get old after a while," she conceded.

"But I wouldn't mind being able to fly."

"Might make up for the lack of fingers."

She threw the last few seeds to the birds, who gobbled them up and eyed us, waiting for more. She began walking toward the palace again, and I fell into step beside her. Her hand slipped into mine, and I squeezed.

I'd take hands over wings any day.

I dared to hold on as we wandered through one of the butterfly gardens full of daisies and goldenrod and milkweed. She was so much smaller than me, the golden crown of her head barely reaching my nose, and her fingers delicate under my touch. It would be easy to think of her as a soft, decorative thing, and anyone who did so underestimated her at their peril. I made a silent wish that Duke Remington would appreciate every facet of his bride, from her optimistic spirit to her vast knowledge of botany and literature to the sense of compassion and duty that colored her every choice. He would never know what she'd sacrificed to be his wife and the queen Floris needed. Even so, I hoped he'd recognize her generosity and love her for it.

As if he'd been conjured by my thoughts, the Duke of Thornton's head appeared beyond a stand of rose bushes. I dropped Lilian's hand, and a moment later, the rest of him emerged, striding toward us with purpose.

"My darling," he called. He held out a hand as he approached and offered me a wide smile. "Mr. Gilding, how are you?"

"I'm well, thank you, Your Grace." I shook his hand and bowed my head.

Lilian, her face a little flushed, smoothed her riding skirts. "Garritt, I didn't think I'd see you again until supper. Papa said he was going to show you the armory first."

"So he did." Duke Remington held out his arm, and Lilian took it. "We also had a wonderful conversation." They moved down the walkway, and I lingered behind to give them room, but the duke glanced over his shoulder. "Walk back to the palace with us if you like, Mr. Gilding. The whole kingdom will know what I have to say soon enough."

I fell into an awkward step just behind them.

"I told your father how much I've enjoyed getting to know you," Duke Remington said. He paused, took Lilian's hand, and raised it to his lips.

My face heated, and I looked away until he laced her arm back through his and resumed walking.

"As neither we nor our parents have raised any objections from our week together, your father and I agreed it's time we move to the next step of our betrothal."

I couldn't see the duke's face from behind, but it was clear from his tone that he was wearing an enormous grin. I gritted my teeth together and stared straight ahead, past Lilian and the duke, and toward some imaginary point in the far distance.

"You mean—" Lilian started.

"Announcing our engagement." Enthusiasm bubbled from his voice. "Your father has already arranged to have our photographs taken tomorrow so the newspapers can share the good news on the third of the month."

"So soon!" Lilian said.

The duke didn't catch the hesitation in her words. How could he? Lilian had been trained in diplomacy from infancy. But I heard it, and I bit my tongue to stop myself from interrupting.

This wasn't my conversation. This wasn't my decision. Lilian wasn't my bride.

"Isn't it wonderful?" The duke glanced over his shoulder again. "And, no doubt, the palace will be glad to know they can start planning the wedding."

"I'm sure the heads of staff will be glad for all the advance notice you can give them," I said as if we were talking about something other than the end of the world.

"You are pleased, aren't you, my dear?" the duke said, looking down fondly at Lilian.

She smiled, and only I saw the tightness at the corners of her eyes. "How could I be otherwise?" she said. "This is exciting news for all of Floris."

"I hope you don't mind that your father and I made the decision without you," he said. "He assured me you would have told him if you weren't ready to proceed with our marriage."

Lilian hesitated for the briefest of instants before patting the duke's arm. "My papa knows me well. Have you told your parents yet?"

I couldn't stand another second of this.

"Excuse me," I blurted. They turned, startled, and I bowed deeply enough to hide my face. "I have to stop by one of the tool sheds. Please continue without me, and congratulations on your engagement."

"Thank you, Mr. Gilding," the duke said brightly.

“Thank you, Deon,” Lilian murmured.

It was everything I could do to walk away without breaking into a run.

2ND APRIL

I signed the bottom of the Flower Festival map and handed it back across my rarely-used desk to the Horticulture Council secretary. He tucked the paper neatly into his green leather folio.

"Here's a copy for you to keep." He was a tall, thin young man who hadn't quite grown into his knees and elbows. He reminded me of myself: tasked with important responsibilities and anxious to perform his tasks well.

I accepted the paper, which showed the palace's display areas, sales tables, and warehouse assignments. Each of our reserved parcels of fairground space was outlined in red ink and labeled *Palace* in a tidy scrawl.

There were so many of these little rectangles, each one destined to be filled with horticulture displays or crates of tulip bulbs for sale. A week ago, the thousands of details that ensured each flower and staff member would end up in the right place at the right time had overwhelmed me. Now, I wished that was all I had to worry about.

The secretary shuffled his papers and pursed his lips. Finally, I cleared my throat.

"Is there anything else?"

"No," he said abruptly, then, as if he'd had to dare himself to ask, he added, "I don't suppose you can tell me anything new about the blight that's been affecting the kingdom?"

I bit back a sigh. I couldn't blame him for asking, but I rather wished I'd thought to have cards printed up informing people that asking was as pointless as trying to identify the disease was turning out to be.

"We've got all our best minds working on it," I said. "I'll share anything I learn with the Horticulture Council, as I hope they'd share with me."

It was nothing, as answers went, but the secretary put his hat back on and shrugged as if to say he'd had to ask.

"That's what the king said at his meeting with them yesterday," the secretary said. "Or so I hear."

I held out a hand to stop him from leaving. "King Alder met with the Council?"

"Yesterday." The man frowned a little. "Didn't you know?"

"I must have forgotten." I waved the paper he'd handed me. "So much to think about. Slipped my mind."

The minute the secretary left and closed the door behind him, I slammed the paper down on my desk. Why had King Alder gone to see the Horticulture Council? He hadn't talked to *me* about all this, and I'd been trying to get an audience with him for days. He was aware of the problem, clearly.

Sticks and stones, I had to be doing something wrong if he didn't even want to talk to his Head Gardener about the blight. Or maybe he just knew that I'd kissed Lilian a few days ago, and that was reason enough to avoid me.

Lilian had been right. We should have run away. Even if we managed to stop the plague spreading across the kingdom, it seemed like I might not have a job here for much longer anyway.

Before I could get my composure back, someone knocked on my office door, then opened it without waiting for an invitation. I stood and prepared to remind whichever of my staff members it was that they shouldn't just barge in even if they *did* think a spotted garden slug would do my job better than me, but the words died on my lips.

"What are you doing indoors on a beautiful day like this?" Hedley asked. He laced his thumb behind one of his suspenders. "Thought I taught you better than that."

"Am I glad to see you!"

I greeted him with a big hug and invited him to sit down. Sliding into my chair on the other side of the desk was surreal. These roles were supposed to be reversed. He was supposed to be in the big chair, and I was supposed to be the one coming to visit him.

"I like what you've done with the place," Hedley said with a chuckle.

The office was as bare as if Hedley had just moved out, the only proof of my presence the scattered pile of papers on my desk and the bottle with black ink smeared down the side.

"Can't say I spend much time in here. I keep meaning to get a houseplant or two, but I haven't been able to get one of those clever Forge lamps yet." The office had one window, but it sat in the shadow of another wing of the castle for most of the day. There wasn't enough light to keep so much as a common ivy happy. The office of Hedley's day had been filled with greenery and lamps that simulated sunlight.

My office would eventually look like his had, assuming I didn't get thrown out on my ear first.

"I didn't think you were going to be here until closer to the Festival."

Hedley's silvery eyebrows drew down. "Afraid I couldn't wait that long," he said, resting his hands on his stomach. He'd always been a muscular man from years of hard work in the gardens. In retirement, his wife's good cooking had softened his frame and given him the start of a belly. "I came to the capital yesterday to see this blight for myself. In the ground, not just in that specimen jar you brought to me."

"It hasn't gotten as far as Goldenrod yet, then?"

"Not yet," he said. "Seems it's only a matter of time."

I sighed. "We'd be fools to think otherwise. What have you learned?"

"Problem's worse than I feared," he said. "I'll admit I hoped the newspapers were blowing things out of proportion."

"I wish that's all it was."

"Would you permit me to examine the palace grounds?"

I leaned forward. "Of course. Please."

"Only I don't want you to think I'm overstepping my bounds."

"Stars, Hedley." I ran a hand through my hair.

"Overstep all you like. This situation is beyond me. It's beyond any of us."

"You sure Jonquil isn't prepared to solve the whole thing with a wave of his hand?"

Hedley's face didn't change, but his eyes twinkled. He knew the garden staff as well as I did, probably better, and Jonquil's moods had never been all daisies and sunshine.

"I threatened to fire him," I admitted.

Hedley laughed and tapped the edge of the desk with a closed fist. "Oh, I'd have liked to have been there for that. How'd he take it?"

"Not well," I said. "He's been worse than usual since you left, but the stress of this past week's been getting to everyone."

The light in Hedley's eyes faded. "It's not just the staff," he said. "Everyone's being hit by this blight." He rubbed his short, well-trimmed beard. "These flowers we grow, they're not just Floris's main export. They're tied to the happiness of the people."

"We're all happier surrounded by plants," I said. "Especially ones that aren't doing their best to die on us."

He shook his head. "No, it's more than that." He let out a long breath and fixed me with his gaze. "Much more. About eighteen years ago, the people of Floris were miserable."

I raised an eyebrow. It seemed like an odd way to begin a story, but it was clear he was starting one. He leaned back in his seat and settled in, fixing me with his gaze.

"You likely don't know much about it, because folks don't like to talk about their mistakes. But Floris was full of mistakes. So were the rest of the kingdoms."

I remembered that from my history lessons. The kingdoms had been prone to disagreements, from diplomatic standoffs over trade embargoes to outright wars. That had all changed shortly after King Alder took the throne. He had reached out to leaders of other nations and proposed friendlier relations between the kingdoms, and they had been receptive.

I knew that. Everyone did. But I wasn't about to interrupt Hedley just so I could tell him that.

"We didn't have a Flower Festival back then," he continued. "No point. Nobody wanted to come to Floris, and nobody from Floris wanted to let foreigners in. Besides, everyone was in such a bad mood in the other countries that they weren't about to spend their money on frivolities like *flowers*."

He scoffed a little. Flowers weren't a frivolity, every Florian understood that. Beauty was critical to happiness, and nature was the balm of every spirit. That message was our gift to the world—a message that we shared at every Flower Festival.

"Then, things changed." Hedley drummed his fingers on his stomach and watched me. "It was sudden. Floris had always been full of greenery, but when the king and queen married, the flowers bloomed like we'd never seen. The colors grew more vivid. Blossoms hung from trees for months, then grew into the juiciest apples imaginable. The fragrance that filled the kingdom..." He trailed off and pursed his lips a little. "Well, you wouldn't be aware of how different things became. You live with that sweetness in the air every day, and you've never known any different."

He was leading me somewhere with all this. I narrowed my eyes.

"Why did it happen when the king and queen

married?" I said.

Hedley tapped the side of his nose. "That's an interesting question, isn't it?"

"And you think the blight is making people unhappy again?" I said. "Like they used to be?"

He sat, waiting for me to form my own conclusions. I tilted my head and searched his face for clues. He believed what he was saying, that much was for sure. And he'd believed what he'd said about a curse.

"You think the flowers are being cursed, and that's making everyone miserable?" I said. "Who would be that upset at our kingdom?"

"Maybe no one," he said. "Maybe we weren't cursed. Maybe we got blessed."

He nodded toward me, and I remembered something else that had happened eighteen years ago. I frowned at Hedley, but he was still watching me in silence, waiting for me to connect the dots.

"I showed up right after the royal marriage, too," I said. "That feels odd, doesn't it? Like too much of a coincidence?"

He raised his eyebrows just slightly, and I couldn't tell whether he was interested or had already formed these conclusions himself.

But that couldn't be right, either.

"More likely, it's *all* just coincidence," I said. "King Alder married Queen Rapunzel and just happened to inherit the throne a few months later. He started building relations with other kingdoms, and someone in Floris thought he was a good enough king that they could drop a baby off on the doorstep and trust it would be taken care of. Floris didn't change because of magic. We just got a good king."

"Also a possibility," he said.

"You don't believe it, though, do you?"

He shrugged and laced a thumb behind one of his suspenders. "Haven't decided yet. That's part of why I'm here. I need to see this blight for myself, maybe see the queen."

"Good luck."

He squinted a little. "What do you mean?"

"I mean, good luck." I couldn't stop the frustration from leaking into my voice. "The queen won't see anyone. Not even Lilian."

"Makes it all the more important that I see the spread of this disease for myself." He clapped his hands onto his knees and stood with a soft groan. "I don't suppose you have time to show me around? All worries of blight aside, I'd like to see what you've done with the place."

It didn't take long for Hedley to get the lay of the land. He knew these gardens like they were his own name, and he spotted the first instance of blight even before I did.

He crouched and yanked the daffodil out of the ground. Its petals were fading from yellow to a sick gray, and it drooped like all the life had been siphoned out of it.

"It's like root rot and mold and whiteflies all put together," I said. "Can't find a cause, can't find a cure."

"Can't cure a curse."

"I still don't think it's a curse."

Hedley straightened, the dying flower in his hand. "What do you know about your arrival at the palace?" he said. "When you were an infant?"

I raised an eyebrow, but Hedley was busy examining the flower from every angle and didn't see my expression. He waited, and finally, I shrugged.

"Some woman brought me to the palace," I said.

"Perhaps my mother, perhaps not. No one knows who she was."

Hedley poked his finger down the daffodil's bell and peered inside it as if the secret to the blight might be hiding down there with the pollen.

"The king and queen could have sent me to an orphanage, but they took me in." It was a kindness that still surprised me. I wasn't sure what I'd do if someone showed up on my doorstep with a babe in arms. But from the way Queen Rapunzel told it, they hadn't thought twice. "You know the rest. I was schooled alongside Lilian and tried my hand at different career paths until I ended up as a gardener."

"Have you ever tried to find your real parents?"

"Once or twice. There was no paperwork. Didn't seem to matter much in the end."

I'd been curious about where I'd come from, of course. Nobody could help that. But whoever my parents had been, they hadn't wanted or been able to care for me. The king and queen and Hedley had stepped in and been there for me in every way that mattered. It felt almost ungrateful to look for more.

"You think I had something to do with all the flowers blooming brighter?" I said. "Like maybe I was part of it somehow?"

Hedley made a noncommittal noise and bent to examine the healthy daffodils that had been closest to the blighted one. His movements were slow and methodical, and I suspected his eyes saw more than mine, trained as they were by decades of experience.

"Maybe whoever brought me left some magic in the kingdom," I said. "I don't have magic myself, but you said the gardens do. Perhaps it's wearing off."

He made another noise, which was as impossible to

decipher as the first.

"Or maybe—"

I was cut off by the sound of raised voices. I paused, listening. They seemed to be coming from the palace—or, rather, from the other side of the nearest tower. I took off at a jog toward the noise, and Hedley followed.

When I rounded the tower, it took a moment for my eyes to make sense of the nightmare in front of them. People, swarms of them, were walking all over the palace grounds, spilling off the paths and into the flower beds on every side. They walked across beds of petunias and through rows of seedlings. They climbed over low garden fences and leaned against tree trunks. A man wearing a navy blue hat picked one of my flowers, smelled it, and tossed it on the ground.

Hedley came to a stop just behind me. I didn't have to hear his sudden stream of curses to know he was angry; the rage fairly crackled from him.

It was nothing against mine.

I strode forward into the crowd. A number of them had cameras, and those who didn't were clutching notebooks and pens. I grabbed the arm of the nearest person.

"What in blazes is going on?" I growled.

He blinked as if he couldn't fathom why someone would ask him such a question. "We're here to report on the blight." He scrabbled in his jacket pocket and pulled out a wrinkled piece of paper. "Here, here's my press pass."

"I don't give a damn about your press pass. Get off this flower bed."

He glanced down and started. Clearly, the imbecile hadn't realized he was standing *on* a flower bed.

"Sticks and stones," Hedley muttered behind me. He

yanked a couple of journalists out of a bed of irises. I'd never seen him this angry; his face was red, as though it was taking everything he had not to deck them across the face.

I looked around for guards or tour guides or anyone who might have a semblance of authority over this mob, but the journalists and photographers seemed to be utterly without supervision or basic human decency. I whirled on a woman in a trim violet suit.

"The palace grounds are closed," I said. "Get off this property."

She narrowed her eyes at me and raised her notebook. "And you are?"

"Deon Gilding, Head Gardener," I snapped. "These are not the public grounds, and press passes were never used for this kind of... *destruction.*"

She didn't even hesitate. "And what can you tell us about the blight spreading from the castle grounds?"

"Nothing," I said. "Not one thing. Get out."

"This press pass gives me access to the palace grounds until six this evening," she said, flipping her notebook to show me the pass clipped to her page. "Do you have a response to the accusations that your gardeners are the ones who spread the disease from the palace to neighboring farms?"

I shouldered past her. They were turning the garden into wreckage faster than the blight, and I needed someone with the authority to get them out of there.

I didn't bother trying to see the queen. That was a lost cause. Instead, I wasted ten minutes trying to track down the king before finally learning from a housemaid that he was visiting with the queen and wasn't to be disturbed.

I balled my fist to keep myself from driving it into the

nearest tranquil landscape painting and thanked her with gritted teeth.

"Sorry," she said, offering an apologetic smile.

The disaster area outside wasn't her fault. I forced myself to smile back and made a beeline for the front doors.

"I know," the palace guard standing at the top of the stairs said before I could open my mouth. I knew him, at least in passing. Kale had worked at the palace almost as long as I had, and we'd always been friendly. "I sent a few guards over to deal with the problem."

"They have press passes." I couldn't get the sarcasm out of my voice.

Kale nodded, jaw tight. "So they told us." He jerked his chin out toward the palace driveway, which was unexpectedly light on reporters who thought the rules of civilized society didn't apply to them. Only a couple of journalists stood out there, talking to each other and glancing around the driveway with vaguely lost expressions. "I made it clear that press passes can be revoked at the palace's convenience and that vandalizing the palace's grounds was certainly cause for termination. Unfortunately, there are a lot of them, they're tenacious, and we can't use any significant force on the press without the royal family's permission."

"I've already tried to find the king."

His jaw twitched. "I didn't bother."

"What about Princess Lilian?" I said. "Couldn't she do something?"

He gave it a moment of thought, then let out a sharp sigh. "I'd be willing to risk acting on her orders," he said. "You're not going to have any luck reaching her, though. Her Highness's schedule has her doing engagement photos all afternoon."

"Where?"

"Throne room," he said. "I can't imagine they'll take kindly to an interruption, though."

"Well, I don't take kindly to people destroying the grounds."

I spun on my heel and marched inside. Lilian and her entourage were easy enough to find; the lights from the flashbulb bounced off the wall in the corridor opposite the throne room doors. I paused in the entryway. Lilian and Duke Remington stood together in front of a window. They were locked together in a half-embrace, facing toward one another with their hands on each other's arms. The photographer danced around them, snapping pictures from different angles, then nodded at them.

"Now, Your Highness, I want you to turn around," she said. "Your Grace, put your arms around her waist like so, and now look up and smile."

They followed her instructions like obedient puppets, and the photographer lit up the room with another series of flashes. Lilian blinked a few times, and the duke leaned forward a little to say something to her. She replied and laughed a little. Jealousy flared inside me.

I slipped inside the room and caught Lilian's eye. She narrowed her eyes in question, and I waved her toward me. She held up a hand and asked the photographer to wait a moment.

The duke caught her arm and murmured something to her, and she smiled up at him and nodded. He disengaged from her arm and came toward me, and before I could say anything to stop them, Lilian, the photographer, and the photographer's two assistants all bustled off to another room.

"Lilian is terribly busy today," the duke said. "Did you need something?"

His voice was cooler than it had been the last few times we'd spoken. The hairs on the back of my neck stood up, a silent caution I didn't know how to interpret.

"I need to speak with her," I said. "There's a situation outside, and only Her Highness has the authority to help."

"I daresay I might be able to assist." Everything about him seemed civil. Still, unease prickled across my skin. "After all, I'm about to become Lilian's husband."

"To tell you the truth, I need the king," I said. "But Lilian's the next best thing."

His eyebrow raised, and I realized I'd called her *Lilian* instead of by her title. My face heated, but I stood tall.

"There's an absolute mob of press outside," I said. "They're all over the grounds destroying things. The guards won't use force to remove them without the approval of someone in the royal family, and these journalists aren't going to go anywhere without force."

The corners of Duke Remington's mouth tightened. "You would seek to restrict their access to the palace? I've always been opposed to censoring the press."

"I don't want to censor them; I want them off my tulip beds."

Immediately, I regretted the way I'd spoken. My tone was too loud, too sharp—too much to have come from a gardener toward the future king of Floris.

"Sir," I added, much too late.

The duke frowned at me. "It seems that the palace guards shouldn't need the princess's command to handle so simple a disturbance."

"As I said—"

"*Princess* Lilian is having photographs of her

engagement ring taken now," he said. "She has a very busy day, and I'm certain palace security doesn't need her assistance with such a simple matter. Keeping rabble-rousers from the grounds is their job. I suggest you stop over-involving yourself and let them do it."

I stared at him, my brain sputtering at the accusation. How could I *over-involve myself* in *my gardens?* It was my job to nurture and protect every blade of grass in these forty acres, and part of that included pest management, whether that meant beetles or snails or reporters who thought they were important enough to go trampling all over the plants they claimed to be reporting on.

The duke leaned in toward me. His voice remained polite, but there was an edge to it now. "I understand that the king and queen have allowed you a good deal of freedom to impose on Lilian's time and good graces. But you're not children anymore, and Lilian's attentions are on more important matters now. You're a good man, Deon. Let her enjoy her engagement and don't bother the princess with such petty concerns."

I opened my mouth, but nothing came out. More important matters? Petty concerns? I couldn't tell whether he was joking or had just taken leave from his senses.

He seemed to take my silence as agreement. He offered a smile and clapped me on the arm.

"Your hard work is appreciated, Deon," he said, as if he had any right to make such a statement on behalf of the crown, and strode away before my mind could put any of my confused disbelief into words.

3RD APRIL

The guards never did get the journalists to leave the palace grounds. Instead, after they'd all but destroyed several flowerbeds and torn up the grass in a rose garden, the reporters and photographers appeared to have gotten what they'd come for and filtered out.

Their spoils were on full display in the next morning's papers.

BLIGHT OVERTAKES PALACE GROUNDS, read one headline, above a series of pictures of gray flowers, trampled tulip stems, and glowing burn barrels. *PALACE GARDENER DENIES ALLEGATIONS,* read another, above an unflattering article that painted me as a liar and a buffoon. This one was accompanied by a spread of photographs of dying crops, and the article was loaded with claims from anonymous sources that insisted that the blight had been carried from the palace to a nearby tomato farm by an unnamed apprentice gardener.

The articles were full of lies and misinformation and wild assumptions, and it would have been impossible to filter truth from guesswork if I hadn't been the most well-informed person in the world on the subject of the blight at the palace.

I stabbed a sausage and turned the page of the paper in front of me. A housemaid across the table glanced up at me and went back to the sports section of the paper.

They all knew what was going on. None of them were foolish enough to bring it up.

Like a fool, I hoped that the next few pages might contain other news—an update on the construction of the new luxury hotel on the coast, a human interest story about a dog that had rescued a bunny, a scandal featuring one of the opera singers who always seemed to be falling in and out of love with each other. I scoured the page for anything that might brighten this morning, and my eyes landed instead on an enormous photograph of Lilian and Duke Remington smiling up at each other with Lilian's enormous new ring winking on her finger.

Stinging nettles.

Reed dropped into the seat next to me before I could turn the offending page. He pulled a pitcher of strawberry juice toward us.

"She doesn't look too happy, does she?" he said.

It took me a second to realize he was referring to Lilian. He nodded down at the paper, and I realized with a start that he was right.

She was smiling, but the smile was the one that usually graced her face during boring dinners or tedious diplomatic affairs. Her lips were drawn into a perfect expression of happiness, but her eyes were dull as they gazed up at the duke.

It was a wonder I hadn't noticed it before.

Then again, I wasn't in the best of moods this morning.

"Her lady-in-waiting's ladies' maid's assistant said the same thing," one of the housemaids, Daisy, said. It took me a second to make sense of that particular chain of command, and then I tilted my head at her, asking for more.

She didn't need convincing.

"Word among the ladies' maids is that Princess Lilian isn't too excited about her upcoming marriage. Some of them think she's not looking forward to having his parents as in-laws. A few people think she doesn't like *him*, but that doesn't hardly seem possible. Personally, I think she's worried about her mother." She glanced around the table and lowered her voice. "You do know the queen is ill, right?"

Murmurs rippled among the servants at the table, some of them surprised and others smug at having already been in on the gossip.

Daisy cleared her throat and buttered a slice of toast, her movements grand as she happily held court. "It's nothing serious, or at least, that's what the king and queen say. Only no one's seen the queen in absolute *days* now, and isn't that odd?"

"It's true," one of the kitchen maids piped up. "Willow and Hazel both took food to the queen's rooms recently, and neither one of them was so much as allowed in."

"That doesn't mean the queen's doing all that poorly," another kitchen hand objected as he poured himself another cup of coffee. "Just that maybe she doesn't want to be bothered by a bunch of gossipy serving girls."

Daisy gave him a severe look. "Be that as it may, it's odd that she's hiding away and odder still that the king is joining her."

I glanced up. "What do you mean?"

She raised an eyebrow at me. "You can't tell me you haven't noticed His Majesty is nowhere to be seen lately. And meanwhile, the Duke of Thornton is swanning around the castle like he owns the place, meeting with the Horticulture Council, and volunteering to step in for the opening of the new paper mill over in Rootstock. It's like he's trying to take over as the king before he's so much as married the princess."

"He met with the Horticulture Council?" I blurted.

"Day before yesterday," she said. "His valet's laundress's apprentice said he's likely to start meeting with them regularly in the king's place."

I felt Reed's eyes on me, but I couldn't think of anything to say. So I stood instead, scooped up my dirty dishes, and marched out of the servant's dining hall, leaving the papers behind.

I was barely out of the dining hall when Lilian almost ran into me. I grabbed her shoulders to keep us from colliding.

"Lilian." I hesitated, taking in her pale face and wide eyes. I let my hands drift down her arms. "Are you okay?"

She didn't spend a lot of time in the servant's quarters these days. It was odd to see her here now, dressed in one of her calf-length dancing dresses and with pink ribbons in her hair.

"I left my dancing class early," she said. "I had to see you."

"What's wrong?"

"I don't know," she said. "Nothing. Everything. I feel like I'm losing my mind."

I pulled her in for a hug, and she buried her face in my shoulder. She smelled of magnolias.

"What's going on, Lils?"

"Mother is sick," she said. "I mean, *really* sick, worse than I thought. I don't know what to do."

She didn't pull away from our embrace. I didn't, either.

I couldn't pretend to be entirely surprised. It was strange for the queen to stay abed with illness, and stranger still for her to refuse visitors. No matter what King Alder said, somewhere in the back of my mind, I'd known that things couldn't be all right.

Still, hearing it from Lilian made my stomach lurch.

"What's happening?" I said. "Tell me all about it."

I glanced behind me. No one had followed me out, but it was only a matter of time. I didn't need Daisy or one of the others witnessing Lilian and me together like this.

"On second thought, let's go somewhere we can talk. Let's go walk in the gardens."

She shook her head. "My rooms. I don't want to be around people right now."

We slipped up a back staircase that was usually reserved for the housemaids. When we were safely in Lilian's sitting room, she dropped onto the sofa and curled up with her legs underneath her. One of her small dogs jumped up from where it had been sleeping on a cushion and leapt onto Lilian's lap, aware that its mistress needed comfort. She pulled the pup in close and buried her nose in its fur.

I sat down next to her, a bit closer than I probably should have, and waited for her to be ready to talk.

"I went to go see Mama," she finally said. "Father told me not to bother her, but it's been days and..." She swallowed, and her eyebrows drew together in consternation. "I just wanted to *see* her," she finally said. "It's not as if I was trying to force her to go riding with me or anything like that. I just wanted to visit and make sure she was all right. And Papa wouldn't even let me in the door! I've never seen him act like that, Deon. He was *angry* with me. And then the court physician arrived, and Papa wouldn't let him in, either. If he's not even letting Mama's *doctors* in now, what does that mean? I don't think it can be plague. It wouldn't be plague, would it? Only if it *were* plague that would explain why Papa wouldn't let doctors in, since they can't really do anything against plague and it's horribly contagious and--"

She burst into tears.

I would have moved heaven and earth in that moment to stop those tears. But they were unstoppable, and I remembered Hyacinth Hedley's lecture from a few years ago that one should never try to *solve* a woman's problems if he could *listen* to them instead. That didn't make sense to me, but Hyacinth understood women a sight better than I did. So I slid across the couch and took Lilian in my arms. The dog, annoyed at being displaced, shifted and pawed at her skirts.

"I'm so sorry, Lils." I rubbed her back as she cried into my chest. I felt utterly useless, just sitting here while I could be out murdering her problems instead, but she clung to me and seemed to be taking something from my presence.

When her sobs slowed to hiccups, I finally ventured to speak.

"I don't think it can be plague," I said cautiously.

"Last time there was a plague scare, the different parts of the palace were quarantined, remember?"

"Now, *Mother's* being quarantined." Lilian took a deep, shuddering breath, and it seemed she was on the verge of another wave of tears.

"*Doctors* put quarantines in place," I said. "This one sounds like it's just being enforced by your father. He gets overprotective of the queen. He told me that."

She sniffled and looked up at me. Her eyes were red, and her eyelids were puffy, and the sight of them triggered an overpowering urge to protect her from the world. I settled for tightening my arms around her.

"Papa does tend to hover when either Mama or I are sick," she admitted. "It drives Mama crazy."

"There you go," I said. "Most likely, she's got a bad cold, and your father's taking it too seriously."

She patted her skirts and muttered something about pockets. I reached into mine and dug out a handkerchief. She took it with a grateful sniffle and blew her nose.

"You don't think anything's really, truly wrong, then?"

I hadn't said that. But I wouldn't have told her as much, not for the world.

"I think if it were serious, your father would tell you."

Did I believe that? I wasn't sure. I bit my lip and dropped a kiss on Lilian's head.

"I wish he'd collect himself, then," she said. "Ever since Mama started feeling under the weather, Papa's been avoiding everyone and everything, even his duties. He's letting Garritt be in charge instead. Garritt says they spoke about it, and Papa agreed it would be a good opportunity for him to develop his leadership abilities. He's going to be king someday, after all, and Papa thinks he ought to get a little practice in. That's what

Garritt says, anyway. I think Papa just doesn't want to be bothered now that Mama's ill."

She wiped her nose on the handkerchief, and her dog jumped up to lick at the tear marks that still streaked down her face.

"Things are going to be all right," I said as if I had the power to promise any such thing. "I'll bet the queen is up and back to normal within the next week. In fact--"

I was cut off by the sitting room door opening. Duke Remington looked at us, from Lilian's tear-streaked face to my arms tightly around her, and his jaw hardened.

"What are you doing here?" he demanded.

I let go of Lilian and scrambled to my feet. I bowed to the duke, my face hot and my stomach churning.

"Your Grace," I said. "Forgive me, I was assisting Princess Lilian with a..." I trailed off and glanced at Lilian, whose face was as red as mine felt.

"He was talking me through something," Lilian said. The dog on her lap eyed the duke with caution and kept looking back at Lilian's face as if to be sure she was all right. "I asked him to come up here. I didn't want to make a scene in front of the servants."

"All but one, it seems." The duke tried to play the comment off as a joke, but there was no disguising the coldness in his face as he glared at me. "I don't think I need to tell either of you how inappropriate this looks."

Lilian set her dog aside and stood, still clutching my handkerchief. "I'm worried about my mother," she said. "She won't see me, and I'm afraid her condition is worse than my father will admit. Deon was just trying to help."

The duke gave me a dirty look and then smiled gently at Lilian. "My love, I hope you know you can always come to me for comfort."

Lilian hesitated just a second too long. “Of course,” she said. “I should have done that first. I’m just so accustomed to turning to Deon for things. He and I have been friends for such a long time. You understand.”

“I do.” The duke stepped toward Lilian, and she seemed to tense. He wrapped an arm around her shoulder, his limb taking the place where mine had just been as easily as if he owned her. “With all due respect to both of you, and to the apparent depth of your, ah, *friendship,* I think it’s time that we all establish some boundaries around what’s appropriate and what isn’t.”

“We weren’t doing anything--” Lilian started, but he interrupted her.

“I’m sure you weren’t. And yet, I’m also sure you understand how it might look if, say, one of your housemaids were the one to walk in on that scene instead of me?”

I bowed to him again. “My apologies, sir. I’ll excuse myself.”

“I think that’s a good idea,” the duke said. “In fact…”

He let silence hang in the air for a long moment. Dread rose up inside me, thick and heavy.

“I think it might be best if you were to stay outside the palace for the next little while,” he said. “Clearly, you can’t stop yourself from taking liberties with your princess, and it appears she’s too good-natured to stop you. A little distance would be good for everybody.”

I took a step toward him. “I’m the Head Gardener.”

“So, perhaps that’s where you ought to stay,” he said, the coldness in his voice turning to ice. “In the garden. Guard!”

The sentry outside Lilian’s quarters appeared in an instant, tense and ready for action.

“Remove Mr. Gilding from the palace,” he ordered

crisply. "See that he doesn't set foot inside this building except on my orders."

"Garritt!" Lilian cried. She rushed out of the duke's embrace and grabbed my arm as if she had the strength to pull me away from the guard if it came to that. She turned to her sentry. "Leif, don't touch him."

The guard bowed, lips tight. "Forgive me, Your Highness, but His Majesty made it clear we're all to follow Duke Remington's orders."

"I'm your princess!"

"And your father is my king, Your Highness," he said with another apologetic bow.

He grabbed my arm. I wrenched it away from him.

"I can walk on my own, thanks," I said.

"You'd better do it, then," the guard said, although his voice didn't carry much of an edge.

"Garritt, don't you dare," Lilian said, turning back to him with a scowl that would have stopped me in my tracks.

He only smiled. "You'll thank me for this later," he said. "After all, I'm about to become your husband. Our marriage will be happier if we don't have a gardener between us."

The guard nudged me, and I marched out of Lilian's quarters with my head held high.

"He talked to her like she was a *child.*" I stormed across the room and slammed a terra cotta pot onto the worktable. It shattered into three large shards. I swore and threw the pieces in the bin. "And then he ordered me marched out of the palace like a criminal. I'm not even allowed back into my *bedroom* without his say-so.

Where am I supposed to sleep, a garden shed?"

"He did find you cozied up with his betrothed," Hedley pointed out from his seat on the edge of a raised bed. His calm, reasonable tone set my teeth on edge.

"She was *crying*."

"That might have made it worse."

"It's not my fault she came to me for comfort!"

"That definitely made it worse," Hedley said. "He's a man, Deon. He's not going to take kindly to the realization that his bride might prefer another."

"We weren't doing anything wrong," I snapped, setting another pot down on the worktable with slightly more care. "It wasn't as if he caught us in the throes of some passionate embrace. She was sad. I was patting her back. Someone alert the presses."

Not that the presses wouldn't have had a field day with that. They'd found enough to yammer on when it came to the palace grounds. Anything that happened in the princess's chambers was likely to send them into hysterics.

"I can't just stop being friends with Lilian," I said.

"Are you friends?"

There was too much truth buried in the question. Lilian and I weren't friends. Or, rather, we were friends, but we were more, too. Companions and confidants and playmates and everything but lovers, and that hung between us so heavily, it might as well have been strung up in lights for all the world to see.

"I'm not going to abandon her." I dumped a spadeful of light, chunky soil into the pot. "Especially not when Duke Remington has turned out to be such a colossal..." I trailed off, trying to find the right word. Nothing I could come up with felt insulting enough.

Hedley stood with a soft grunt and came over to me.

He pulled down a second pot and began filling it with the same thick soil, full of bark and little white pearls of perlite.

"I don't like to be the one to tell you this, but you have bigger problems than those of love."

I snorted. "Trust me, I don't need the reminder."

"What are you planning to do about it?" he said.

I sighed and pulled on some thick leather gloves. "I was hoping you would have some ideas. I'm at dead ends everywhere I turn. I don't suppose you've had a breakthrough on this blight?"

"No breakthroughs," he said. "Which suggests it might be time to confirm an earlier theory."

"Oh? And what's that?"

I picked up a tiny, prickly cactus from a tray filled with them and set it atop the soil. A few more, and this would be a beautiful arrangement, ready to sell at the Festival to anyone with a penchant for exotic greenery.

"I think you need to go see the queen."

I laughed, entirely without humor. "You're funny, Hedley. You really are."

"I'm serious is what I am." He arranged a small, prickly cactus into his pot. He didn't look at me, and I had a feeling that was intentional. Hedley had never looked straight at me when he'd been delivering important advice, whether it had been on how to handle an aphid infestation in my herb garden or just him telling me that I needed to gather up my courage already and speak to my apprenticeship supervisor before the man worked me into the ground.

"Out with it," I said.

He continued to pack dirt around the base of the cacti, his movements measured.

"The thing is, nothing you've tried so far has worked,"

he said. "When that's the case, best to change course, eh?"

"I would love nothing more," I said. "But she won't see me. She won't even see Lilian. That's half of what Lilian was crying about, in fact, which His Graceless might have learned if he'd bothered to listen instead of throwing me out on my ear."

Hedley stayed silent. It was a long pause, full of unspoken disapproval, and I finally sighed.

"What are you suggesting, then?"

"I'm not suggesting anything," he said. "Only pointing out that you need to see the queen pretty badly. You can't get past her guards and through her door, so perhaps it's time to consider other approaches."

"What, you think I should climb in through her window?"

I was joking, but again, Hedley paused for a long time. I tucked a succulent into my arrangement and turned to him.

"I'm not climbing into the queen's rooms through her window."

Another long silence. "Of course not," he finally said.

"Hedley. I'm not."

"That would be the act of a desperate man."

"I'm not that desperate."

4TH APRIL

I paced the wall of the castle, eying its various ornaments and ledges and staggered roofs. There was a path, lit by the bright waxing moon. There were handholds and gaps small enough to jump, and there, on the third floor, stood the windows of the monarchs' quarters.

"You're mad, friend," I muttered to myself. "Absolutely stark, raving mad."

The other part of myself--the part that *was* desperate, that *was* willing to try anything--ignored the insult.

At least, if I died trying to see the queen, Hedley would take care of the gardens until a new Head Gardener could be chosen. He'd promised he'd stick around at least that long. He'd also told me I was being melodramatic and that his services wouldn't be needed, but now, looking up at the distance between the ground and the queen's windows, I wasn't so sure.

Still, scaling this castle wall would be a far sight easier than living with myself if I let the gardens die without doing everything in my power to stop the blight. It was visible around me, even now, in the moonlit darkness—great patches of bare soil and gray, drooping plants that wouldn't be collected until morning. We didn't have enough apprentices to keep them going around the clock in every part of the garden. That, at least, was working in my favor. I'd reassigned everyone on duty in this part of the grounds to go keep an eye on the seedlings in the greenhouse and the king's prized rainbow tulip garden. Both were far enough from the queen's quarters that, I hoped, no one would see me trying to scale the wall like I was some kind of incompetent lizard.

I propped up the ladder I'd dragged across the gardens and shifted it until the top nestled in a crack between the great stone blocks that made up the castle. The feet sank a few inches into the damp earth, and I carefully climbed onto the first rung, then the next. This ladder was tall enough to let me step sideways onto a thin ledge that marked the top of the first floor

A very thin ledge.

I balanced my weight on the narrow strip of stone and pressed my body against the wall. My stomach swayed. I'd never been scared of heights, not like some people were, but I'd also never been this far above the ground with less than a hand's width of shelf separating me from a broken leg--and there were two more floors to go.

I grasped a drainpipe that carried rainwater from the roof to a collection barrel cleverly hidden behind a lilac bush, then pulled myself hand over hand up toward the nearest window ledge. Halfway there, the pipe creaked, a horrible sound that made my heart skip several beats. I froze, but no one inside seemed to have heard the noise, and the pipe didn't tear itself from the palace wall.

"Good enough," I muttered. The sound of my own voice was strangely comforting. Unlike my current predicament, it was familiar and predictable.

"All right, you've got this," I said under my breath as if I were encouraging someone else. I almost believed the lie.

The window ledge above me looked like nothing more than a thick shadow in the moonlight, but I'd seen it from the ground and knew it would hold me. I grasped the stone windowsill with both hands and heaved myself up. Years of hard work in the gardens made the movement easy, if not smooth, and I scrambled up onto the ledge.

The window was dark and curtained, which, in addition to its proximity to the drainpipe, was why I'd chosen to come up this way. From here, there was another climb up a stone carving of a rose vine, then another heave up onto the queen's windowsill, and then--

I couldn't think past that. Every time I tried, I wanted to run in the other direction. Violating the queen's privacy was a horrible thought. Intruding late at night, when she was unwell enough that even her daughter had been banned from her chambers, made me feel sick. The most comforting thought I could reach for was that she was a queen and had access to dungeons if she happened to want to throw me in one. It would be well within her rights, and I might feel a little better if I was properly punished for what I was about to do.

Just as long as she listened to me first.

The rose carving was smooth under my fingers and full of convenient hand- and footholds. It gleamed dull silver under the moon, its head fat with petals and the shadows between them. I reached the top, my stomach still churning with the height and my nerves, then hoisted myself up onto the queen's windowsill.

Light shone from within her chambers, filtered through a gauzy curtain that faded in color from apricot to deep plum. I had only been inside the monarchs' apartments a few times when I was still quite young, but my memory had served me well. Through the curtains, I made out a bed.

A bed, and a queen, sitting amid its blankets, her hair bound for the night by a purple silk handkerchief and a book propped up against her knees. The king was nowhere to be seen.

I hesitated and watched her for a long moment through a gap in the gauzy curtains. The lamp next to the queen's bed burned brightly enough to illuminate the whole room, and it was easy enough to make out everything from the framed embroideries on the walls to the stack of novels sitting on the queen's bedside table.

She smiled a little and turned the page of her book. She was as beautiful as ever, her skin touched with roses and her eyes bright with interest in whatever she was reading. She seemed normal. Happy.

Healthy.

I crouched on the windowsill and leaned in against the glass as if a closer look would reveal the truth behind her perfectly ordinary appearance. But that only confirmed one thing: If my eyes were any kind of reliable judge, the queen was fine. Better than fine. She looked in the peak of health.

It didn't make sense. Queen Rapunzel liked to be out and about, and she would never step away from her hostessing duties, especially not when her guests were also her future in-laws. Not unless something was horrifically wrong.

Perhaps the threat wasn't to the queen's health. Maybe there was something else afoot--a threat on her life, perhaps, from another kingdom that had tired of the peace between the nations. Or perhaps the illness was a strange one that didn't follow the course of normal illnesses. Perhaps this one attacked from the inside, and didn't affect the appearance of health until the very end. Or maybe she had already recovered, and King Alder had simply asked her to stay in bed for a few extra days to be sure she was well before she resumed her duties.

That had to be it. Anything else was too ludicrous.

And if she was almost well, that meant Lilian would be able to see her soon, and I would be able to ask her about the blight. All would be well if I could only wait a couple of days.

And yet...

I sat, watching the queen through the window, my mind churning. If she would be well in a few days, I could leave without knocking on the window and having what was certain to be an awkward and difficult conversation. But if I was wrong and the queen didn't emerge from her chambers soon, the gardens might pay the price.

And I couldn't allow the gardens to get worse, not if anything else was in my power. I glanced down from the window ledge. The devastation was enough to take my breath away. Off in the distance, the burn barrels carried by roving apprentices glowed orange as they eradicated what had already been destroyed. Closer, it was easy in the moonlight to make out the patches of bare earth.

The gardens had never looked like this, not ever. They were dying. Under Hedley's watch, they had thrived. Under mine...

I took a deep breath. I had to have the awkward conversation.

I turned back to the window. Inside, the queen turned another page of her book. She seemed tranquil, content--entirely unlike someone who would be glad to be interrupted by a young man perched on her windowsill.

I raised my hand to knock anyway.

And then she shifted. She sat up and turned to adjust the pillow behind her back. Her loose purple scarf slipped at the movement and tumbled to the floor, revealing her gleaming golden hair. She twisted to bend over and pick it up from the floor.

My breath caught in my throat, and I jerked back. My left foot slipped off the ledge. My stomach dropped in sudden terror, and I reached out to grab hold of anything that could break my fall--but there was only the smooth glass of the queen's window, and it wasn't enough.

The weight of my body forced me from the ledge. I reached out with desperate fingers to grab onto the carved rose that twined up the palace wall. My fingers met stone, but it was smooth, too smooth to grip. I clung to it, searching for a crag, but each one my fingertips landed in shallow enough to only slow my fall, not break it.

I reached out for the narrow ledge that marked

the first floor. It was too thin, too delicate, and then I grabbed it, my body dangling as precariously as a broken branch hanging from a tree.

My breath caught in my throat, and my blood roared in my ears. I forced myself to breathe slowly until my vision cleared and the rapid-fire pounding of my heart slowed to hard, steady beats.

Carefully, slowly, I inched down the ledge toward the ladder. My foot landed solidly on the top rung. And then, too quickly, fueled by the relief that rushed through me in an instant, I dropped my whole weight on the ladder.

The ladder jolted. My foot slipped. The ladder wobbled and fell, taking me with it as it crashed sideways onto the lilac bush. A blinding pain tore through my ankle.

I held absolutely still, waiting for my body to tell me whether I'd died or not. After a few moments of hot agony radiating up my leg, it was clear that I had made it back to the ground with life still coursing painfully through my veins.

It took some time to disengage from the lilac bush, and all the time, my ears stayed perked for the sound of a window opening overhead or guards rushing toward me. But it seemed that Queen Rapunzel either hadn't heard the cacophony of my descent, or she'd decided her window had just been hit by a very stupid bird, and the world around me stayed quiet except for the sound of lilac leaves rubbing against one another as I tried to free myself and the ladder from the prickly branches.

On the bright side, I was going to smell marvelous when I got out of here. I swatted a blossom away from my face and managed to wriggle down the side of the bush. I landed on my feet, and another round of pain shot up my leg.

I didn't have time to feel sorry for myself. I tucked the ladder on my shoulder and hobbled back toward the greenhouse.

~

Hedley was where I had left him, carefully watering seedlings with a clever misting fan from The Forge. Artificial lights and oil lamps filled the greenhouse with pleasant yellow light, and the scent of orchids from the back wall drifted through the room and met me when I pushed open the house's glass door.

The blight hadn't been as bad in here as it was elsewhere. The disease seemed to prefer flowers that were already in bloom, and these seedlings meant for sale at the Festival were still young and weeks away from putting out their first buds.

I hopped down a row of curling sweet pea seedlings toward Hedley, who observed me with one of his thick silver eyebrows crooked.

"How did it go?" he said.

I resisted the urge to make a smart remark and hoisted myself up onto a wooden worktable instead.

"I think I sprained my ankle."

Hedley's other eyebrow went up.

"What did you do?"

"I thought it was a good idea to climb three stories up a palace wall, is what I did," I said. "I violated the queen's privacy, broke a ladder, and just about murdered a lilac bush while I was at it."

"Sounds like a productive evening."

I narrowed my eyes at him, and the corner of his mouth tightened as if he were suppressing a smile.

"Did you speak to her?"

I shook my head. "Didn't have the chance, not before I fell off the window sill. But I'm not sure I needed to. Something *is* wrong with her. Horribly wrong."

The hidden smile faded, and Hedley's face settled into an expression of worry.

I'd never really seen Hedley worried before. He was too calm and competent for fussing of any kind, but the concern on his face was impossible to misinterpret.

I took a deep breath, trying to picture exactly what I'd seen. There had been no mistaking it.

"Her hair," I said. "It's gray."

The words did nothing to explain the horror of the sight. My ankle throbbed, and frustration tightened the dread building in my chest.

"That's not what I mean. It's not gray like hair is ordinarily gray." I shook my head, annoyed at my inability to tell him what I meant. "Everyone loses color in their hair eventually. Some people started finding silver hairs years before anyone would have expected it. The queen's hair isn't like that."

I chewed on the inside of my cheek while Hedley watched me, waiting with infinite patience for me to find the words.

"It's like the flowers," I finally blurted.

That was the truth. That was the reality that sickened me to admit.

The queen's hair wasn't turning from gold to the equally dazzling silver of age. I hadn't discovered a few white hairs threaded through her sparkling tresses. Queen Rapunzel's hair was decaying, the dull colorlessness of blight creeping up her hair from the tips inexorably toward her scalp.

I couldn't bear to imagine what would happen when the gray met her skin.

Hedley took a deep breath. His gaze didn't flinch. He didn't swear or exclaim or smash things around. He just stood there, letting the horror of it sink in, and his stillness made goosebumps rise on my skin.

"I think it's going to kill her." My voice was dead, colorless, just like the rot covering my grounds and creeping towards my queen. "This disease... It's not a blight. It's a plague."

Hedley nodded, and the single tiny gesture hit me like a thorny branch to the face.

Queen Rapunzel was dying.

Lilian's mother was dying.

The land, this beautiful country of flowers and fruit and sweet-smelling air, was dying.

My throat closed up.

"It's as I feared." Hedley's voice was low and steady. "This is no ordinary pestilence, and magic is to blame. Magic, or the lack of it. I told you that all the world seemed to get brighter after the king and queen were married. Now it seems that the queen is linked to the life of the flowers, and the flowers are linked to the happiness of the kingdom."

"And what's happening in our kingdom will eventually happen throughout the world."

Hedley nodded wordlessly.

I dropped my head into my hands, and we stayed, suspended in horror and silence, for a long, long time.

I couldn't sleep. The throbbing of my ankle was partly to blame, and some of my restlessness had to do with the fact that my new bed was a pile of unicorn manure bags covered with blankets I'd gotten one of the maids to sneak out of the palace for me. I'd lied about why I was sleeping and eating outside now, and had a feeling the palace was full of gossip about how the Head Gardener felt so badly about the blight that he'd decided to penance himself by sleeping on what was essentially a pile of droppings.

That was still better than anyone knowing the truth. It seemed that Duke Remington and Lilian's guards had all kept their mouths shut about why I'd been thrown from the palace, most likely because the duke's fragile ego couldn't stand the thought of anyone knowing that Lilian hadn't turned to *him* for comfort.

Even if I'd had my bed, though, I suspected I wouldn't have been able to sleep. Every time I closed my eyes, I saw blight--on my flowers, in Lilian's strawberry patch, creeping up the queen's hair. I tossed and turned, and finally, when it was close to midnight, I got back up and pulled on my clothes.

Sharp pain danced around my ankle, and I welcomed the pain. It stole attention away from the aching in my heart, and its pain was something I knew would pass with time. I bound the swollen joint with a few scraps of landscaping cloth to keep it from twisting, then headed out into the cool spring night.

The apprentices were easy enough to find, but I walked past a few of them in the darkness until I spotted someone who looked like he could use a break. Purslane was one of the youngest of the apprentices, barely thirteen years old, and he walked around the gardens with his glowing burn barrel like someone in a trance. His eyes were glazed, and his eyelids kept drooping, but still, he kept moving and pulling up blighted plants.

I tapped him on the shoulder, and it took him a second

to react. When he realized who I was, he straightened and blinked a few times as if trying to force himself into alertness.

"Mr. Gilding, sir," he said.

"Purslane," I said. "You're doing good work out here. I want to help, but all the burn barrels are being used. Would you be willing to let me take yours for the rest of the night? And then you can go to bed?"

He couldn't hand the barrel over to me fast enough. He waited long enough to help me secure the straps over my shoulders with the glowing barrel down near my stomach, then shifted from foot to foot.

"Are you sure, sir?" he said, words slurring a little. "I can keep working."

I bit back a smile. His earnestness was at odds with his body, and the boy looked like he was about to topple where he stood.

"I'm sure," I said. "Thanks for letting me borrow your equipment. I appreciate it."

He offered an awkward and unnecessary little bow before nearly sprinting away toward the palace.

He was a good kid. He didn't deserve the devastation that was coming.

The weight of the small barrel was enough to make my whole leg throb with every step. I moved slowly but steadily through the garden, bending every so often to pull up a blighted flower by its roots and toss it in the glowing coals. Each time, enchanted flames rose to lick the plant into bright, pulsing ashes, and the magically cool metal of the barrel against my stomach flared for a moment into heat.

I passed apprentices now and again, and each time, we exchanged glances and nods. Everyone was tired, and everyone was equally committed to doing their part to keep this disease from spreading. Our efforts seemed futile, but we had to make them anyway. To do otherwise was to admit that we were powerless against the blight.

I couldn't admit that. Not yet. Not when it meant giving in to a future in which Lilian had to survive without her mother, and in which we all had to learn to live without the colorful flowers that formed so much of our culture and identities.

And our happiness, if Hedley was to be believed.

I'd never faced a gardening problem that Hedley couldn't solve. But tonight, in the greenhouse, when I'd finally broken our long silence to ask what I could do to help, he had only shrugged.

I moved slowly through the gardens. Ahead, along a walkway of sparse tulips, a familiar figure crouched, his figure lit by the flame of an oil lamp that sat on the cobblestones next to him. I hesitated and turned to go in the other direction, but Jonquil had already seen me.

He raised a hand in an unusually civil greeting. There was nothing for it but to keep walking forward and trying not to limp.

"What are you doing up?" I said.

"Couldn't sleep." He gazed across the tulip bed lining the walkway. The blight was visible here, in the empty spaces between tulips and the wilted leaves sitting where the plants' sharp green blades should have been. A pile of sickly, rotted plants sat on the cobblestones next to him. "You?"

"Same." I crouched and tossed the flowers from his pile into my barrel one at a time. They flared and died down, each one a blinding reminder of the devastation we couldn't stop.

"I can't figure it out," Jonquil said. "I know more

about tulips than anyone in the kingdom."

It could be argued that a few of the other specialists were a little ahead of him, but I didn't say anything.

He sighed. "I've tried everything. Nothing even slows the spread of the disease."

"I know," I said, and thought back to the time I'd tried to use magic I didn't even possess to heal the spreading sickness. "I've attempted dozens of interventions, and each one is as useless as the last."

"Does burning the plants seem to be helping?"

For once, his voice wasn't edged with aggression. It was a real question, and I hated the answer.

"I don't think so," I said. "But I'm not willing to stop long enough to find out for sure."

"I wouldn't be either." He glanced up at me, his expression cautious, but he seemed too tired or discouraged to start one of his usual arguments. "The situation is getting pretty dire."

I nodded and threw the last of his plants into my barrel. The flames rose and licked their way up the soggy stem, devouring the damp plant with as much magic as fire.

Jonquil's jaw twitched as he stared out at the devastated flower bed. I followed his gaze, scanning the area for any hint of gray he'd missed. He turned and looked up at me, his eyes hard.

"You'd better find a way to fix this," he said, his voice equal parts plea and threat. "You've got to."

5TH APRIL

If I'd thought the brief moment of peace between Jonquil and me was a signal of cooperation to come, I'd been sorely mistaken.

I looked out across the fire garden. It was a gloomy sight, the usual array of blazing daffodils and yellow freesia and flame-like orange irises now a mass of gray death.

"It is what it is," I said, voice loud and blunt with exhaustion.

My body practically vibrated with the coffee I'd chugged this morning in an effort to stay awake. I'd been up most of the night wandering the palace gardens like a spirit of destruction, tearing up plants and burning them with an intensity I had regretted the moment I'd opened my eyes this morning. My body ached. My swollen ankle throbbed. My eyelids scratched against my eyes with every blink. Two of the general gardeners, Rue and Ash, stood next to me with their arms folded.

"We have nothing for the Flower Festival," Rue said, panic edging her voice.

Ash shifted from foot to foot, a constant, restless movement that annoyed me. "We were supposed to have an entire display. The fire garden takes up an entire booth every year. It's one of the highlights of the festival. There's *nothing left.*"

"I can see that." Immediately, I regretted my tone. I was tired, and their fear inflamed mine. I took a deep breath. "We're going to have to cancel the fire garden this year."

"We've already arranged for the Draconis Fireflame plants to be brought in," Ash said. "What are we supposed to do about that? It's too late to cancel; they're already being transported."

"I don't know." I ran a hand through my hair. "We can still have the Fireflames. Just... put them in a different display. There has to be some gilded goldenrod still alive around here somewhere. Change the theme from fire to treasure."

"The goldenrod's gone," Rue said quietly. "I've already looked. It was supposed to go in our display."

My heart raced, and I couldn't blame it all on the coffee. I wasn't usually given to anxiety, not like this, but it was hard not to get alarmed when the world was falling to pieces all around me. I forced myself to count to five before I spoke again.

"Give me some time to think about it," I said at last. "We'll figure out something to do with the dragons and the space. Maybe we could do an educational booth on the different types of compost we use in the gardens."

Rue nodded, although it seemed more like she was trying to encourage me than like she actually thought it was a good idea. Ash narrowed his eyes at the devastated garden as if he could revive it with the power of his stare.

I had hardly left their garden when Chervil accosted me. I tensed up as soon as I heard his voice. After Jonquil, he was one of the hardest to get along with. He'd wanted my job, and his resentment of my youth and position was impossible to miss.

"I need to speak with you," he said without preamble. "Burning the blighted flowers isn't helping. My apprentices have wasted enough of their time on a lost cause. I've pulled them back to help me work on the flowering herbs that are left."

I frowned and kept walking. Every step hurt, but the pain was still less than I usually felt from trying to have a face-to-face conversation with Chervil.

"We can't stop burning the plants," I said. "For all we know, that's the only thing stopping the blight from spreading faster than it is."

"Jonquil says otherwise. He thinks burning the plants is a lost cause, and he tells me you all but admitted you agree."

Irritation flared. "I said I don't know for sure," I said. "That doesn't mean your apprentices can just *stop*."

"It's a waste of their time."

I stopped and turned to face him. "What do you do with any other kind of blight?"

His mouth twisted. "Destroy the infected plants. But--"

"That's right. And we have infected plants."

"Burning them doesn't seem to--"

"I'm not going to risk the contagion spreading any

faster than it is."

"My apprentices are tired."

"I'm tired," I snapped. "We're all tired. My ankle is sprained, and I shouldn't be walking on it, but we have a Festival to prepare for." He opened his mouth to argue, but I kept going. "Yes, everyone is putting in extra hours. Yes, we're all worried. Yes, there is no guarantee that destroying these plants is helping. And no, you're not permitted to just stop doing it. Put your apprentices back on burn duty, or I'll find someone else to supervise them."

He glared at me, and I glared back at him until he looked away like one of Lilian's puppies after it had been caught misbehaving.

"Yes, sir," he muttered.

"Thank you."

He walked away. Guilt and anger and frustration bubbled inside me. I had a feeling I'd handled that all wrong. Or maybe I'd handled it all right and it didn't matter because everything was going to die anyway.

Unless we found a way to stop it.

The tiniest hope still burned inside me. In spite of everything--in spite of the death and the hopelessness and the sight of the queen sitting there while decay crept up her hair--the outcome of this disease was still undecided.

As long as a single plant remained alive in the kingdom, there was the possibility of restoring our future to something resembling our beautiful past.

But I couldn't just choose that future.

Not alone.

~

I couldn't run, not without blinding pain, which meant sneaking into the castle and hightailing it to Lilian's quarters was out of the question.

Which left me back at my foolproof plan of harassing the women of the Florian royal family via their windows.

I squinted up at the many rectangles that marched along the palace wall in an orderly line. The glass reflected the morning sunlight, obscuring anything that might have been within. It was still early; chances were good Lilian was taking breakfast in her rooms. Lilian preferred breakfast in the small conservatory adjoining her sitting room, although sometimes she ate in front of her bedroom fireplace if she'd been up late the night before.

She never ate breakfast in bed. She hated the crumbs.

The conservatory jutted out slightly from the rest of the building. Its windows were placed closer together, and only narrow frames separated the large panes. I stepped back, made my best guess, and took aim.

The pebble bounced off the window with a light clink. I waited, but nothing changed. I tossed another stone, this one a little larger, and winced when it hit the glass. The window held up, though, and it only took a few more pebbles before one of the panes tilted outward, and Lilian's face peeked out.

The concern on her expression faded the moment she saw me.

"That's one way to do it," she called. A slight smile danced at the edges of her lips.

I held out my hands in a shrug. "I can't come in. I figured you might be able to come out."

Lilian's expression hardened. "You can't come in, my left *ear*. Have you really not been in the palace since he threw you out?"

I shook my head. "The guards stopped me when I tried. Your duke's taking my banishment pretty seriously."

"He's not *my* duke. I mean, he is, but that doesn't mean I have to like him right now." She sighed, and then, in typical Lilian fashion, she tried to see the best in everyone and added, "I'm sure he'll come around."

I didn't say anything. There was no guarantee the duke would change his mind about me--and anyway, did it even matter? Their engagement had been announced. The photos had been published, and the alliance between the two prominent families was all but secured. The only thing left was to set a date.

"I need to talk to you," I said. "Somewhere private."

Lilian pursed her lips and tilted her head. "What did you do to your ankle?"

I glanced down. The cloth I'd wrapped around the joints had come untied. Besides that, the swelling felt like it had to be visible from the moon.

"It's a funny story," I said. "I never plan on telling it to anyone."

"You'll tell it to me."

My stomach did a little flip at the smug confidence in her voice.

"Never."

"I'm coming down." She closed the window partway, then opened it again. "Give me a few minutes," she called. "I'll bring a salve for your ankle. Where should I meet you?"

"Come to the little storage shed by the gardenias and peonies."

Something like pain passed over her face. There weren't many peonies left, or gardenias. Still, she knew where they were supposed to be blooming.

"Don't let anyone see you," I added. "The last thing we need is someone seeing us together. Forget the palace--the duke will kick me right out of the gardens."

"If Garritt tries, he'll remember who his princess is very quickly."

The threat had no teeth. The king had left the duke in charge, and, for some reason, the idiot guards had decided that was enough reason to listen to him instead of their princess. Still, knowing Lilian was ready to ride to my aid on a white charger made me smile.

"Just don't get caught," I said. "I'll see you soon."

"Deon?" she said as if worried I was going to run away before she could speak. I couldn't leave quickly, not with my foot like this. And I wouldn't have anyway. I never left first if I could help it, not if the other option was watching her grow smaller as she walked gracefully across the grounds or seeing that last glimpse of her golden hair as she disappeared around a corner. Or, in this case, getting in one final glimpse of her perfect, rose-blushed face.

"Lils?"

She drew her eyebrows together as if thinking seriously about the words that should come next. I waited, my heart in my throat.

"I miss you," she said at last.

I bit back a grin. "Then come down and see me."

"No, Deon, I mean…" She trailed off, then shook her head in annoyance. "I mean, I *miss* you."

"I miss you, too, Lils," I said.

"All right, then," she said. "I just wanted to make that clear. I'll be down in a minute. With the salve. And a pastry."

"You *do* love me!"

It was a joke, but one colored with so much truth that I wanted to kick myself in the damaged ankle the second the words were out of my mouth. I gritted my teeth, hard.

"I'm an idiot," I added.

"You were born that way," she said. "It can't be helped."

Her eyes twinkled, and everything inside me leapt and twisted and fell all at once.

"Just bring the salve," I said.

"And the pastry?"

"Always the pastry."

The shed door creaked open, letting in a slice of morning sunlight. Lilian slipped inside and blinked. The only windows in this shed were a high horizontal slit in the wall on either side, and it seemed to take a few moments for Lilian's eyes to adjust to the relative darkness.

Then she furrowed her eyebrows.

"That's not where you're sleeping."

I patted the blanket-covered pile of manure sacks next to me. "Have a seat, Your Highness."

"What's under there?"

"Unicorn poop."

"Deon."

"Lils."

I stared at her, fighting the laugh that wanted to erupt from me at the look on her face. She narrowed her eyes at me, trying to decide if I was serious. I lifted a corner of the blanket to reveal a burlap sack printed with the words *Woodland Stables Finest Unicorn Manure* in dark violet letters.

Lilian's nose wrinkled a little. "At least it smells all right."

"That's why I picked this pile," I said. "We've got another shed of steer manure, and it's not nearly so nice."

Delicately, she sat on the makeshift bed next to me. She pulled a small jar out of her pocket and smoothed her pale blue skirts over her knees.

"Let's see that ankle."

"I'd rather have the pastry."

She smirked and took a wrapped package from her other pocket. I reached for it, and she held it up and away from me.

"No fussing when I put on the salve," she said.

"I can put it on." The thought of Lilian touching my ankle made heat rise to my face.

She raised her chin and eyebrows in a stubborn expression. "Give me your ankle," she said sternly. "No fussing about the smell."

"What does it smell like?"

"Deon?"

She held the pastry away from me, the threat unmistakable. I collapsed my shoulders in defeat.

"Fine."

"Give me your ankle."

My stomach flipped. I lifted my foot and angled my body toward her, careful not to touch her immaculate skirts with my dirty boot.

She grabbed my leg and plopped it across her lap, then handed me the paper-wrapped package. The sweet scent of cinnamon and apples filled my senses, mingling with the faint lavender scent of the manure beneath us.

I ate while Lilian carefully removed my shoe and thick woolen sock, then unwound the fabric that bound my ankle and pushed my trouser leg out of the way. My skin thrilled at every touch of her slender fingers.

She opened the jar of salve. Instantly, the sweet scent of the apple pastry was replaced with an acrid herbal odor that seemed like it was trying to claw its way up my nose.

I recoiled. “Sticks and stones, that’s awful.”

Lilian grabbed my leg and pressed it firmly into her lap. “Hold still.”

She dipped her fingertips into the foul mixture and massaged it into my ankle. The salve tingled wherever it touched, first hot and then cold, and it stained my skin with streaks of deep, muddy green. It stained Lilian’s fingers, too, and when she was done and had capped the jar, she considered her fingertips with a calculating expression and then wiped the lingering salve off on one of her petticoats.

“My maids are going to murder me,” she said lightly. “How does that feel?”

“Better,” I said. “I think.”

Although it was impossible to tell whether the gentle, comfortable throbbing in the joints was due to the salve or just a relic of the delight of being touched by Lilian.

My face grew hot, and I realized with a jolt that I was staring at her. She bit her lip and stared back.

Stars, she was beautiful. The strain of the last few days had paled her skin and added lingering lines of worry at the corners of her eyes, and even so, she was so lovely it almost hurt to look at her.

She giggled, and my skin flushed even hotter. Was it possible to get a sunburn just from blushing? If so, I was in trouble.

"Thank you," I said, too loudly.

"You're welcome."

"Stop looking at me."

"No." She leaned forward, blue eyes intense. "You're the nicest thing I've seen all day. Especially when you turn red like that."

"I'm not red," I said as if objecting to reality would do anything to change it.

She laughed. The bubbly feeling in my chest subsided, and so did her smile. We gazed at one another. Her lips parted slightly, the rose pink of them gleaming under the thin coat of perfumed beeswax she used to keep them soft. Her lashes trembled.

I pulled away.

"I can't get too close to you, Lils."

"I know." She drew back, too, and settled her hands tightly in her lap. "Stars, Deon, I'm sorry. I keep thinking I'll be all right, and then I get close to you, and..."

She swallowed. She didn't need to finish the sentence. I knew how it ended, with butterflies in my stomach and tingles spreading across my skin.

"You still want to run away?" The words escaped me before I had the chance to think them through, and my breath caught after the last one as I waited for her answer. A tantalizing hope glimmered at the edges of our lives, a hint at a future where happiness might be within our grasp.

Her chest rose and fell in a heavy sigh. "I want to," she said.

The *but* was there as loudly as if she'd said it. I smiled a little if only to let her know I loved her anyway.

"I would. Honestly, if things were different, I would." She glanced at me, and a rueful smile twisted her lips. "Or, at least, I like to think I would."

I knew what she meant. Whatever our hearts said, Lilian and I shared more than just our love for one another. We also shared a sense of duty that ran as deeply inside us as the roots of an ancient oak.

"I can't leave so long as Garritt is in charge." A shudder passed across her face, so faint I could have tricked myself into believing it wasn't there. "Deon, it's awful. He's controlling everything. He's gone to all sorts of meetings with the Horticulture Council, and he's talking about firing the Head Cook because he doesn't like that she trained in Badalah instead of Floris, and he's just awful to the housekeeping staff. He wasn't like that the first few days, but then Papa told him he was in charge, and he's just turning into this hideous person. He's always sweet to me, but he's *not* particularly civil to my maids."

Her mouth tightened to a thin line. I winced inwardly. No one who wanted to be in Lilian's good graces could get away with treating her maidservants with anything less than respect. She had no patience for people who were unkind to the palace staff.

"Have you talked to your father?"

"He won't see me," she said. "I haven't got the faintest clue what's wrong with him, but he barely looks at me, and he's started taking all his meals with Mama, who's still locked up in her rooms." Her voice shook at the last word, and she clenched her jaw. I reached across the space between us for her hand. She squeezed mine tightly enough to all but crush my fingers, and I stroked the back of her hand with my thumb.

"And on top of *that,* all the flowers are dying," she said, then shifted to look at me straight-on. "I'm not blaming you for that."

"I know."

"It's just that everything seems to be falling apart all at once." She turned to face me, and worry etched deep lines into her forehead. "Mama's sick. Something's wrong with Papa. The entire countryside is turning gray. You've been thrown out of the palace, and even if you hadn't been, we're still not free to marry." She made a frustrated sound, something between a growl and a curse. "And Garritt is swanning around like he owns the place as if nothing matters but all his newfound power."

My stomach turned more to lead with every word. It was a grim prospect, all the worse for its truth.

Lilian wiggled closer to me and rested her head on my shoulder.

"I don't know what to do," she said in a small voice. "It's like everything is dying."

I dared to put my arm around her. She gave a contented little sigh and snuggled in closer as if I could actually provide her with any protection in this terrifying new world.

I couldn't even keep my flowers from dying. How was I supposed to protect a princess?

"Hedley thinks it's all connected," I said.

She sat up straighter. "You've talked to Hedley?"

"He's here," I said. "Hasn't he seen you?"

She shook her head. "Garritt has been keeping me from seeing anyone or doing anything useful. He claims I ought to be focused on my dancing lessons and on going to fittings for my wedding gown." She grimaced. The thought of her wedding dress, which I'd noticed women often liked talking about even if they didn't have a wedding in sight, seemed to fill her with dread.

The constant spark of anger that had glowed inside me over the last few days grew into a small flame. It was a good thing Duke Remington had kicked me out of the palace. If we passed each other in the hall now, I was liable to tell him exactly what I thought of his treatment of Lilian, and everyone else--and I had a feeling it would be my fists rather than my mouth doing the talking.

"Well, Hedley's here," I said, fighting to keep my tone calm. "He came to see how the blight was affecting the grounds, and he's staying through the end of the Festival. The Head Housekeeper gave him a room in the servants' quarters, so he didn't have to pay for lodgings in the city, and Hyacinth's going to join him before the Festival starts."

"Oh, I can't wait to see Hyacinth." Lilian's body softened a little under my arm. "She was always so kind to me when I was little. Remember when she caught us playing in the flour bin?"

It was a memory I hadn't thought of in years. I snorted. Lilian and I couldn't have been more than four or five years old, and one of us had somehow figured out that flour was even more fun to play in than the sand in Lilian's sandbox. Hyacinth had caught us in the pantry, covered head to toe in flour, and proclaiming that we were now cloud people.

"She wasn't even mad," I said.

"She was mad! She warned us that she'd never bake raspberry jam tarts ever again!"

"She was laughing while she said it."

Voices sounded outside the shed. I froze, and Lilian held her breath. They were too far away for me to make out what they were saying, although I was fairly certain one voice was Chervil's. The voices grew closer, then faded as they walked away.

I turned to Lilian and slipped my arm off her shoulder, the mirth from a moment before gone.

"We probably shouldn't stay here too long," I said. "Someone might come looking for you."

"I told my maids to tell Garritt I'd gone riding along the willow walk if he asked," she said. The winding dirt path was on the other side of the gardens, as far from the palace as one could get without leaving the grounds. "He's too busy being a domineering brute to come looking for me."

The acidity in her voice was too pronounced to ignore, and I choked back a laugh. Few things in this world were quite as satisfying as knowing Lilian disliked the same people I did.

It would have been more satisfying if she hadn't been engaged to *marry* this one.

"What did Hedley say?" she said. "Before I go, what did you mean? That things are connected?"

"The flowers and everything else that's happening," I said. "He's got this hare-brained theory. I mean, I don't know that it's hare-brained--Hedley doesn't usually go in for that sort of thing--but it seems like he's reaching for magical solutions when the real problems are much more ordinary."

"What's his theory?" she said. "I'm open to hare-brained ideas."

"He thinks it's magic," I said. "That someone maybe cursed the gardens, and that the curse is what's making the flowers die."

She furrowed her eyebrows. "Go on."

"That's it, really. He thinks the flowers are somehow connected to everyone's happiness, and so, if somebody cursed the flowers, they basically cursed everyone. The other possibility we've floated around is that the gardens were charmed eighteen years ago, and now that charm is wearing off. He thinks that's why things got so much better for the kingdom back then. Personally, I think your father is just a good king."

Lilian's lips drew to a thin line. "I'm rather reconsidering my view on that subject right now." I'd never heard her voice quite that icy; whatever her father's reasons for handing the reins of the kingdom to Garritt and disappearing, Lilian wasn't having it.

I hesitated before saying my next words. I would rather do anything than cause Lilian pain, but this next bit was important, and it had to be said.

"He also thinks whatever's happening has something to do with your mother's illness." I bit my lip and straightened my shoulders. "And I agree. They're connected."

"Why?" She narrowed her eyes. "How? What do you know?"

"I don't *know* anything." Goosebumps rose on my arms at the memory of the gray death creeping up the queen's hair. I knew I should tell Lilian. But I couldn't force my mouth to shape the words. I tried, but they stuck in my throat. I couldn't be the one to tell her that horrific news, not without knowing for sure what the queen knew. "You need to see your mother."

"I told you, she won't see me."

"That doesn't matter," I said. "You need to see her and ask her what's going on. I don't know what's going on, but the queen--I think she does." Perhaps more than the image of the queen's graying hair, the way she hadn't seemed upset by whatever was happening to her had stuck with me. She had been reading in bed, cheerful and calm. It didn't make sense. "Your mother knows something, and someone needs to talk to her. You're the only person who might be able to force their way in."

"I tried." Lilian's eyes flashed. "Her guard took my arm and almost forced me away from her door."

The palace guards might have been braver than I gave them credit for. There was no power on earth that could have compelled me to push Lilian anywhere against her will.

"Then maybe don't go in through the door." My ankle twinged at the memory of my clumsy fall from the castle wall, and I hastily added, "Don't go in through a window, either."

She raised an eyebrow. "You think I'm the kind of girl to go through windows?"

I hadn't been the kind of guy to peer through windows, but then, here I was.

"I'm just saying, maybe there's another way," I said. "Could you send her a letter? Claim you're horribly sick and need to see your mother before you die a dramatic death from, I don't know, a sudden walnut allergy?"

The corner of Lilian's mouth twitched. "Have a nervous breakdown the next time a harp string breaks?" Her eyes twinkled. "Throw a tantrum because Cottonpuff keeps having accidents on the carpet and demand the queen use her monarchial powers to order a public puppy execution?"

I grinned. "Insist that you can't entertain the Duchess of Silverseed without your mother there to take on half the burden of her long-winded stories?"

"Refuse to eat or drink anything unless Mama is there to enjoy it with me?"

"Stand outside her door and scream like a banshee until she has to come outside just to shut you up?"

"That one might work," she said. "I'll try."

"Maybe try the letter first."

She winked. "Where's the fun in that?"

The world might be crumbling around my ears. But even in the midst of it all, Lilian shone. I tucked a strand of golden hair behind her ears.

"I love you, Lils."

"I know." She gazed at me as if looking deeply enough could somehow compensate for the endless divide between us. "I love you, too. I just wish it did us any good."

6TH APRIL

Ahead of me in the garden, voices shouted at one another, the argument escalating by the moment. I quickened my pace and ducked through the arch cut into a tall, graying hedge just in time to see Linden step forward and scream into Reed's face.

"Maybe you should back up and let me do my job," he shouted. "I don't have time for your attitude, and I don't have time to argue about water lilies with you."

Reed held his ground. "It's not about water lilies, and you know it. Mr. Gilding ordered us to destroy infected plants. If you can't follow orders, you bet I'm going to step in and do something about it. I'll pick up your slack, but I won't let you treat me like garbage for it."

"I'll treat you like garbage if I--"

"I'll let you do your job if you *do* your job," Reed snapped. "If you'd rather just mope around the gardens being pissy because you somehow think you'd handle the biggest crisis Floris has ever seen better than your boss, you'd better go do that and get out of my way."

"Touch my gardens again, and I swear I'll have your head."

"Oh yeah?" Reed said. He took a step closer, not that there was much room between them. "You try to stop me from taking care of these gardens, and we'll see who has whose head."

"Knock it off."

The volume of my own voice surprised me. I wasn't much of a yeller and never had been, but my body seemed to think otherwise right now.

I stepped toward them and gestured at them to break it up. Linden glared at me.

"You'd better get your staff under control," he said. "If you can't take care of your gardens, you owe it to those of us who are *professionals* to keep some semblance of order around here."

I held up a hand. "I have no idea what you're talking about. What's going on?"

"I'll tell you what's going on: He's being a real--" Reed started.

I cut him off with a sharp gesture.

"Take a deep breath, both of you. What happened? Reed, you first."

"Of course, friends always come first," Linden muttered.

I folded my arms. "Fine, then. You go. I don't care so long as you talk one at a time."

"Reed here has been taking liberties in the water

garden," Linden said. "As you know from the last round of assignments, I'm in charge of that area until the Festival. I told my staff there to stop worrying about destroying the blighted plants and to move the healthy ones into tanks until we can transport them to the Festival. We only have so many hours in a day, and burning the plants clearly isn't a good use of our time. And then *he* decided he needed to spend the entire day pulling up infected plants instead of rescuing the survivors as I ordered."

"We can't just let it spread," Reed started.

I shook my head sharply at him, and he folded his arms and glared at the ground, breathing hard.

"Did the healthy plants get moved?"

Linden scowled. "Not fast enough. We lost three to blight today because Reed was too busy wasting his time disobeying my instructions."

I turned to Reed. "That true?"

"You said to burn the infected plants!" he said. "You're Head Gardener, even if some people can't seem to accept that. Your instructions are the ones I'm following."

I took a deep breath. Reed looked to me for support, while Linden narrowed his eyes and waited for me to side with one of the only people in the garden who had been civil to me over the past few months. I bit the inside of my cheek.

"I am Head Gardener," I said.

Linden rolled his eyes, and I cleared my throat.

"However, Linden is in charge of the water garden. And frankly, he's got a lot more experience than me with both water plants and tulips. We hadn't thought of rescuing and quarantining the healthy plants. It's a good idea. Besides, he's the boss in that garden, and these grounds can't run smoothly if we don't respect each other's authority."

Reed frowned at me as if trying to decide whether I meant anything I was saying or was just trying to stay in Linden's not-wholly-despicable graces.

"If you've got a problem with a supervisor's orders, bring it to me. Otherwise, I think it's best if we assume we all know what we're doing. Linden, keep quarantining. Reed, do what he tells you to do. You'd want the same thing from your apprentices in the stone fruit orchards."

Reed pressed his lips together, and his shoulders stayed tense, but he nodded sullenly at the ground. Linden observed me with skeptical, narrowed eyes.

"Linden, does quarantining seem to be working?"

He nodded, just barely. "We haven't seen blight affecting the plants we moved into a greenhouse, but it's also too soon to tell."

"Keep going with that, then," I said. "Anything you think might save the plants."

He jerked his chin at me in acknowledgment. "Thank you, sir."

He'd never called me *sir* before. I couldn't tell if it was sarcastic.

"Reed?"

"Fine," he muttered. "Sorry, Linden."

He held out a hand, and, with visible reluctance, Linden shook it. Linden strode away, and Reed watched him with a dark expression.

"He's a self-righteous thorn in my side," Reed said, quietly enough that Linden couldn't hear him.

"Yeah, I know. He's right, though. Sorry."

"Nah, you can't take sides just because we're friends. I'm just sick of listening to them all act like you don't know what you're doing. It's not like any of *them* have managed to save the kingdom."

"I'm afraid that might be beyond all of us."

I looked out across the gardens. Every morning over the past week had been worse than the last, but today's sunrise had illuminated a whole new level of devastation. The gardens were gray. The apprentices would never be able to keep up with the spreading death, even if we hired twice as many and kept them all busy around the clock.

Linden was right. We were going to have to stop burning plants entirely. The only thing to do now was try to rescue what was left.

Including my entry to the Festival competition, if it was even still alive.

"I need to go deal with something," I said.

Reed nodded. Gloom darkened his face, and I recognized the expression. I had a feeling I was wearing it, too.

I clapped Reed on the shoulder. "You're doing everything you can. That's all we can do."

My words didn't seem to make him feel any better, and why should they? The stupidity of them echoed in my head as I walked to my private garden alone.

I didn't have hope. No one who was paying attention could possibly have hope, not when the gardens looked like this. Even the grass was beginning to turn, the once vibrant blades fading to soggy, colorless mush on either side of the path. Above me, the sky shone blue and bright, mocking the devastation below.

I hesitated outside the door to my private garden. Memories of the last time I'd seen Lilian here flooded my mind. *That* had been a moment of hope. I hadn't dared set foot inside since. There was too much to do elsewhere, and I didn't think I could bear to see the blight grip the sacred space I had created for myself.

But I had to rescue my competition flowers if they were still alive.

I closed my eyes and uttered a silent wish to whatever distant powers might be listening. Then, heart in my throat, I opened the door and gasped.

~

"It doesn't make sense." I turned around, taking in the dazzling green vines that swung overhead.

Hedley stood in the middle of my garden, his arms folded, and his eyes taking in every last fluttering leaf and arching stem. I'd left the garden at a fast hobble and dragged him back here, partially because whatever was happening in here seemed important and partially because I needed someone else to confirm that my eyes weren't playing wild tricks on me.

"The garden walls aren't that high," I said. "And it's not like walls help anyway. The blight comes into the greenhouses just as well as anywhere else. Did you use some kind of special fertilizer in here when it was your garden? Something that might still be having an effect?"

"Nothing I used could do this," he said.

We stood, marveling at the life around us. Everything here was green--green, or green accented with the bright colors of blooming flowers. More than that, everything was alive. No hint of gray death crept along the branches of the rose bushes or spoiled the delicate white flowers of the trillium patch. Even the moss that oozed up between paving stones was vibrant.

"This is magic," Hedley said at last. "These flowers were grown from magic, and it's magic that's keeping them alive."

I opened my mouth to argue, but what evidence did I have against his theory? This garden certainly wasn't thriving thanks to my efforts.

"Why here?" I said. "If magic is affecting the gardens, why is this the only place the blight hasn't touched? Do you think one of the old head gardeners was a magician? Before you?"

Hedley tapped his fingers against his suspenders. "No, Juniper was no magician. Nor a witch, either. And it's as I told you: The magic I sense in the kingdom didn't arrive until after the king and queen were wed."

I squinted at him. "You're not a secret wizard, are you?"

He laughed. "I daresay I'd have done more to stop the spread of this blight if I were." He focused on me, his smile fading to a look of speculation. "I daresay you might be one, though."

"We've already been through this."

He nodded and clucked softly to himself, like a clock marking seconds. His silvery brows drew together in thought.

"You know lemon daisies don't usually bloom at this time of year?"

I remembered having this same conversation with Lilian only a couple of weeks ago. *This shouldn't be blooming yet,* she had said about a cluster of metallic blossoms that sparkled like gold dust. *Goldenrods don't come on until autumn.*

I told Hedley the same thing I'd told her. "Everything in this garden thrives. I don't know why."

"You don't think you have magic about you?"

"The rest of the gardens wouldn't look as pitiful as they do now if I did," I said. "Whatever's happening here, I didn't do it."

Hedley didn't seem convinced. He walked slowly down the paved path, taking in the cascading blossoms of the sweetspire and the odd, spiky blooms of the bottlebrush shrubs. Every single flower seemed at its peak; even the blooms that were fading were doing so with graceful elegance as if a painter had designed them that way.

"Sure seems like the kind of garden that wouldn't look like this on its own."

"These grew quickly," I said. "But I grew every plant myself. Unless some pixie is sneaking in at night to sprinkle enchanted dust on my flower beds, the magic is either native to this garden or is nothing more than Floris's climate and dumb luck."

Hedley tapped his suspenders again and gazed up at a pink magnolia flower as big as my face. "I don't believe in dumb luck. Do you?"

I sat on the edge of one of the raised beds. "Honestly, I don't know what I believe." I wiped my hands on my trousers; the ever-present film of soil on my hands left faint earthy smears on the brown fabric. "Everything I thought I knew has gone by the wayside these past few weeks. So sure. It's magic. It's just not mine."

He waited, in that quiet way of his that made it clear he expected *more*. I let out a sigh. Embarrassment warmed my face.

"Trust me," I added. "If it was magic, I'd know. I already tried."

This interested Hedley. He examined my face, and I let him look, red flush and all.

"I tried to perform a spell on one of the flowers," I said. "When the blight had just appeared, but after I came to see you and Hyacinth. You said you thought it might be a curse, so I found a charm to remove curses from growing things."

"And?"

I shrugged. "It didn't work."

"Not even a little?"

"Not at all," I said. "The petals didn't so much as twitch."

"And yet," he said. He turned around in a slow, thoughtful circle. "There's not a sign of blight here, Deon. Not a sign. You know what the rest of the kingdom looks like."

I nodded. On the one hand, joy suffused me. My garden wasn't dead. There was still a spot in Floris, however small, where life and color still flourished. On the other hand, all this beauty made me sick. If my beloved private garden still looked like this, why didn't the rest of the kingdom?

"I want you to try something for me," Hedley said.

There was something in his voice: a challenge, or maybe a question. I couldn't tell what he was getting at, not exactly, but it was clear I ought to be cautious.

"You'd better tell me what it is first."

His mouth cracked into a grin. "You never used to be so suspicious."

I had to acknowledge the truth of it, if only to myself. Perhaps watching the blight destroy years of hard work and threaten our future had done it. Maybe it was the way Duke Remington had turned from a decent man to a power-hungry monster all but overnight. Maybe I was just all grown up.

Or maybe I was just bitter from losing Lilian. That sting would take a long time to fade if it ever did.

"I'm willing to try anything you think will help the gardens," I finally admitted.

He gave me a brisk nod and pointed toward a tall

bearded iris, pale blue and in the fluttering shape of a wave that had just reached its crest.

"There's a trick I learned from a magician once," Hedley said. "I was never able to get it to work, not properly. You might have better luck."

"You're like a dog with a bone." I slipped off the raised bed wall anyway and came over to the iris, which sat in another raised bed so that its flower was on level with my eyes. Its sugary, arresting fragrance rose up to greet me.

Stars, I missed these scents. I hadn't noticed it until now, not really, but the world outside these walls had lost some of its sweetness. Even in the depths of winter, the air in Floris had always carried a slight memory of growing green things. Even the scent of decay that came with autumn leaves had seemed bright and alive like the trees were only sloughing off their old foliage in order to make room for the new buds rising to burst underneath. Now, the air smelled like nothing at all--nothing, or the sickly odor of gray rot.

I breathed in the iris's perfume.

"All right," I said, squaring my shoulders. "What do I do?"

Hedley shifted a bit away as if to give me room, though room for what, I couldn't imagine.

"Hold your hand over the flower," he said. "Touch the plant. Give yourself a sense for it."

I did as he instructed. The iris's stem was glossy smooth, almost like rubber, and the moisture inside pressured the stem into an upright, proud position, strong enough to hold its enormous bloom. The edges of the leaves, pointed blades like those that belonged to tulips, scraped against my skin as I skated my palm across their sharp surface. The flower itself, I handled with delicate fingers, cupping the blossom and tracing my fingertips along the edges of the curving petals.

I glanced up at Hedley. "Is something supposed to happen?"

"Focus on the center of the plant."

I frowned. "What does that mean?"

"If you have magic, you'll be able to figure it out," he said.

The spell books I'd looked through days ago had been full of those kinds of cryptic comments. Spells were just scaffolding; a *true* magic-worker should be able to sense the subtle energies that flowed through all things and manipulate them in a way that couldn't be taught.

That sounded like a load of pretentious bunk to me, but I tried to feel into the center of the iris anyway. After a while, although I was pretty sure it was just my imagination, I got a sense for something running through the plant like a thread. It was like the bright core at the center of a young onion, or the green life that lived in the branches of rose bushes that someone who didn't know the ways of roses might have assumed were dead.

"I think I found it?" I said. Hedley ignored the uncertainty in my voice.

"Trace that core down to the roots."

"All right," I said, although I suspected I was just picturing roots in my head. Still, I could almost feel them under my fingertips, the firm bulb with its many tendrils creeping out into the damp soil around it.

"Now, draw life up through the roots and into the stem through the core."

"Draw life?" I couldn't keep the edge from my voice. "What's that supposed to mean?"

“Just do it,” he said. “If it doesn’t work, you can mouth off after.”

His slight smirk annoyed me, but I couldn’t give up, not without giving this my best try. I reached out in my imagination, coaxing water and air from the soil and up the body of the iris. That was all life was in a garden, after all, water and air and nutrients and sunlight. Those simple elements were all it took to feed this world, transformed by the awe-inspiring power of the plants around me.

“I think I’ve done it?” I said after a while.

Hedley grunted softly. After a moment, he said, in a low voice, “Now pull it toward you.”

The effort of imagining all that life trickling upwards toward the flower took enough attention that I didn’t have any left over to give Hedley the skeptical look I thought he deserved. Instead, I tried to pull the energy in my direction. Without my ordering them to, my fingertips twitched inward, as if the stem were under my fingers instead of in front of me.

The flower twitched.

Startled, I lost concentration and jerked backward. I glanced up at Hedley, whose eyes were bright with what looked like victory.

“Look at that,” he said, more to himself than to me. “Did you see that?”

I looked down at my hands, then at the flower. It was swaying gently as if it had just been bumped.

But I hadn’t touched it. No one had.

“It worked.” I squinted at the flower. Had that been me? Or had it just been a breeze? But no wind stirred the garden, and the other irises rising around mine remained still. “It did work, didn’t it?”

Hedley scrutinized the flower for a long moment.

The wheels in his head were turning, the evidence of his thoughts clear in the way his gaze darted around the flower, examining its every dip and curve.

"Aye, it worked," he said. "A bit. The way beginner's magic might. But it did work." It was clear he was suppressing a smile, either because he was deep in thought or because he was trying, generously, not to gloat.

"So that means..." I trailed off. The thought was there, but the words wouldn't form. They were ridiculous. I thought I'd already proved them wrong.

"It means you have magic," Hedley said. "Magic, you might be able to train. And I'd bet my striped calendula collection that your abilities have something to do with why this garden looks the way it does."

I stared at the iris. It had stopped bobbing and returned to its proud, upright position.

"Do you think I could use this to stop the blight?"

Hedley pursed his lips and seemed to be chewing on the inside of his cheek. "I don't rightly know, to tell you the truth," he said. "Still, we know more than we did an hour ago."

"Do you think I could do it again?" I was already focused on the flower, reaching out with my mind for the core of life that flowed through it.

"I daresay you could," he said. "It doesn't hurt to try."

~

I disembarked from the carriage. The palace driver nodded at me, and I offered a few coins, which he accepted politely.

This part of the city felt different from the rest. It was

home to artists and fortunetellers and other Florians who lived slightly outside the margins of ordinary society and clustered together with others of their kind. Magicians lived here, too, and it was these I had come to see.

"Have a sweetie?" asked a short woman in a blue dress. "Half off today only!" She held out a large rainbow-colored lollipop worked into the shape of a daisy.

I shook my head with a smile and moved on. The homes and shops were bright here, their wooden siding painted in vivid shades that seemed so Florian as to have almost gone too far. The rest of the city liked bright colors well enough, but elsewhere there seemed to be an unspoken agreement that shades ought to at least coordinate. Here, all thoughts of visual harmony had been thrown out the window. Sunflower yellow trim marched across a fuchsia house, and the door flared with a bright orange that put me in mind of marigolds and pumpkins. The next building was apple red accented with seven different shades of green, all of which clashed horribly with the house that came after with its striped cerulean and royal purple siding.

As in the rest of the country, every home and shop had window boxes. They were empty, aside from one, which held flowers cut from cardboard and colored with a child's untidy scrawl.

My stomach twisted.

I ducked down a side street and checked the address on the paper in my hand.

"Learn about your future?" asked a woman sitting on the stoop of a navy-blue shop painted with silver stars. "I'll scatter the seeds and tell you who you'll marry."

I already knew who I *wouldn't* marry, and that was quite enough knowledge of the future for me. I shook my head and hurried on.

The office I eventually reached was more understated than I'd anticipated. The two-story building, which looked as if it had once been someone's home, was a reasonable shade of butter yellow, ornamented only by a few white window boxes, which stood as empty as all the rest. A sign on the tiny graying lawn read *Hemlock & Cypress: Magicians for Hire.*

They were two of our best magicians--not just in Tulis, but in all the country. Rumor had it that the king had tried several times to engage them at the palace full-time, but they preferred to run their own private practice and had been working out of this same little office for decades.

I went inside, expecting to find a secretary and a sitting room. Instead, the door opened directly onto a stunning room full of waterfalls and coiling vines. It was as if they'd built a forest in the center of an old house. Water cascaded lightly down from the walls, and the only seats were large boulders that were set on walkways that wandered over rippling pools.

Aside from the profusion of plants and water, the place was empty.

But there *was* a profusion of plants. Hope rose in my chest. These magicians, whoever they were, had managed to keep their plants from dying.

If our experiment earlier in the day had been right, I had some of that same magic, and perhaps the two greatest magicians in Floris could teach me to wield it.

"Do you have an appointment?"

The voice next to my ear was high-pitched and almost buzzing. I jumped and spun around, but I was still alone.

"Watch it!" the voice said.

Motion caught my eye, and a second later, I realized a tiny pixie was buzzing through the air. Her translucent skin was the same shade of pink as her gossamer wings, and she glowed with a faint light of her own.

"I'm so sorry," I said. "I didn't see you."

"Clearly." She was not impressed by my inattention. "Do you have an appointment?"

"No," I said. "I was hoping they could squeeze me in. I'm from the palace."

"Oh, if you're from the *palace,* then," she said.

I suddenly wished I'd kept that part quiet.

"Are either of them available?"

"Perhaps," she said. "I'll let them know you're here."

The pixie zipped away, under a hanging philodendron leaf that was twice as big as she was and through a door on the other side of the strange room.

A few minutes later, an elegant woman in a moss-green tunic and trousers the color of fresh soil entered the room. She wasn't at all what I'd expected. Most magicians I'd seen who had come to the palace were grand--the kind of people who wore velvet robes and arrived with large chests of strange tools and herbs. This woman looked nothing like them, except for a strange sharpness around her eyes that all magicians seemed to share.

"You're from the palace?" she said.

"You must be Madame Hemlock." I bowed deeply.

She stopped in front of me and held out her hand. I took it, expecting to kiss it as I usually did to women who outranked me, but she only gave mine a firm shake.

"You can tell the king I have no news for him," she said. "Moreover, you can tell him I'll let him know if we have a breakthrough. I'm not holding out on him, and he ought to know that by now."

I frowned. “The king didn’t send me.”

The tiny lines at the corners of her eyes eased. “What are you here for, then?”

“I came for,” I started. I fell silent, then waved my hand around vaguely at the vines that surrounded us. “Well, I came for *this*. Your plants are alive. I think I have some magic, and I want to learn how to keep mine alive, too.”

Her lips thinned, just barely, and I realized I’d come at it from the wrong angle.

“My name is Deon Gilding,” I said. “I’m the palace’s head gardener. I’m trying to stop the blight.”

Understanding passed over her face, and her shoulders fell as she sighed.

“I see,” she said. “In that case, I’m sorry to tell you you’ve wasted your time.”

“I can pay you,” I said quickly.

She shook her head. “I mean, there’s nothing I can do.”

She waved a hand as if to swat away the heart-shaped leaf that dangled near her ear. Her hand passed straight through it as if the leaf had been a ghost.

“It’s an illusion,” she said. “That’s all we can do anymore. Did the king not tell you?”

My heart sank, and I fought back the annoyance and disappointment I was sure must be visible on my face. “His Majesty hasn’t communicated much with me of late.”

This seemed to strike a chord. She pursed her lips as if she wanted to laugh or scoff. Whatever the urge was, she didn’t give in to it.

“Perhaps we’d best communicate, then.” She gestured toward one of the boulders. “Have a seat. The rocks are solid enough, at least. I’ll order tea.”

She turned and put her fingers to her lips. She whistled, two bright, distinct tunes. From elsewhere in the building, two other whistles sounded back.

"Cypress will join us in a moment."

Cypress turned out to be a delicate, willowy man dressed in a similar tunic, although his was deep blue. He needed very little explanation from Hemlock to get caught up to speed.

Each of them sat on boulders not far from mine. It was an unusual sitting configuration--unusual, but comfortable, and I preferred it to the formal desks and stiff chairs I'd expected to find here.

Cypress crossed his legs, his back straight but relaxed. Behind us, the pixie zoomed in, carrying teacups that had to have been dozens of times her weight. She dropped the cups from the sky, and we caught them. She lugged in a teapot next and poured the steaming mint tea from what seemed like an impossible height. The streams landed with precision in each of our small cups, creating a head of refreshing foam.

"Anything else?" she asked as if she had far better things to be doing.

"That'll be all," Hemlock said, then added, in a singsong voice, "Thank you, Apple."

Apple zoomed away without a backward glance. Cypress watched her go with an indulgent shake of his head.

"We tried to heal the plants," Hemlock said, without further preamble. "When that didn't work, we tried to stop them from getting any worse. We failed. Utterly."

"We're not accustomed to failure," Cypress said. The way he spoke, it was clear this wasn't a boast. It was a fact, just like it was a fact that my plants had usually flourished before this blight had descended over the land like a funeral shroud.

I sipped my tea. It was sweet and strong and strangely comforting.

"We have messengers throughout the kingdom," Hemlock said. "Pixies, mostly. A few birds. They report that almost a third of the flowers in the kingdom are without color, and the curse is spreading out fast from the palace."

"It is a curse, then," I said.

Hemlock inclined her head. "No ordinary blight would resist our magic like this." She glanced at Cypress. "In truth, no ordinary blight could damage our magic, but this one has."

"It's weakened us," Cypress clarified. "Our knowledge is every bit what it once was, but our skills appear to have withered."

"We're not alone," Hemlock said. "Magicians throughout our community report the same effect. Whatever this affliction is, it's a poison to our magic just as it's a poison to the flowers."

"Can I train my magic anyway?" I said. "I think I have some. Just a little. Do you think learning your craft could be enough to help me keep the palace gardens from dying completely?"

They exchanged glances, a wordless conversation passing between them. Hemlock turned back to me with an encouraging smile, but I'd seen enough of their silent exchange to know she was only being kind.

"You never know," she said. "Perhaps you'll have better luck than us."

It was the kind of *maybe* people gave to children when they claimed they wanted to be unicorns or ogres when they grew up. I swallowed the last of my tea and tried to be gracious.

“Thank you for your time,” I said. “I’m sorry the blight is affecting you.”

“Likewise,” Hemlock said. She searched my face, her expression suddenly cautious. “Tell me, how is the queen?”

I searched hers right back. She knew something, perhaps more than me, but I couldn’t risk it. Telling Lilian she needed to see her mother was one thing; revealing palace secrets to a virtual stranger was another entirely.

“I assume Her Majesty is well.” I set my teacup on the boulder next to me. “I don’t see her often. She’s busy with the upcoming royal wedding.”

“Of course.” Hemlock glanced at Cypress, who met her gaze and looked quickly away. “Of course, and no doubt you spend most of your time in the gardens. How silly of me. Still, if you happen to speak to one of her maids, do pass on our best wishes, won’t you?”

7TH APRIL

"You should know better than to read the news by now," Reed said.

I glanced up from the morning paper, which I was reading in the gardens while I ate the plate of eggs on toast one of the maids had brought out to me.

"Knowing something and having the self-discipline to follow through are two different things," I said.

He sat on the bench next to me and reached for the section of the paper I hadn't read yet. I finished the last few bites of my egg while I skimmed an article on the blight. It confirmed what the magicians had told me: The disease was continuing to spread, radiating out from the palace like the unfurling petals of some poisonous bloom. Farmers' crops were beginning to fail in large numbers, and the Agriculture Office was scrambling to arrange the importation of grain from other countries. Food prices were set to skyrocket, and an Agriculture Office representative encouraged people to begin preserving food, however they could. Bottling produce was best, he said, as there was no guarantee the blight wouldn't find some way to infect apples and potatoes being stored in cellars.

At least we were more or less an island. Our northern coast connected with the continent's capital city of Urbis, but other than that, ocean separated us from other kingdoms. It would be foolish to hope the blight would never find a way to cross the waves, but perhaps, if all the botanists and magicians and farmers and gardeners worked together, we could find a way to fight this plague before it took hold in other lands.

"Grim news on the Festival front," Reed said. "Looks like another kingdom is predicted to win first prize in just about every competition we've got. Smart money is on Elder for best sapling, and it sounds like Enchantia and Skyla might be neck-and-neck for best flower."

I scoffed. "Enchantia always thinks it's going to win best flower, and it never has. Floris owns that title."

Reed glanced at me. A rose petal fell from a blossom on the topiary next to the bench and fluttered onto his lap. "Floris is dying. What flowers are we going to bring? Linden's last fringed tulip just turned gray, and I'm sure you know Briar had to withdraw her entry after her lily hybrids died."

"There are still Florians entering the competition," I said. "Florians from farther away, near the coast. We'll still win."

"That's not what this says." He shook the newspaper,

and the pages rustled with the movement. "Apparently, two of the greenhouses that were supposed to be in stiff competition both closed down this week."

I grimaced. "I hadn't heard that."

"It's not looking good out there. Still, at least, people are coming to the Festival."

I nodded as if I agreed, but it was a small consolation. I'd already received a note from the Horticulture Council this morning, informing me that they were going post inspectors at all the docks to make sure plants leaving the country weren't carrying blight. Their presence was going to be an embarrassment, a sign to the rest of the world that Floris had fallen, but it was a necessary embarrassment.

The Festival was always the highlight of the year, and I'd spent my whole life looking forward to finally being old enough to enter my own flowers into the competitions. This year, not only was I old enough, but I was also the head gardener of the Palace of Floris. It should have been a triumph.

Now, it sounded like Floris would be lucky to have any flowers to show at all.

Still, I had my entry. My blooms, secreted away in my private garden, remained impossibly untouched by the curse that had devastated the rest of the country. I would take them to the Festival. I wouldn't win the first-prize trophy, of course, but at least Floris would be *represented.*

"We'll do the best we can," I said, with far more resolve than I felt. "That's all we can do."

Reed nodded, most likely more to reassure me than because he believed it himself. He was a good friend.

I kept looking at the paper even after Reed left. The articles all had the same tone, a blend of hysteria and gossip that sold newspapers but was justified even so. This article warned about strawberry shortages; that one theorized that a new weed-killing potion was to blame for the blight; a third cautioned readers to stop growing plants altogether.

I shouldn't keep looking at the stories. There was work to do, even in a garden that was a shell of itself. I had blighted plants to destroy and carefully watched seedlings to label. There were seeds from last year's harvest, tightly stored in glass jars in the hopes that would save them from infection, and they all needed to be packaged for sale.

Part of me wasn't sure we should even try to sell our seeds and plants anymore. Even if they didn't carry the blight with them to the other kingdoms, there was a good chance they were all we would have left by the time this sickness had ravaged the land.

On the other hand, maybe it was for the best that we get all our healthy plants safely away. Perhaps, in a year or a dozen years or maybe a hundred, whenever this curse was lifted, we would be able to buy back our seeds and start again.

Stinging nettles, the thought depressed me.

I bundled the newspaper and got up from the bench to throw it away. The roll of newsprint settled atop the other waste in the bin and unfurled itself, revealing part of the headline, *FESTIVAL GROUNDS SHOW EVIDENCE OF BLIGHT,* and the accompanying photo of empty dirt lots where thriving floral displays should have been.

Reed was right. Reading the papers only frustrated me, and it was rare that they provided any news I didn't end up hearing five minutes later from the housemaids and stable boys. Still, I craved those stories. What if one of them held the bit of information I needed to solve this thing?

I cut through a topiary garden on my way to the seed storage shed. I hadn't wanted to come here, but my ankle still hurt with every step and putting weight on it longer than necessary seemed like a fool's decision.

I hadn't spent much time in the topiary garden in the past year, and not at all since the blight had begun to creep its way across the palace grounds. These shrubs and roses had their own team of specialists, who cared for them and kept them trimmed and trained into fantastical shapes, and they hadn't needed my attention.

I remembered running through this area when I was a child, either with Lilian or on my own when Hedley hadn't given me enough chores to do. I remembered towering moss elephants and laurel umbrellas and boxwood bubbles rising from enormous glazed pots. The garden had seemed like a playful menagerie, then.

Now, it was a graveyard. The arches of climbing roses hung like corpses from their frame, the gray blooms heavy and damp on the rotting vines. The shrubs that had once looked like giraffes and unicorns and playful bears were now skeletons. Even the great dragon, once covered in a dizzying array of red mosses and creeping yellow flowers and firetongue sprays, hunched over as if all its flame had gone out.

"I followed you in here," a voice said behind me. "I wish I hadn't."

I held out a hand to Lilian. Running in the other direction would have been wiser, given her future husband's feelings about me, but here, surrounded by the gloom of whimsy turned to rot, I needed the warmth of her palm against mine.

She laced our fingers together. "I hadn't seen this

garden yet," she said. "I think I've been avoiding it."

"Me too." I'd examined almost all the others by now, if only in passing. This one, though, hurt me worse than the rest, if only because it had once been a place of such safety.

"How are things?" she said.

I laughed, mostly so I wouldn't end up yelling or crying. "About the same. Which is the problem."

"I know exactly what you mean."

Of course, she did. She always knew.

"I discovered I might have a bit of magic after all, though." The delight of the discovery had faded out a little. It was hard to stay excited when the world around me looked like this. "It's not enough to matter, but Hedley thinks I might be able to train it up eventually."

"That's brilliant." Interest illuminated her face, casting out some of the unsettling aura that permeated the garden. "How did you find out? What did you learn?"

I started to speak, but she quickly shook her head.

"Stars, Deon, I'm acting like things are normal," she said. "I'm sorry, I want to hear everything, but we haven't got time."

She was right. Even here at what felt like the end of the world, we didn't have the luxury of ordinary conversation. Not when she was a princess, and I was a gardener, and I'd been banished from the walls of her home.

"I found something out," she said, hesitating over the words like she wasn't sure she wanted to say them. "About Mama. I'm supposed to be writing thank you notes for the engagement gifts people have sent, but I had to come tell you."

I tensed. Here it was, perhaps: the key to the blight and the elusive piece of information that might give me the power to solve it.

"I went to go see her," Lilian said.

She was interrupted by a booming voice.

"My love," Duke Remington said, striding around the corner of a limp hedge and into the garden.

I flinched and jumped away from Lilian. But it was too late; he'd already seen us and had been, perhaps, watching us for a while.

"Garritt," she said, with a composure I envied.

My face reddened; my palms began to sweat. I balled my hands into fists and tucked them quickly behind my back. I stood at attention like one of the palace guards, pretending an innocence we all knew didn't belong to me.

"I thought we discussed this, dear," the duke said, giving Lilian a look that chilled my blood.

She stood up straighter, her posture ramrod-straight and incongruent with her lacy blue dress.

"I need to speak with Mr. Gilding," she said. "No one has told me a thing about the situation in the gardens. I'm tired of being kept in ignorance."

"You simply don't need to be bothered with such troubles." His tone was sickly sweet.

My skin crawled. The thought of him being alone with Lilian filled my mind, and I tightened my hands behind my back, gripping one of my wrists in a vain attempt to shackle myself.

"I can see what's happening in the garden with my own two eyes," Lilian said. "Preventing me from speaking with *my* gardener is not going to somehow shield me from the reality of what's happening on my grounds. It's only going to irritate me."

She had never used a voice that cold with me, not even when we'd been in the middle of our biggest arguments. I never wanted to be on the opposite side of her.

It didn't even seem to faze the duke.

"Such things are not for princesses to trouble their heads with." He took her arm and twined it with his, a posture that suggested tranquil evening strolls and entrances at grand balls. She tried to jerk it away, but his limbs were like iron. "Now, let's go back to the palace. I'd hate for you to catch a chill."

All this time, he had barely so much as looked at me. Now, his gaze cut into me like a knife.

I shuddered inwardly. Forget being allowed in the palace. I needed to watch my back, or I'd end up on the streets of Tulis--or worse.

He strode past me, Lilian's arm shoved firmly up against her side. She glanced back as he dragged her from the garden.

Don't, she mouthed.

I was too angry to listen.

I followed after them, but at a distance, ducking behind walls at every opportunity. The duke only checked behind himself a few times before he seemed assured that I'd remained in the topiary garden like a good little servant.

He was in for a rude awakening.

I crept up the walkway where the duke marched Lilian, still resisting, toward the palace. He walked her around to the front of the palace, perhaps thinking that the eyes of the guards would be enough to dissuade her from making a scene. She yanked her arm free from his grasp and said something to him. I couldn't make out the words from this distance, but her demeanor made clear exactly what she thought of him and his behavior.

I couldn't imagine Lilian being married to such a

brute.

And then, horribly, I could imagine it. She would hate being tied to this man. He would force her into a tiny box, make decisions without consulting her, tell her that she didn't need to worry her pretty little head about things like plagues and crop failures. He would creep in on her authority until the crown princess of Floris was forced to take a back seat to her consort unless she was willing and able to fight him every step of the way and then some.

And Lilian would fight. But it enraged me that she would *have* to.

King Alder and Queen Rapunzel should be here. They should know the kind of man their daughter was about to marry. The king and queen I knew would have never encouraged this kind of alliance, but now, even if Lilian decided she wanted to break off the engagement, it seemed her parents were nowhere to be found.

Anger burned inside me. That Lilian should be in this position, that I should be so unable to help, that the love of my life was a princess and therefore a prisoner to the constraints of class and duty--it was enough to make the edges of my vision cloud until the only thing I could see was the duke, smiling calmly down at Lilian as she told him exactly what she thought of his behavior.

I wasn't going to murder him. I was a gardener, committed to creating life, not destroying it.

But sticks and stones, I was going to make him regret he'd ever laid his hand on her.

My sprained ankle throbbed in pain as I hobbled toward them. I wasn't trying to conceal myself anymore, and it didn't matter, because the duke wasn't paying attention anyway.

He reached for Lilian again. He wrapped an arm

around her shoulder in a gesture that should have been loving but instead looked like a prison.

"This kind of behavior won't do, my love," he said. "You are a princess, Lilian. A future queen. You can't be seen cavorting with your filthy gardener plaything. It's uncouth. How do you think your father would feel if he saw what I just saw?"

Lilian wrenched herself away. "My father trusts and respects Mr. Gilding, as do I. As will you if you want to be part of this family."

He leaned forward. "Is that a threat?"

"It's a warning. You'd do well to take it."

Her face flushed. This conversation was taking courage and anger and dedication--it was taking everything she had, at a time when worry for her mother and her kingdom had already consumed her strength.

Perhaps I would kill him after all.

"If you feel the need to manage the affairs of the garden yourself, perhaps we could compromise," he said. "Marriage is all about compromise, is it not?"

She folded her arms. "What do you propose?"

"Regular meetings," he said. "Ones, we both attend." He sneered, the ugliness twisting his face. "It would be a shade more productive than seeking out his company in the gardens like some common harlot."

Lilian's eyes flew open in outrage, and she stepped back. "Were I a harlot, you can rest assured that there would not be enough coin in the world to tempt me to be with you."

Stars, I loved that woman.

"Our engagement is over," she said. "I refuse to be tied to anyone who would disrespect me as you have."

I expected anger, or surprise, or outrage, or perhaps even sudden apologies and a subdued tone, but the duke leaned in toward Lilian with smugness all over his infuriating face.

"I think you'll find that decision is no longer up to you." He put a gentle hand on her shoulder, and she swatted it away. "I've already spoken with the court physician. He's a reasonable man, in spite of all those troublesome gambling debts. He agrees with me that you've become hysterical with worry for your mother. We all know the queen is sicker than anyone outside the palace would like to believe. You're in no condition to abandon such a long betrothal, especially not when you'll be happiest if you seek the company of your devoted future husband."

Lilian's face drained of color. "You can't do that."

"I already have, my dear. You're to be confined to your room until you feel better. We all believe you need good care and a firm hand right now."

"I want to speak to my father."

"Your father is in Urbis," the duke said in a measured voice. "He's left me in charge. You'll see him again at our wedding."

I'd heard enough. I ran toward them, adrenaline and fury silencing the pain in my ankle, and flew at the duke before he knew I was coming.

My fist cracked across his face with a satisfying thud. I hit him again, landing a blow on his jaw.

Lilian screamed and backed out of our way, but she didn't tell me to stop.

The duke made a feeble attempt to hit me back, but he hadn't spent his life digging up tree roots and hauling bags of manure. His fist slamming into my face was enough to make me blink but not much more than that. I hit him with a solid punch to the gut.

Then I was being dragged back, a strong pair of arms

around my chest and another pair wrangling my wrists. I fought them, but it did no good; the palace guards who had come to the duke's rescue were as strong as me, and there were two of them.

Duke Remington stumbled back, massaging his jaw. His hair was disheveled, and hatred burned in his eyes.

"Take him to the dungeons."

"Don't you dare," Lilian said. "I'll tell the whole kingdom what you are. You might have gotten my father out of the way, but I promise you, you don't want a rebellion on your hands."

They locked eyes. The people loved Lilian. And now, with the nation in crisis and fear of the blight making tempers high, rebellion was a real possibility.

Finally, the duke turned to the guards.

"Take him to my office," he snapped. "Mr. Gilding and I need to have a chat." He narrowed his eyes at me. "You get one more chance. One. Fail that, and you'll wish I'd only thrown you in a cage."

They dragged me, none too gently, to an elegant room with a desk and a fireplace. I'd seen this room before--I'd seen every room in the palace at some point or other, during Lilian's and my rambling adventures--but it had been updated since I'd been here last. A shiny new desk sat under a wide window, and a thick red carpet muffled my footsteps as the guards shoved me across the room.

I didn't recognize either of these men. They were rougher around the edges than the palace guards I knew. It seemed Duke Remington had acquired more than just a new desk and rug.

They left me standing in the middle of the room and took up their places guarding the door. We waited in silence for a long time. The duke had been right behind us a few moments ago. I imagined him pacing the hallway outside, killing time just so I would feel the weight of his power. Or perhaps he'd turned his attentions to Lilian and was off somewhere continuing to berate and intimidate her.

Anger bubbled inside me, hot and roiling like one of the cook's spicy red pepper stews.

Finally, when I had started considering the merits of smashing through the window to escape, the duke came in. He closed the door behind himself, his movements slow and intentional. His footsteps sounded on the polished wooden floor, then the carpet. I stared straight ahead, refusing to acknowledge his presence.

Then he was in front of me, glaring at me with a bright red spot blooming on his cheek.

I wished I'd aimed for one of his eyes. He'd have looked better with a shiner.

"Mr. Gilding," he said.

I jerked my head at him in the tiniest of nods. This man didn't deserve a bow of respect.

"Well," he said.

He let the word hang in the air for a long time. I bit back the urge to say, *Well, what?,* because I knew it was what he was after. After a long silence, he leaned back against his desk.

"I hope you enjoyed yourself out there," he said. "It's the last thing you'll enjoy on these grounds."

I remained silent and continued to stare past him.

My silence seemed to annoy him, and I clenched my teeth to force back a smile. I wanted to annoy him. I wanted to punch him again, too, but one couldn't have everything.

"I'm going to explain to you how the next week is going to work," he said. "And only the next week, because after that, your life will be none of my business."

"I look forward to that."

He gazed intently at me, a slight smirk mangling his lips.

"The wedding has been moved up," he said.

My heart sank, but I didn't have time to process the news before he went on.

"All things considered, we think it best to have the wedding now, while we still have the luxury of having the queen and flowers at the ceremony."

I wanted to scream at the slight smile on his face. Anyone who could smile at the thought of losing our queen, of Lilian losing her *mother,* had no soul.

"We're going to be married in just over a week," he said. "Directly after the Spring Flower Festival ends. Many of our invited guests will be in the kingdom for the event anyway, and I see no reason to make them travel all the way here twice." His smile spread as if he actually gave a fig as to whether his guests were inconvenienced or not.

"Has Lilian agreed to this?"

His expression sharpened as if my even using her name affronted him.

"Lilian is a sensible girl," he said. "I'm sure she and I will come to some sort of agreement."

"You mean because you threatened her, right?" I said. "Or blackmailed? Not that I can imagine Lilian would ever do something that would allow you to blackmail her, but you're clever. I'm sure you'll come up with something."

If only I'd known what he was the first time I'd met him in the gardens. If only Lilian had seen through his polite, shy act before she'd agreed to announcing the engagement. If only--but *if only* did me no good. I couldn't change the past.

I couldn't even figure out how to change the present.

"Once Lilian and I are married, you will be fired," he said. "I'm telling you now as a courtesy. Don't expect any kind of reference from the palace. A gardener who strikes his betters is unlikely to be the sort of man most people want to hire. Perhaps you should look into mercenary work. Or piracy."

He thought he was making a joke. I thought I'd rather enjoy being a mercenary, assuming he was the person I'd been hired to take out.

"If you fire me, Floris will never maintain its title at the Festival." We still might make a decent showing this year. My competition entry would see to that. But next year, when the blight had grown roots deep into this land and nothing was alive but the flowers I grew in the walls of my private garden? I was Floris's only hope.

It wasn't just our reputation at risk. It was our crops, too, and our economy. Our nation was built on the bulbs and seeds we sold to the rest of the world.

Without whatever mysterious magic lived in me and in my garden, small and untrained though it was, Floris was doomed.

The duke scoffed. "With all due respect, Mr. Gilding, as little as that may be, I doubt we'll maintain our title with or without your help." He gestured out the window, where the once vibrant gardens sulked in shades of gray and faded green. "I don't know if you've noticed, but our gardens haven't exactly flourished under your care."

"Lilian will never let you get rid of me," I said. "Neither will her father, or the queen. I've been loyal to this family since I was born."

"But you haven't been loyal to *me,*" the duke said.

"Not at all. And soon enough, when Lilian and I are married, and the king has given up his throne entirely to tend to his ailing wife, I will be the head of this family. You see our conundrum."

There was no conundrum. There was only a towering pile of human rot, one that put the plague out in the gardens to shame.

"I know you and my bride think I'm trying to break your hearts or some such nonsense," he said. "In truth, I'm doing it for Lilian. I love her, and it's my responsibility to take care of her. That includes getting her away from..." He hesitated, overly delicately. "Polluting influences."

He wasn't thinking about love. He was thinking about power, the kind of power only kings could hold. It was all over his face, in the way he raised his chin to look down his nose at me, and in his shoulders, which he held stiff and broad as if taking up space was all it took to take over a kingdom.

"The gardens will never recover without me," I said.

He raised an eyebrow. "And why should I care?" he said. "I'm here for the princess, not some tulips. You'd understand that kind of affection if people of your class were capable of such elevated feelings."

I ground my teeth together. I was going to punch him again. I was going to send him flying through that window, down to the putrid ground. I was going to smash my boot into his sneering, slimy face, and then I was--

"Take him away," Duke Remington barked.

The guards' vice-like hands closed once more around my arms, and I was yanked, struggling, from the room.

THRONE OF ENCHANTMENT

8TH APRIL

I threw a shovelful of thick, aromatic mulch onto the ground. It landed with a muffled thump, and the mulch was quickly raked into place by one of the apprentices.

We'd stopped trying to pull the blight from the gardens. It had been no use; the disease that was quickly destroying every green thing in the kingdom spread like fire, jumping from one flowerbed to another with a speed that made me dizzy.

Instead, we'd resorted to removing the healthy plants, few and far between though they were, and storing them under domes of enchanted glass. This had been Hedley's idea. My old mentor had been the first one to suggest the plague tearing its way across the kingdom was magical, rather than biological, and I'd stumbled back to the shed that passed for my bedroom last night to learn he'd already started the apprentices working on saving what they could.

"I hoped you wouldn't mind," he had said, as I'd tumbled onto my makeshift bed, my wrists aching from where the palace guards had yanked them around and my sprained ankle still throbbing in pain. "Not trying to step on any toes."

I'd told him to do as he liked. Nothing I'd tried had so much as slowed the blight. I had a few plants yet that were thriving, but whatever magic was keeping the flowers in my private garden alive clearly wasn't strong enough to rescue the whole of Floris.

Now, a few apprentices walked past, each drawing a small wagon along the brick walkway between the poppy field and one of the palace's many tulip beds. Each cart held as many glass domes as the apprentices had been able to cram inside, and each dome held a single bright, precious flower.

Hedley had only been able to obtain a few hundred domes, although he'd promised me he was working with some magicians to create more. They would all end up at the Spring Flower Festival, which was approaching with an alacrity that terrified me.

This annual festival was everything to this kingdom.

And while we might not have the kind of displays the world usually expected, we would have *something.* I couldn't save Lilian from her upcoming marriage to a power-hungry brute. I couldn't save her mother from the gray plague that was creeping up her hair like the approach of Death himself. But I'd do what I could to save her kingdom's reputation, at least, for this one year.

“Beds fifty-four and fifty-six are cleared,” a voice said at my elbow.

I stopped shoveling and turned to face Linden, who was standing stiffly next to the cart of mulch.

“Thank you,” I said. “How many flowers were you able to save?”

“One hundred and seventy-two.”

The number made my heart sink. Most years, we had thousands and thousands of tulips on display, raven wings, and silk flutter reds, and the iridescent purples the rest of the world loved so much.

This year, we’d be lucky to have a thousand flowers in total.

“Are we really going to spread mulch on the grounds and leave them like this?” Linden asked.

Ordinarily, the question would have been a criticism, coming from him. Now, he just sounded sad.

“Unless someone comes up with a better idea,” I said. “There’s no point in wasting seeds when we know they’ll just die.”

He didn’t answer. He didn’t even nod. His shoulders just fell.

“How are we on bulbs?” I asked.

“We have enough,” he said. “As many to sell as most years.”

“At least, the blight doesn’t seem interested in bulbs.” I drove my shovel into the ground and leaned on the handle. My body ached, mirroring my bruised soul. This curse, whatever it was, only seemed interested in things that were actually growing. Our seeds and bulbs were safe.

For now.

“I’d like to hold a few extra crates back,” he said. “Just in case someone finds a way to fix things. I want to be sure Floris has enough bulbs to replant this fall."

The rest of his words remained unspoken. *If the blight is cured by autumn. If this nightmare can be solved. If there's any hope of the future looking like the past instead of like the wasteland it's turning out to be.*

There was no point holding extra bulbs in reserve. The blight wasn't going away any time soon. But the grief on his normally cynical face wounded me.

"That's a good idea," I lied. I might as well pretend I still had hope. The apprentices helping with the mulching were listening to every word we said; I wouldn't be the one to tell them everything was doomed. "Let the other supervisors know they can keep however many seeds or bulbs they think reasonable. Just remember that this festival brings in money for the kingdom."

My words remained unspoken, too: *Make sure we sell enough, in case we lose everything of value and have nothing to sell to the rest of the world. Make sure we save enough to get us through what's sure to be a long, dark winter. Don't let us starve.*

He touched the brim of his straw hat in acknowledgment and walked away, his narrow shoulders still drooping.

The people in this garden were starting to look as bad as the plants.

I went back to spreading mulch over the earth. It went on like a blanket, and I hoped, like a blanket, that it would protect the ground underneath until it was safe to plant again.

If that day ever came.

I could only try to break my back with mulching for so long. Eventually, the cart was empty, and the apprentices had to go refill it. I watched the cart go, and then I turned on my aching heel and went in the other direction, toward the seedlings greenhouse where I knew Hedley would be waiting.

My mentor was standing over a tray of delicate seedlings, peering at them through a magnifying glass.

"No sign of blight," he said as I entered the room.

He spoke as if this was a good sign, but I knew better.

"It doesn't usually show up until the first true leaf appears." I gave the tray a dirty look it didn't yet deserve. "It's like this blight wants to make sure to give you hope, just so it can destroy it."

Hedley straightened and set his magnifying glass down with a clank.

"Who blew on your dandelion?" he said.

I scowled. I couldn't help it. The anger bubbling inside me had to go somewhere, and a grumpy expression seemed like a better outlet than trying to poison the future king of Floris might have been.

"Lilian's marrying a monster," I said.

Hedley's lips thinned just a bit. "I thought we decided you needed to spend a little more time focusing on your gardens and a little less on the princess's love life."

"It's not a love life," I said. "She's practically been imprisoned by that overgrown flea beetle."

His bushy silver eyebrows drew together. "How do you mean, imprisoned?"

I sighed. I hadn't had the heart to tell him all about it last night, but now, the story poured out of me: How Duke Remington had found Lilian and me speaking in the topiary garden, how he had manhandled her away, and how I had ultimately done everything in my power to knock him unconscious before the guards had leaped to his rescue.

"He's going to fire me after the wedding," I said. "Which is now in just over a week."

His eyebrows jumped up like surprised caterpillars. "When did they move the wedding up?"

"Right after I landed one on his jaw, I assume," I said.

Guilt roiled in my stomach. I had tried to save Lilian and only succeeded in moving up the date of her lifelong imprisonment.

"And the king is in Urbis," I said, unable to keep the frustration out of my voice. "When we need him most right here."

As usual, Hedley refused to get worked up. He picked up his magnifying glass and moved to the next tray of seedlings. "I imagine His Majesty is searching for solutions like the rest of us."

It was likely the truth, but it didn't soften my anger. Hedley raised a hand and gestured at me to come stand by him.

"Come redirect your thoughts, if you can," he said. "I'm curious as to whether this magic of yours can help these seedlings."

If this mention of my newfound abilities had been a ploy to get me to stop raging and sulking, it worked. Hope lit in me whenever I remembered the iris I'd managed to make move, real hope that seemed untouched by the blight or the duke. I gave Hedley a begrudging smile and leaned toward the tray.

"What should I do?"

"That's the question, isn't it?" He touched one of the seedlings with one broad, calloused finger. The tiny green plant yielded, then sprang back the moment he moved his finger away. "I wonder if you might make those true leaves grow a little faster."

It was a worthwhile test; these seedlings were still a day or two from the growth that would mark them as real, viable plants rather than delicate babies. I held my hand out and tried to feel into the core of the plant, as Hedley had coaxed me into doing before.

The magic that ran through these seedlings was easier to find than it had been last time, either because I knew what I was feeling for or because the seedlings, full to bursting with the energy that had been stored in their seeds, were somehow *louder* than the iris had been. I focused on one seedling, the one that seemed smallest and furthest away from any kind of growth spurt, and reached out with my thoughts into the fountain of life that pulsed at the center of the tiny green thread.

I thought about leaves, as if thought was all it would take to bring a thing into reality, and tried to sense the potential in these plants.

"Lilian said she learned something about her mother," I said abruptly.

The connection between the magic and me dropped, the brightness I'd sensed inside the plants disappearing as if I'd blown them out like a candle.

Hedley folded his arms. "You have a one-track mind that would astound even the most reclusive scholars."

"Sorry." I glanced up at him anyway. "Still, you're the one who told me the queen might have answers. That's why I was with Lilian in the topiary garden, by the way. She was trying to tell me something that might have stopped the blight. That's what His Gracelessness interrupted. For all I know, we could be halfway out of this mess right now if he'd minded his own business."

"Deon," Hedley said, warning me.

"I'm just saying."

"I doubt she learned anything from the queen that could have changed the fate of the nation overnight." His voice was a study in exaggerated patience. "Seedlings.

Please."

I turned my focus back. The line of magic was still easy to find, but controlling it--that was something else. I could imagine leaves. I could feel the way the energy within the plants might help them form. But I couldn't make it happen.

The thought of Lilian trapped inside her own palace didn't help. Even as I tried to focus, a chattering voice in the back of my mind warned me she was in danger and urged me to rescue her. Perhaps I could climb the palace wall. I'd done that before, and I hadn't died even if I did only have a sprained ankle to show for the attempt. Or maybe I could bribe a guard.

"Focus," Hedley said.

I tried. I stared and sensed, and finally, for the slightest moment, I felt something spring to life inside the seedling. I held my breath, ready for a leaf to uncurl, or even to bud.

Nothing happened. The hint of possibility faded away. Perhaps it had been nothing more than a lingering shred of optimism buried somewhere inside my otherwise battered soul.

Finally, Hedley sighed and drummed his finger on the top of the worktable. In front of us, the tray of seedlings sat, stubborn and still.

"It was a good effort, Deon," he said. "At least, we tried."

We worked in silence for a while, tending the seedlings that would be sold at the festival and placing each tray back under a dome of enchanted glass when we were done.

There was no guarantee the glass would work. We'd only been trying it since yesterday. Still, nothing under glass had met a horrible, moldy death since yesterday, which put its success rate far higher than any other intervention we'd tried.

"I would like to know what Lilian found out," Hedley said eventually. He spoke quietly, as if to himself, but I caught the words. The princess's name always captured my attention.

I watered a fragile crystal bell seedling with an eyedropper, carefully wetting the soil but not allowing water to so much as touch the plant's stem. These were delicate, enchanted flowers, usually grown only by fairies. If we could have a few of them for sale at the festival, the world would know we still, at least, had the skills to grow *some* plants of note.

"I couldn't tell if she saw her mother or just learned something," I said. "The queen's maids have barely been allowed into her chambers, and none of them have seen her, but maybe one of them noticed something anyway?"

Hedley didn't answer, and I let out a sigh I felt like I'd been holding for days.

"What do you know about the queen's past?" Hedley said after a while.

I shrugged. "Same as anybody else, I guess. She was a lady from near the coast. The king met her while he was touring the kingdom, and they fell in love and got married. I heard the king's father was a little annoyed she wasn't a princess but gave his blessing anyway."

"That's all true," Hedley said, in a way that made me think that perhaps it wasn't.

He wasn't forthcoming.

"What?" I demanded.

"It's all true," he repeated, then added, "on a technicality."

I gave the crystal bell its last few drops, then

examined Hedley's expression. He was thinking about something, and thinking hard if the little lines between his eyes were to be believed.

"What is it?" I said. "You may as well tell me if there's anything to know. I can keep secrets."

He unspooled a length of fine twine from a ball and clipped off a piece, pondering all the while. He removed the glass dome from a tiny elfin climbing rose and tied its newest tendrils to the diamond-patterned trellis behind it, and I watched. There was no way on earth to hurry him up; the best I could do was to avoid distracting him while he considered.

He replaced the dome, and, decision made, looked seriously at me.

"This isn't to leave this conversation," he said.

I held up a hand as if he'd asked me to swear an oath.

"I won't tell anyone."

"It's not that you strictly *can't,*" he said. "It's just that the way King Alder and Queen Rapunzel did things... when it came to them being wed... Well, it's not how things are done."

This intriguing pronouncement made, he leaned back against the worktable and laced one of his thumbs behind his suspenders.

"The royal family of Floris has always married within the nobility," he said. "Or within royalty from other nations."

I nodded. Everyone knew that.

"What you said before is right, the queen was a lady. But only in the sense that she's a woman, and she has a fine, mannerly way about her."

I set the dropper down. This was too interesting for any half-listening.

"And the king did meet her on a tour, but her family home wasn't exactly one of the prescribed stops. As it happens, His Majesty was going on an unattended ride through the forest when he met her. You know how the king values his private time," he added. "He's always been one of those quiet family-man types, even before he had a family of his own. The ribbon-cutting and baby-kissing that comes with being a prince wore him down, though you'd never know it from the polite way he behaved, and he used to go off a lot to think about things and just be on his own."

I listened, utterly silent. It was rare to hear anyone speak about the king as a young man, and rarer still to learn things that wouldn't have been obvious to anyone who knew their history books.

"While he was riding, he came across a tower in the woods. It looked old and worn-down, and like it maybe shouldn't have been there, but it was there all the same. And Queen Rapunzel was up in the tower."

I held my breath as if the slightest sound would make him change his mind about telling me this.

"She wasn't a queen then, of course. She wasn't a noble lady, either, or even a wealthy merchant's daughter or skilled craftswoman. She was a prisoner, the adopted daughter of the witch who'd kidnapped her at birth."

I immediately forgot my attempt at silence.

"The daughter of the *what now?*" I exclaimed. "Kidnapped her from who? When?"

And stars, *why?*

"The witch used to go up and down the tower using Rapunzel's hair, see," Hedley continued as if my outburst hadn't happened. "It was longer then, impossibly long, and it gleamed like... Well, you've seen it. She keeps her hair at a manageable length now, but when she was young, she had to let it grow so the witch could go in and out as she pleased. And King Alder, he was so fascinated by this mysterious woman that he figured out how to climb up and down her hair, too, and that's how they got to know each other."

I blinked. Hedley's image didn't waver or do anything else to indicate I'd lost my mind.

"What do you mean, he climbed up and down her hair?" I said. "That's ridiculous."

"Magic often is," Hedley said, steady as ever. "One thing led to another, and the two young people fell in love. The witch wasn't happy with it, and she tried to keep them apart." He frowned a little. "Well, that's a long story. But in the end, they got married. Alder's father didn't appreciate the idea at first, but his health was failing, and I think he decided a bride he liked well enough was better than a bride he'd never met, so he gave them permission to go ahead with the union."

"What happened to the witch?"

"Still sulking in her tower, no doubt," Hedley said. "The point of all this is that Queen Rapunzel's hair has magic, just like your garden does. I don't know if it came from the witch or if the hair is why the witch wanted her in the first place, but I suspect whatever's happening with the blight has something to do with her hair and something to do with your garden." He took a deep breath and let it out slowly. "How the pieces connect? That's the part I don't know. Still, it seemed like information you should have."

I tried to imagine it, the queen locked in a tower in a forest, and King Alder coming to visit her by climbing her hair like a rope. I couldn't quite envision it, not without the image seeming too ludicrous to be real.

Still, Hedley had never lied to me. Nor had I ever known him to speak on a subject he didn't fully know about. Even his guess that I had some kind of magic buried deep inside myself had turned out to be correct, even if it hadn't proved as useful as he'd hoped.

"Does Lilian know?"

He shook his head. "I doubt it. Doesn't seem like the kind of thing she'd know and not have told you already."

It was a decent point. Lilian was decent at keeping secrets, but she'd never been any good at keeping them from *me*.

A dozen questions swirled through my head. I picked one at random.

"Who were the queen's real parents?"

Hedley tapped his suspenders. "No one knows, not even her," he said. "She spoke to me about it once. Said she tried looking for them but never came up with anything. Likely they died. Then you arrived on her doorstep, and she decided she'd rather focus on building her current family than focusing on the one she'd left behind." He scratched his cheek in thought. "I always thought it was strange, them taking in a baby so soon after they got married. But I suppose it makes sense. She was raised almost totally alone. Imagine that, for a woman who loves people as much as the queen. I don't think she could have sent you to the orphanage once she'd seen your face, not when she could give you a good life instead."

She'd given me a wonderful upbringing, one of the best. Picturing her now, hidden away in her room with her golden hair turning gray, hit me like a punch to the gut. She deserved better.

I couldn't figure out how to give it to her.

"Do you think it's the witch's fault?" I said. "Is she the one cursing the kingdom now?"

Hedley shook his head. "King Alder was able to put that witch in her place. A sorceress that our king could best, doesn't seem powerful enough to curse a kingdom, don't you think?"

It made sense and was almost the more frustrating for that. Having someone to blame meant we'd have someone who could fix this situation.

"She might not be able to curse a whole nation." I glanced up at Hedley. "Think she might be able to curse a single duke?"

Hedley groaned, and I bit back a smile. Getting Hedley to actually make sounds of annoyance took work. I was almost proud of myself.

"Deon," he said solemnly. "If you march into the forest to find a wicked witch when the festival is mere days away, I will disown you. See if I don't."

I ducked my head to hide my smile and busied my hands pulling down the next covered tray of seedlings.

"Of course, if you wanted to find her after the festival is over, that's your business," he added under his breath.

I looked sharply up at him. "You don't approve of him, either," I said. "I knew it."

"There's not much to approve of, is there?" he said. "I don't like the way you say he treats Lilian."

"You believe me, then?" I said. "You don't just think I'm, I don't know, some lovesick youth blinded by grief?"

Hedley's lips twitched. "That's a bit dramatic."

"It's how it feels," I muttered, pulling the bell off the seedling tray.

"I know you better than that." He shrugged, his broad shoulders barely moving. "You'd support the princess to the ends of the earth. If her betrothed were a good man, you'd stand aside, knowing she was in good hands. If you say she's being mistreated, I daresay that's close enough to the truth."

Hedley's trust in me warmed the pit of my stomach. Nobody seemed to trust me these days--not the duke, not my staff, not the journalists who kept swarming the palace grounds for evidence of my failure in holding back the blight.

But Hedley believed in me. So did Lilian.

We went back to work, each quiet with our own thoughts. I turned over the strange story Hedley had told me, trying to match it up with what I'd heard of the king and queen. He'd been right, what I heard did match up in technicalities. It was the nuance beyond those that had my head spinning.

Their story made sense, though. Or, at least, it made the queen's actions make sense. It was strange that she and the king had taken in a foundling child so soon after their wedding, and stranger still that they'd raised me with such love instead of merely bringing me up as one servant among hundreds.

But when I considered what the queen's past had been, her choices were no longer surprising. However unlikely it seemed, I had a feeling Queen Rapunzel saw herself in me: an orphan child, with nowhere to go, in need of a loving home. I could imagine her surprise at finding an infant on her doorstep. Just as easily, I could imagine her impulse to take care of me, to ensure I was raised in a home where I would never be lonely. When Lilian had come along, she had always encouraged our friendship and seemed to delight in watching us play together.

Or perhaps I had it backward. Perhaps, I saw myself

in her. We were both separated from our true parents. We had both made a home here at the palace. We both loved Floris, and the gardens, and Lilian.

Strange as it was to consider, I was more like the queen of Floris than I was different.

And now the queen was in danger of the blight that threatened to take everything we loved.

I glanced at the tray of seedlings. I would learn to focus my magic. I would learn to use it. And I would try to save the kingdom before it was too late.

9TH APRIL

The morning before the festival dawned clear and cool. I saw it happen because I had already been up for hours, supervising the last crates of bulbs and seeds that were being taken over to the festival grounds.

I heaved a wooden crate of bulbs onto the back of the wagon. Reed loaded another, and I called to the driver to go ahead. The cart rolled forward, and the next one, just arrived from the grounds, pulled up to take its place.

"We must have a few seeds left if it's taking this many loads to get everything over there," Reed said.

I acknowledged his optimism with a smile but didn't explain that it was because I'd held almost all the seeds, bulbs, and seedlings back at the palace until the last possible moment. With the blight frightening everyone in the kingdom, theft was a real concern.

I could have always pulled a few palace guards to keep an eye on everything over at the festival grounds, of course, but I didn't dare. Too many of the guards the duke had brought in were loyal only to him. I didn't trust them not to destroy the crates themselves just to spite me or win points with their boss.

"Do you think we'll have a festival next year?" Reed asked.

The way he quickly glanced away told me it had taken a lot of courage to ask the question--courage and fear. I smiled ruefully.

"I don't know," I said. "I think, yes. Even if we have to import all the flowers from elsewhere."

I didn't add that it might not be up to me. Lilian would try to stop him, but the duke had warned me I'd be fired as soon as the festival was over and he was married. The alliance would solidify his powers, and there was little I could do to stop him.

Lilian was the princess of Floris and would inherit the crown from her father. But the Florian custom had always been almost total equality between the monarchs and their spouses. In Floris, a king was a king and a queen was a queen, no matter who had married into the family.

Duke Remington was a born and bred Florian, and he would know this better than anyone. He wanted the power of the throne, and he would use it.

I was as good as gone.

"I'll admit, a festival full of flowers from The Forge would be impressive," Reed said. He'd taken my comment as a joke, and I was glad. "All those wild blooms with their zany colors."

"We'd be in danger for our lives," I said. The Forge was home to an impressive variety of venomous and carnivorous plants. Hedley hadn't allowed me near the ones in our greenhouse until I was thirteen for fear I'd lose a finger. "I wouldn't mind it if Skyla provided most of the flowers, either. We'd have to hire hot air balloons just so people could keep up with all the flying blossoms."

"Come to think of it, I'm not hating this idea." He grinned. His good cheer was nearly indefatigable, provided someone like Linden wasn't around to push his buttons.

When I was gone, I hoped the palace would consider promoting Reed in my place. He didn't have the experience, and he'd mentioned before that he didn't particularly want the job, but I knew he'd do it well. Or, at least, he wouldn't be an absolute tyrant, which wasn't something I could say about many of the more experienced gardeners on the staff. Myrtle would be good at the job, too, if she weren't so single-minded about her tulips. Hollis should be considered, too. She'd always been professional, and she had the organizational skills to manage the palace's forty acres.

"You all right?" Reed asked.

I jumped and realized he'd already started loading the newest cart while I'd been staring ahead, contemplating the depressing reality of a palace where I wasn't allowed.

"Just making sure I haven't forgotten anything," I lied and got to work loading.

Hedley came by to help us before the cart was full. He threw himself into the labor, and the final cart was loaded before I knew it.

The morning was starting to warm up. Reed wiped

the sweat off his forehead and turned to Hedley.

"You do know you don't work here anymore, right?" he said, still grinning.

Hedley scoffed. "What else am I going to do, get underfoot in the kitchens? No, Hyacinth doesn't arrive until this evening. I might as well make myself useful."

I tried to contemplate a world in which Hedley *wasn't* useful. I couldn't conjure up anything so ridiculous.

"If you need work to do, I can give it to you," I said, nodding at the cart. "I'm headed to the festival grounds to help set up the last displays."

"I'm at your disposal," Hedley said with a nod. It was almost funny, my old mentor showing me any kind of deference, but I appreciated it at a level I couldn't have explained. There were so few people who thought I was worth anything these days, but so long as I had Hedley and Lilian's respect, I could manage.

"I'll join you in a bit," Reed said. "I need to go drain the water garden now that it's empty."

Discouragement hid behind that simple statement. The water garden was never empty. But this year, everything that had survived had already been taken to the festival grounds, and we had little hope of growing anything new there.

"I'll ride with you." Hedley climbed onto the back of the cart.

I followed, and we arranged ourselves among the wooden crates. The morning sun kissed my cheeks and the back of my neck, its warm light ordinary and surreal because of it. The driver got us moving. The palace grounds spread out on either side, so drained of color, I could have tricked myself into thinking the world around me was nothing more than a black and white photograph.

"I'm glad I caught you alone," Hedley said in a voice low enough that the driver wouldn't overhear us under the creaking of the wheels. "I heard a bit of news this morning you ought to be aware of."

I propped an elbow on one of the crates and rested my head on my hand. A sudden fatigue pooled in my bones.

"I'm not going to like this, am I?"

Hedley grimaced. "It would appear that Duke Remington has been asked to be one of the competition judges."

My stomach lurched in a way that had nothing to do with the bumpiness of the ride. "You're joking."

I didn't have to ask which competitions the duke would be judging. Hedley's face said it all.

"Who asked him?"

"The Horticulture Council."

No doubt he had them wrapped around his little finger. It sickened me.

"Thanks for the warning," I said dryly. "I was afraid this week was going to be too good."

Hedley normally had little patience for my moods. To my surprise, he made a soft noise somewhere between a laugh and a snort and leaned forward on his crate.

"We really are in a pickle, aren't we?" he said.

He was as pessimistic as the rest of us, then, in his own way.

"Is the enchanted glass helping?" I asked.

"Perhaps," he said. "Still too early to tell."

"If it works, maybe we can get some magicians to enchant a whole greenhouse."

He thought about this for a moment, then gave the idea one decisive nod.

"It wouldn't be enough to restore the kingdom to what it ought to be," I said. "But if we were to set up a few greenhouses here, and maybe enchant every greenhouse in the kingdom, we could grow enough to keep the people fed."

"It might come down to that." He sighed and stretched his arms, then laced a thumb behind one of his suspenders.

"Maybe I could find a job growing food," I said. "When I'm not at the palace anymore."

Hedley shook his head. "The duke's a fool if he goes through with that threat of his. Firing you isn't going to help the gardens, and it'll drive a wedge between him and the princess he won't easily be able to fix."

"I don't think he cares," I said. "Lilian isn't important to him. Just the throne."

"Yes, I heard his parents gloating about it." Hedley's voice took on a shade of distaste I wasn't accustomed to hearing from him.

I leaned in closer. "You've met them?"

"Better than met," he said. "I overheard them when they were walking through the palace yesterday."

I realized that I hadn't seen the duke's parents in some time, nor any of the other nobles and courtiers at the palace. The gray grounds had chased them all indoors. I envied them.

Although, in truth, that might have just been because my late-night baths in the lake--a cold necessity now that I'd been barred from the palace--were starting to lose their charm.

"What did they have to say?" A hard edge crept into my voice. It was bad enough that the duke had invaded

Lilian's home, but it felt somehow far worse to know his parents were swanning around the castle while Lilian's parents had all but disappeared.

"Just a good deal of nonsense about how their son had finally reached the position to which he had always been destined." Hedley paused, then continued, with more caution, "They also seemed to think Princess Lilian isn't being as gracious of a hostess as they'd expected."

A laugh burst from me, sharp and at risk of becoming hysterical. "They think they deserve better, do they?" I exclaimed.

Hedley cleared his throat and jerked his chin toward the cart's driver. I swallowed the rest of my outrage.

"They're lucky Princess Lilian hasn't thrown a little nightshade in their tea," I muttered. "Luckier still, I'm not allowed in the palace, or I'd do it myself."

Threatening the lives of the future king's parents, even in jest, seemed like the kind of thing I probably shouldn't risk, but I was past caring. Duke Remington had already taken everything he could take from me.

Almost everything, anyway. And he'd steal the last few things soon enough.

"I don't care if he's judging the flower contest, I'm going to win," I said. "This is the only flower festival I'm going to get. I had one year as head gardener, and I'm not going to go out by losing to some poppy fanatic from Oz."

Hedley nodded slowly, the movements keeping a regular time against the irregular jolts of the cart against the cobblestones. We were passing through the city now, where the blight was only visible in the empty window boxes and the small gray lawns and bushes that had once brought life to the homes along this route.

"I've seen your entry," Hedley said. "You have a shot."

A shot. It wasn't a guarantee. But nothing in life came with guarantees, especially not when the Duke Remingtons of the world were in charge.

"This is my last chance," I said. "I couldn't protect the gardens. I couldn't save Lilian. I couldn't even earn the respect of my gardening staff. The *one* thing I've managed to do since this nightmare started is to keep those flowers alive. If I'm going to go down in history as the palace's worst gardener, I want the record to show that I did one thing right."

Hedley smiled a little, the gesture tightening the apples in his cheeks. "You've done plenty right, my boy. You've just had a bad year. Don't let it sour you. You're a good gardener and a good man. No one could have handled this crisis better."

That was far from the truth. Thinking back, I could think of a dozen things I should have done differently. I should have plucked out the blight the instant it appeared, instead of waiting until the next morning. I should have seen who Duke Remington was, instead of being blinded by his gracious manners like everyone else. I should have gone to see the queen the moment she fell ill, should have put my foot down with Linden and Chervil and all the other gardeners instead of letting them walk all over me, and I should have run away with Lilian when she'd given me the chance.

I was in a situation as dire as any I could imagine, and it was my choices and failures that had led me here.

I had only a few hurdles left on which I could try to prove myself. There was the festival, feeble as it was likely to be this year. And there was the flower competition, which would pit me against the best gardeners and breeders in the world combined with Duke Remington, the last man on earth to give me a fair chance.

"You're going to do just fine today," Hedley said. He leaned back and tapped his suspenders. "And if not, I suppose I can always find you a job out in Goldenrod shoveling manure or running Hyacinth's errands."

I tried to give him a severe look, but couldn't stop myself from chuckling. "That's low."

"Wouldn't want you to think no one's looking out for you."

"She wouldn't even let me run errands; she'd just feed me until I looked like a kingdom pig."

"It's the only thing you'll be good for if you don't win this contest," Hedley said with a serious shake of his head. "Seeing as how you're past your prime and all. The Shame of Floris. The worst human being to ever mar this great land. The first man since the infamous Lord of Larceny and his great tulip con to truly bring ignominy upon the royal family of Floris. The greatest disappoi--"

I plucked a clod of dirt from the floor of the cart and threw it at him. It hit one of his suspenders and bounced onto his lap in a shower of dust while he grinned at me.

"All right," I said. "You don't have to go on about it."

He winked, and the cart slowed to a stop before the festival ground gates.

~

Given the dull gray of the blight, a black-and-white garden seemed in bad taste. But we'd been planning and growing flowers for this display for a year, and we had too few displays to back out of anything now.

A bed of onyx tulips and midnight calla lilies danced together from their pristine white pots. Black satin irises fluttered in the breeze, and black widow columbines stretched their pointed spurs in every direction. Snow ivy crawled up an oiled ebony trellis, and striped black-and-white hellebores clustered alongside beetle pansies and void roses. Throughout the display, white petunias and hibiscus added light from their gleaming black pots.

A chessboard of alternating patches of stone clover and white candytuft stood in front of the display, covered in chess pieces made of wire grown over with black and white moss. Similar moss-covered sculptures as high as my knees sat to either side, shaped to look like a pair of skunks considering the board and reaching toward the pieces.

I set the last pawn onto its place on the board, and the apprentice helping me carefully pinned it into the ground with a curved metal stake.

I stepped back and took in the view. The blooms were big enough to stand out from their green foliage, and the solid-colored pots added to the overall effect.

"I like it," I announced.

On the other side of the display, arranging the climbing vines of a variegated shadow rose, Hollis pursed her lips.

"It's not what it should have been," she said.

Briar, one of the younger gardeners, shoved her hands into the pockets of her sturdy overalls. "It'll have to do," she said. "It's not as though we've got anything else."

I frowned at her. It really did look good. I'd seen black-and-white gardens before, and this one held its own. "Why the long face?"

She sighed. "Sorry. It's just been a long couple of weeks. I never thought one of our flower festivals was going to go like this. I don't even have a display to contribute this year."

We'd had to completely scrap her forest of miniature flowering trees. Too many of them had died, and her one remaining apple tree was under lock and key in her chambers back at the palace. We didn't have any reason to believe bringing flowers indoors would stop the blight from spreading, but I had a hard time blaming her from wanting to keep it close.

"Not having anything is better than having a display like mine," Hollis said. "I've been coming over here every week since autumn to grow the rose maze, and now, it's so thinned out, it doesn't even qualify as a maze. It's just a sad little walk."

"It's still something," I said. "Your Thornton reds are still better than any in the kingdom."

Of course, the Thornton reds had survived. They were Duke Remington's preferred flower.

"That's nice of you to say," Hollis said, although she clearly didn't believe a word of it.

Mace arrived a moment later, carrying a shallow box precariously loaded with waxy white geraniums in black pots.

"This is the last of them." H**olding** out the box for Hollis and Briar, who took the first two pots and arranged them in their places among the other flowers, **Mace** glanced at me.

I rankled under his sidelong gaze.

"The tea garden is almost finished," he said as if he'd rather not be speaking to me at all. "Glad the tea bushes arrived in time, humiliating as it is to have to ship them from outside Floris."

I grimaced. "We've all had to make concessions this year."

“I’m not complaining,” he said in a patronizing tone. “It’s just that one doesn’t really expect *Floris* to have to source the plants for its displays from elsewhere.”

“One doesn’t expect blight, either,” I said tersely. “We do the best we can.”

“Of course, no one would ever argue with that,” Mace said. “I just wonder if maybe there had been a better way to handle this festival than to try to make it go off like it always does.”

“No one needs your backhanded comments, Mace,” Briar said tersely.

He stepped back as if she’d slapped him. He’d always had a flair for the dramatic. “I have no idea what you’re talking about, Briar. If you want to interpret my comments in a negative way, that’s your decision. It’s not my fault if you choose to be offended.”

“Oh, shut up,” she muttered.

Hollis clucked her tongue, caught Briar’s eye, and shook her head.

Briar rolled her eyes. “No, I’m sick of listening to you acting like this is anybody’s fault. This entire festival is a nettle-stung disaster. We all know it. But those of us with functioning brains *also* know we need to band together if we want any hope of not humiliating ourselves in front of the entire world.”

“It’s a little late for that, don’t you think?” Mace snapped. “This is already an embarrassment. We all know what a Spring Flower Festival is supposed to look like.” He swept a hand toward the festival grounds. “This isn’t it.”

“The grounds look fine,” Hollis said. “There are fewer displays than usual. So what? The rose maze looks bad, I’ll admit that, and we had to source plants from outside Floris. It’s not the end of the world.” She glanced at me, and it was clear she was trying to back me up, even if that meant taking a position she didn't really buy into.

She thought the festival was a failure. But what did that matter? I thought the festival was likely to be a failure, but I was here anyway, doing what I could to make the best of the situation.

"Briar is right," I said. "Either we work together without complaining, or we may as well not bother."

"I was leaning toward *not bother,*" Mace muttered.

Briar's hands balled into fists. "Mace, I swear to the fairies, I will--"

"Stop it." My voice was hard; it had taken on an edge of authority I wasn't used to wielding. "We're wasting time bickering. People have already traveled across the world for our festival. We can't just ignore this event. So either everyone here needs to stop feeling sorry for themselves and get to work, or you can decide this isn't the right career for you and go home."

I met each of their gazes in turn. Hollis pursed her lips and gave me a tight nod. Briar chewed on the inside of her cheek, sighed, and then she nodded, too.

Mace held my gaze for a long moment, a simpering little smile on his lips, but finally, he broke eye contact, and the smile faltered.

"Fine," he said. "I'll do my best. But I'm just trying to look out for you, Mr. Gilding. You're the Head Gardener. People are ultimately going to hold you responsible for all of this." He gripped the edges of his box tightly enough that his fingers paled. "I just think, maybe, that you should consider skipping the competitions and festivities this time around. Go home after the opening ceremonies. People are going to have some unkind things to say about Floris's offerings this year. I just thought that maybe you'd want to avoid hearing that."

I didn't like Mace. I knew Hedley would have taken objection to his suggestions, and Lilian would have given him a talking-to he wouldn't soon forget.

To me, though, the words made sense. They sounded an awful lot like the ones that kept creeping into my mind in quiet moments.

"Don't be an idiot," Briar said, snapping me back to the conversation. She looped her thumb behind one strap of her overalls and made a face at Mace like he was a particularly dim child who had just suggested one of us go solve the blight by dancing on the moon. "Deon's the one good thing we've got going for us." She held out her hands and wiggled her fingers. "Give me that box. I'm sure you have some apprentices to bother."

"Briar." I put a hand on the back of my neck and furrowed my brow at her. "Come on. Teamwork. Remember?"

"I'm doing my best." She grabbed the box from Mace, and the few remaining pots rattled. She caught my eye, and so quickly I almost missed it, winked. She spun around, and Hollis, who seemed happy enough to escape the conversation, hurried to help her place the last few plants.

Mace clasped his hands behind his back. "I'm only trying to look out for you."

"I appreciate that." I gave him a smile as insincere as the ones he usually gave me. "And I'd appreciate it even more if you could make sure the bulb cases in the tulip tents are being arranged properly."

He searched my face, trying to figure out if I was arguing with him or not. For someone as indirect as Mace, every conversation, no matter how innocent, came with the possibility of a veiled attack.

Living like that sounded exhausting.

I widened my smile, and this time it was for real. "I know the festival isn't what it should be," I said, more gently. "But we're all going to do our best, and I know that includes you. Thanks for caring so much about the kingdom's reputation. It's good to know you're so passionate about your work."

My sincerity seemed to confuse him even more. He hesitated.

"Thanks," he finally mumbled, and he wandered off toward the tulip tents.

I bit back a smile and watched him go.

Hedley had been watching the whole thing. I didn't realize it until I turned around, but then, his slight smile was impossible to miss.

He waved me over, and I fell into step with him. I expected him to make some quiet comment about how Mace had always been hard to manage or a confirmation that the black and white garden did, in fact, look all right.

Instead, he leaned in so only I could hear him.

"Mace is right," he said. "You should go back to the palace after the opening ceremonies."

I stopped in my tracks. "Why would you say that?"

Hedley had always been my biggest supporter, aside from maybe Lilian. I had worked so hard to make sure the festival was as good as it could be under the circumstances. And now he was siding with Mace?

"Are the rest of the grounds so bad?" I said. "They're not what they should be, I know that, but we've been working hard, and I think we've done a decent job--"

Hedley cut me off with a sharp shake of his head. "It's not the festival," he said. "It's the duke. He'll be at the event all day."

I snorted. "Very funny. If you think I'm going to

run and hide from Duke Remington, you've seriously underestimated the level of pure contempt I have for that man."

"It's a sentiment I share," he said, still quiet. He stopped speaking as we passed a group of gardeners, their arms laden with wire and greenery. Linden was in the group, and he gave me a very slight nod as they passed.

Hedley turned onto a walkway that quickly gave way to a bridge that floated at almost surface level with an artificial lake, and I stayed with him. Beautiful sea grape bushes rose up from the water, their branches heavy with fruit, and a merman who was arranging saltwater lilies waved as we crossed the lake.

On the other side, the path reached land again and abruptly descended and twisted back the way we'd come, this time as a wide ramp sloping gently underground.

The air cooled as soon as the last traces of daylight disappeared. Blue light danced on the walls of the dark corridor ahead of us, and then the path opened onto the Atlantice Tunnel.

A glass ceiling curved above our heads, revealing a vibrant underwater world on every side. The Atlanticeans had outdone themselves this year. A few humans and merpeople had arrived a week ago to establish plants in the lake's sandy bottom. Now, brilliantly colored fish darted between swaying ribbons of bull kelp and an octopus slept in the crevice between boulders. Its arms curled and drifted in the underwater currents. I wondered what filled its dreams.

Other than the sea creatures and the merman, whose tail I could see far overhead, we were alone in this bubble, and the glass would protect us from curious ears.

"I think you need to go back to the palace after the opening ceremonies," Hedley repeated, "because Duke Remington will be here, filling in for the king. And if Duke Remington is *here,* he will not be *there.*"

I let out a sharp breath. Of course. I was a fool.

"If you've been looking for an opportunity to speak with Lilian, this is the best one you'll get. I can get word to her easily enough to claim a headache and retire to the palace, and chances are good the duke's new cronies will be too busy escorting him around the festival grounds to realize they're leaving their posts at the palace unguarded."

It was a brilliant idea and the only chance I'd get for a moment alone with Lilian.

It was also impossible.

"I can't leave the festival," I said. "Not until the flower competition is over."

Hedley's eyebrows drew down a little. "I think the current situation warrants you missing a flower contest."

"Not this year," I said. "Not when I might win. You know I have a chance. You've seen my flowers."

"It's not a question of whether you've got what it takes." His lips thinned a little. "It's a matter of priorities."

I shook my head. In the distance, past Hedley's shoulder, a school of dazzling silver anchovies flitted by, followed by the sparkling flowers of silver seagrass that drifted through the water in their wake.

"It's not about me." I tasted the lie on my tongue as soon as I said it, and I shook my head quickly. "I mean, it *is* about me, I'm an idiot and a liar if I claim my ego's not in this somewhere. But it's also about Floris. Everyone already knows we're struggling. What if we lose the flower competition for the first time in the festival's history?"

Hedley tucked a thumb behind his suspenders. "That's a point," he admitted.

"Everything is riding on me winning this," I said. "I represent the palace and the royal family. If I don't win, how's that going to reflect on them? There's already talk of other kingdoms refusing to renew their contracts with some of our flower producers. Enchantia is already in talks to cancel its annual order of snow lily bulbs. You know how much money that brings in."

Hedley didn't like it, that much was clear. He pursed his lips and made a thoughtful tutting sound.

"There's too much at stake," I said. "I have to be here."

Hedley was silent for a long moment, thoughts steadily forming in his head like seedlings peeking out of the soil and unfurling their leaves. I knew this process, and I waited.

"I could try to talk to her," he finally offered. "Find out what she knows, pass it to you."

"That could help," I said. "You know as much about this as anyone."

"She won't tell me as much as she'd tell you," he said. "I might get the facts, but I won't get her real opinions. She's forever the princess, even with me."

I smiled, and something in me softened. "She knows her duty," I said. "Always, no matter what it costs her."

"Floris has much to be grateful for," Hedley said. "It would have still more if she wasn't under the thumb of that incompetent blowhard."

It was the strongest opinion I'd ever heard Hedley express, outside of his feelings about brown-backed root beetles. I bit back a grin.

"We can't do a thing about the duke," I said. "Not unless King Alder gets back before the wedding, and we somehow manage to catch him in time." I didn't have high hopes; getting the king's attention was something even Lilian hadn't been able to accomplish lately. "But if we can keep our kingdom's reputation from falling apart *and* figure out what Lilian learned about the queen, I'll consider that a good week in what has otherwise been a month of pure and unmitigated hell."

"Hold onto that youthful optimism, Deon," Hedley said dryly. "I'd hate to see you get jaded."

I laughed, but there wasn't much humor in it. Beside us, a patch of vivid green seaweed shimmied in the current, and I squinted as the light played tricks on my eyes and brushed the tip of one graceful frond with the faintest hint of gray.

10TH APRIL

Whatever cynicism Hedley had accused me of dropped away the moment I arrived at the festival grounds.

I had been to the festival every year since before I was old enough to form lasting memories. And every year, opening morning took my breath away. I'd seen the grounds a dozen times in the past week alone, but it was different this morning now that thousands of Florians and guests from around the world were clustered outside the wrought-iron festival gates. Women in bright floral dresses and men with hats piled high with precious flowers milled all around me. I caught a glimpse of a group from Enchantia, recognizable by their sleek white clothing and flawless posture. A younger woman stood with the group, but while her clothing shared the same sleek tailoring as the others, she was clad in jet black. She felt me staring and glanced over, and one side of her mouth quirked up in an amused smile.

I recognized her from the newspapers; this was Princess Kelis of Enchantia. Lilian had met her a couple of years back and taken an immediate liking to her. According to Lilian, she was "not at *all* like one of those stuffy princesses who're too scared to make a joke lest she be accused of having a sense of humor." Her eyes had the same gold ring around the iris as mine. It was unusual, to be sure, and that was probably why I felt drawn to her. But I didn't have time for princesses, at least, not another princess.

I slipped forward through the crowd and took my place on the raised dais set to one side of the gates. Lilian was already sitting there, along with Duke Remington and several members of the Horticulture Council.

I didn't dare look at Lilian for more than a second. The duke's gaze fixed on me immediately, and I knew that if I so much as tried to wish her a good day, we'd both pay for it.

"Glad you could make it, Mr. Gilding," the duke said, in a voice that was even cooler than the morning breeze that ruffled our hair.

I'd been on the grounds since before the crack of dawn, making final arrangements, but I didn't bother trying to explain that to him. I just gave him a deferential nod and turned to gaze resolutely out at the crowd.

The large bell set into the top of the iron gates rang out, marking eight o'clock. The bell was draped in rose garlands, and I silently prayed that no one would notice half the blooms were silk.

The crowd's excited chattering settled to silence.

Lilian rose from her seat and stepped toward the

microphone that amplified her voice with a clever combination of magic and technology from The Forge.

"Welcome, citizens of Floris and distinguished guests. We are honored to welcome you to the annual Spring Flower Festival." She looked out over the crowd, her gaze catching here and there as she made contact with some lucky individual. Her pink dress softened her, but her back was straight, and she held her chin high.

Hedley was wrong; she wasn't every bit a princess. She was a queen or, at least, had it in her to become one. My heart fluttered, feeling for all the world like just another flounce on her rosy dress trembling in the breeze.

Stars, I couldn't lose this woman.

The backs of my eyes prickled, and I closed my eyes firmly and shoved down the sudden grief that threatened to engulf me.

It was a beautiful morning. The festival was here. Lilian was radiant. I had no right to fall apart now.

"As many of you know, Floris has faced challenges in the past month," Lilian continued her voice strong and clear. "I am delighted to be able to show you today that we have met this challenge head-on. I am also inspired by the displays brought to us from around the world. The festival is a unique opportunity for the kingdoms to come together in a celebration of life and beauty, and I think you'll be dazzled today by the astonishing creativity and hard work reflected in these gardens. Although I should caution you to please, keep your hands to yourself when you pass through The Forge's birdcage garden. The signs warning you to keep your fingers away from the Cheshire flytraps are no joke."

A laugh rippled through the assembled crowd.

"Thank you all for being here. Your support means more to Floris and to me personally than you can possibly know." She placed a hand on her heart, and her face lit with a smile to rival the rising sun. "I now pronounce the Spring Flower Festival open!"

The bell pealed again, and a roar rose from the crowd. The Horticulture Council members placed on either side of the gate pushed the intricate doors open, and the thousands of visitors rushed forward like a meadow rippling in a sudden gust of wind.

I watched them push forward. An atmosphere of celebration filled the air, and I breathed it in. I hadn't felt joy like this in a while, and I wasn't sure when I'd get to experience it again.

Lilian caught my gaze and read my mind. She smiled, blue eyes sparkling.

And then the duke took her arm firmly in his and shielded her from my view.

I waited until the last few people trickled in through the gates **and** tried to fall in with them. But Duke Remington's voice stopped me.

"It's a shame the festival isn't what it should be, Mr. Gilding," he said.

Lilian hushed him, but he ignored her. The voices in my head shouted at me to ignore him, but I turned around anyway and gave him a polite nod.

"I agree." I wouldn't let him bait me. Not today. "Still, I hope my staff have done their best to do right by Floris."

"I'm sure they have," Lilian said. "I toured the grounds early this morning, and I think the displays are beautiful."

"If only most of them weren't from other kingdoms," the duke said.

Lilian raised one eyebrow, her face otherwise the picture of neutrality. "On the contrary, I think it's lovely that the festival represents such cooperation between nations. That is why the festival was started, after all, to give us a chance to mingle and share the things that make our lands beautiful."

"Certainly." Duke Remington acknowledged her with a polite nod.

To the side of him, Minister Saffron from the Horticulture Council eavesdropped with her eyes slightly narrowed.

The duke patted Lilian's hand and continued, in the kind of polite voice I could only assume someone like Mace aspired to. "One just wishes Florian's farmers had more to contribute, as a matter of national pride. As you know, my love, I can be patriotic to a fault when it comes to our great kingdom."

"Of course," I said. "Your opinions stem from *patriotism.*"

Lilian shot me a warning look, and I bit my tongue. I gave them both a bow and made as if to excuse myself, but the duke cut me off.

"My concerns should be nothing to yours, Mr. Gilding," he said with a tense smile. "After all, this entire festival is a reflection of your abilities. I saw that you still intend to enter a flower in the competition. Let's hope it's enough to redeem you. After all, one never knows when you'll need to rely on your reputation when it comes to finding work."

He gloated down at me, his hand still firmly atop Lilian's. Her expression remained pleasant, even neutral, but she couldn't disguise the tension in her shoulders.

I bowed again. "Enjoy the festival, Your Grace," I

said. "Your Highness."

"Her Highness will not be staying. She is to head back to the Palace while the judging takes place."

I nodded my head to both of them, but my stomach roiled. He was keeping her from the judging. The judging was the main part of the festival.

"Then, enjoy the festival yourself."

He opened his mouth to make some unpleasant retort, but I was halfway through the gate before he could get a word out.

~

Now that the festival was here and running smoothly, I almost didn't know what to do with myself. Every tent and display hosted by Floris was already staffed and scheduled, and the displays being managed by other kingdoms didn't need anything from me.

So I wandered. I felt as light as a dandelion seed on the wind, now that I had the freedom to drift around without the strain of the festival weighing me down. Even the duke couldn't keep me down for long, and by the time I reached the potted forest hosted by the kingdom of Elder, the sense of wonder and excitement filling the festival grounds had recaptured me.

The displays felt different, now that these walkways were filled with people experiencing their beauty for the first time. A little girl in front of me babbled to her even littler brother about how she could probably climb these trees all the way to the top because she was so strong, and an elderly man leaned on his cane to one side of the walkway and stared dreamily up at the puffy white flowers adorning the branches of a wolfhair pine. The trees captured both the imagination and a sense of beauty, and it was a deep privilege to be allowed to witness them affecting the people all around me.

A man in a shabby but well-brushed three-piece suit bumped into me. He stopped in his tracks and put a gentle hand on my arm.

"My apologies, my good man," he said. He bowed, and his top had slid ever so slightly down his forehead. He settled it back into place.

The hat's shape put me in mind of fancy cameras and electric lights. I held out a hand. "That's quite all right. Welcome to Floris. You're from The Forge, right?"

"I certainly am." His polite concern warmed into a smile. "Dr. Wit Lapin. Your servant, sir."

His manners were so impeccable that I almost laughed; he was a sharp contrast against the duke's insincerity.

"Mr. Deon Gilding," I said. "Literally, a servant. I'm the Head Gardener at the palace of Floris. Thank you for coming all this way for the festival. I'm always honored by the number of people who show up for this event."

Dr. Lapin touched his lapel, in what seemed like a tidy reflex. "In that case, I must admit that I didn't come solely for the festival. I've been here for several weeks researching your medicinal plants. I'm fortunate that my timing coincided with this wonderful event."

I cringed inwardly. "That's generous of you to say," I said. "If you've been here for a few weeks, you've had a front-row seat to all our problems."

"We all have our challenges," he said kindly. "It's been a pleasure to see so many people rise to this one with grace. Yourself included, Mr. Gilding. These displays are astonishing, given the circumstances. I recognize your name from the event program. You still intend to enter this afternoon's new breed flower competition, isn't that right?"

A lump rose to my throat. Whether I won or lost today, his kindness gave me hope that the palace wouldn't have reason to be shamed by my entry.

"I hope you'll make it to the contest," I said. "I expect to face stiff competition from The Forge. Your kingdom has developed some incredible plants in the past few years."

We fell into an easy conversation about The Forge's unique flowers and the medicinal plants he'd come to Floris to research. By the time we reached the end of the potted forest, I felt as if I'd made a new friend.

"Best of luck today, Mr. Gilding," he said when we parted.

"Thanks." I shook his hand, halfway feeling as if I ought to give this polite man a hug instead. "I'm glad to have met you."

The confidence he'd given me only lasted another hour or two. Then it was time to collect my flowers and go to the competition tent.

I clung to the covered bell jar that held my entry. The atmosphere that pervaded the grounds seemed to shift from excitement to anxiety as I walked, although I knew better than to think my sudden nerves belonged to anyone but me.

By the time I arrived at the contestants' seating area beneath the enormous tent, I was practically vibrating. It felt distinctly like the time Reed had dared me to consume several pots of coffee, back in our teens. I'd done it, on account of being a teenage boy with more bravado than sense. Lilian hadn't let me live that choice down for months.

The white canvas tent diffused the afternoon sun, and tendrils of jasmine and wisteria that climbed up the tent poles filled the air with sweet perfume. People milled around behind me and slowly took their seats on the folding wooden chairs. Next to me, contestants on numbered seats shifted and exchanged nervous smiles. A beautiful woman whose clothes suggested she was from Badalah clutched her covered bell jar and tapped her toes. I offered her a smile, and she gave me one back, although neither of us could hold onto the expression for more than a few seconds. On my other side, a famous breeder from The Vale kept letting out long, steady breaths as if to calm himself. I'd met him last year, in passing, but couldn't remember his name. He seemed to recognize me, but we didn't do more than exchange pleasantries before we got back to our separate worrying.

Finally, when I was about ready to crawl out of my skin, Minister Balsam from the Horticulture Council stood.

Everyone fell quiet. The delicate sounds of skirts shifting and chairs squeaking hovered in the air, along with the occasional whisper.

From his seat behind the judges' table, the duke met my gaze. He smiled. I clutched my bell jar.

Minister Balsam made the opening remarks. They didn't mean much to me, just words that were hard to hear over the pounding of my heart. Then the first contestant was called up.

"Jinan Barakat of Badalah, gardener to the noble family of Asal." The slender young man bowed as he introduced himself **and** approached the table. He removed the colorful embroidered fabric that had covered his jar, and I hissed in a sharp breath.

It was stunning, a succulent with a fat, vivid green body that looked like a pincushion and a single enormous flower rising from the center. The central flower was the color of polished white granite, iridescent and cool.

"This is the Star of the Sands," Jinan said. "The flower blooms white during the day, and the internal central petals, which you can see are now curled, bloom again at night, creating a layered pattern." He pointed at the center of the flower, where I assumed the second round of petals was visible. "I encourage you to savor the fragrance; its lightness is being explored by our physicians for its possible euphoria-inducing properties."

I hoped my new friend, Dr. Lapin, was somewhere behind me so he could hear this.

Jinan passed the bell jar to the first of the judges, a delegate from Skyla. She examined it, made notes on the paper in front of her, and passed it down. The judges conferred for a moment when they'd all had the chance to examine the bloom, and then Minister Blackwood handed it back to Jinan.

The next three people went, displaying a vivid yellow flower that bloomed, budded, and bloomed again all within a minute; an enormous purple iris that was nearly as tall as me and smelled of sugar; and a dahlia with a delicate red-and-white honeycomb pattern all across its sturdy petals.

Then it was my turn. I took a deep breath and stood. My legs wobbled beneath me.

"Mr. Deon Gilding, Head Gardener at the palace of Floris." I bowed, and a ripple of interest passed through the crowd behind me.

Minister Blackwood gave me an encouraging smile and gestured me forward.

With trembling hands, I lifted the silk covering my jar and shoved it in my back pocket. Minister Balsam's eyebrows **rose** in interest, and the visiting judge from Enchantia leaned forward to get a better look.

I had already named my flower, but with the duke glaring down at me, I thought it best to use one of the other names I'd considered, at least for now.

I cleared my throat. "The Gilded Lily," I announced and held up the jar.

Inside, the petals of my creation winked and glinted as brightly as Lilian's hair under the midday sun. The silver leaves and stem that supported it held nothing of the gray that had plagued our kingdom these past few weeks; instead, they shone with hints of moonlight**,** and stardust**,** and the twinkling scales of the fish in the Atlantice dome. The bloom itself shone. An impossible light emanated from the pistils at its center and cast translucent patterns of light onto the white canvas over our heads.

Minister Acacia put a hand to her mouth. The judge from Draconis narrowed his eyes in interest. A muscle in Duke Remington's jaw twitched.

"This flower brings light in the darkness," I said. "The golden luminescence at the center of the bloom grows throughout the day and becomes brightest at night when its glow is enough to serve as a gentle lantern. The flowers close up at dawn and open again during the course of the morning." I pulled a series of small glass vials all chained together from my pocket. "When the flower blooms again, it holds a few tiny drops of dew. I think the dew tastes a bit like strawberries. I've collected some over the past week so that you can all have a taste and form your own opinion."

Minister Blackwood smiled, and her piercing black eyes took on a twinkle. She tucked a strand of bright red hair behind her ear and gestured at me to hand the plant to the judges.

I gave it to the judge from Skyla, along with the chain of vials. The judges passed my lily between themselves and carefully tasted the dew.

Minister Blackwood handed the flower back to me when they were through. She opened her mouth, clearly wanting to say something, then closed it again and shook her head just barely.

I took my flower, covered the jar again, and returned to my seat.

The last few flowers passed in a blur. Relief at having gotten through my presentation flooded my body and turned my perception of the world a little fuzzy. But then, at last, it was time for the winners to be announced.

"The Star of the Sands," Minister Acacia announced.

As one, the judges raised the cards they'd used to score Jinan's flower. An eight, a seven, two more eights, a nine, and another seven.

Jinan stood and bowed in appreciation. The representative from Skyla passed their detailed score sheets to an assistant off to one side, who handed them to Jinan.

The next few flowers received similar scores. Then it was my turn.

My heart thumped hard enough to shake my rib cage. My stomach churned, and my skin prickled with a thousand sudden goosebumps.

This was my flower, the one I had tenderly cared for and shaped over the course of years. It was my last great offering to Lilian, a flower that shone with her beauty, tasted of her favorite fruits, and paid homage to her name.

They weren't just judging my flower, or my gardening

abilities, or my work as the head gardener of the palace of Floris.

They were judging my love, and I prayed with a silent *please, please, please* that I wouldn't be found wanting.

The judge from Skyla raised her card.

Ten.

Minister Oleander: Ten.

Minister Acacia: Another ten.

I swallowed, and tears rose and prickled behind my eyes.

And then Duke Remington raised his hand. He fixed me with a glare that could have turned the earth barren.

One.

I smiled. It was the best score I could have hoped for from him, and in a strange way, I was honored to receive it.

The delegate from Draconis raised his card to reveal another ten, and then, after a teasing pause, Minister Blackwood revealed the final perfect score.

Five tens and a one. With Duke Remington at the judge's table, I couldn't have asked for a better result.

I swallowed, fighting to keep the tears from flooding my eyes. I stood and gave them a deep, grateful bow.

My lily beat the last few scores by a healthy margin. I watched it happen, the celebration in my head drowning out the sights and sounds around me, and I watched myself go up to the judge's table afterward and thank them over and over again.

And then, before I could be mobbed by well-wishers or reporters or other gardeners asking for my secrets, I shoved the lily into Hedley's waiting hands. He met my gaze, and I didn't have to speak. He already knew.

I had to go.

~

Hedley had been right. The palace was virtually unguarded today; they were all back at the festival grounds, following the duke around or enjoying the festival under the guise of keeping the peace.

It was easy enough to sneak in through one of the servants' doors, dart through the kitchen, and make my way up a back staircase. By the time I arrived at Lilian's chambers, she was already in our old schoolroom waiting for me.

I closed the door behind me and turned the lock. She stood near the window, her golden hair framed by the sunlight, and stared at me.

"Deon, that was the prettiest thing I have *ever* seen."

Warmth rushed through me. "You were there?"

"You dolt, of course, I was there! Garritt didn't want me to be, of course, but I ducked in the back after the judging had already started. He couldn't do anything about it without making a scene."

"And here I thought the duke loved making scenes."

"Not in public," she said. "It's the one thing I've got going for me." She shook her head, like someone shaking away a fly.

"How did you know I was going to be here?"

"Hedley told me, of course." A smile lit her features. "Deon, honestly, that was the most beautiful flower I've ever seen in my life. How did you do it? How did you keep it from getting ruined by the blight? Any why on earth haven't I seen it before?"

She sank onto a cushioned stool in front of a screen of needlework and stared up at me, eyes wide and ready for explanations. I settled onto the floor across from her and looked up to her perfect face.

"It was for you, you know."

"Of course, I know," she said. "You made that for me, and it's the best gift--I was going to say it's the best gift I've ever been given, but it's not. It's the best gift I've ever even heard of."

I grinned. "It's just a flower."

"Yes, and we Florians don't care at all about those."

I drew up my knees and wrapped my arms around them. "I've been working on it for years. You've almost seen it a couple of times, but I al**ways** managed to distract you at the last moment. And I don't know how I kept it from the blight, except that my entire private garden looks like that."

Her blue eyes widened. "It's all lilies?"

I laughed. "It's all alive, I mean. It's some kind of magic that's either in the garden or in me. We don't know. Hedley and I are trying to figure it out."

She twirled a lock of her hair around one of her fingers. "I wish you would. We need a miracle, and soon."

"I know." I sighed. The euphoria of winning the contest was still with me, but it was tempered by the reality that my beautiful flowers might soon be the only ones left. "I met a doctor today who reminded me how important our plants are. Not just to us, but the world. He's from The Forge, but he came here to study our medicinal plants. What if we lose them? There are flowers and herbs that only grow here, and if they all die out, what does that mean for the rest of the world? We can import grain, and I suppose we could live without beauty if we had to."

Lilian made a face, and I nodded my agreement.

"But what about medicine? What about the magical

plants the rest of the world relies on Floris for?"

"That poor doctor," Lilian said. "To come to research our herbs and then to find all this."

"He was gracious about it," I said. "I just feel bad for him and everyone like him."

"Glad *you* met someone with manners today." Lilian's face took on a disgruntled expression, and I bit back a laugh, even though I hadn't heard the story of what had annoyed her yet. "I met a prince today who was the most obnoxious, conceited person I have ever encountered. He was *charming,* I can't deny that much, but I should inform you that you and Garritt both have competition for my affections now that he's in town and ready to, and I quote, 'teach every woman in Floris exactly what she's been missing.'"

I snorted. "Sounds like a winner."

"He was infuriatingly handsome, and it was everything I could do not to throw my lemonade in his face. Prince Fallon of Aboria," she added, in a simpering voice. "Thinks his beauty is a gift from the gods, and he personally informed me that I ought to marry him instead of Garritt because he has looks, money, *and* phenomenal taste in fine wines, while Garritt only has money."

"Just imagine what he'd say if you told him you preferred the gardener."

Lilian's annoyed expression softened. "I really do."

I tried to keep my voice light. "You just don't want to lose my superior plant-breeding skills to some fancy capitol greenhouse."

She didn't take the bait. She furrowed her brow a little. "I don't want to lose you at all, Deon. I already miss you too much as it is, and you've only been banished as far as the grounds."

My heart twisted. If she missed me now, I could only imagine how she was going to feel when her betrothed fired me in a week.

"Are you really marrying him so soon?" I said.

She blew out a long, tired breath. "I don't want to marry him at all. But I can't get out of it now. Prince Fallon was right, the duke *does* have money. Thornton is our richest province. And we're going to need that money if we have to start importing all our food. I have to do what's best for my people."

But what about what was best for her? Could she really be expected to sacrifice so much, just because she had been born into such responsibility?

I bit the questions back. I already knew the answers.

"I admire you, Lils," I said. "Always will. Keep that flower I created around to remind you, will you?"

"Of course I will, I want a whole garden full of them. It would be visible for miles at night." The corner of her mouth quirked. "But *Gilded Lily?* Really?"

I leaned back on my palms. "It was supposed to be called the Lilian," I said. "Then I took one look at Duke Remington's face and figured I should name it something else."

She grimaced. "Sticks and stones, he's a menace." She leaned forward. "And he's likely to come looking for me any minute now. I'd prefer to spend the whole day just talking with you, but we can't waste time."

I scrambled forward onto my knees and scraped my way across the carpet until I was close enough to her that we could speak in lowered voices.

I was close enough to reach out and brush my hand along the exposed skin peeking between her golden slippers and her flounced hem, too, but I thought better of that. If I touched her now, I wasn't sure I'd ever be able to stop.

"Tell me what you learned," I said. "Tell me everything."

She leaned in toward me. "I saw Mama," she said. "I managed to slip in when her guards were changing shifts. She's not sick at all, not really. Only it's somehow worse than that." She inhaled sharply, then, as if she'd had to dare herself to speak, said, "Her hair is gray."

I bit the inside of my cheek and nodded. "Yeah, I know. That's why I wanted you to see her."

She tilted her head. "How did you know?"

"You don't want the answer to that, I promise," I said. "I'll tell you someday. How far up has the blight gotten?"

A line appeared between her eyes. "It's all gray."

"All of it?" I said. "Up to her scalp?"

"Even her eyebrows," Lilian said.

I let out a sigh of relief. Then the poison reaching her skin hadn't killed her.

Not yet, anyway. It was too soon to rule anything out.

"She said it happened quickly."

"You spoke with her, then."

She nodded. "We had a long talk. She says she should have told me everything earlier, but Papa's been too worried about her. He convinced her it was better to stay out of sight while he fixed things. Except he's not fixing things. Mama doesn't think he can."

"Does she know what's causing it?"

"It's a witch." She shook her head at her hands in her lap, clearly overwhelmed. "Mama's past is so much more complicated than I thought."

"She's adopted," I said. "Like me."

Lilian glanced up. "You knew?"

"Only recently," I said. "Hedley told me. She was raised by a witch in the forest."

"Abused by a witch in the forest, more like." Lilian's voice hardened. "The creature insisted she was Mama's mother, but she was controlling and neglectful, nothing like a mother ought to be. Mama said she'd been about ready to jump out of the tower before Papa showed up, and he saved her."

"Hedley doesn't think that witch is powerful enough to do this." I nodded toward the window, **in** a small gesture to indicate the vastness of a kingdom. "He said she's been hiding in the forest ever since your parents escaped her."

"Mama disagrees," Lilian said. "She thinks Gothel--that's the witch's name--has enough power and more than enough rage to accomplish something like this. Hedley's right about one thing, though: Gothel hasn't been seen in eighteen years now. Apparently, Papa's sent military parties into the woods more than once to try to find her or smoke her out, but she's always evaded them. She's still in there, though, and the proof is the good soldiers Papa lost."

"So what do we do?"

Lilian looked at me, her wide eyes open and hopeless. She shrugged and spread her hands, and then her shoulders dropped as if someone had tossed a great cape over them.

The weight of all this hung on her like a physical thing. I had thought I'd been worried about the kingdom, what with the festival and my responsibility for the plants at the palace.

But Lilian--she was responsible for a *nation.* People depended on her--human beings and fairies and immigrant races like the Munchkins from Oz. They all relied on the royal family to keep them safe, but the king and queen seemed every bit as lost as me. And if the monarchs couldn't figure out how to stop this curse, with all their vast authority and resources, what hope did a princess have?

I didn't have enough magic to fight the blight, nor the knowledge to hunt an evil witch. All I could do for Lilian was to stand beside her through these dark times.

And if Duke Remington had his way, I wouldn't even be able to do that.

I held out a hand. Lilian took it and laced her fingers between mine. I squeezed, and she sighed, and we sat there together in our old schoolroom and tried, pointlessly, to think.

11TH APRIL

The next morning, before I could make my way to the festival, Hedley woke me by barging into my shed with an enormous gold trophy shaped like a bouquet of tulips under his arm. Reed skittered in behind him and held up my glowing lily in its glass jar. The petals were tightly closed, sheltering the gathering strawberry dew.

I blinked groggily, glad I'd taken to sleeping in warm clothes that covered more than the nightshirt I'd favored back when I'd lived indoors. "What are you doing?"

Hedley opened his mouth to answer, but Reed burst forth instead.

"You won!"

I sat up and stared at them. Memories from yesterday flitted through my head like petals drifting from a cherry tree, flashes of color as I remembered the displays and the princess from Enchantia and the swaying seaweed in the Atlantice dome and Minister Blackwood's smile as she'd examined my lily.

"I know?" I said slowly. I rubbed the sleep from my eyes and squinted up at them. The pre-dawn sky outside the open door glistened soft periwinkle, and a breeze floated in and ruffled my tousled hair. "I was there?"

"No." Reed dropped heavily onto my unicorn manure bed. He winced at the stiffness of it and glanced curiously down at my blankets, then, already over it, turned back to me with excitement dancing in his eyes. "I mean, *you won.* You won the whole blooming thing. You left before all the other competitions yesterday. I don't blame you, given the way the duke was looking at you," he added. "I get the feeling he doesn't like you much, but it's not *your* fault a blight is destroying his kingdom."

Hedley cleared his throat, and Reed leaned in toward me, the golden lily jar still clasped between his hands.

"I mean, you *won,*" he said. "Grand prize. Best of Show. The whole thing. The scores were added up last night, and the twelve representatives from all the kingdoms voted, and they *all* voted for you."

I rubbed my eyes again, and my mind clutched at the holes in Reed's story.

"I can't have won," I said. "The duke was on the grand prize judging committee. He wouldn't have let it happen."

Reed shook his head, grinning. "That's the other thing. King Alder came back. He showed up at the last minute, and I guess Minister Yarrow just acted like; of course, the duke would offer to yield his seat to the king, so what could the duke do? He offered it up, King

Alder accepted, and they all voted *unanimously* that your lily was the best thing at the whole festival. Linden thinks it was a pity vote since we're having such a hard time with the blight, but I think Linden's just full of sour grapes. The one last tulip he saved from his beds wasn't enough to win him the Bulb Flowers Division contest, and he's in a bad mood about it."

"The point is," Hedley said, his calm voice a slow cadence against Reed's excited yammering. "You won Best in Show, and the king has returned. We thought you'd like to know."

I met his gaze, and it was pregnant with meaning. Suddenly, I was wide awake.

"I won," I said. "The king is back. Stars, I need to get some clothes on."

"We'll leave you to it," Hedley said.

Reed was too busy grinning like a lunatic at me to move, but finally, Hedley cleared his throat. Reed jumped, laughed, and shoved the lily at me before jumping to his feet.

"You did it, Deon," he said. He shifted from foot to foot, too worked up to stay still. "We're facing the worst plague in history, and you *still* showed every kingdom in the world who's in charge."

"No need to insult the rest of the world over it." But I couldn't help grinning. My lily had bought us more time and told the rest of the world that it wasn't time to write us off just yet. Hope rose up in me like dandelion heads turning to the sun.

Reed beamed, and finally, Hedley turned to him. "Why don't you go tell the kitchen staff the good news?" he said.

He didn't need to tell him twice. Reed was gone in a flash, but not before showering me with another beatific grin.

Hedley watched him go, smiling softly and shaking his head.

"Young people," he said.

He closed the door behind Reed. The soft morning light faded to near-darkness, and I heard rather than saw Hedley approach. He settled onto the bed as my eyes adjusted. The golden trophy shone a little in the dim illumination from my high window, the lines of the tulips and their golden vase etched with my name and the name of my flower just visible in the gloom.

"Did you have any success yesterday?" Hedley asked in a low voice.

I nodded, then realized he probably couldn't see me well enough **to know it**.

"I spoke with her."

Hedley set the trophy on the small shelf next to my makeshift bed, and I allowed myself just a moment to stare at its elegant form.

Then I turned back to him and quickly related everything Lilian had told me. Hedley listened, taking in each word. When I was done, he sat for a moment, allowing the information to churn and process at its own pace.

When he finally spoke, his question surprised me.

"They're still going ahead with the wedding, then?"

I frowned. Of everything I'd told him, I hadn't expected that to be the most interesting bit of information.

"She doesn't see a way around it," I said. "That might change now that King Alder is home, assuming she gets a chance to see him, but I don't think she'll push too hard. The province of Thornton has money. Floris needs money right now."

"That's a shame."

He didn't need to tell me. The euphoria of learning I'd won faded quickly, like a flower cut and left on the grass, and Hedley noticed it going.

He clapped a hand on my knee.

"There's still time for a miracle or two," he said brightly. "In the meantime, I suggest you put on some clothes and take that trophy and your lily for a stroll. There are some people gathering at the front of the palace who might want to see them."

By the time I had dressed in the nicest clothes I owned--a shirt with only a single discreet grass stain on the sleeve and trousers with relatively un-worn knees--Hedley had returned to my shed with a mirror in hand. I brushed my hair as the sun crept over the horizon, and he fixed the back for me when a few dark strands refused to lie down.

When he pronounced me presentable, I picked up the heavy tulip trophy and my enclosed lily, and we walked to the front of the palace. I had expected a few supporters and perhaps a member of the Horticulture Council.

Instead, I heard the crowd before I saw them.

The driveway in front of the palace was crowded with visitors. It was like the time journalists had invaded the grounds to ask about the blight, except this time, almost all my gardening staff was on hand to usher them away from the flowerbeds.

Not that it mattered. The palace grounds were utterly barren by this point. Every surviving flower had been whisked away to the festival or quarantined in a greenhouse under an enchanted glass jar.

Still, seeing them all work together to corral the crowd warmed my heart. It meant they were on the same page as me about something, for probably the first time since I'd taken over this job.

"Mr. Gilding!" someone exclaimed, and in an instant, hundreds of eyes and half as many cameras were trained on me. My heart skipped a beat; I'd never had so much attention in my life.

I glanced up at Hedley, and he smiled and gave me an encouraging nod.

"Go tell them all about your lily," he said. "You've earned this." He dropped his voice to a murmur. "But maybe don't mention the magic. Not yet."

I nodded and stepped forward toward the crowd.

"How long have you been working on the Gilded Lily?" one journalist demanded. A child rushed forward with a newspaper clipping and enchanted quill in her hand, begging me to sign it. A group of ladies holding a sign reading *TULIS TARTS: WOMEN'S FLOWER CLUB* jumped up and down and waved at me, while a few other reporters interrupted one another with questions to the point that I couldn't form their scrambled words into sentences.

My head spun a little, and I took a deep breath and forced myself further into the crowd. People grabbed at me and reached in to brush their fingers against my trophy and the lily case, but I pressed forward to the palace steps where I might have half a chance of seeing them all and hearing what they had to say.

One of the guards--a man I recognized, who had served the palace long before Duke Remington had arrived--jumped in to shield me as I made my way to the stairs. Once I was safely out of the reach of the crowd, he clapped me on the arm and stepped back.

"How did you protect your lily from the blight?" someone called out.

I cleared my throat. "We've been working with Florian

magicians to…"

But my words were drowned out by the ocean of questions and exclamations. Everyone, it seemed, had something to say, and I couldn't shout over them all.

"What did the king and queen think about your entry?"

"Will you be selling the lilies anytime soon?"

"How similar is your variety to the sunglow lily created by Lark Aspenwood a few years ago?"

I blinked out at the crowd. There was a reason press conferences were usually held with microphones. I needed a moderator, and something to amplify my voice, or at least a way to shout louder than the rest of them. I glanced out at Hedley, who was held back by the sheer volume of the crowd, and he shrugged.

I was on my own, then.

The guard who'd ushered me through the audience stepped forward and leaned in so I could hear him.

"Perhaps this would be better conducted in the throne room?"

"I'm not allowed in there."

"I daresay this might be an excellent opportunity to push the duke on that particular boundary, Mr. Gilding, sir."

I glanced sharply at him. His expression hadn't changed, but a muscle in his jaw twitched.

I wasn't the only one unhappy with the way things were being run, then.

"Let's give it a try." I gave him a quick nod of thanks, and he returned it. He gestured at the guards standing on either side of the front doors to open them. One moved immediately, but the other shook his head at first. He and the guard who'd been speaking with me exchanged glances, and some kind of conversation or argument seemed to take place between them in the space of a moment.

Then, as if something had been decided, the guards opened the front doors.

“Members with press permits, please proceed in an orderly manner to the throne room,” the guard barked in a loud voice I envied in this moment. “Anyone not following standard procedure will be escorted from the premises. Those of you without press permits may remain here, and Mr. Gilding will return in the course of half an hour to visit with you.”

He glanced at me, and I nodded my agreement. Some in the crowd groaned or sighed, and the journalists and photographers pressed forward, but with a touch more organization than they’d shown a moment before.

I turned to go inside the palace, but before I could take more than a few steps, the duke was standing in front of me with his hands clasped behind his back.

“Mr. Gilding is not permitted inside the palace,” he said.

The guards again looked among themselves. The one who’d been helping me seemed to hold his breath for a moment, then he straightened his shoulders.

“The throne room is traditionally the space used for palace statements to the press, Your Grace,” he said, with utmost politeness in his tone and bearing. “As a security matter, I advise we stick to established protocol.”

“Mr. Gilding is not a member of the royal family, and therefore, not qualified to give statements on behalf of the palace.”

The duke narrowed his eyes at me. It was everything I could do to not swing my heavy trophy right at his head, but I’d already gotten in trouble for whaling on him once. Instead, I took a hint from my guard and stayed calm.

Someone came up behind the duke, and the air around us shifted subtly.

"I think this might be a fine time for an exception," a familiar voice said.

I bowed deeply before I caught a glimpse of his face. "Your Majesty," I said. "Allow me to welcome you home from your travels."

"Thank you, Deon." The king's face was lined; he looked years older than last time I'd seen him. But he also wore a warm smile, and he held out a hand to me. I shook it, and he clasped both his hands over mine. "You've honored us all," he said quietly. "Thank you."

"My privilege, sir."

"Please show Mr. Gilding to the throne room," King Alder said loudly. "Ensure a broadcasting system is set up. My secretary will be there shortly to facilitate questions."

"Thank you, Your Majesty." I took a small step toward him. "Sir, if I may, I'd like to speak with you--"

"I'll see you soon," he said quietly, his lips barely moving. "I'll find you. After."

He offered the assembled crowd a broad smile and turned to leave. I watched him go, studying the lines of his shoulders and back for a hint of what he'd found--or not found--in Urbis.

~

The press conference passed in a blur. I answered questions as well as I could with my lily and trophy sitting on either side of me atop the king's polished wooden lectern and the duke glaring at me from the back of the room: Yes, the enchanted glass domes would be available to gardeners outside the palace as soon as we could manage. No, my plant wasn't a stable hybrid, but I planned to get there eventually. Yes, the bulbs would eventually be for sale, but only after I'd ensured they would grow reliably. No, the king and queen hadn't helped with the breeding process, although I gave all due credit to their support and encouragement over the years.

I spent another hour talking to people outside, signing autographs, and posing for photographs with the handful of nobles who had brought their own cameras. I wondered if this was what things were always like for Lilian when she stepped outside the palace and experienced a flush of gratitude for the guards who often accompanied her into the city.

And then, finally, when my hand hurt from signing my name over and over, and my face ached from all the smiles, I turned around to find the king waiting for me atop the palace steps. Quickly, I excused myself from the remaining stragglers, who took one look at the king and, awestruck at his nearness, let me go.

"Walk with me," the king said.

I checked the corridor behind him, but the duke was nowhere to be seen. We fell into an easy step, passing through the entrance hall. I kept pace with the king and turned when he turned, and eventually, we found ourselves in a broad hallway full of landscapes and empty meeting rooms. This wing of the castle was rarely visited by palace residents unless the palace was holding a convention of some sort.

"I'm glad to see you doing so well," King Alder finally said. "It seems you've been blessed by some god."

I almost snorted. I hadn't felt *blessed* over these

past few weeks.

Then again, he was right. The whole kingdom was suffering, but I had, at least, had a moment of brightness to lift my spirits. I suspected many in the nation hadn't even experienced that. I hoped the news of my lily would spread if only to give the rest of the kingdom hope that we could still grow beautiful things.

"I'm proud of you, Deon," the king said.

My face grew hot. The king wasn't a father to me, not exactly, and he hadn't raised me in the same way Hedley had. But he had always been kind, and his opinion of me was one of the most important in the world.

"Thank you," I said. "I wanted to represent Floris well."

"You did," he said. "Better than well. The Horticulture Council tells me they've never seen such a promising entry from someone your age, and given the circumstances, that lily of yours is just what we need right now."

"Thank you, sir," I said again.

The king kept walking slowly down the corridor, past paintings of rolling hills and colorful meadows. They showed Floris as it should have been. My heart hurt, looking at them.

"I'm sorry I haven't been around much," the king said.

I glanced up, surprised. He realized he'd been absent, then.

"The queen is still unwell." He hesitated, looking over at me as if my face was a puzzle he wanted to solve. "I understand Lilian broke in to see her. I suppose she told you? She seems to tell you everything."

There was no point denying it. "She did," I said. "It seems the blight affects more than just flowers."

"To my grief, yes." His lips pressed into a thin line, and he blinked at the painting before us with more force than usual. "Rapunzel's spirits remain high, but--well, you've seen what the blight's done to the rest of the kingdom."

"Perhaps it will only affect her hair," I said.

The king smiled, but it was a sad smile that didn't reach his eyes. He was trying, for my sake and his wife's, but I saw how heavily the queen's condition weighed on him.

"I feel I've been neglecting my duties," he said.

"I understand, sir. We all do. We all love the queen."

"And yet, I'm not just a husband," he said. "I'm also a king. And as a king, I appear to be failing on many fronts. I missed most of the festival. I've barely seen my daughter this month. And I haven't the faintest clue how I'm going to support all the people who are going to turn to the palace for help." He touched his fingertips to his lips and looked over at me. "I'm sorry, Deon, I shouldn't burden you with this."

"With respect, sir, it's a burden we already share." I nodded at the painting before us, which glowed with a wheat field rippling in a sunset breeze. "Mr. Hedley and I have been talking about how we might use enchanted glass greenhouses to grow food. And I've already sent a letter to the Horticulture Council advising them to discuss starting a seed bank with other kingdoms. If the blight is going to poison every plant in our kingdom, we should do what we can to avoid letting them go to extinction."

The king watched me carefully, his eyes trained on my face. He was listening--listening closely.

It was my chance to bring up the other issue, the one that really mattered.

I opened my mouth, searching my mind for the words to explain what had been happening with the duke and how Lilian really felt about him, in spite of all her gracious behavior.

"Sir?"

I jumped. A servant had appeared at the end of the hall. The king straightened his shoulders, the focus in his eyes gone.

"Hill?"

"The queen has asked to see you," the servant said. "If you're available."

The king glanced at me. He didn't need my permission, but he had it anyway.

"Queen comes first," I said with a smile. "Give her my best. I'd like to talk with you later if you're able?"

"I'll try." He shook my hand. "Thank you, Deon. It's good to know we have you on our side."

Light flute and harp music floated up from the corner, mingling with the clink of silverware against golden plates and the happy chatter of a hundred voices. It seemed the entire court had shown up to celebrate our festival win. The tables were laden with pastries and meats, as well as the jewel-like fruit salads that would become a precious rarity if the blight continued its march across the land.

Tonight, everyone was pretending the blight didn't exist, and I was glad to join in on the collective denial.

"Mr. Gilding!" one of Queen Rapunzel's ladies-in-waiting gushed. She leaned over the back of my seat at the high table and gave me a gentle, unexpected embrace.

I set my fork down and turned to look up at her. I bowed my head as deeply as I could without standing. “Lady Jessamine.”

“Congratulations,” she said, squeezing my shoulder with one of her gloved hands. “You did Floris proud.”

“Thank you.”

A few seats away, Duke Remington scowled at me. His mother, Duchess Annemie, prattled on as if she still had his full attention.

“Princess Lilian is so delighted with your Gilded Lilies,” Lady Jessamine said. “She’s talking about having an entire enchanted greenhouse built just to house more of them.”

“I hope we have the resources for that,” I said. “Of course, food should come first.”

“What use is food without beauty?” she said.

“Or beauty without food?” I countered.

She gave me a bright smile. “I sincerely hope we’ll be able to keep growing both. If not, please know that you’ve given us all a good deal of optimism today. We’ve been sorely in need of some good news.”

I was tempted for a moment to ask her if she’d seen Queen Rapunzel recently, or knew about the queen’s graying hair and the witch who might be to blame. But the queen’s condition was to remain a secret for a while longer, it seemed, and anyway, this was neither the time nor the place.

Lady Jessamine gave my shoulder another quick squeeze and made her way back to her seat. Across the room, Lady Calla beamed at me, and Lord Narcissus inclined his head in respect.

It was strange to sit here at the high table with the royal family and their honored guests. I’d eaten with Lilian probably hundreds of times before, but never at her family's table at a royal function. It was an honor to be here. If I were truthful with myself, though, I rather preferred our picnics in the gardens--and not just because those didn't usually include the addition of Duke Remington, who now sat directly to Lilian's left. The gentle curve of the head table gave him plenty of opportunity to glare at me whenever possible, and I wasn't the only person to notice.

"He doesn't seem to like you much," a young noblewoman from Atlantice observed. She was one of several visitors who sat between Lilian and me.

I took a sip of my wine. "How did you guess?"

"Everyone's talking about it." She adjusted the blue satin cuff of her sleeve and glanced sidelong at the duke. "A string of tens, and then he gives you a one? That's not a horticultural judgment. That's personal." She tucked a strand of hair behind her ear. "Not that it's any of my business, but what's the situation?"

I grimaced. "I'm friends with the princess. He doesn't like it."

Her eyes widened. "Romantic intrigue!"

"I wouldn't say it's romantic," I lied. "Lilian and I are just friends. But he won't be convinced."

"Well, if he makes it too unbearable for you, perhaps you'd be interested in coming to Atlantice," she said brightly. "We'd be delighted to have you."

Warmth flooded through me--not because I had any intention of leaving Floris, but because it meant that when the duke did fire me and throw me from the palace grounds, I might not be a complete pariah.

We fell into a pleasant conversation about Atlantice's gardens and the abundance of unique sea plants in the waters surrounding the island. I'd only ever met a few merpeople before, but this woman spoke about them as if they were scarcely more remarkable than people with brilliant red hair or particularly blue eyes.

I glanced up the table at Lilian. Her eyes were the bluest. I wished they would land on me.

I took the wish back before it had fully formed; I didn't want the duke to catch her looking.

As servants began clearing the dinner plates to make room for dessert, the king stood and cleared his throat. The hundreds of conversations around the room died out, and all eyes turned expectantly toward the head table. Some of their gazes landed on me from people curious about the palace gardener or, perhaps, hopeful that the winning lily might mean something **favorable** for the fate of their home.

King Alder said a few words, thanking everyone assembled for joining us in celebration and paying tribute to our honored foreign guests. And then he turned toward me.

"Mr. Gilding," he said. "Would you please stand?"

My face flooded with heat. My stomach churned as if it wanted to reject every morsel of the delicious meal. I stood, keeping my fingertips on the table for stability.

"Mr. Deon Gilding has been a valued member of our staff for eighteen years now," the king said.

Out in the crowd, I caught a flicker of movement. Hedley and Hyacinth were out there, and Hyacinth was giving me a tiny, excited wave and beaming at me as if she was trying to outshine the sun.

The nerves in my stomach settled just a little.

"Queen Rapunzel and I have had the honor of seeing him grow from a curious, intelligent boy to a young man of remarkable kindness and talent. He has served as our palace's head gardener for the past year, and has been both the youngest to hold that position in the kingdom's history and a worthy successor to our own valued Sheldon Hedley."

The king inclined his head toward Hedley, who nodded in return.

"And now," the king continued, "we have the honor of seeing him named the grand champion at this year's Spring Flower Festival. At a time when our future feels uncertain, Mr. Gilding's green thumb has given us hope."

He raised his wine glass toward me. The heat in my face only grew, and I had a feeling I was turning as red as one of Lilian's strawberries.

"To Deon Gilding," the king said.

Hundreds of glasses raised toward me, and hundreds of voices repeated the toast.

I wanted to crawl in a hole and die.

"Thank you," the king said to me, quietly enough that only those of us at the high table could hear.

A few seats away from him, the duke glared at me and crumpled a napkin in his hand.

12TH APRIL

I had planned to sleep in the next morning. It was the first chance I'd had in months to really rest, without a thousand festival tasks waiting for my attention the moment I opened my eyes.

But when the first gleaming of dawn filtered through the windows of my shed, my eyes popped open. Excitement coursed through me, running through my veins with my blood and forcing me from my bed.

I had won.

The king had come home.

A few plants were still alive on the palace grounds, safe within the confines of my private garden.

And perhaps, given everything that had happened, the duke wouldn't dare try to fire me. Now that the first confused rush of winning the festival had passed, I was thinking clearly, and it was obvious that, of course, King Alder would never let his future son-in-law fire me.

He probably wouldn't let me live in a shed, either. I made a mental note to inform him of my living conditions. But that could happen later. For now, I had energy—energy, I could try to harness.

I jumped up and threw on my clothes, then sat cross-legged on my manure bed with a few wilting sprigs of lavender in a glass jar filled with water. I'd plucked these last survivors of the blight from the garden a few days ago and left them in my shed, thinking that perhaps I could try to figure out if the magic that kept my private garden alive had attached itself to the garden or to me.

The results were inconclusive; the lavender hadn't turned dull gray, but it hadn't stayed as bright as it should have, either.

Of course, that could have been due to the depressing lack of sunlight in this shed.

No matter. My magic, whatever amount of it I had, should work on the things either way.

I held my hands a few inches away from the sprigs and closed my eyes. I burrowed my attention into the plants, trying to go deeper and deeper, from the surface of the delicate purple blooms to the cells that made them up to the water that supported the cells. There wasn't much water left--the wilting was evidence of that--but I tried to feel for it anyway and for the core of bright energy that still ran through the center of the stems.

I breathed deeply and focused, slowly, the way I'd focused the lens of my science tutor's microscope back when Lilian and I had studied botany together. I remembered the intricate green webs of leaves and the coral-like texture of pollen and the fine-bubbled texture of a rose petal, and I tried to get a sense for what this wilted lavender might look like up close.

Slowly, gently, I began to draw water up the stem. I tried to force the water into the plant's cells, then stopped and backed off. That didn't feel right; the lavender resisted me, in a strange way I couldn't explain. I took another deep breath, then, feeling my way through the words as if I were saying a prayer to a goddess I'd never met, asked the flower to please take a drink.

The lavender seemed to inhale.

But it wasn't taking in air. It was taking in water, sucking up moisture through its stem and letting it flood throughout the silvery leaves and the delicate blossoms.

I opened my eyes. Before me, in the dim light from the high windows, the lavender was straightening and stretching like it had been woken from a long sleep.

Joy flooded through me. I'd done it.

It was a small step, to be sure. Plants *wanted* water, and reviving a few wilted but healthy sprigs was nothing like curing a plant of a cursed blight.

But stars, it had still *worked.*

I kept my focus deep within the lavender, holding the strange connection I'd created with this plant. If I could ask it to drink, what else could I do?

I felt down toward the cut stems. Perhaps I could ask it to root. Perhaps I could propagate these cuttings and use my magic to protect them from the blight. Perhaps I could accelerate their growth and coax the plant to adulthood before the curse reached it, even without the help of enchanted glass. Perhaps--

The door burst open. I jumped. My connection with the lavender snapped like a taut string, and like taut string, the end of attention I'd been holding recoiled back toward me. A blinding headache crashed between my eyes, and my head throbbed.

I squinted against the too-bright light pouring in from the doorway.

"Reed, I was in the middle--"

I cut myself off.

That wasn't Reed.

Duke Remington stared down at me, his eyebrows arched in distaste, and his lips twisted in a snarl.

He was so different from the polite man I'd first met in the gardens. He had rotted just as quickly as the blight, but I had a feeling his transformation had little to do with a curse. He was just a good actor, and I'd failed to see through his lies.

I hoped I'd seen all of him now. If there was an even worse monster buried beneath this facade, I feared for Lilian.

"Can I help you?" My voice was curt, even cruel. I didn't recognize that tone; it wasn't me.

The duke threw a newspaper at me. It hit my shoulder with a *thwack* and tumbled to the floor, sending loose sheaves across the dirty boards.

"Are you happy now?" the duke snarled. "Congratulations. Get ready to pack your bags, Mr. Gilding, and don't expect to find a warm welcome elsewhere."

I stared at him, but I couldn't make sense of the words. I wasn't about to bend over to pick up the newspaper. Taking my eyes off that monster was as good as asking for a thump to the head.

I stood and straightened my shoulders. He was a hair taller than me, but I was broader, and I had the muscles that came from years of hard work.

"Are you done?" I said.

He eyed me, sizing me up. Then, wisely, he seemed to realize his precious guards weren't here to protect him.

"I hope you enjoyed your celebration last night," he spat. "It was the last you're likely to get." He glanced at the papers spread across my floor. "It's a shame," he added, voice suddenly sickly sweet. "You had such a promising career ahead."

He left as quickly as he'd come, slamming the door behind him and leaving me in darkness.

I bent to gather up the sheets of newspaper, then, after making sure the duke had actually left, cracked the door to give myself enough light to read by.

It wasn't hard to figure out which article he had meant for me to read.

ACCUSATIONS OF CHEATING ROCK SPRING FLOWER FESTIVAL, read the headline splashed across the front page. Right underneath it was a huge picture of me, grinning like an idiot in the throne room between the enormous tulip trophy and my gleaming Gilded Lily.

The kingdom of Floris was rocked late last night by accusations of cheating at the Spring Flower Festival, the article read. *Representatives from multiple kingdoms have accused Mr. Deon Gilding, the eighteen-year-old Head Gardener at the Palace of Tulis, of cheating in this year's New Breeds flower competition. Mr. Gilding was named both New Breeds and Grand Champion winner at this year's festival, a surprising decision in light of Floris's recent struggles with the plant disease various horticultural experts are calling the Florian Blight or the*

Gray Death.

"The existence of the Gilded Lily in a nation everyone knows was crippled overnight is suspicious, to say the least," said one source from Oz, who requested that her name be withheld. "Anyone who thinks that lily was real ought to come see me; I've got a bridge I'd like to sell them."

Minister Saffron Blackwood of the High Horticulture Council of Floris vehemently denied accusations that the lily was artificial.

"Every judge on the panel examined the Gilded Lily in detail," she said in a statement early this morning. "We found no evidence that the plant was in any way faked, nor that it was enhanced by magical means not explicitly allowed by contest rules, which permit the use of unicorn manure, pixie dust, and other common biological additives."

Some, however, claim that the festival judges themselves are to blame for the lily's unfair win. Rumors of bribery abound, with the most prominent accuser coming straight from the palace itself.

"There's no way the other judges were unbiased," said Mr. Sorrel Valerian, a palace guard. "The discrepancy in judging makes that clear. A string of tens in any of the competitions is unusual, but that's what Mr. Gilding got, aside from Duke James Remington's score. I know Duke Remington personally. He's a man of honor and as much of an expert in horticulture as many of the others on the panel. The fact that he scored Mr. Gilding's lily so differently from the other judges gives me pause. Duke Remington is above bribery or blackmail. Can the same be said about the other judges?"

This morning, representatives from the nations of Atlantice, Elder, and The Forge have lodged a formal request for an inquiry into the Gilded Lily and Mr. Deon Gilding's participation in the festival. Other nations are expected to lodge their own complaints in the coming days.

King Alder departed to Urbis via private train late last night and is not expected to return until Princess Lilian's wedding on the eighteenth of this month. Other palace representatives could not be reached for comment.

I stared at the last paragraph, and the words seemed to blur before my eyes. Then I glanced back up at the paragraph from Valerian. He was one of the duke's new guards. I wondered how much the duke had paid him to go to the papers.

Sticks and stones, I should have known it was too good to last. I threw the paper down onto my bed. On the shelf, my tulip trophy gleamed down at me in mockery, my winning Gilded Lily winked out its first hint of golden light through a crack in its otherwise tightly furled petals.

I had planned to send it up to the queen today as a gift, and then to send the next most-beautiful Gilded Lily in my private garden to Lilian.

Now, it seemed I would have to submit this one for scrutiny by every representative from every kingdom who put stock in these ridiculous rumors, all the while running the risk that the duke or one of his cronies would find a way to get to my flower. They'd do something to the bloom to make it seem less real and magical than it was. Such a thing wasn't impossible. The duke had guards on his side; I had no doubt he could find an unscrupulous magician to do his bidding, too.

Outside, raised voices babbled in the distance. They grew closer until I could make out the slow, reasoned tones of the one and the tense comments of the other.

Reed barged through the cracked door without knocking. He met my gaze with his own grim expression. Behind him, Hedley stood with a face like thunder.

"I take it you've heard the news," he said, taking in the papers on my bed.

I nodded wordlessly. All the joy and excitement I'd felt when I'd first woken up was gone, replaced by a dull ache that sat in the pit of my stomach. The feeling was as heavy and gray as lead, or perhaps blight.

"The press is here." Reed's jaw tightened. "You're expected in the throne room."

~

My first press conference had passed in a quick blur of excitement and surprise. During this one, I felt every moment.

I stood in front of the assembled reporters, who filled the throne room in quickly arranged wooden seats, with their notebooks and cameras at the ready. A flashbulb went off, and, like the first person to start a round of applause, it triggered several more to follow. I flinched back and blinked against the brightness.

"What do you say about the allegations that you brought a false lily to the flower festival competition?" someone shouted.

Lord Agave, the palace's Officer of the Press, gripped his Forge-made microphone. "Mr. Gilding will read a prepared statement," he said, and the enchantment on the microphone threw a blanket of silence over everyone else in the room, leaving his words alone to ring through the space. "There will be plenty of time for questions later. You may take photographs, but please keep flashbulbs off until after the press conference."

I nodded my thanks, and he acknowledged the nod but didn't smile.

I shifted from foot to foot and looked down at the paper that had been thrust at me before I'd entered the throne room.

"I am here to deny any rumors or accusations of cheating at the Spring Flower Festival," I read. "My festival entry adhered to all restrictions and requirements and is a flower whose properties are all biological and inherent."

"But what about the blight?" someone called.

I looked up sharply. The gears in my head spun. I couldn't tell them about my magic. Not yet, and especially not with the duke sitting in the front row with an awful grin on his face, his parents on either side with their arms folded and the same expression on their faces. On the duke's other side, Lilian sat, her face pale, and her hands clenched tightly in her lap.

"As you will know if you've been paying attention to palace statements, we've had some luck using enchanted glass domes to protect plants from the effects of the blight," I said. They could interpret that how they would.

"So you kept your flowers alive and let the rest of the kingdom die?" someone spat.

I opened my mouth, but Lord Agave shook his head at me and gestured discreetly at my paper: *Stick to the statement.*

I looked back down and kept reading. "The Horticulture Council of Floris, as well as all delegates from the twelve kingdoms nominated to serve as judges in the competitions, were unanimous in agreeing that my Gilded Lily is a real, legitimate breed of flower and was subject to no tampering. I also absolutely deny any allegations of attempting to bribe, blackmail, or otherwise influence the judges. Thank you."

That word, *unanimously,* glared at me from the paper. It hadn't been unanimous. The duke was the one spreading these rumors.

But, of course, he wouldn't be foolish enough to do that on his own.

"Why did Duke Remington give you such a low score?" someone shouted.

Lord Agave stepped to the microphone. "Keep order." He waited for a long moment, then looked out at the assembled crowd with warning on his face. "Mr. Gilding is *now* open for questions. One at a time, please."

This said, he nodded at the person who'd spoken before. She stood and cleared her throat.

"Mr. Gilding," she said, now that she had the attention of the whole room. "There was an obvious discrepancy in the judges' scores. If you deny that you cheated or attempted to influence the judges, how do you explain Duke Remington's decision to give you such an unusually low score?"

I glanced at the duke. He narrowed his eyes at me, daring me to speak.

I couldn't say anything about him, not here. Not when everyone was already prepared to tear me into pieces. Launching a verbal attack on the future king of Floris wasn't going to get me in anyone's good graces.

"I can't speak for Duke Remington's decision," I said. "However, the detailed scoring sheets given to me after the competition indicate that His Grace thought the Gilded Lily was too flashy and lacked originality, given the similarity in its coloring to the common gilded goldenrod. I can only conclude the discrepancy in scores came down to a matter of personal taste."

The duke looked like a cat who'd just caught a bird. I wanted to punch the smug look right off his face. I clenched my fist on the edge of the lectern instead.

The reporter who'd asked the question didn't look entirely satisfied, but she sat back down. A dozen hands flew into the air, and Lord Agave pointed at one of them.

"Will you submit your Gilded Lily to a review by independent parties?" asked a heavyset man with spectacles too small for his face.

I glanced over at Lord Agave, who gave me the tiniest of nods.

"I would be happy to submit my flower for review," I said. "I have nothing to hide. My only request is that the flower is treated with care; I have very few of them, and, given our current situation, I'm concerned about losing the breed to the blight."

The man nodded, content, and sat back down.

The next man to stand glared at me. He shook strands of his blond hair off his face like he was about to get into a fight. "A lot of people find it suspicious that you prioritized the health of your competition lily over the hundreds of other rare and valuable flowers that could have used your attention. You claim you used enchanted glass to protect it. Where was your enchanted glass when it came to the birdcage gladiolus or the silver-threaded passion iris?"

I opened my mouth, but he wasn't done.

"I don't know if you know this, but leading botanists confirmed two days ago that the sunspot tulip is extinct. It's one of the only flowers in the world that changes color under sunlight, and its genetic code has been terrifically valuable to breeders throughout Floris. As I'm sure you know, as the *head gardener* of Floris, the sunspot tulip has not been permitted to leave our borders since its development, given its value to the flower breeders whose work supports the economy of our beautiful nation. That means the flowers were here and *only* here, and that means that since all the ones here are *dead,* that species is gone. Forever. The sunspot tulip is *over.*"

He breathed heavily and stared at me like he thought he might be able to burn a hole through my head with the power of his rage.

I swallowed, heat creeping up my neck. "I'm sorry, what was the question?"

He barked a laugh like he couldn't believe the idiot standing in front of him. "Where was your enchanted glass?" he demanded. "Why was your attention on your frankly unremarkable lily and not on any of the plants that *keep Floris afloat?*"

"I didn't know." My voice was small, and I hated myself for it. "If I'd known the sunspot tulip was at that kind of risk, I would have worked with them to save it."

I cringed at my arrogance. As if I could have *saved* anything. My lily was alive due to a fluke in magic, nothing more.

"You should have known," he said.

Lilian shot to her feet and spun around. "Mr. Gilding is our palace gardener," she said, voice sharper than I'd ever heard. "He is not responsible for the wellbeing of every plant in Floris."

The duke tugged on her arm, but she yanked it away and continued glaring at the reporter.

"Mr. Gilding has been working nonstop to learn about this blight," she snapped. "It's thanks to him and our previous Head Gardener that we know about the enchanted glass at all. He protected his lily because he determined that it was likely to be one of the most valuable plants on the palace grounds, and he showed good judgment in doing so. The loss of the sunspot tulip is *tragic,* but I would argue that, given the excellent response from Festival judges and attendees, the Gilded Lily is *just* as valuable to our nation and deserves our protection."

The reporter might not have been convinced, but he was cowed. He inclined his head respectfully at the princess and sat back down. She watched, stone-faced until he had settled back into his chair, and then she turned back around and sat with absolute dignity.

She raised her chin and nodded at Lord Agave that he could proceed.

She didn't look at me.

And I was glad because I wouldn't have been able to wipe the grin off my face if she had. My Gilded Lily may have been beautiful enough to impress twelve kingdoms and inspire accusations of cheating, but this brilliant, fiery, terrifying, wonderful woman put it to shame.

Duke Remington leaned over to Lilian and muttered something at her. He looked furious, and she looked as if she could not have cared less.

Lord Agave pointed to the next person ready to launch a question or accusation at me. I took a deep breath, straightened my shoulders, and prepared to answer.

~

"Psst."

I glanced up. The garden around me glimmered in the soft twilight. The days were getting longer, and I didn't know how long I'd been out here, staring at the grass that had turned the same dull gray as the pebbles in the walkway.

"Psst," the voice said again.

I spotted Reed, crouching behind a skeletal rosebush we hadn't yet pulled up. A few remaining leaves hung, limp and dark, and a single rose dangled like a hanged corpse.

"What are you doing?"

"Shh," he ordered. "Head to the servants' entrance on this side of the palace. I'll distract Remington's stupid guards. You're needed in the servants' dining hall."

"I don't want to go in there," I said.

"Remington won't find out."

"I don't care if he does," I said. "There's just nothing for me in that palace. Why are you hiding behind a bush?"

"I don't want anyone to see me talking to you."

"Great," I said. "Accused of cheating, and now, my very presence is enough to ruin other people's reputations."

I hated the words as soon as they came out. They were sulking and sullen, reminding me more of the teenager I'd been and less of the man I was supposed to be these days.

"Wow," Reed said, his thoughts clearly mirroring mine. "Wow, Deon. You're handling this great."

"Shut up." I couldn't stop a slight laugh from bubbling up. It wasn't amused, exactly, but it hadn't crossed the line into hysterical, either. Thank the stars for small mercies.

"Hedley wants you inside," Reed said. "So does everyone else."

My neck and shoulders tensed. "Why, are they lying in wait to murder me?"

“Yes,” he said flatly. “Everyone’s going to murder you. It’s a surprise attack. Daisy’s waiting with a butcher knife and Petunia’s got the other maids all lined up to strangle you with twine. Of course, I wouldn’t send you in for something like that, you dolt.”

I sighed. Whatever was waiting for me inside couldn’t possibly be worse than the thoughts that had been running through my head.

Reed waited until I was moving toward the palace, and then his dark shadow darted ahead in the twilight toward the doors. He started shouting and pointing wildly, and the guards exchanged confused looks and then ran in the direction he was pointing.

Reed raised his thumbs at me and then took off after them, shouting something about a wild boar that had attacked one of the peacocks that roamed the grounds.

I slipped in through the servants’ entrance. The familiar scent of stone and fires burning hit me, reminding me of a time when I’d been allowed within these walls--when they’d provided me with a home.

It hadn’t been that long ago. Even so, it felt like a lifetime.

I cracked open the dining room door, then stopped. The room was packed, as if every servant in the palace and gardens was here, squeezed into every corner.

I poked my head in, scanning the faces for Hedley. “Someone needed me?”

Linden clenched his jaw. And then, stone-faced, he began clapping.

The others joined in.

I flinched. Today had been bad enough. I didn’t need the sarcasm of everyone I worked with piled on top of it.

But it wasn’t sarcasm. Linden wasn’t scowling at me, not exactly. And the maids were outright beaming.

One of the kitchen hands raised his fist in support, and the cook pursed her lips and applauded, nodding at me like I'd done something to merit her approval. Alongside one wall, Chervil clapped slowly and angrily, a veritable storm on his face, and Myrtle set her chin as if she was ready for someone to punch her. Even Jonquil was applauding, his claps, a stark contrast with his expression of disgust.

Slowly, I stepped into the room and looked around at their faces. Hedley was here, too, and Hyacinth, both staunchly clapping like someone had dared them not to.

"What's...?" I hesitated, searching their expressions for more clues, but I couldn't make sense of the applause or the widely varying looks on everyone's faces. "What's going on?"

"You won the Spring Flower Festival on behalf of the palace, and that self-important cocklebur upstairs won't give you a shred of credit for it," Jonquil said.

I stared at him. Out of everyone in the kingdom, Jonquil was the *last* person I would have expected to support me.

Well, second to last.

"We're none too pleased with what happened today," the cook said. "We know you didn't cheat. And we thought you ought to know that *we* know."

Myrtle nodded, jaw still set in a square line.

"You'd never do something like that," Daisy said with absolute conviction. "The duke's only acting like that because the princess likes you, and he's jealous."

Another of the maids elbowed her in the ribs, and she stumbled to the side and hissed "*What?*" at the girl who'd nudged her.

I gaped around the crowded room. A lump rose up in

my throat, but there was confusion there, too. I looked from Jonquil to Chervil to Linden and shook my head a little.

"I don't understand," I said. "You guys hate me."

Linden pressed his thin lips together. "That might be," he said. "You and I don't always see eye to eye."

"That's one way of putting it," Jonquil muttered.

Linden spoke over the interruption. "Even if we don't agree with the way things have been run lately, we know you're doing your best. You wouldn't cheat, not at something like this."

"An insult to you is an insult to us all," Jonquil said.

"Basically, they're saying that *they're* the only ones that can call you names," Reed said.

I jumped. I hadn't heard him come in behind me.

"You represent Floris," said the head housekeeper, Mrs. Almond, "and Floris does not cheat in flower competitions." She smoothed the front of her skirt. "We don't have to."

I blinked around at all of them. "Thank you. All of you."

That didn't seem like enough, those little words. I opened my mouth, searching for more that would convey the sense of surprised warmth blooming in my torso, but Hedley, seeming to see I was in trouble, clapped his hands.

The cook waved at someone on the other side of the room, and the crowd parted to make way for a couple of kitchen hands bearing an enormous cake covered in white frosting and topped with an enormous marzipan recreation of my Gilded Lily.

I swallowed again, hard, and Hedley caught my eye. He winked, and Hyacinth took his arm and beamed at me.

“Don’t let anyone get you down, love,” she said. “All will come right in the end.”

I had no reason to believe her. But just now, in this moment, with this enormous cake and a room full of people who seemed willing to believe in my basic decency, whether they liked me or not--that felt like plenty for now. I’d have been selfish to ask for more.

13TH APRIL

Another polished wooden wagon traveled up the palace driveway, pulled by a team of black horses with manes and tails that bounced with every step. The words *Cinnamon and Sons Event Services* was written on the side in gleaming black letters adorned with silver flowers. It was the fourth in a string of identical wagons that had arrived this morning, and I had a feeling I'd see more before the day was out.

The palace events coordinator routed the wagon around to the side entrance closest to the throne room. The wheels dug into the ground and tore up the grass, but it didn't matter. The grass was gray, the earth beneath it incapable of producing life. The grass around the castle would all be pulled up and replaced with artfully painted stones before the wedding, anyway. Most of my apprentices had been pulled away from their usual duties to help paint colorful flowers onto rocks the size of my palm, and I hadn't been able to complain, given how little there was for them to do these days. We only had so many enchanted bell jars, and it would be weeks before the next shipment arrived from the magicians Hedley had hired to make more. Those of us who had years of gardening experience were more than capable of taking care of the few seedlings we'd managed to keep alive under glass.

Lilian's wedding should have been a beautiful affair out in the gardens, not in some stuffy throne room that also played host to terrible events like press releases.

But there were a lot of ways Lilian's wedding *should* have been different. Her mother was supposed to be healthy, for one. Her father was supposed to be here, watching his daughter's joy at the preparations, instead of off in Urbis doing the gods knew what. And Lilian should have been happy because she should have been marrying the man of her dreams instead of a monster who held her hostage through some miserable combination of duty and the money that would feed the kingdom through the blight.

The duke's parents, Duke Markus and Duchess Annemie, followed the wagon up the driveway. Now that the gardens were all but dead, they'd taken to taking their daily air by walking between the various pieces of architecture the gardens had to offer: a gazebo here, a lattice trellis walkway there, a few old ruins that had been brought to the grounds in the days of King Alder's great-grandfather.

I couldn't fathom why they chose to walk together every day. They clearly detested one another; Duke

Markus talked to his wife like she was an idiot, and Duchess Annemie responded by sniping and moaning about everything that crossed her path.

I watched the duchess's dull purple skirts shift as she walked up the drive. Had she been like Lilian once, beautiful and clever, and just been worn down by her awful husband? Or had she always been like this? I hoped it was the latter. I couldn't bear the thought of Lilian being married to the duke, but imagining her as bitter and dried-up as this duchess--it made ice run up my spine.

Lilian wouldn't lose herself like that. She was strong. She wouldn't let it happen. I had to believe that.

The duchess seemed to sense me watching her. She looked up sharply, and her eyes met mine. I bowed in respect and returned to the flowerbed I was working in. I'd already removed the last gray stems and creeping roots, but it still needed to be tilled.

I couldn't stop the blight from killing everything that grew in this soil, but I could try to, at least, keep it aerated and groomed until the day we could put seeds in the earth again.

When I next glanced up, the duke and duchess were much closer--and headed directly for me.

My stomach sank, and I staked my tiller in the soil.

"Duke Markus," I said with another low bow. "Duchess Annemie."

The elder duke stood erect, his hands behind his back. He looked down at me, and I could *feel* him trying to intimidate me. He straightened his shoulders and puffed out his chest and stepped slightly closer to me than normal courtesy allowed.

It was almost funny, the retired Duke of Thornton trying to throw his weight about to impress a mere gardener.

"I suppose you've read the papers," Duchess Annemie said, voice and expression both cool.

"I haven't, Your Grace." I inclined my head in what I hoped was a respectful gesture.

"Then I suppose you know what they're saying about you."

"Well enough, Your Grace."

She waited for more, eyebrow arched, but I wasn't about to get drawn into a conversation with Duke Remington's mother.

"Everyone thinks you cheated."

"I didn't."

"But everyone thinks it."

I glanced at the duke as if he might provide some clues as to what she was getting after, but he only looked down at me with a smug half-smile.

"I've already made my statement," I said. "My lily is being reviewed by the Horticulture Council and the Festival delegates. I await their decision."

"You have more flowers, though, don't you?" The duchess's eyes sharpened.

My skin prickled with warning.

"We've managed to grow several new seedlings under glass," I said. "I'd be happy to have one of my gardeners give you a tour if you'd like."

She narrowed her eyes. "Not under glass. You have a private garden, don't you?"

My spine stiffened. I fought to keep my expression calm.

"Yes, Your Grace. The Head Gardener always does."

"And it's got flowers in it."

I didn't answer. I didn't have to. The triumph was bright on her otherwise cold face.

"I heard Lilian talking to one of her ladies about it," she said. "Apparently, you have quite the green thumb."

I nodded as if acknowledging a compliment.

"You still have flowers."

The idea of denying it flashed across my mind, but it faded just as quickly.

"I've managed to keep a few alive, yes." I shoved my hands in my pockets to prevent their twitching from betraying my sudden nerves. "The enchanted glass has been promising, and we've been running other experimen--"

"Cut them," she ordered.

I shut my mouth and stared at her.

"Your flowers," she said impatiently. "The ones you've kept alive. Cut them, put them under your fancy glass, and bring them to the palace florists. We require them for the wedding."

"They decided to paint rocks, Your Gr--"

"Bring them," she said. She didn't raise her volume or sound anything other than polite, but goosebumps prickled down my arms anyway. She narrowed her sharp eyes at me. "Either you can bring the flowers and attempt to save the root systems of your plants, or I'll have other servants harvest them who might not be so careful."

"It's my garden," I said. "Lilian wouldn't--"

"*Lilian* is not the only one getting married," the duchess snapped. "That girl is too soft to require her servants to do anything. It's a wonder she bothers to keep them around at all. I, however, am not so easy to push around. Lilian and her maids need bouquets. The hall needs decoration. We are in *Floris,* Mr. Gilding, and a royal wedding in Floris requires flowers. You grow flowers. On royal grounds, may I remind you, and at the pleasure of the royal family. Bring them to the florists, and perhaps we won't have to pull my Garritt into this."

I pressed my tongue to the back of my front teeth, hard. Words I shouldn't say fought their way up, and I shoved them back down. Duke Markus shifted just a hair forward, and I edged back so I wouldn't give in to the urge to shove him that was building in my arms.

"Yes, Your Grace." I didn't sound like myself. This person was angry and as cold as the duchess.

Perhaps it wasn't *Lilian* changing I had to worry about, after all.

"I'll bring them to the florists the night before the wedding," I said, keeping my voice on the tightest possible rein. "You'll want them as fresh as possible."

"You'll do it today. The florists need time to do their work. And besides, we can't have you doing something to the flowers just to spite my son."

I took a deep, silent breath. "Yes, Your Grace."

The duchess held her arm out, and her husband took it. She gave me a smile that didn't go anywhere near her eyes. "You made a good choice not to cross me, Mr. Gilding. Whatever the Council decides, you'd do well to remember that you are still a servant."

"Yes, Your Grace."

"Know your place, Mr. Gilding." She cut her eyes at me. "You're lucky to be here at all."

I snipped the stem of a gorgeous blood peony and put it in the bucket I'd filled with cold water and pixie dust. Hedley added another of the giant red flowers and covered the bucket with the largest bell jar we'd been able to find while we moved to the next flowerbed.

"I hate her," I said. "I thought I hated the duke, but I *really* hate his mother."

"You don't hate anyone," Hedley said. "You're not capable of it."

He was teasing me, or trying to, but the lightness in his voice sounded forced.

"What does Hyacinth think of all this?"

"Hyacinth is inclined to murder anyone who so much as looks at you wrong." Hedley knelt next to a trellis covered in amethyst sweet peas. "Any use in cutting these? I can't imagine they'd hold up well in bouquets."

"They're delicate." I stared at the curling green vines and the jewel-like purple flowers. Their fragrance was light and almost too sweet. This was how springtime was supposed to smell in Floris. "Lilian loves sweet peas," I finally said. "Cut them."

Hedley didn't argue, just took his shears to the fragile stems and began clipping them with care.

The sound of the blades rubbing against one another made me wince every time. I would have gladly given up this garden to Lilian.

But not for her wedding. Not like this.

"I think I'm going to ask if the Horticulture Council will let me work on the enchanted glass efforts after this," I said. "They seem to be on my side. Minister Blackwood is, anyway, and Minister Yarrow will be once she's confirmed my lily is real."

"I thought you were planning to run away to Atlantice?"

I lugged the bucket over, then knelt next to Hedley and began trimming the thread-like sweet pea vines. "I can't leave. I won't be allowed to see Lilian after this, but I won't be able to keep an eye on her from Atlantice."

"You think you'll be able to keep an eye on her?" he

said. "Sounds painful."

I snipped a vine and placed it carefully in the water, draping the stem over the bucket's edge. Several of the flowers weren't blooming just yet; they would be perfect when the wedding arrived.

"Everything's painful." The words should have sounded dramatic and self-indulgent. But Hedley only nodded in silence as if he agreed.

I sat back on my heels. "You're worried, aren't you?"

He cut another vine and handed it to me so I could put it in the bucket but didn't meet my eyes.

"I'm worried," he said after a moment. "The blight's taken the farthest reaches of the kingdom. The flowers in this garden are the only ones for hundreds of miles, as far as I can figure. Over half the flowers in the kingdom are gray, and crops are failing everywhere but at the farthest coasts. It's only a matter of time."

"At least, it's spring," I said. "It's not too late to start new food crops."

"Assuming we can grow enough of them under glass," he said. "Assuming our greenhouse idea works."

"It should. The bell jars do."

"As far as we know," he said. "It might not stop the blight, only slow it. Enough time hasn't passed to tell."

"You're not making me feel any better about this, Hedley," I said.

He sighed. "Not helping myself much, either. We're far away from most of the other kingdoms, at least. There's no word of the blight spreading beyond our borders. If we're going to fall apart, maybe with luck, we won't take the rest of the kingdoms with us."

"This is getting cheerier and cheerier."

"I'll put in a good word with the Council for you," he said. He snipped the last sweet pea vine and handed it to me. The bed in front of us looked like it had gotten a bad haircut, with only a scattering of spiky green stems to indicate the beauty that had been here moments before.

"I wish I'd discovered my magic earlier," I said. "Maybe I could have done something about all this. I doubt I'll ever be good enough to stop the blight, but I'll bet I could figure out how to turn the duke into a toad, given enough time."

I picked up the bucket with its bell jar and dragged it awkwardly down the path to a bed filled with swaying orange silk poppies. I loved looking at them. I felt starved for color these days.

"With all due respect to His Grace, I don't think he needs to be turned *into* a toad," Hedley muttered. "Although that might be an insult to toads."

There was a distinct kind of pleasure in knowing Hedley disliked the same people I did. I grinned and dropped to my knees at the edge of the poppy bed.

We worked in silence for a while, and then Hedley leaned back with a grunt and rolled his shoulders. "I don't know how this is all going to shake out," he said. "I worked at this palace for a long time and saw a lot of changes. I can usually predict how a thing will go. This breaks all the rules." He rubbed his chin and looked over at me. "I hope you figure out your magic, too. Or maybe we ought to take another look at that witch the queen thinks is responsible."

"I don't have enough power to take down a witch."

He was silent for a long moment. The gears were turning in his head at their own pace, and, as always, I waited.

"You can't kill her," he finally said. "But a crossbow might."

He sounded like he was trying to figure out the best solution for a beetle infestation. I laughed. Nothing about it was funny. Nothing about this situation had been funny in a long time.

But the world was all shaken up, and Hedley was still here, solving problems in his own ponderous way, and something about it was hilarious.

Hedley gave me a concerned look, one of his bushy eyebrows drawn up. I only laughed harder and slipped from my crouch hard onto my backside.

"It's not funny," I said, laughing.

"You need a drink," Hedley said flatly. "The pressure's turned you mad."

He was right. I'd gone crazy, and the world was going to hell.

It was what it was.

I just kept laughing.

~

Everything was stupid.

My bout of laughter, combined with the devastating sight of my garden without a single flower in it except for a few of my prized lilies--which were *not* going to Duchess Annemie, no matter what threats came my way--was enough to knock something loose in my head.

Suddenly, all these problems--these dramatic, awful problems--seemed ridiculous. The normalcy of my life was over, and all that was left was an obnoxious family from Thornton, an empty outdoor room where a garden should have been, and the absolute knowledge in the pit of my stomach that I had to do everything in my power to stop this blight.

Even if that meant breaking into the queen's

bedchamber.

You'll get caught, warned the cautious little voice in my head.

But so what? I'd lose my job? The love of my life would marry the worst man on earth? My kingdom would turn gray, and I'd get accused of cheating in the Spring Flower Festival, and everything I'd ever worked for would be as dead as the flowers of Floris?

At this point, getting thrown in the dungeons would be a welcome break.

Getting into the palace ended up being easier than I'd expected. After all, I was working under orders of Duchess Annemie, and who in these circumstances was going to *stop* the man whose arms were full of fresh, living flowers?

"These get delivered straight from my hands to the Head Florists' or not at all," I said firmly to the guard at the front doors who tried to stop me. "I'm not going to risk one of you blockheads crushing these amethyst sweet peas. Do you have any idea how delicate these blooms are? The vines *alone* are--"

"You can go in," the guard interrupted with an annoyed scowl. "Straight to the florists' chamber, then straight back, do you hear?"

"What, you don't want to put an armed guard on me?"

I regretted the words immediately, but, for the first time in a month, luck was with me.

"Guards are all at the docks searching festival visitors," he growled. "Can't have blight leave our shores."

I raised my eyebrows. "Smart idea. Must not have been yours."

I bit the inside of my cheek. I'd gone too far. But I'd

been talking back to Remington's guards for a while now; it would be suspicious if I let up today.

"Florist's chamber," he barked. "Then out."

I gave him a mock salute, which wasn't easy given the two enormous buckets hanging from my arms and the giant bell jars strapped to my back. I looked like the world's strangest beetle, and I could see the guard trying to formulate a remark that would condemn me for it. But my feet worked faster than his brain, and I was inside the entrance hall before he'd figured out the words.

I hurried the flowers to the florists' chamber. The open, airy space had once been filled with colorful blooms on every day of the year, and the Head Florist herself had once commanded an army of assistants who made arrangements, placed them around the palace, sent them to local nobles and charities with the royal family's compliments, and traded out bouquets the moments they started to wilt.

Now, that same army sat in the room, along with several of my apprentices, painting rocks. Everyone was chatting, but the atmosphere in the room was oppressive. It seemed they all felt the same way I did about replacing living flowers with painted stones.

The gloom lifted when I entered the room. Several pairs of widened eyes stared at me, and the Head Florist rushed forward, looking like I was about to hand her one of Lilian's newborn puppies.

"How?" she stammered. "Where?"

"We managed to keep a few back for the wedding," I lied. "These are the last you'll see in a while. Treat them well and keep them under the glass as much as you can."

She took one of the buckets from me, and her

assistants rushed forward to relieve me of the other bucket and the jars. They touched the blooms like they were priceless jewels--and, to even the most average Florian, these were more precious.

I slipped from the room before my apprentices could get too curious about my appearance in the castle and slipped into one of the narrow servants' corridors. It led me to Lilian's room, and I let myself into our old schoolroom and then found her in the conservatory. She was sitting with a book but staring out the window instead of at the pages.

"Lils," I whispered.

She jumped and spun around. The book tumbled to the floor as she rushed at me. Her arms flew around me, and she nuzzled her face into the hollow of my shoulder. The magnolia scent of her hair dazzled me.

"What are you doing here?"

"I need your help," I whispered. "I need to get into your mother's rooms."

She searched my face for a brief moment.

"Don't talk to her about Garritt," she said. "I don't want to worry her. I can handle him."

"I need to ask her about the blight," I said. "How we can fight it."

Lilian gave me a brisk nod. "I'll distract the guard."

A few moments later, we were one corridor down from the queen's chambers. I crouched behind a massive, now-empty golden vase, and Lilian, halfway down the corridor from me, threw herself to the floor and started screaming.

The guard was at her side in an instant. Lilian clutched her ankle and wailed about having twisted it, dramatically enough that I was surprised he believed her.

As soon as I was sure he was focused on the princess, I sprinted down the corridor and to the queen's door. I slipped inside and shut it silently behind me, then rested against the door and waited for my heartbeat to slow.

When I glanced up, the queen was looking at me from a sofa with her eyebrows raised and an amused smile playing on her lips.

"It's good to see you too," she said lightly.

Her hair was wrapped in a pink scarf today, patterned with cherry blossoms on delicate branches. Despite the gray peeking from beneath the silk, she appeared healthy. Her skin had its usual glow; her cheeks held their usual flush.

"Your Majesty."

I dropped into an awkward, too-sudden bow. Her smile twitched.

"Are you and Lilian playing hide-and-seek?" she asked lightly. "I remember that being a great favorite about ten years ago."

It had been a favorite. The castle was enormous; even when we'd restricted the game to a single wing or floor, it could take us hours to find one another. Once Lilian had tracked me to the inside of an old oak chest, only to discover me fast asleep atop some priceless woven heirlooms. She'd called me Tapestry Boy for a week.

"She did help me get in here," I said.

"Have a seat," she said, patting the couch beside her.

It should have been uncomfortable, a grubby gardener sitting like an equal next to a beautiful queen. But Queen Rapunzel had always made me feel at home. I settled next to her, and she held out a hand. I took it.

"You're still strong," I said, watching the tendons

shift under her creamy skin as she squeezed my hand.

"I'm not sick," she said. "But I suppose you already figured that out."

I looked at her more carefully, and she gave my hand another squeeze.

"Lilian has never been able to keep from spilling all her secrets to her best friend," she said. "I suppose she told you she came to see me?"

I nodded.

"I'm quite all right. We weren't certain what would happen when the gray reached my head, but it seems to be... nothing." She pulled at the scarf, and it slipped easily from her hair, which was still long, gray, and dull as rough stone. "But Alder and I agree, I can't be seen like this. Not when the kingdom is already under such stress."

"That's all?" I said. "You're just hiding your hair?"

I frowned at her. That didn't seem like enough to keep someone like Queen Rapunzel locked in this room for so long.

"I wouldn't think you'd be willing to get locked in a tower again," I said cautiously. "Not over something so simple."

She started, and her hand slipped away from mine. The queen's gaze darted back and forth between my eyes. Her eyes were as blue as her daughter's, but darker, the way Lilian's sometimes looked under the dappled shade of a tree.

"You know, then," she said. "About my history. Who told you?"

"Hedley."

The fine lines on her forehead softened. "Oh, of course. Yes, he was there for all of it."

"Is that why you're hiding?" I said. "Is that why

you're staying up here, really? Are you trying to hide from the witch?"

She blinked a few times as if she wasn't sure how to take the question. I tensed, worried I'd insulted her.

"I don't think I could hide from Gothel," she said at last. "She knows who I married. And she was always so overprotective. I daresay she's kept a closer eye on me than anyone would assume." She twisted the silk scarf in her lap. "No, I'm not hiding from Gothel. I'm trying to hide Gothel from the rest of the kingdom."

I squinted at her, trying to make sense of it. She let out a heavy sigh.

"It's my fault the flowers are dying," she said. "If Gothel is causing this--and I'm almost sure she is--then she's doing it to spite me."

"Would she do that?" I said. "After so long?"

The queen looked steadily at me. "No one else's hair has turned gray."

I bit my lip. This was no great mystery, then, if the queen and Hedley's suspicions were to be believed. A single wicked witch in the forest was responsible for all of this.

It was simple. And the solution was simple, too.

"What can we do?" I said. "How do we find her?"

The queen's jaw tensed. "We don't," she said.

I stared at her. On the side table beside her end of the couch, a bouquet of silk roses sat in a crystal vase.

Florians never used silk flowers, not for ordinary decorations. Their presence here felt artificial and sickly.

"We have to destroy her," I said. "We have to stop the blight."

"We will not." The queen's voice was firm, almost harsh. Then, slowly, her face fell. "Not until we've tried everything else," she added softly. "She's dangerous, Deon, terribly so. And in spite of it all--she's my mother."

She stared at me, willing me to understand.

And I didn't understand, not really.

But I loved the queen, and I trusted her.

"We're going to just fight against her magic, then," I said. "Not her."

Queen Rapunzel's face relaxed. "That's my hope."

"What if the people starve before then?"

"They won't," she said. "Alder has been running projections and budgets nonstop. We have enough grain in storage to last the people a while, and Enchantia and Draconis have already agreed to provide us with regular shipments of fresh fruits and vegetables. The cost will go up, but the palace is prepared to subsidize the imports. We can do that, thanks to Lilian's marriage."

"That should buy us enough time to figure out how to grow in the greenhouses," I said.

She nodded. "I heard about those. They were a clever idea."

"It was all Hedley."

"And the Gilded Lily was all you," she said, her smile returning. "I heard about that, too. Congratulations."

"The win is being contested."

She rolled her eyes. "It won't hold. Minister Yarrow is furious that anyone even brought their judgment under question."

A long-standing tension in my shoulders unknotted itself a little. "That's good to hear." I shifted a little. "Your Majesty, where is the king? We need him here."

The temptation to tell her about the duke and his hideous parents flared inside me, but I ignored it. I'd promised Lilian, and unlike *some* people, I respected Lilian and thought she could make her own decisions.

The queen pursed her lips a little. "He's in Urbis," she said, which I already knew.

"Looking for a cure to the blight?"

A tiny dimple appeared at the corner of her mouth. "Looking for a wig," she admitted. "I have to appear at Lilian's wedding. I can't do it wearing a scarf."

She laughed at the look on my face.

"A wig?" I said. "*That's* why he keeps disappearing?"

"He's talking to magicians too, of course," she said. "But yes, a lot of it's about the wig."

"You have servants for that kind of thing."

"Servants gossip," she said. "I can't risk it."

"Can't he find wigs in Floris?"

I realized the idiocy of the question as soon as I asked it. Wigs could be found in every kingdom, but none that would pass for Queen Rapunzel's famous locks. Outside of the queen and Lilian, I'd never seen hair that gleamed like sunlight or shifted like a waterfall of gold with their every move. The queen's hair was special; her wig would have to be, too.

"Never mind," I said. "Forget I asked."

"We've rejected human hair, horsehair, silk, enchanted cornsilk, Enchantia cotton strands, and hammered gold threads," she said. "Alder is now pursuing pegasus mane and elf-spun gold. Failing those, I'm going to have to find an absolutely *spectacular* scarf or risk wearing a witch glamour for the day."

She made a face, clearly not liking this last idea. I wondered whether her adopted mother had ever used glamours.

Footsteps sounded outside the door, along with Lilian's raised voice and the lower tones of the guard.

"I'd better go," I said.

The queen glanced at the door. "I can just add you

to my list of permitted guests," she said. "It seems you know everything anyway."

"No," I said, too quickly.

She looked startled, and I shook my head.

"It would be better that no one sees me coming and going," I said, coming up with the excuse as I said it. "If people know I've seen you, they'll ask questions."

"Just help me back to my room," Lilian said, much too loudly, from outside the door. "But let's walk up and down the corridor here for a few minutes first. I don't think it's actually sprained, and I don't want to trouble the court physician until I'm sure."

The queen raised an eyebrow at me. I smirked.

"She's a good accomplice," I said. It would take the guard at least ten minutes to get to Lilian's quarters and back--more if Lilian managed to stall him as long as I knew she'd attempt. "Is there anything else you can tell me? Anything that might help me stop this blight?"

"The blight is my fault," the queen said, lines appearing on her forehead again. "I'm responsible for fixing this. Just please, do what you can to get the greenhouses built quickly. You're the Head Gardener and the winner of the Spring Flower Festival," she added, forcing a smile. "If anyone can get the rest of the kingdom on board with this new way of doing things, it will be you."

Not when I get fired next week, I thought, but the queen didn't need to know about that. Not yet. She had enough on her plate, and I couldn't go into why Duke Remington hated me without going into his troubled relationship with Lilian.

"Thanks, Your Majesty," I said.

Impulsively, I leaned in and gave her a quick hug. She squeezed me back, the embrace as warm and loving as the rest of her.

"Thank you, Deon," she said. "I'm so glad we have you."

"Can I ask you a question?" I said. "Since we have a few minutes."

She pulled back, but we stayed sitting close together, and she kept her hand resting lightly on my forearm. She was so like a mother, even if she wasn't really mine.

"Of course, Deon," she said.

"How did I come to the palace?" I said. "I've been wondering lately. About me, about where I come from." I swallowed, debating on how much I should say. But I already knew too much about her. It only seemed right that she should know about me, too. "I think I have magic," I said. "Just a little. I think it's how I managed to keep the Gilded Lilies alive."

Her gray eyebrows shot up, and delight illuminated her face.

"Did you know my birth parents?" I asked before I could lose my nerve. "Do you think they were magicians, or something else, maybe? Elves?"

"I don't know." Her face tightened in concentration, and her gaze grew distant as if she were looking for memories in the space behind my head. "I don't think they ever told us," she said at last.

"They?"

"The people who brought you to the palace." She reached for my hand and held it, her skin warm against mine. "You were brought in the middle of the night, right at the end of Alder's and my wedding celebration. We had no idea what to do with a baby at first." She laughed a little. "Of course, Lilian arrived nine months later, so we figured it out pretty quickly. But those first few days, we just stared at you."

“Why did you keep me?” I said. “Why didn’t you send me to an orphanage?”

“I couldn’t,” she said wide-eyed. “Goodness, I wasn’t about to let you go. Complete strangers brought you to me--to us. It seemed cruel to send you back out into the world. You were so tiny, and trusting, and...” She trailed off, and finally shrugged with a little laugh. “I don’t know, I suppose you were cute. And Alder and I had already overcome so much. It seemed only right that we should share our good fortune with everyone we could, starting with you.”

“So, you kept me.”

“We didn’t adopt you.” She tilted her head a little. “I suppose we should have, but it never crossed our minds. You were such a surprise. We decided to raise you even so, and at first, you loved tagging along behind the housekeepers--they adored you--and then you and Lilian both decided you were going to become stablemasters when you grew up, and then you discovered the gardens. You showed an aptitude for it.”

“I remember that,” I said. “It felt like I’d finally figured out what I was supposed to do with my life.”

The queen burst into laughter and patted my hand. “Yes,” she said. “*Finally.* After years and years of struggle, maybe as many as five.”

I flushed, but I laughed, too. I had been pretty young.

“Stars, you were a joy to watch,” she said. “The way you took to the earth and toddled after Hedley like a loyal puppy. I knew from the beginning you’d be a great gardener.”

She glanced toward the window. Not much was visible from this angle besides sky, but I knew what the grounds looked like.

The queen did, too. Her smile disappeared.

"I wonder if maybe you're connected to all this," she said. "Somehow. You arrived just as my life was becoming beautiful. Perhaps your arrival was what gave us so many wonderful years."

I shook my head. "Floris was pretty before me."

"I'm afraid I've ruined it," she said. "I should have stayed in my tower. It would have kept Gothel from taking out her rage on everyone else."

I held the queen's hand tightly in mine.

"You're not to blame for this," I said firmly. "We're going to fix it. Somehow. Floris *will* be beautiful again."

Her eyes filled with a sudden rush of tears. She blinked, hard, fighting them back.

"I'll help you," I said. "This blight won't last forever."

It was the height of hubris, assuring her of something like that. I didn't know how to fix this problem. I'd tried, and every tiny success we'd had so far was thanks entirely to Hedley.

But I couldn't bear the grief and fear on her face. She was my queen; more than that, she was the closest thing to a mother I'd ever known.

The voices outside the door grew louder, culminating in Lilian saying, "Fine. Let's go back to my room, then."

"I'd better go," I said in a low voice. I met the queen's gaze. "Floris *will* be beautiful again," I said as if I could guarantee any such thing. "I promise."

14TH APRIL

"Deon," someone whispered.

I turned over on my unicorn manure mattress. The bags had taken my shape over time, creating a perfectly formed hollow that was good for sleeping but made it hard to sit up.

I sat anyway, though, because I knew that voice.

"Come on in," I called softly.

The door creaked open, and Lilian peeked in. The sky was still dark behind her.

"What time is it?"

"Too early," she said. "The maids aren't even up. Mama wants to see you. She sent her guard on some dumb errand, so you have a while."

I scrambled out of bed, rubbing sleep from my eyes. Lilian closed the door again to allow me privacy to get dressed, and then we slipped across the dark, empty grounds like shadows.

The queen was waiting for us in her chambers. She wore a tunic and slender trousers and was illuminated only by a few dim lamps from where she stood in front of a darkened window. Her hair was uncovered today, bound back in a tight gray braid that gave her a severe look. I narrowed my eyes to take her in better.

"Are you going somewhere?" I asked, keeping my voice down.

"No," she said. "But I have news that might interest you."

The queen looked to Lilian, who touched my arm lightly.

"I'll keep an eye outside the door," she said. The curiosity on her face was plain, and I nodded slightly at her, promising to tell her everything afterward.

Lilian closed the door quietly behind herself, leaving the queen and me alone in the deep gold darkness.

"I couldn't sleep last night," she said. "I kept thinking about what you said about killing Gothel."

I stepped toward her. "We don't have to go that way," I said. "You said--"

"I know what I said," she murmured. "I also know I'm letting my own feelings for her get in the way of what's best for the kingdom."

Her face hardened. It was the same expression Lilian wore when she talked about the duke; it was clear where Lilian had gotten her sense of duty and commitment to her people.

"I don't want to kill her if we can help it," she said. "That's not the Florian way, even aside from my feelings on the subject. I'll do what I must if it comes to that, but I'd like to talk to her first. She's not entirely evil.

She can be reasoned with."

I raised an eyebrow. This witch had damaged an entire kingdom to get back at her daughter if our suspicions were correct, and she'd done it as the result of an eighteen-year-old grudge to boot.

But the queen knew her better than I did. I trusted her judgment.

"I have informants all over the kingdom," she said. "They've kept me apprised of Gothel's movements over the years, as well as they could."

"Hedley said she lives in the forest," I blurted. "He said no one can find her."

"Hedley is not privy to *all* my secrets." Queen Rapunzel winked, so quickly, I wasn't sure I'd seen it at all. "I received a telegram early this morning. It seems Dame Gothel may be in Urbis. She was seen near the City Archives."

I furrowed my brow as the pieces connected quickly in my head.

"King Alder is in Urbis."

"Yes," she said. "And I need to find out if Gothel is there, via someone I can trust."

Her gaze bored into me, and I knew without being told what she was asking.

"I can go," I said. "I'll find him and tell him."

"I don't want you to find him." She glanced at the floor, then up again. "I want you to find *her.* Confirm my suspicions. Lilian's wedding is soon, and if Alder thinks he might be able to track down Gothel, I'm worried he'll go running after her and miss his daughter's big day." She widened her eyes as if we were both in on a secret. "I don't know if you've ever noticed, but Alder gets single-minded about things. I'd rather he not spoil Lilian's wedding by getting murdered before he gets the chance to walk her down the aisle."

I bit back a smile.

"Are you sure you'll be able to leave the gardens?" She clasped her hands together and examined my face as if she was suddenly worrying she might be inconveniencing one of her servants. She was so much like Lilian. And whatever Duchess Annemie thought of their considerate natures, I loved them both for it.

"There's very little for me to do in the gardens right now," I said.

"But the enchanted glass..."

"Reed can manage it," I said. "Hedley's got him working with some of the magicians in Tulis."

She frowned. "Hedley is still here?"

"He's as worried about the blight as the rest of us. He and Hyacinth decided to stay in town while he runs tests."

The queen's face fell a little. "That's kind of him. I feel terrible that he's not able to enjoy his retirement."

"Most of his retirement was about his garden," I said grimly. "There's nothing of that left."

She bit her lip and nodded. "I'll make sure Lilian talks to the gardening staff. We can put him back in charge and say you've gone to, I don't know, do some research."

"Tell them I'm visiting the library in Urbis," I said. "They have a good horticulture section, or so I've heard."

"I'm so grateful for you, Deon," the queen said. "I'd go myself, but..." She waved at her head as if that was the only thing preventing the queen of Floris from traipsing off to track down a witch.

"I'll find her," I said.

I was full of promises lately. At least I might be able to follow through on this one.

"I've written you a note with instructions," she said. "It tells you a bit about Gothel and what to do if you find her. Don't reach out to Alder until you've heard from me."

"I don't even know where he's staying," I said.

"The City View Hotel," she said at once. "Top floor. Password is *tulips.* It's all in the note."

She picked an envelope from the side table near the sofa. My name was written on it in the queen's graceful hand.

I accepted it from her. The heavy paper brushed against my fingers like the sturdy petals of a zinnia. She handed me a coin purse, too, made of thick blue canvas embroidered with tiny silver flowers.

"That should cover your expenses. Can you leave today?"

"I can leave this moment," I said. "Although I'd prefer to pack some clothes first."

A broad smile spread across the queen's face. "You've always been so ready to help," she said. "You've always been there for me, for us, for Lilian. I'm so proud of the man you've become."

My face turned red. I wasn't sure whether she could see it in the dim lamplight, but I felt the heat blooming in my cheeks.

"I'm just doing my job, Your Majesty."

"You have never settled for just doing your job," she said. "You've always gone above and beyond, and you've always been there for my family. You *are* my family." She took my hand. "I'm so sorry to be sending you into danger like this."

"I'd be hurt if you asked anyone else," I said with a shrug.

"I wish we'd adopted you that night you first showed

up," she said. "We should have, and I'm sorry we didn't understand that then. You're better than any son I could have imagined."

It was one of the kindest things anyone had said to me. Even so, I was glad they hadn't taken me in as an actual son. It would have been way too weird to have Lilian as a sister.

"You're my family, too," I said. "I'll find her. I promise."

She pulled me in and held me close. Her hair, gray and dull as it was, still smelled like lilacs and honey.

"Don't tell Lilian," she said. "Or do, because I know she'll pester you otherwise--but please try not to frighten her. She's getting married in a few days, and I want this week to be as normal and wonderful as it can be."

Again, I wanted to tell her everything--the way Duke Remington kept grabbing Lilian's arm like he could control her, their heated conversations, his threat to fire me.

But Lilian wanted to deal with him on her own. I had to trust her.

"I don't want her to worry, either," I said.

The queen stood on tiptoes kissed the top of my head. She'd done that often, back when I was still shorter than her and running around the palace with Lilian on my heels. The gesture still filled me with warmth.

"I'll handle this," I said. "And I'll be back before you know it."

Lilian followed me back out to my shed. The first hints of dawn were shimmering **on** the horizon, so we ducked inside. Lilian lit the lamp and held it up while I went through the clothes that now lived in a wooden crate at the foot of my manure pile.

"Don't you find spiders in your clothes?" she said.

I shrugged. "Sometimes."

She shuddered.

"They're usually just cellar spiders," I said. "Totally harmless."

"Still creepy."

"I wouldn't do this job if I didn't get along well enough with them." I laughed at the horrified look on her face. Lilian had a soft spot for most creatures, but arachnids had always been an exception.

I folded the clothes as best as I could and tucked them inside a carpetbag Lilian had brought from the palace. It was dark brown with a pattern of delicate golden vines and smelled of dust and cedar oil.

I told Lilian the bare bones of my conversation with her mother: that I was going to Urbis, that I was supposed to track down a witch the queen thought might be responsible for the blight, and that I would come home straight after without trying to engage with the witch or do anything else foolish. Lilian listened with her eyebrows furrowed.

"I wish I could come with you," she said at last. She frowned. "Wait, why is Papa not doing this?"

I grinned. "Apparently, your mother doesn't trust him to chase after the witch *and* make it to your wedding on time."

Lilian scoffed but didn't look surprised. "My parents are so overprotective of each other."

"I think it's kind of sweet."

"It is sweet," she said. "But they're ridiculous."

"I like it." I tucked my last shirt into the bag. "Lils, will you water my Gilded Lilies while I'm gone?"

Understanding passed across her face, and she

grinned. "You kept some."

"Of course, I did," I said. "I wasn't about to hand them all off to the Horticulture Council, and I'm not cutting them down for your wedding, either." I frowned, not liking how that had sounded. "Unless you want me to. You're welcome to them."

She placed a hand over mine and stood next to me, resting her golden head against my shoulder. "Keep them," she said. "I'll take good care of the lilies and everything else in your garden."

I grimaced. "There's nothing else left."

A scowl crossed her face. "You didn't cut everything down? Not for the wedding?"

"I had to," I said. "Duchess Annemie would have had my hide otherwise."

Lilian's soft lips hardened to a frown.

"It's all right," I said. "I want your big day to be beautiful. I might not be back from Urbis by then, so at least that way, you'll have a little of me with you."

"I don't want to marry him." She spoke in the same way children did when announcing *I don't want to eat my vegetables*, or *I'm not tired* and *I don't want to take a nap* as if she needed to register her protest but didn't have any hope of anything coming from it.

I wrapped my arm around her. "Are you going to be all right? He's not kind to you."

"He's not a fool, either," she said. "I'm still the princess, and the people love me."

"That doesn't mean he won't be a complete cocklebur in private." I pulled her close and buried my nose in her hair. "Has he ever hurt you, Lils?"

She was silent for a long moment. My heart clenched, dreading her answer.

"No," she said at last, sounding thoughtful. "He's

never touched me like that. It's not to say he won't, but I won't hesitate to get the guards involved if he tries."

"He already owns half the guards."

"And I own the other half. And if push comes to shove, my half will win--especially if I go to the press. If there's one thing Garritt is scared of, it's losing power. The press holds a lot of power in Floris."

"You don't have to tell me," I muttered.

Lilian giggled. "They were awful to you," she admitted. "But you don't need to sulk about it. Your lily is perfectly real, and everyone will know soon enough. And aren't you glad you live somewhere accusations of cheating are taken seriously? It sounds much better than the alternative."

"That's because they didn't accuse *you,*" I said, but I wasn't angry. She was right, as usual.

I kissed the top of her head, and she let out a soft little sigh that made my heart twist. Was this the last time I'd be able to kiss her--the last time I'd be able to hold her in my arms?

I turned her around to face me, and she laced her arms around my neck and pressed herself against me. She smelled sweet, like Floris should have, and the softness of her cheek against mine reminded me of how petals had felt, back when the world was all right.

"Be safe," Lilian said. "Don't do anything stupid."

"I'll do my best."

I kissed the top of her head again.

~

I'd assumed I'd be able to board the last train out of Tulis without incident.

But the first journalist staking out the palace

who'd attached himself to me had been joined by two others, and the three of them kept hovering and asking questions and trying to take photographs with small hand-held cameras.

"Is it always like this?" Hedley muttered, hiking his satchel further up onto his shoulder.

He'd volunteered to come with me the moment I'd told him what the queen had asked. I hadn't even had to float the idea: He had just given me a nod, told me he'd need a few minutes to gather his things and inform Hyacinth, and he'd be ready to go.

"I haven't left the palace grounds since the festival." I glanced at one of the journalists, who was trying to write on a notepad while he kept pace with us.

Hedley edged toward me as he walked and ducked his head so he could talk without being overheard. "Do they spend all their time lurking outside the palace? You'd think they'd have something better to do."

I thought back to Lilian. "At least we have a free and open press," I said. "That's good, right?"

He grunted, not quite agreeing.

We reached the Tulis Central Station, a beautiful stone building with sparkling domes and tall windows that revealed a glimpse of the steam engines within. I counted out the coins the queen had given me and quietly purchased a pair of tickets from a tired-looking woman sitting in a booth behind a brass grille. I gave one to Hedley.

"Where are you going?" one of the journalists asked brightly.

I ignored him and shielded the tickets from his curious gaze.

We traipsed into the station, an odd crowd of me, Hedley, and the three hangers-on we were clearly trying to avoid. The security guard gave the reporters a curious look, but as they weren't technically breaking any rules, he didn't seem inclined to do anything about them.

I walked briskly across the marble floors, which were set in the patterns of giant flowers. Billows of silvery steam poured from the train, and I managed to board it in record time, Hedley following close behind. The reporters boarded the train right after us.

"I didn't see you buy any tickets," I said to the nearest one.

He shrugged and gave me a cheeky grin. "Couldn't. Don't know where you're headed."

"Shame." I opened the sliding door under the number *11* and held the door for Hedley. The reporter made as if he was going to follow Hedley in, but I blocked him. "This is a private compartment."

"Are you going to the coast?" another reporter asked.

"Or to Goldenrod, perhaps?" the third suggested. "Are you returning home, Mr. Hedley? Where is your wife?"

Hedley's face twisted with contempt. "You leave my wife out of it."

Down at the other end of the carriage, the conductor appeared and opened the first compartment door to check tickets.

I waved at him. "Sir?" I said loudly. "Sir? These gentlemen don't have tickets. They're trying to enter my private compartment. I paid for this space, sir."

One of the reporters, the youngest one, seemed inclined to try to argue his way out of it, but the others knew better.

"Fine, fine, we're leaving," one said, holding up his hands.

The two of them left, and the youngest, after giving the hard-faced conductor a moment of consideration, decided he didn't want to take his chances. I watched them go.

The conductor turned to me without a smile. "Tickets?"

"Right here."

Eventually, Hedley and I ended up settled in our compartment, each of us with a long bench to ourselves. There was something to be said for letting the palace foot the bill.

I leaned against the window, kicked off my shoes, and stretched my legs out on the bench. Hedley leaned back and rested his hands on his belly.

"So," he said. "We're after the witch, are we?"

"After her location," I said. "Nothing more."

"Did Her Majesty tell you where in the seedy underbelly of Urbis we should begin our search?"

A gust of steam billowed by my window. The train inched forward.

"Not the seedy underbelly at all, it turns out," I said. "The witch was spotted at the city's Central Archives."

Hedley raised one of his thick eyebrows. "Bold of her."

"She can afford to be bold if she's as powerful as the queen seems to think."

Hedley gazed out the window. The train picked up speed, and the station slipped away as the train dove headfirst into the night. The lantern light from our compartment escaped the window and shimmered on the moving ground beside the tracks.

I shifted, trying to angle my back more comfortably toward the corner. "You still don't think she's causing the blight."

"I don't know." He drummed his fingers on his belly. "The Gothel I heard of wasn't strong enough to create a problem like this. Not by herself."

I shrugged. "The queen must know things we don't."

"She must," he murmured.

I followed his gaze to the city outside the window. The storefronts were closed, and the pubs were open, spilling their light and noise out onto the walkways. I caught a glimpse of a large signboard outside a closed shop bearing the advertisement *Royal Wedding Commemorative Tea Set, Special Price Tomorrow Only!*

"The Central Archives aren't a bad place to start, regardless," Hedley said, oblivious to the painful reminder we'd just passed. "Whether or not we track down the witch, I'd like to search for any information on plant curses. Maybe we can learn something about this blight yet."

"Maybe," I said. "It can't hurt to try."

We passed another sign: *Royal Wedding Party Apparel Here!* And then another, *Celebrate the Royal Wedding with our Fine Collection of Thornton Rose Jewelry!*

The train rattled over the tracks, and the lantern hanging above our heads rocked with the gentle movement. After a while, Hedley began to nod, and then to snore.

It would be several hours before the train stopped, and we transferred to the Urbis Express. We could have caught it directly from Tulis, of course, but then the reporters and anyone else watching would have known exactly where we were headed. At least this way, we had privacy and time to rest.

So I waited for sleep to take me as images of Lilian being married to that brute filled my head.

And waited.
And waited.

GOD OF LOYALTY

16TH APRIL

Back in Floris, wedding preparations were in full swing. Maids and footmen scurried from wagons to the palace's front doors, bearing armloads of silk or tree branches draped with tiny sparkling fairy lights. I wasn't allowed in to see for myself, but the maids I'd managed to talk to had said the entrance hall and all the corridors leading to the throne room and ballroom were being hung with silk garlands, and well-rationed flowers from my garden already stood in crystal vases at intervals.

The wedding was going to be beautiful. I wished I could have said the same about the marriage.

I dodged behind the gray branches of a dead rose bush to avoid a cluster of photographers who were being led into the palace by a guide. They were getting a sneak peek at the wedding decorations in advance of the big day, which put them one step ahead of me. I held my breath as they passed, then, when no one noticed me, let it out again.

I wasn't ready to make another statement to the press, not until the Festival judges had ruled on my lily.

On either side, gardeners and apprentices raked the bare dirt of former flowerbeds and coated the gray grass with green paint, sprayed from clever little Forge contraptions that distributed the coloring in an even coat across the blades. Nearer the driveway, apprentices and assistant florists arranged the rocks that had been painted with flowers.

It wasn't an unattractive scene, on the whole. But it wasn't as elegant as a princess's wedding should have been, and it wasn't very Florian.

Still, all we could do was our best. I knew Lilian wouldn't blame anyone if it didn't look quite right in the end.

"Mr. Gilding."

I started, jerked out of my reverie, and was surprised to see Jonquil standing a few feet away, his hands resting behind his back. He didn't usually call me *Mr. Gilding,* not when *Deon* or a sarcastic *sir* would do. But his face didn't bear any of his usual contempt.

My stomach turned over. "What is it?"

He shifted from foot to foot. I'd never seen Jonquil looking nervous before, and he'd certainly never seemed like that around me.

"The blight isn't improving," he said.

I waited for the accusation that was sure to follow, but he fell silent.

Finally, I nodded. He shifted again and held an

envelope out to me.

I took it and raised an eyebrow when I saw my name on the front.

"What's this?"

"It's my letter," he said. "Of resignation."

I jerked my head up to stare at him. He wasn't joking. It wasn't a threat, either. If anything, he looked sad.

"I've been offered a position in Draconis," he said. "I start in a couple of weeks. It's a good opportunity. And with things the way they are here..."

He trailed off. He didn't need to explain.

"It's a chance to keep working," I said. "That's not something you're going to get in Floris, not anytime soon."

"I hope you'll convey to the king and queen that this isn't any reflection on the palace," he said. "I know Their Majesties are doing their best."

I allowed myself a slight smile. "I'll bet you'll be happy to get away from me, though, right?"

He didn't deny it, but, with uncharacteristic graciousness, he didn't agree outright, either.

"We could use your help setting the kingdom up with enchanted glass," I said. "But I suppose you've thought about that."

"I considered it. At the pace we're going, it'll be months before I have enough to do. In Draconis, there's a chance for advancement."

I couldn't blame him, not in the slightest. I'd played with the idea of escaping, too.

"It sounds like you have the job in the bag," I said. "But I'll be happy to write you a reference if you end up needing one."

His eyebrows went up. He hesitated, then said, awkwardly, "I didn't think you'd, uh..."

I didn't have to offer him anything. He'd been a thorn in my side ever since I'd been promoted, and I couldn't honestly recommend him as a cheerful addition to any team.

But he was a talented gardener, and hurting his chances of finding something better in the future sounded like something Duke Remington would have done.

And I was no Duke Remington.

"You were good enough to get a job at the palace," I said. "I'd hate to see those skills go to waste."

He frowned, trying to make sense of me. Confusing him like this was almost more entertaining than firing him on the spot would have been.

I held out a hand. "I'll pass your regrets on to Their Majesties. I hope it works out for you."

His handshake was firm, and while I couldn't truthfully say I'd be sad to see the back of him, it was a gift to end on a decent note.

"Do me a favor?" I said.

He put his hands behind his back again and nodded.

I grinned. "Be a little nicer to your next boss."

I watched him walk back across the gloomy grounds--I couldn't rightfully call them *gardens* anymore--and wondered how long it would be until the next notice came my way. A few of the apprentices wouldn't last much longer. Chervil would drag his feet and complain a bit, but then he'd likely go, too. I'd try to talk Olive into finding a position abroad if she didn't end up pursuing one on her own; she was too young and talented to remain a gardener in a kingdom with no flowers.

And the rest of them--I'd figure that out as I went. There was no reason to keep an army of gardeners at the palace anymore. Once we figured out our greenhouse situation, perhaps some of them would be willing to go out into the country and teach the people in small cities and villages how to grow their own food under glass.

~

I made my way to the biggest of our greenhouses. Reed was inside, as I'd known he would be, but he wasn't alone. Two figures were with him, and it took me a moment to place their elegant figures.

"Mistress Hemlock," I said, walking forward. "Master Cypress."

Hemlock greeted me only with a sharp glance. Cypress, though, smiled and held out a hand. I shook it, and his skin was as smooth and cool as a river stone.

"What are you doing here?"

"Magic," Cypress said. "Or, at least, that is our intention."

"We *are* performing magic," Hemlock said. "The question is whether it's going to do any good."

Hemlock cupped her hands on the outside of one of the bell jars and seemed to fall into deep concentration. A tiny shard of light flashed in the glass, and she let go.

"Is that how you enchant them?"

"Stars, no," Hemlock said, waving a hand. "That has to be done in concert with a glassmaker. This is just an extra boost to encourage the plants to be productive. If this works, we'll use it on the greenhouses, too."

She nodded at Reed, who took the bell jar and placed it over a small terra cotta pot that held a couple of seedlings. Their tender green stalks looked so delicate. They were young and fragile, and it seemed impossible that they could survive against the onslaught of the blight.

I watched them work for a while. The process seemed simple, but I couldn't imagine what they were doing. Reaching into the core of a plant and feeling for its life energy made sense in an intuitive way I couldn't quite pin down. But reaching into glass--that seemed different. I bit my tongue and resisted offering to help. I didn't have those kinds of abilities, and they didn't need to be teaching magic to a child. And anyway, Reed still didn't know I *had* magic, and this didn't seem like the time for a big reveal.

So I stood, useless.

I had been useless a lot lately. Even going to Urbis, exhausting as the quick trip had been, hadn't actually done any *good.* Everything I did, from raking dead flowerbeds to combing through an already-pilfered archive, felt like a lot of work for very little result.

Even so, the queen deserved to know what had happened.

I waved at Reed to excuse myself in silence. Hemlock and Cypress, intent over their jars, didn't notice me leave.

It was easy enough to slip inside the palace. All I had to do was fall into step with a bunch of delivery men, and use their bodies as a shield until I was through the entrance hall.

Getting up to the queen's rooms, on the other hand, required a bit more stealth. I tried sneaking through the usually-quiet servants' passages, but they were crowded today with maids rushing from the laundry to guest chambers with arms full of fresh bedding. I pressed myself to the wall and waited for a group of them to pass before Daisy, one of the senior housemaids, caught me lurking.

"You," she said loudly, pointing at me over a bulky

tulip-embroidered comforter. "Out."

"I'm just trying to get upstairs."

"It'll be our hides if the duke finds out you were here," she said in a low voice. "He was very clear that anyone who spots you inside is supposed to report you."

"You wouldn't turn me in."

"Of course not," she said with a dismissive wave. "But how many other people do you think have seen you already? I can tell you, if Violet or Primrose or any of the other girls notice you're here, Duke Remington will be at your elbow before you can say sticks and stones." She made a face. "Suckups will get us all in hot water. Scram."

She wasn't wrong about the other maids or the duke, but Daisy and I had always gotten along. "I thought we were friends," I tried.

She rolled her eyes. "If you're my friend, you'll get out of here before someone spots us talking. I'm already on Duchess Annemie's bad side. I don't need the duke's attention on me, too."

I sighed. I was going to be in trouble with the duke no matter how I sliced things. It wasn't fair to take anyone else down with me.

"Fine, I'm going."

She gave me a crisp, approving nod and rushed down the corridor. I was nowhere near the queen's quarters, and how did I think I was going to get inside without help, anyway? Lilian wouldn't be there to distract the guard this time, and with the wedding so close, there was no way to get her attention.

Just like Urbis, I'd wasted time and effort for nothing. I sighed and made my way briskly back downstairs and outside where I belonged.

~

I couldn't see the queen. I couldn't enchant glass jars, or magic away the blight, or track down an evil witch, or even attend to the ordinary work of the gardens.

But there was one thing I could do.

Now that the blight had ruined everything that had once been beautiful on the palace grounds, the stone walls of my private garden hulked like a giant child's block dropped unceremoniously in the middle of a lawn. The ivy that had once grown up the outer walls was dead, with only a few gray stems and soggy leaves remaining, and the stone underneath was old and worn and covered in blight-spoiled moss. The inside was no better. Barren flowerbeds stared at me when I opened the heavy wooden door, each one an ugly gash in the earth's skin. Raised beds sat empty, their architecture dull and uninspiring without their usual cloaks of greenery. With my flowers gone, the sweet smell that had always filled the garden had been replaced by the poisonous perfume of decay that pervaded the rest of the palace grounds.

This garden had once been my heart. Now, it was empty and broken.

"Exactly like my heart's going to be after the wedding," I muttered to a sparrow sitting on the top wall of the garden. The bird was thinner than it should have been, emaciated as a result of the blight. "Seems a little right on the nose, don't you think?"

I reached into my pocket for a bit of leftover scone from breakfast and scattered the crumbs on the ground, hoping the bird would hop down for an easy meal. It only fluttered away, startled.

It would come back. I had to hope so, anyway.

What would the kingdom look like when all the birds were gone? We wouldn't be able to afford to feed them all, not when everything was being grown under glass.

On the far side of the garden, my few remaining Gilded Lilies shone with their enchanting golden light. It was hard to believe I'd created something so beautiful. Whatever magic lived in this garden must have helped me. I moved toward the lilies, each step heavy with the risk that if I got just a little closer, I'd catch sight of a hint of gray on a petal or an unwelcome droop of a leaf.

But they were just as healthy and beautiful as ever. Their light had stayed warm, their shimmer, strong. They were everything I had hoped for, and it was time to dig them up.

I took tools from my small shed and got to work. The feel of the earth under my fingers soothed me, and the scent of the rich soil reminded me of better days. One of Lilian's and my tutors had once told us that smell and memory were linked, and that was why flower scents were so highly prized in Floris. A whiff of lavender could remind one of calm; a note of gardenia could trigger memories of a loved one. And dirt--rich, dark, fertile dirt--took me back to my earliest memories, of filth under my nails and Lilian grinning at me. We couldn't have been more than four or five the day we'd gotten into Hedley's petunia beds. He'd just spread compost all across the beds, and we'd been unable to resist the light, fluffy texture and the way it squished and crumbled between our fingers.

We'd never gotten in as much trouble as we should have. Looking back, I wasn't sure if it was because Lilian was a princess and exempt from the usual punishments or just because Hedley was kind and loved me.

I'd been blessed here in Floris, with love and family, the likes of which no orphan foundling should have been able to expect.

It would be over soon, but I couldn't leave without making sure my lilies were safe with their rightful owners. I repotted a few for the queen and a few for Lilian, then reserved the rest for myself. Wherever I went after this, whether to somewhere in Tulis or another kingdom entirely, I'd have to be able to keep working to make the Gilded Lily into a stable hybrid. My work would be the only thread I'd be able to carry from my old life to the new one. I doubted Duke Remington would allow me to write to Lilian once they were married. Seeing her would be out of the question. My lilies--and whatever waves I might be able to make in the press or in horticulture journals--might be the only connection I would have with Lilian going forward.

Stinging nettles, I was going to start crying like a child if I kept thinking like this. I blinked back the prickling behind my eyes and took a few steadying breaths.

The future was coming for me, whether I was ready for it or not. The best thing I could do now was to use these lilies to get inside the palace. I'd give them to the queen and the princess.

I'd say goodbye.

~

The silence of the garden was absolute, aside from the sound of my spade scooping soil into the pots to stabilize the lily roots. So when the door creaked suddenly open, I jumped and spun around.

"Sticks and stone, Reed," I exclaimed, before realizing that it wasn't Reed.

My stomach dropped, and I became acutely aware of the lilies sparkling behind me.

"I thought my mother told you to dig up all your flowers for the wedding," Duke Remington said. His smile was friendly, which only made his words the more chilling.

I clutched my spade. The idea of using its heavy wooden handle against the side of his head flashed across my mind. I dismissed the image as soon as it arrived, though the temptation that accompanied it couldn't be denied.

"Your Grace." I bowed. "Yes, she did." I didn't have to scramble far to find the lie. "The Gilded Lilies are particularly delicate, so I'm taking them to the florist last."

"Not cutting them, I see." He strode casually forward and spoke like we were having a normal little Florian chat about gardening.

"I haven't experimented with using them as cut flowers. Sir," I hastily added. "I don't know how well they'd hold up. I trust the florists will be able to conceal the pots or paint them to match the wedding decorations."

He leaned forward and touched one of the petals. His finger was delicate, and I felt a moment of surprise that he was capable of such gentleness.

But, of course, he was. It was all I'd seen when he'd first arrived.

Even if his persona at the beginning had all been an act, I hoped he'd revert to it soon, if only for Lilian's sake.

"They are real," he said. "I suppose you've heard. The Festival judges are almost ready to release their statement. I signed it this morning."

I scrutinized his face for hints of what he meant, and his smile broadened. I would have mistaken him for a friend if I'd been watching this moment from the outside.

"I was happy to add my approval to the statement," he said. "After all, it was very clear, after closer scrutiny, that the flower is real, and any similarity to other breeds was ruled coincidental."

I stiffened. "And the accusations of bribery?"

"Flatly denied, with no evidence to support them," he said. "The gossips who started that rumor must have been mistaken."

I ground my teeth and fought to keep my face neutral.

"That's good news, sir," I said.

"It should help you find a new position quite easily."

He stepped toward me. It was a difference of an inch, but it was enough to raise the hairs on the back of my neck. I took a deep breath and resisted the urge to step away.

I couldn't let him win, even in this little way.

"You're still getting fired," he said, voice still pleasant. "In fact, consider this your pre-emptive notice. In two days, Lilian and I will be married. We'll leave on our honeymoon, and you'll be gone by the time we get back. We won't hear from you again."

I stood up straighter. My fingers were so tight on my spade handle, it was a wonder they still had any feeling.

"If I accept a job at the Horticulture Offices?"

"You'll find a way to be absent from meetings with the royal family," he said. "I suppose we'll end up at social functions together now and then, should you end up in yet another high position you haven't really earned. If that happens, I trust that you'll find a way to keep your distance."

Anger boiled under my skin, heating my blood and sending a flush to my face.

"Keep my distance from you, sir?" I said. "Or your wife?"

He didn't twitch. He didn't flinch. If anything, his chilling, friendly calm only deepened.

"After the wedding, you will never speak to Lilian again," he said. "If you do, your reputation will be the least of your worries."

He let the threat hang in the air for a moment, then he glanced over the lilies with that same smile still playing over his lips.

"The lilies will be a beautiful addition to the ceremony," he said. "Thank you for creating them."

He cast his eye across the flowers, and one corner of his mouth rose.

"In fact, it seems you're about finished here," he said. "There's no need for you to have to lug these all the way up to the palace. I'll deliver them for you."

"They're very fragile. I'd rather--"

"I insist." His smile widened, showing his teeth in a snarl like a wolf's. "It's the least I can do."

Panic rose up in my stomach, churning and heaving like I'd eaten something rotten.

"There are too many flowers for one person to carry," I blurted.

"Good thing you have so many apprentices," he said.

"I can carry--"

"No," he said. "You can't. Wait here while I fetch help."

He stopped at the garden door and looked back to where I stood, frozen, with my heart beating like a drum in my ears.

"You and those lilies had better be here when I get

back," he said, voice as warm as I'd ever heard it. "Or else you'll come to know the true meaning of the word *regret*. Do we understand each other?"

I swallowed. "Yes," I said.

His eyes narrowed, and I straightened my shoulders and gave him a bow that felt as if it would crack me in two.

"Yes, Your Grace."

17TH APRIL

I was peering over Cypress's shoulder in our largest greenhouse the next morning when the door opened. I glanced up, and my heart skipped a beat.

Lilian was there, wearing a simple riding tunic and fitted trousers, with her golden hair pulled back with a green ribbon. She slipped inside the greenhouse, bringing the sunshine with her.

I put a finger to my lips, warning her not to disturb the magician's concentration, and she came to stand beside me in silence. A light flared within the bell jar, and Cypress let out a deep breath and relaxed.

"What are you doing?" she said, eyes alight with interest.

I couldn't answer. Seeing her here, after I'd lost the

opportunity to bring her one of my lilies yesterday, was enough to make my heart feel like it had grown three sizes and was threatening to burst from my chest.

She listened to Cypress explain the process with interest. I knew I should be listening. I'd come to the greenhouse this morning specifically to learn what I could of his magic, partly to improve my own fledgling abilities and partly to take my mind off how quickly tomorrow's wedding was approaching. But I couldn't focus on anything he said, not with the love of my life standing so close to me with the scent of magnolia rising from her hair. Her forehead glistened with a slight sheen of sweat, a familiar sight that told me she'd been working her horse hard this morning.

"So this doesn't stop the blight?" she said after Cypress had finished. She stood on tiptoes to see better and rested her hand on my shoulder for balance. My whole body tingled at her touch. "But it increases yield?"

"Exactly, Your Highness."

She graced him with one of her dazzling smiles. "That's so clever! I love that you're attacking this problem from multiple angles. The glass was a wonderful breakthrough, but I've been concerned about yield."

"We hope this will help," Cypress said. "We're still testing."

"Let me know if you need anything from the palace," Lilian said. "I'd like to help with this as much as I can."

Cypress smiled at her, clearly charmed by her interest. "Perhaps we can discuss some ideas after your wedding, Your Highness," he said.

My heart twisted.

But that was selfish. I should be glad that I was leaving this effort in the capable hands of my gardeners and the magicians, and glad that the princess of the realm felt such a deep concern for their work. I should be grateful. I should be able to think beyond the panic and grief that clutched at me with icy fingers.

Lilian beamed up at me, and a little of the ice melted.

"I'd love that," she said, her eyes still fixed on me. "For now, though, I was wondering if I could have a moment, Mr. Gilding?"

My insides went to war, torn between the promise of conversation with her and the agony of having her refer to me so formally.

I bowed, keeping up the pretense. "Of course, Your Highness."

She led me from the greenhouse, and it wasn't until we were safely ensconced behind a potting shed that she spun around and took my hand.

"He's gone," she said.

I knew who she meant without asking, but it took my mind a second to catch up with her words.

"Gone?" Hope rose up in me, champagne bubbles that fizzed through my veins and set my heart to racing. "What do you mean?"

"Not for good," she said quickly. She set a hand on my arm, quelling my sudden irrational optimism. "He'll be back late tonight. But today--we have today."

Our gazes met, and I didn't need her to explain more. I pulled her close and kissed her forehead--gently, chastely, with a restraint I didn't really feel.

"What about the guards?"

"My ladies-in-waiting distracted them." Her eyes twinkled. "One of them lit a compost pile on fire at the far end of the grounds, and the others are busy making trouble disguised as wedding preparation. Hedley's got a few of them busy investigating a couple of shattered bell jars, too. He's blaming them on what I believe he's calling 'young hoodlums' and making a very un-Hedley-like fuss."

I stared down at her. "How long have you been planning this?"

"Only since this morning," she said. "When Garritt told me he had to leave town on some secret business or other." She wrinkled her nose. "Apparently, it was *men's work,* and I didn't need to bother my head about it." The disgust on her face didn't last long; it was replaced in a moment with the tell-tale gleam of mischief. "My ladies all came together rather splendidly. Which means we have a day together. One day."

"And then I have to leave."

She hardened her jaw. "Only for a time. I'll get you back somehow. I'm not giving up."

"You've got bigger things to worry about." I rubbed her back lightly as I spoke. Her tunic was perfectly tailored, the gentle contours of her shoulder blades giving way to the small of her back under the fine green wool. I could have spent forever exploring those curves. "You've got a whole kingdom in trouble."

"And how am I supposed to face that without you?" she said. "You're my best friend. We can't be together, not as we'd like. But we can be friends."

I brushed a loose strand of hair behind her ear. "I don't want to be your friend, Lils."

"Yes, you do."

She smiled up at me, but not before I saw the flash of pain in her eyes. I could have kicked myself; I wasn't the only one about to face enormous loss. I should be taking the burden from her, not making it heavier.

I stood up straighter and forced a smile. "You're right," I said. "You know what? We are friends. Always will be. So let's take today and make some memories."

"You read my mind." She put her hands on her hips and grinned up at me. "Race you to the stables."

Twenty minutes later, we were flying across the barren palace grounds. Lilian's horse soared over a line of decayed, cut-down lilac bushes, and mine carefully skirted around them. Lilian brought her mount to a stop and looked over at me, laughing.

"What, too high for you?"

I shook my head. "I thought you already went riding once this morning. Your poor horse."

"That was just to look busy while Garritt was leaving," she said. "This is a different horse. And this round is just for fun."

I was nowhere near as comfortable in the saddle as Lilian, but I would have spent all day trotting alongside her if it meant I got to enjoy her expression of total focus and joy every time her horse soared over some obstacle. She leaned forward and stroked her mount's neck, and it leaned into the affection.

There was very little cover in the now-empty gardens. That made the grounds wonderful for riding--Lilian never would have galloped her horse over the lawns and flowerbeds when they'd been in their full glory--but terrible for hiding. I saw a figure in the distance and tensed, waiting to be caught with the princess by one of the duke's guards or informants.

The figure waved, though, and I realized it was Hedley. Lilian nodded at me, and we trotted toward him. He shielded his eyes from the sun and looked up at us as we came to a stop.

"You might want to clear out of this area." His voice was serious, but the corners of his eyes creased in a hidden smile. "The guards are about to be alerted to another broken bell jar. There might be theft afoot."

Lilian laughed, and I narrowed my eyes at him.

"You're not *actually* destroying jars, are you?" I asked. "We need those to grow food."

"They are bell jars," he said, eyes still twinkling. "But they are not enchanted. Cypress has agreed to swear up and down that they have magic residue, though."

I tilted my head. "Cypress is in on this, too?"

"You have more friends than you think, Deon," he said. "Besides, every inhabitant of this kingdom would do anything for the princess."

"You're going to make me blush." Lilian held out a hand, and Hedley took it. She squeezed, giving him one of those grateful smiles that always made my stomach do backflips.

Hedley patted her hand. "You'd best make yourselves scarce. Your picnic has already been delivered."

I raised an eyebrow, but it was clear neither of them was going to let me in on the plan. And that was just fine. I was ready to follow Lilian anywhere.

Still, some idle part of me wondered how Hedley could be so happy. A few stolen hours or not, I was still about to lose her, and the kingdom was about to fall under the clutches of the unfortunately wealthy Duke of Thornton. He dreaded that moment almost as much as I did, but his face held no concern.

And perhaps that was for the best. I had one day with Lilian. I shouldn't waste it fearing for tomorrow.

Lilian gave Hedley one last dazzling smile and galloped off toward the edge of the grounds. I clicked my tongue at my horse, and it followed, turning the gray earth to a blur underfoot.

This edge of the palace grounds was bordered by a high, stone wall that separated the landscaped grounds from the wild forest beyond. Some king many generations ago had signed a decree marking this area as protected hunting land, but King Alder didn't venture here often. Hunters from Tulis came here sometimes, and it was rumored that a few solitary witches lived and practiced their earthy craft deep within the protection of the trees, but the area was large enough that it was easy to get lost and rare to run into anyone else.

It was clear the moment we passed out of a small gate in the wall that this was why Lilian had chosen it. She glanced over her shoulder at me, her blue eyes darker under the dappled shade of the gray branches overhead. I urged my horse forward.

I followed Lilian down a meandering deer trail that wound between undergrowth and heavy, ancient trees. The forest was strangely beautiful, even stricken by the blight. The scent of decay was thick here, and the carpet of fallen leaves and pine needles seemed to squish under our horses' feet. But the trees around us hadn't given in to the blight, not completely. Most of their leaves were gray, but the ancient trunks seemed to be putting up a good fight. The bark of the oldest trees was still rich brown, and some of them persisted in putting out tiny green buds as if to spite the disease all around. Those tender leaves would die soon enough, but their resistance warmed me.

The trees would keep fighting. We would, too.

We rode in silence. Birds called overhead, their songs more sparse than they had once been but still there. Lilian seemed to know exactly where she was going, and after a while, I caught the sound of a brook bubbling alongside us. The thick forest opened a little to reveal a beautiful little pond, ringed with pale purple mushrooms that had somehow retained their color. A picnic basket sat atop a flat boulder, holding down a picnic blanket the same warm green of healthy moss.

We stopped our horses, and Lilian looked over at me.

"What do you think?"

I blinked, waiting for the purple of the mushrooms to fade. The color stayed vibrant. "They're alive."

"Interesting, isn't it? I had to show you."

She slid from her horse and tethered it to a tree. I did the same, and the horses began nosing through the underbrush, looking for anything still alive that they could eat.

I bent to examine the fungi. They had the same ruffled appearance of oyster mushrooms, interspersed with tiny purple toadstool-like caps that held a faint crystalline shimmer.

"These are amethyst mushrooms, aren't they?" I knelt to get a closer look. My knees sank into the soft ground, staining my trousers with mud and bits of blighted moss. "I'd heard they grow here, but I've never seen them before."

"One of my ladies found them a few days ago." Lilian crouched next to me.

I glanced up at her. "Do your ladies often wander deep into the woods?"

She bit her lip. "A gentleman might have been involved."

I grinned. "Scandalous."

"But aren't they incredible? The blight hasn't touched them. I thought you might be able to learn something from them that could help your efforts. Do you think we could, I don't know, combine them with other mushrooms? Or grow them as a food source? Are they edible? I don't even know. They're so rare."

"They're rare but magical." I glanced over at her.

"Can I try something?"

Her gaze sharpened with curiosity. "Of course."

"I've been practicing my magic," I said in a low voice. Even though we were alone, it still felt like something I should keep quiet. These abilities I had were special; I didn't want anyone else to find out about them before I was ready.

Lilian's eyes widened in interest. She leapt up and grabbed the picnic blanket, then nodded at me to move. She folded it in half and set it down next to the mushrooms, giving us a comfortable surface to sit on.

I glanced at my muddy knees. "I probably should have thought of that, huh?"

She shrugged. "I like you covered in mud," she said. "You always seem your happiest when you're a complete mess."

"Thanks," I said. "Thanks a lot."

She giggled and sat down, then patted the blanket next to her.

I sat cross-legged. The mushrooms shimmered, their crystalline skin inviting me in for a closer look.

I leaned in toward the fungi, sensing in the air for any hint of magic that might invite me deeper.

"Cross your fingers," I said. "Let's see what we can learn."

Lilian sat in still silence while I stretched my attention into the mushrooms. The dappled sunshine frolicked across their thin, sparkling skins, and the magic that radiated from them like a reflection was so strong I found it in an instant.

I took a deep, calming breath and tried to tune in to the magic. I let my attention play against its frequency, slipping around the mushrooms' particular strain of magic, much like I might have let my voice slip up and down a scale in an effort to match a musical note. The energy was vibrant and easy to fall into, and I slid down, through the shimmering heat of the magic, until my attention landed on the fungi's glittering surface.

And then it stopped.

I tried to reach deep within the plant and find the life at its core, but I couldn't. I held my hands out around the mushrooms in an effort to guide my mind, but no matter where I searched, and no matter how deeply I breathed, I couldn't find an opening.

Not even the mushrooms' gills would let me in. That sparkling purple skin was a shield--one so strong my energy couldn't begin to penetrate it. I narrowed my eyes and focused, trying to force my way through, but whatever abilities I had were nothing against that delicate-looking barrier.

I leaned forward, imagining my attention as a knife that could break through that tender skin, but it was no use. The knifepoint only slipped sideways, and the mushrooms stood, totally tranquil and impossible to break.

Lilian put a hand on my arm. I jumped. My attention snapped back from the microscopic world of the mushrooms and back to the graying forest. My head throbbed, and I blinked, trying to stop the sudden swaying of the earth underneath me.

"Sorry," Lilian said, drawing back her hand as if she'd been burned. "So sorry. I pulled you out, didn't I?"

I closed my eyes and let out a breath. Slowly, the world steadied.

"It's all right." I stared at the mushrooms twinkling innocently before us. "I wasn't getting anywhere."

"What did you see?" she said. "You were a million

miles away."

"I..."

A warm breeze drifted through the clearing, rippling the glassy surface of the pond. The mushrooms' reflections undulated lazily, and I stared at the movement. I could make a tulip droop or rise or spin its head around, but I hadn't been able to make the mushrooms so much as budge.

I looked at Lilian, who was watching me with concern.

"Nothing," I said. "I saw absolutely nothing."

Her forehead wrinkled. "What do you mean, *nothing?*"

"I mean, I couldn't get in. I couldn't get close to them." Gently, feeling as if lightning might strike if I touched one of their purple caps, I ran a finger across the top of a mushroom. Nothing happened. It was smooth and soft.

Ordinary.

And anything but.

"We need to get some of these back to Hemlock and Cypress," I said. "Or maybe we should bring them here. Is it the mushrooms or the clearing?"

I looked around wildly, the possibilities suddenly spinning through my head so quickly I couldn't keep up. Lilian put her hand back on my arm, but that wasn't enough to steady me.

"It's the mushrooms," I said after a moment. "It has to be the mushrooms. The rest of the clearing is all gray. But we should take some of the soil, too. Mycelia can cover vast distances. We need to be sure whatever's happening isn't just at the surface."

"But *what's* happening?" Lilian said.

I stared at her, my heart fluttering wildly. "They're immune to the blight," I said. "Or... not immune, I can't say that, but..." I gestured at the ruffled fungus closest to us. "The skin. It's a shield."

Lilian met my gaze, and her eyes lit up as if she was reading my mind. "We could use this."

"Maybe."

"We could at least research it."

"Absolutely."

"Do you think we could use these to stop the blight?"

I shook my head. "I have no idea. But we should definitely try."

Suddenly, I knew what I was going to do after the wedding. These mushrooms were a gift--a promise, like my Gilded Lilies, of work that could save me from the grief of losing her.

And they were a gift from her to me, a blessing that might save the kingdom and might just save my heart.

"I really love you," she said. "Your face when you get excited is one of my favorite sights in the world."

Her voice was light and cheerful, but mine, when I spoke, seemed barely louder than the whispering of the brook that fed into this pond.

"Memorize it," I pleaded.

The enormity of the moment--of what she'd found, of the wedding that was about to cleave us apart, of the knowledge that something, somewhere in Floris, was strong enough to fight the curse--flooded me with pain, and with hope.

I reached out and brushed my fingers against Lilian's cheek. Her face was as soft as a peach, as warm as a rose on a sunny day, as bright as the light from one of my lilies, the ones that should have been named for her. I searched every curve and corner of her face, from her dark brown eyelashes to the lightest dusting of freckles across her cheeks to the luscious pink curve of her lips. I explored the gentle hollow below her bottom lip, the tiny mole on her right cheekbone, and the tiny, almost imperceptible scar above her left eyebrow from a long-ago fall down the stairs.

I memorized her, storing every bit of her I could gather, praying this moment would somehow be enough to last me a lifetime.

"I'm not going to forget you, Deon," she promised. Her hand settled over mine, as light as a butterfly. "We'll still be friends."

"We won't," I said. "We can't. You'll be a married woman, and me? I'll be well and truly banished from your grounds."

"My parents won't let that happen."

"What good would their protection do?" I said. "Do you really think we'd be able to stay away from each other? I won't be the reason you break your wedding vows."

She scowled. "Some vows. I'm marrying him for his money, and he knows it. Whatever we say at that ceremony tomorrow will be a sham." Her face flushed, and she swallowed as fear descended over her features like a shroud. "I don't want to marry him."

"I know."

"But I have to feed our people." Her gaze fluttered away from mine and down to the glittering mushrooms. "These might be a solution. But we don't know yet. We won't know fast enough. Our stores of grain will last another season, and then..."

"I know, Lilian."

"I can't let people starve on my watch."

"I would never ask that of you."

"You're really going to leave, then?"

"I don't have much choice."

Her eyebrows furrowed. She couldn't meet my eyes.

"Please don't tell Mama and Papa why. Papa's already so worried, and Mama..." Her lips trembled, and she pressed them together and took a long, steady breath. "Mama says she feels well. Maybe she does. But..."

"But she would never stay in her rooms like this if she was at her best," I finished gently.

"You know her. She can't stand to be cooped up. Even when she's ill, she always has visitors going in and out to keep her mind off things."

"Maybe she really is just hiding her hair," I said. "She seemed healthy enough last time we saw her together."

Lilian stared at me, and after a moment of that intense blue stare, I stopped pretending.

"I know it's more than that," I said. "I know it is. I won't tell her anything."

She frowned up at me. She was so young, but the strain of these past few weeks and the enormous responsibilities she held weighed on her, giving her the look of someone years older.

"You want food?" she said at last, dejected.

I shifted on the blanket to kneel facing her and took both her hands in mine.

"I do want food," I said. "And I want to spend the rest of this day eating and talking together just like we always have. And then tomorrow, when everything changes, you can go into the future with today in your pocket. Today we are ourselves. *Today* is how I will always feel about you."

Lilian spread the blanket out on top of the flat boulder, and I unpacked the picnic basket. We didn't bother with the plates someone had neatly folded inside cloth napkins, and instead ate together from the same dishes of fried potatoes and egg salad and spicy roasted pigeon.

“How did you get all this out here?” I asked, scraping the bowl for the last creamy bits of the egg salad.

“You can thank Lady Iris. She brought it during her morning ride.” Lilian reached into the basket for a paper-wrapped parcel I hadn’t yet touched. She untied the string and unwrapped the package to reveal a napkin full of fluffy pastries oozing with strawberry jam. “And you can thank Lady Camellia for these. She’s becoming an exceptional baker.”

“Were all your ladies-in-waiting in on this?”

Lilian smirked. “Every single one.”

I accepted one of the pastries, which immediately shed flaky crumbles onto my fingers. “You’re not worried one of them will tell the duke?”

□I may have a dreadful fiancé, but I have excellent friends.□ She raised a bottle of lemonade, the cook□s special brew flavored with mint leaves and orange rinds. □To friends. And to best friends. And to boys, I□d rather marry in a world where I wasn□t a princess, and you weren□t a gardener, and the entire kingdom wasn□t being threatened by a blight that□s turned a forest into...□ She glanced around and waved her bottle generally toward the gray canopy overhead. □Well, this.□

I laughed and raised my drink. “To friends, best friends, and girls I’d rather marry.”

We clinked bottles, and I downed a long swig of the sweet lemonade. Lilian sipped hers, watching me, and then said, looking over the top of the bottle, “You know, it really is too bad that you ended up a gardener. Not that you’re not brilliant at it, but... Goodness, if only whoever left you at the palace had left you at Thornton manor instead!”

I snorted and almost coughed on my lemonade. “You

think the duke's family would have adopted me?"

"All right, well, not *Thornton* manor," she said. "But some other noble house. They could have adopted you, and we could have met at a ball or something, and then I could just marry you instead of awful Garritt."

There were a thousand ways that plan could have gone wrong, from my being sent to an orphanage to my adoptive noble family not being rich enough for Lilian's present circumstances to the simple possibility that she might not have loved me so much if I hadn't been raised under Hedley's love and discipline.

None of them mattered. If we were doomed to take separate paths from here on out, I was glad that at least we'd had eighteen years of walking side-by-side.

I grinned. "Your mother said she should have adopted me."

Lilian tilted her head and smiled a little as if she found this sweet, and then her eyes widened in horror.

"Oh," she exclaimed. "Oh, *no*. No, that would not have been good."

I cracked up, and she turned bright red and shook her head. A golden ringlet that had escaped her ribbon bounced against her cheek.

"You don't want me as a sibling?"

She shuddered, laughing. "Stars, no. If we have one blessing in all this, you not being my *brother* has got to be it."

Crinkles danced at the corners of her eyes, and the blush faded slowly from her skin. Watching her was like watching a sunset, each second slightly different from the last and every change beautiful.

The day slipped away too quickly for me to track. Every second with her seemed shorter than it should have been, and before long, the shadows of the gray-laden branches overhead had shifted clear across the little clearing.

Off in the distance, bells chimed. It was time for the daily moment of gratitude, where every Florian took a moment to feel thanks for the blessings in their lives.

The bells had struck me as ironic some evenings during this past week. What with the blight and the duke and all the hubbub around my lily, there had been days when I hadn't felt as if I had much to be grateful for.

Today, though, I was full.

Lilian knelt up on the blanket and offered me her hands. I took them. Tradition sat with us like an old friend.

"Know what I'm grateful for?" I said.

"Let me guess." Lilian pulled her hand away long enough to wipe a stray crumb from my cheek. She held it up, the telltale red of a strawberry pastry on her finger. "You're grateful for strawberry preserves." She wiped the crumb on the blanket and took my hand again.

"Correct," I said. "I'm eternally grateful for strawberries." I ran my thumb gently across the back of her hand. I secretly preferred the taste of raspberries, but strawberries were Lilian's favorite, and that made them mine, too. "And I'm grateful for horses." I glanced at the mounts we'd brought with us. One had wandered a ways away and was still nosing among the undergrowth for anything that hadn't turned gray. The other seemed to be dozing while standing. "And I'm grateful for puppies."

A dimple appeared at one corner of her lips.

"And dimples," I said. "And I'm grateful for picnics, and lessons in your schoolroom, and eyes the color of the sky."

She laced her fingers through mine and lifted one of my hands. "I'm grateful for dirt under fingernails," she said quietly. "And the way some people's hair runs wild when they sleep."

"I'm grateful for gardens."

"I'm grateful for lilies that cast light onto tent ceilings."

I inched closer to her. Evening birdsong sounded in the distance, followed by the rustling of the few surviving leaves. "I'm grateful for forest clearings."

"And purple mushrooms."

"And you."

She closed her eyes and took a deep breath. I watched her soak in the moment and said a silent prayer that it would stay with her always.

I pressed my forehead against hers, and she sighed and leaned against me.

"And I'm grateful for raspberry tarts," I said.

Her eyes flew open. "You're *always* grateful for raspberry tarts, Deon."

I kissed her, and I tried, hopelessly, to make it last forever.

3
18TH APRIL

The next morning, I watched people scurry to and from the palace, readying the final preparations for the wedding ceremony. I watched a crowd gather outside the palace gates, silk flowers on their hats and colorful flags waving in the air. I watched wedding guests arrive in decadent carriages and clattering Forge vehicles.

I watched it all, and it all meant nothing. It was as if a curtain had been drawn between me and the world, rendering it distant and me numb.

"You all right?" Reed asked, coming up beside me in the staff quarters' bathroom, where my reflection stared grimly back at me from the long mirror over the sinks.

I'd been allowed inside the palace for the day to make myself presentable before I sat in the area of the throne room that had been reserved for heads of staff. The one suit I owned was stiff and smelled of the cedar chips it had been stored in. The last time I'd worn it had been almost a year ago, at the palace's annual servants' ball. My shoulders must have grown broader since then, judging from the way my dress shirt strained across my chest and the small of my back.

I ran a damp hand through my hair and tried to tame it with a comb, aware of Reed's gaze on me through the mirror.

"I'm fine."

It was such an obvious lie that Reed didn't bother to call me on it.

"I know you and the princess have always been

friends," he said, a little awkwardly. "You knew she had to get married someday, right? And it's not as if she can marry her gardener."

"I'm aware, Reed, thanks," I said tightly.

"Sorry," he said. He shifted from foot to foot and gave me a clumsy clap on the arm. "I just... You know I'm here for you, right?"

I ran the comb through my hair one last time and gave up.

"Yeah, I know," I said. "You always are. I appreciate it."

"We still have the gardens," he said. "And the enchanted glass. Just look ahead to that, maybe."

I didn't have the energy to pretend everything was still all right and under control. I felt like one of the lingering plants out in the garden, drooping and with a gray stem that couldn't hold my head up. "I'm not going to be here after this week," I said. "Remington fired me."

Reed was silent for a moment, then burst out with a furious, "*What?*"

"Or he's going to fire me," I said. "I've got until they get back from the honeymoon to clear out."

He sputtered. "That's just nonsense. The gardens can't get along without you, and the king and queen would *never*--"

I stopped him with a hand on his shoulder. "I know," I said. "But I've already thought it through. It's all right. I can't stay here anyway. Not with..."

I trailed off. The image of Lilian standing at the altar with that monster flashed through my mind, and I winced in physical pain.

"I just can't," I finished. "But I'll stay in Floris for a while. We can still work on the glass together. It'll be fine."

He stared at me, but finally, he gave me a slow nod. "Whatever you say, boss."

I gave him an impulsive hug. I clapped him on the back, and he held on tight, for longer than he might have normally.

I wiped my eyes as I pulled away, quickly, before he could see.

"That's that, then," I said, forcing myself to be brisk. "Guess we'd better take our seats."

Reed frowned, still taking in the news. "Guess we'd better."

We went our separate ways outside the throne room door, me to the pews that had been set aside for heads of staff and Reed to the balcony that had been erected in a crescent at the back of the room for servants.

Most royal weddings, at least in other kingdoms, didn't include the presence of the palace's entire serving staff. But including the help in weddings and christenings had been a long-standing Floris tradition, and it seemed fitting for someone like Lilian, who had always treated her servants as friends.

Who had always treated *me* as her friend.

I swallowed, straightened my shoulders, and found my seat in the pews. Hedley had promised to save me a spot. He wasn't here yet, but Hyacinth was, and she grabbed my hand and gave it a strangling squeeze as soon as I arrived. I wondered how much Hedley had told her, then realized he didn't need to say a thing: Hyacinth had always seen right through me. I bent and gave her a quick kiss on the cheek before taking my seat.

If time had sped up yesterday in the forest, now it crept along, slow with dread. Elegant Florian nobles and royals from other kingdoms filtered in as a small harp and violin ensemble played traditional Florian wedding songs. People greeted each other and remarked on the beautiful decor and how happy they were for the beautiful young couple. Silk draperies covered the walls, decorated with arrangements of flowers from my garden. The air smelled sweet, the way Floris always should. And amid it all, the seconds ticked by, each one heavier than the last.

"Your flowers look lovely," Hyacinth said.

I murmured a thanks. They were beautiful. I wondered which ones the florists had decided to put in Lilian's bouquet. At least, she would walk down the aisle, holding something I'd grown.

The giant silver clock at the back of the room chimed ten. The room stilled in anticipation of the wedding. At that moment, Hedley slid quietly into his seat next to Hyacinth.

"I was beginning to think you weren't going to make it," she whispered.

"So was I," he said in a low voice.

The doors at the back of the room opened, and Duke Remington took his place at the head of the room next to the officiant. The duke was handsome, dressed in a deep blue suit and looking every bit like the kind of elegant, rich, gracious man a woman like Lilian should marry.

The musicians struck up the first few notes of "Poem for a Sylvan Spring," a traditional Florian ode to the endless renewal of our nation's forests. It was usually used as a wedding song, with the trees acting as a metaphor for long-lasting love, but it held extra meaning in the middle of the blight. It was a reminder to all of us that frosts could kill and fires could ravage, but the life that sustained us would always prevail.

Flower girls in frothy pink gowns walked down the aisle, scattering rose petals, a precious extravagance in this land without flowers. Lilian's ladies-in-waiting followed. One of them, Lady Iris, caught my eye as she walked past, and her smile faltered for the briefest moment. Her eyebrows tensed, a silent message of support, and I nodded my thanks.

Hyacinth, watching the flower girls at the front of the room, pulled a handkerchief out from beneath the neckline of her gown and dabbed at her eyes. Hedley pulled a handkerchief from his pocket, too, and held it out across Hyacinth's lap toward me.

But no, it wasn't a handkerchief. It was a scrap of paper, small and yellowing and torn on three edges.

I glanced at him in question, but he stared resolutely ahead and shook the paper a little. I took it, and then the swelling first notes of the Tulip March sounded as Lilian appeared at the back of the room with her parents standing on either side just behind her, a symbol that today, the most powerful people in the realm came after their daughter.

We all rose to our feet, and I stood on tiptoe to get a clear look at the bride. Tears flooded my eyes, and goosebumps tingled all the way down my arms. Stars, she was beautiful. Her bare shoulders floated above a gown of cream and palest pink, embroidered with thousands of golden flowers. The draping, off-shoulder sleeves of her gown were so light they seemed to be made of spider silk, and her equally delicate veil floated down her golden hair and trailed the ground behind her. It obscured her face, but only barely; beneath the gossamer, her eyes stared straight ahead, and her lips stayed in a fixed, graceful smile.

The smile wasn't real. But her beauty was, just like

her sense of duty and her unfailing loyalty to her people.

Stars, it had been an honor just to know her.

She moved forward, each step in time to the melodic march. The dancer in her was visible in every elegant motion, and her parents followed behind, both beaming. A lacy veil covered the top of the queen's head, but beneath it, a wig designed to mimic her famous hair shone like spun gold.

Lilian's eyes landed on me as she approached my pew. They stayed fixed on my face for what seemed like an eternity but could only have been a few seconds, and then she blinked and returned to staring straight ahead at the duke. I held my breath as she passed.

Hedley reached across Hyacinth and nudged me. She swatted his hand away and nudged me herself. I tore my eyes from Lilian and glanced down at the paper in my hand.

It was a newspaper clipping, the words printed in a style that suggested this paper had come from another kingdom far away. The text was too small to read without bringing the article closer to my face, but the photograph was large.

Duke Remington of Thornton smiled up at me from the crinkled photo, wearing a pale suit. A woman with dark hair and a dazzling smile held his arm.

No, not just a woman.

A bride.

I stared. The paper swam before my eyes. At the front of the room, Lilian took her place opposite the duke, and her parents sat in the front row next to his.

My mouth opened, then closed again without a sound. Tingles ran up and down my body, and the room seemed to spin under my feet.

I clutched Hyacinth's hand for support, and she

beckoned me to lean down.

"We had to check that he was still married before we told you," she whispered into my ear. "Couldn't get your hopes up."

I gaped at her. I knew the words she was saying, but they refused to coalesce into something resembling meaning.

Even so, something like joy was about to burst inside me.

"I don't..." My mouth still wouldn't work. I stammered and gripped the paper so tightly it crinkled under my fingers.

At the front of the room, the officiant invited everyone to sit. The pews creaked as we all settled back in our seats, but their sound was drowned out by the heartbeat thumping in my ears. The officiant began a reading of a love poem from a great Thornton writer. Lilian stood absolutely still, her posture perfect but stiff.

"I needed to find out whether he was divorced," Hedley said, leaning in so that he could speak without being overheard.

A man standing in front of us glanced backward as if trying to decide whether to hush us. Hedley fell silent, then leaned back in to me. "He's not."

"Not married or not divorced?" I mouthed.

"Not divorced," Hedley said.

The implications of this filled my head. They were obvious, but I couldn't quite make sense of them.

Hyacinth patted my hand. "I called in a favor yesterday," she murmured. "Had a friend who works for the Remingtons contrive an emergency out in Thornton so you and Lilian could have the day together. Turned out not to be necessary."

"He's *married?*" I whispered, my voice barely above

a breath. I repeated it, my lips lingering over the words as if that would make them more real. "He's *married.*"

"A few years ago in Arcadia," Hedley said.

"The marriage went bad quickly, and they've been living apart since only a few months in, but she won't grant him a divorce," Hyacinth added. "Seems he's just been pretending she doesn't exist."

"Do his parents know?"

"Of course, they do," she said, rolling her eyes. "They're just as morally bankrupt as him."

"But he's *married?*"

The man in front of us turned around and shushed us with a scowl. We fell silent. My heartbeat made my whole rib cage jump.

Miracles didn't happen. Not in the real world. Not like this.

At the front of the room, the officiant droned on about love and commitment and fidelity. Lilian smiled fixedly at the duke, and he gazed down at her. Anyone who didn't know him could have mistaken the expression for one of love.

I clutched the paper. The bride and groom in the photograph beamed up at me.

I stared back.

The king and queen's heads were just visible from here. The queen's hair flowed down the back of her chair, no doubt cascading onto the ground. The wig they'd acquired must be impressive if she was willing to let it be seen by the people directly behind her.

I shook my head, trying to clear it of irrelevant thoughts. The queen's wig had nothing to do with this moment--with this absurd, wild, unbelievable situation.

Hedley beamed at me. An answering grin spread itself across my face.

“This marriage is a sacred oath,” the officiant declared. “Today, you make promises not only between each other but between yourselves and your nation, to lead with examples of love and kindness, always treating one another with the respect you wish to see throughout the kingdom.”

He scanned the audience. Somewhere amid a cluster of pastel hats, someone blew her nose. He looked down at the large book in his hands.

“To that end, if anyone here knows any reason, legal or moral, why these two may not be joined together in marriage, let them speak now.”

Silence descended, a fragile moment that had never been broken in hundreds of years of royal weddings.

I took a deep breath.

And then I shot to my feet.

“I object.”

A thousand eyes turned on me. Cries of horror filled the air, and Lilian and the duke spun to face me. Remington’s face clouded with rage, and Lilian’s wide blue eyes bored into me through her gossamer veil.

I raised the newspaper clipping high into the air. “Duke Garritt Remington of Thornton already has a wife.” My voice boomed through the room. “A wife who is currently living.”

The officiant faltered.

“Well,” he said mildly.

He looked around the room, and his attention caught briefly on the king and queen, who seemed as startled as anyone else.

“Well,” he repeated. His book snapped shut. “I suppose we’d better take a pause, then.”

King Alder stood and strode to the front of the room. He exchanged a few tense words with the duke, then turned to Lilian. She shook her head, eyes still wide. Throughout the room, people seemed torn, unsure whether to stare at the gardener in his ill-fitting suit or the princess whose wedding had just been destroyed.

The king turned back to face us all. His eyes met mine for a brief second, and I hurriedly sat back down.

"This is a claim that clearly requires investigation," he said, in that collected tone that reminded me that he led a country. "We'll suspend the ceremony for an hour while we speak with the gentleman who raised this objection. You are all invited to retire to the ballroom; in the meantime, to enjoy tea and cakes."

Down the row from me, the Head of Housekeeping muttered an expletive and slipped out of her pew. The Head Cook followed right after her.

The king looked to me again, and this time he held my gaze.

"Those who have reason to participate in this conversation should meet immediately in the antechamber behind me."

The small, windowless room was already full by the time I arrived. Plenty of floral brocade chairs lined the walls and surrounded the fireplace, but so far, only Queen Rapunzel had taken a seat.

I was the only one here who'd been sitting near the back of the room, and the only one besides the palace's Officer of Law who wasn't related to the bride or groom. My stomach churned with nerves.

The lawyer, Mr. Ficus, appraised me, his cool gray eyes neutral. King Alder stood beside the empty fireplace with his hand on the mantel, and Queen Rapunzel sat beside him on a cushioned chair, her face etched with lines of worry. She searched my face as if hoping to find answers there.

"I'll be the first one to speak and say that this is ridiculous," Duke Remington said.

Lilian frowned up at him. Her gown took up an astounding amount of floor space, and she shoved part of her train aside and stepped toward him.

"Is it true?" she demanded.

"Of course not," Duchess Annemie said. She looked to her husband for support, but Duke Markus stayed silent. The duchess pulled a fan from the reticule on her wrist and began flapping it wildly at herself. "Garritt, married? That's preposterous. This gardener has no right to disrupt a royal wedding like this. His relationship with the princess has always seemed inappropriate to me, but *this?* If anyone needed evidence--"

"Annemie, hush," Duke Markus snapped.

Mr. Ficus rested his hands behind his back and observed us all with an impassive expression. "I suggest we learn more about the claim. Mr. Gilding, is it?"

"Mr. *Gilding* is a dirty gardener and can't be trusted with royal affairs any more than I'd trust my chambermaid to throw a Thornton ball," Duchess Annemie said.

Lilian shoved her veil from her face and opened her mouth, but before she could speak, King Alder cleared his throat, The duchess pursed her lips but fell silent.

"Mr. Gilding is a loyal and valued member of our staff," the king said firmly. He glanced at Mr. Ficus, then nodded at me. "Deon?"

Lilian sank into a chair beside her mother. Her gown ballooned around her and slowly deflated, the massive train still covering the floor in front of her. Queen

Rapunzel took her daughter's hand.

I stepped forward, careful to avoid the embroidered fabric on the floor.

"I acquired this via the Central Archives in Urbis," I said. "It's a newspaper clipping from Aboria."

The duke blanched and clenched his teeth. Murder gleamed in his eyes.

The king took the newspaper clipping. He was a carefully trained diplomat, and his face gave nothing away as he scrutinized the photograph and read the article fragment underneath. Silently, he handed the paper to Lilian, who read it with Queen Rapunzel peering over her shoulder.

Lilian was not as reserved as her father. A dozen emotions passed across her face; shock, and anger, and disbelief. When she was finished, she handed the paper to Mr. Ficus without looking at him.

I had expected to see joy on her features, or at least relief, but she seemed overwhelmed. She couldn't look at me.

"Is this real?" she asked, in a voice that was utterly emotionless.

Mr. Ficus examined the paper.

"This is from the Central Archives, you say?"

"Yes, sir," I said.

"And you have no reason to believe His Grace is lawfully divorced?"

"No, sir, I believe him to be still married."

"That will be easy enough to confirm if it's true." He turned to Duke Remington. "What say you, sir?"

The duke reddened. "This is an insult."

"Perhaps," Mr. Ficus said, still the picture of calm. "But is it true?"

The duke's color deepened.

"A search of Aboria's marriage records will turn up everything we need to know," Mr. Ficus said. "However, if we have to go that far to make an official pronouncement on the wedding, you could easily be charged with intent to defraud both the royal family and the kingdom of Floris. We could charge you with that either way, of course, but a confession at this point would do a good deal to keep you out of prison."

"Prison?" Duchess Annemie drew herself up and puffed out her chest like an indignant bird. "How *dare* you, sir? You are speaking to the Duke of Thornton."

"Yes, ma'am," Mr. Ficus said pleasantly. "And I represent the Crown of Floris."

She sputtered and clutched at her husband's arm. Duke Markus jerked it away.

"I said this was a bad idea," he muttered.

"You're married," Lilian said.

All eyes turned to her, and she stared at the duke for a long, bewildered moment. She stood, shoving the bulk of her gown behind her. She advanced on him, and he, in what might have been his first-ever moment of good sense, stumbled backward. "You're *married,*" she said, bare arms trembling with rage. "You lying piece of pond scum."

"My so-called wife is a tart and a strumpet," he snapped.

Duchess Annemie froze, and Mr. Ficus pressed his lips together and slipped the newspaper clipping into his jacket pocket.

"She was hardly the right girl for a man like me," Remington spat. "It was a foolish dalliance, and I regretted it the moment it happened. It's not my fault the bull-headed woman won't grant me a divorce."

"You admit it, then," Lilian said.

"Of course, I admit it," he said. "And if you dare try to throw me in prison for it, I'll--"

"You'll what?" She stared him down, lightning and fury in her eyes. "Tell me, Garritt, what? You'll take over the throne? You'll harass my maidservants and throw my Head Gardener out of the palace? You'll stride around like you own the place and marry me just to gain a little more power in your wretched, miserable life?" She drew herself up to her full height, and even though she was a full foot shorter than her former fiancé, she seemed to tower over him. "No amount of money is worth that, and I'm ashamed I ever thought otherwise."

He sputtered, almost purple now, and a muscle in his jaw clenched. His hand tightened into a fist, and his arm jerked as if it took everything he had not to strike her.

Lilian held her ground. She took a tiny step toward him.

"Get out of my palace."

He froze for a long, terrifying moment.

And then he spun on his heel, elbowing her in the process, and threw open the antechamber door. He marched out, and the door slammed behind him.

We stood in stunned silence for a long moment while Lilian stared at the closed door, breathing heavily.

"That sounded like enough of a confession to me," Mr. Ficus said briskly.

Duchess Annemie burst into tears and rushed after her son. Duke Markus stood as if torn, then, with a sigh that sounded like it weighed a million pounds, trudged out after her.

"Lilian, darling?" the queen said, voice quiet and full of caution. "Would you care to explain what just happened?"

"I would love to," Lilian said. She swallowed, and finally--finally--she looked over at me. "But first, I would very much like to take a walk with Deon."

~

We wandered in silence through the garden. It was still a wasteland, forty acres of barren ground broken only by dull gray stems that protruded from the earth like stubble. It was also the most beautiful place I'd ever seen.

Lilian slipped her hand into mine. She had changed from her voluminous gown to a simple pink dress and had traded her veil for a single ribbon that pulled her hair back from her face.

"He's married," she said after we'd been walking for the better part of ten minutes.

I nodded and gazed out onto the grounds before us. The ballroom was on the other side of the palace, which meant it was unlikely that anyone looking out the windows would notice us strolling through the empty landscape even without the usual protection of bushes and tall grasses. We stopped underneath a young poplar tree.

I knew this tree; I'd planted it with Hedley a few years ago. The blight had hit it hard, and gray leaves now dripped from the branches like wet rags. Still, the trunk was still brown.

I wondered whether the tree would ever come back and whether a thread of life still ran through its core.

"Garritt is married to someone else," Lilian said slowly, looking up at me. "He's not married to me. He'll never be married to me."

"Not ever," I said.

She leaned against the tree trunk. "I'm so happy."

"You don't look happy," I said. "You look like you just got thrown off a horse and haven't hit the ground yet."

A laugh bubbled from her. "That's about the truth, isn't it?" She ran a hand through her hair, pulling strands loose from her ponytail.

I stepped forward and untied the ribbon. Her hair fell in a cascade of gold around her face.

"Turn around," I said gently. "I'll braid it for you."

Her hair was like silk beneath my fingers, light, and smooth, and warm near her scalp. My fingers dove in and out of the waves in practiced motions, coaxing strands together to form a thick, glossy rope. She relaxed with my every motion, and I allowed my fingertips to brush against her neck and shoulders and back until the braid was completed. I tied it with the ribbon, and she turned back around to face me.

"I feel terrible," she said as if confessing to an enormous mistake. "I'm so happy."

"Why would you feel terrible? He's *married.* He lied to you." I frowned. "In addition to being a general all-around jerk, I mean."

"Not about him," she said. "Well, the money. It's a shame to lose that. I don't know how we're going to manage. But even now, think about the wedding. People came from so far away, and there's supposed to be a giant reception this afternoon and a party tonight and then a great feast tomorrow, and all the food's been made, and we don't exactly have food to waste right now."

It was profoundly Lilian-like to stand in the middle of the drama of her life and still be consumed by the duties of her role.

She continued, words picking up pace like a train gathering speed. "And you cut down all your flowers--I can't believe she made you cut down all your plants, it's a *sin*--and the hall's been decorated, and it's just an outrageous amount of money and effort that's all going to waste, and everyone's been working so hard, and--"

I pressed my finger to her lips. She clamped them shut and raised her eyebrows at me, waiting for me to somehow soothe the giddy panic in her eyes.

And I knew how. Because I knew Lilian, and always had.

"Breathe," I ordered.

She did, taking in a huge lungful and letting it out slowly while I smiled at her.

"I put those mushrooms your lady-in-waiting found in my private garden," I said, trying to sound reasonable and measured. "So not all the plants are gone. These might even help us feed everybody. If we're lucky, really lucky, you won't need Remington's money."

She nodded, somehow willing to rely on my reassurances.

"As for the wedding feast."

Lilian stared at me, breath suspended, waiting to see if I would dare to take the next step.

And I dared.

Stars, I dared.

I took both her hands in mine and slowly, aware of my every heartbeat, sank to one knee.

"Lils," I said. "My beautiful, clever, fierce girl. Will you marry me?"

She stared at me, blue eyes enormous.

My stomach fell. I'd done it all wrong. Of course, she couldn't marry me. Of course, the princess of Floris couldn't marry her gardener. Her parents would never allow it. She would never do something so foolish. Just because this wedding had fallen through, I didn't deserve--

And then she pulled me up, spun me around, and pinned me against the trunk of the tree.

"Yes," she breathed.

Her soft strawberry lips covered mine. She kissed me more deeply than she'd ever dared before, and I kissed her back, our lips mingling and dancing like flowers in a sweet spring breeze. The scent of the still-fragrant earth rose up around us, and she pressed her delicate little hand to my chest and held me against the tree I'd planted and kissed me until the stars swam before my closed eyes.

19TH APRIL

As long as I lived, I would never forget the look on the king and queen's face when we returned to the palace.

Last night, after we had kissed one another until even coming up for breath seemed futile, we had made our way back to the castle. For the first time in a long time, the guard standing outside the queen's chambers let us in without a fuss.

It was clear when we entered, hand-in-hand, that we had interrupted an intense conversation. Queen Rapunzel was sitting on the sofa, and King Alder was pacing back and forth in front of her.

"Darling," Queen Rapunzel was saying. "I daresay Lilian isn't too devastated. Whatever just happened down there, it seems things have not been quite rosy between her and that duke." The last words were filled with a disdain I'd rarely heard the queen direct at anybody. "Of course she'll be upset for a while, but--"

Lilian cleared her throat. Her parents both jumped. They took in Lilian's face, then mine, and then their gazes traveled down to our entwined fingers.

King Alder's eyebrows shot up. The queen's mouth dropped open a little bit, and then, to my utter amazement, a smile crept onto her features.

"It seems we've overlooked even more than I thought," she said, still smiling but also looking as though she'd been stunned. "Am I right in thinking you two have some explaining to do?"

So we did. We sat on the sofa opposite the queen and told them everything: how double-faced the duke had been, how Lilian had been willing to marry him anyway to help the kingdom, and how Hedley had come to our rescue at the last moment with evidence of the duke's fraud. And we told them about our feelings for one another and that I'd asked Lilian to marry me, and that she'd said yes.

"But we still need your blessing," I finished, squeezing Lilian's fingers tightly between mine. My heart raced, and the king and queen's bewildered expressions did little to soothe the way my stomach swayed like treetops in a high wind. "It's never been done before, a princess marrying her gardener. I know I don't have much to offer. I don't have anything, really."

My heart pounded. I was a fool for thinking this was possible.

But I couldn't give up now. Not with Lilian here next to me, her hand and her hopes all tangled up with mine.

"I know I'm not a duke or a prince or even a knight.

I don't have money or land or a title. And of course, I'm not asking to be king someday. Lilian is more than capable of ruling on her own. All I want to do is support her and make sure she knows she's loved every single day. That's all I can offer. I know it's not much."

The queen's features softened. "But that's everything."

She glanced back and forth between us, her eyes lingering on Lilian's face.

I dared to look, too. Lilian's cheeks were flushed, but she was clear-eyed and held her head high. She met her mother's gaze.

"Darling, that's all we've ever wanted for you," the queen said. "To be loved. To have a partner who can stand by your side the way we've stood by each other."

She reached for King Alder's hand, and he took it without even seeming to notice he had.

"We thought you liked him," King Alder said. He still looked as bewildered as I'd ever seen him. "Sweetheart, we never would have encouraged your marriage if we'd known what he was like. We chose him because he seemed kind and considerate. He seemed like the kind of man who could serve Floris at your side."

"It's almost as if we shouldn't be arranging royal marriages anymore," Queen Rapunzel said lightly, but in a way that made me think this was a conversation they'd already had more than once.

King Alder glanced at her. "Yes," he said. "It is almost like that." He looked to Lilian. "It seemed to work in the past. Your grandparents adored one another."

"It might have gone better if the duke was the kind of person he pretended to be," Lilian said gently. "I was willing to marry him, even if he wasn't Deon." She glanced at me. "I would have tried my best to be a good wife and to care for him, even if I already loved someone else."

"But darling, if you already loved someone else, there was no need to find you a husband," the queen said. "We just... We didn't know."

Lilian frowned. "Mama, he's been my best friend since I was born."

The king cleared his throat, eyebrows furrowed like he was still trying to think this all through. "You two have always been more like... well, like siblings."

Lilian tried to suppress a laugh, which only came out as a snort. I pressed my lips together and silently shook my head.

"Not siblings," I said. "Never siblings."

The queen stared at us. "Why on earth didn't you say something?"

I hesitated. But she seemed genuinely puzzled. So did the king. He was watching us like he was waiting for one of us to start speaking a language he understood.

"Your Majesties," I said, cautiously. "I'm a *gardener.* Lilian is a *princess.*"

The queen's eyebrows drew together. They had been coated in gold, but hours after the interrupted wedding, hints of gray were beginning to peek through.

"What does that have to do with anything?" she said.

Lilian looked to me, but I couldn't make sense of these people in front of us, either.

"My darlings," the queen said. "I was a forest hermit before I became a princess. You can marry whomever you like."

I stared at her. It couldn't be that easy.

A broad smile spread across her face. "You love each other. You respect each other. And we all *know* Deon is exactly who he claims to be." She leaned against King

Alder and smiled at me. “You’ve always been our family. I can’t imagine anything more wonderful than to make you part of it for real.”

“And of course, you should be king eventually,” King Alder said as if he’d been puzzling over this question through most of the conversation. “You’ve already had the best education Floris can offer. You’d be an excellent king. Much better than that pretender from Thornton.” He scowled at Lilian. “Did he really harass your maids?”

She nodded. I silently promised myself to never, ever mention that he’d also tried to shove Lilian around.

“We were thinking,” Lilian said. “All the guests are already here, and we’ve spent so much money on the celebration. I already have a dress. Could we just... go ahead with the wedding?”

The queen considered this for a moment.

“Tomorrow.” She glanced up at King Alder. “We can have the ceremony in the morning and go straight into the other celebrations afterward.”

The king had taken only a moment to consider, and then a broad smile had spread across his face.

“Tomorrow,” he agreed.

He turned to me and leaned over, offering me a hand. I took it, and he shook my hand, his grip firm and warm as an embrace.

“Welcome to the family, Deon,” he had said, clasping my hand in his. “Welcome, at last.”

Now, it *was* tomorrow. And in moments, I would walk through the throne room doors, take my place at the front of the room, and marry the love of my life.

~

Reed nudged me. I'd asked him to be my impromptu best man, and while he'd been utterly bewildered at the news that I was about to marry the princess, he'd agreed and was now right at my side.

"The lilies are taken care of," he said. "Being in the shed didn't seem to hurt them any. Glad you hid a few from the duke."

"I'm just glad they survived." I stretched my arms, trying to relieve the nervous tension building in my neck and shoulders. At least, the suit the palace had provided me with actually fit today.

"A couple of dark days isn't enough to kill anything," Reed said. "Least of all, a lily that makes it own light."

"Sir?" someone said.

It took me a moment and another nudge from Reed to realize the assistant had been talking to me. He bowed and gestured toward the door.

"It's time to take your place."

I took a deep breath, and Reed and I walked into the throne room. All the guests from yesterday were there, dressed again in their wedding finery, but now, Hedley and Hyacinth sat in the place of pride on the front row, next to where the king and queen would sit when they arrived. Hyacinth smoothed her hair and beamed at me, and Hedley gave me a slow grin.

Music floated through the air, and the doors at the back of the room opened. Flower girls entered, but they didn't carry baskets of petals. Instead, each little girl carried one of my Gilded Lilies in a silver pot. The flowers' petals had just opened for the day, and each blossom cast rays of dancing golden light onto the girls' faces. People gasped and murmured as they walked up the aisle.

When they arrived at the front of the room, the

girls placed the lilies on small marble pedestals that surrounded the altar in a crescent shape. The littlest girl, one of Queen Rapunzel's ladies' children, stumbled as she tried to lift the pot. I darted forward and steadied her, and together, her chubby hands next to mine, we set the lily on its stand.

The little girl grinned up at me and ran to her mother, who was waiting in one of the front rows.

Lilian's ladies-in-waiting came next, each one in a beautiful gown of pink and gold.

And then, as the music changed to the swelling tones of the Tulip March, Lilian appeared at the end of the aisle.

I had seen her in her gown yesterday. I knew the way her shoulders floated above its loose sleeves. I had already witnessed the lines of the bodice skimming her beautiful curves. There was nothing new about the gossamer veil that covered her face or her golden necklace with its glass heart resting between her collarbones, or the shimmering slippers that peeked out from the hem of her voluminous skirt.

I had seen it all before, and still, she took my breath away.

She grinned at me, and it was nothing like the fixed smile that had graced her features before. Her parents walked behind her, both of them sharing in her joy. The queen's enchanted wig shone beneath a delicate lace veil, and King Alder gently touched the small of her back as they reached the end of the aisle. The king kissed the top of Lilian's head before taking his seat, and the queen stopped to kiss my cheek before joining him.

Lilian took her place next to me and lifted her veil. The golden light from my lilies frolicked first across the fabric, then across her creamy skin.

"Dearly beloved," the officiant began. "We are gathered here today to join together this man and this woman in marriage."

I met Lilian's eyes, and his voice seemed to fade away. For a moment, time stood still, and there was only this spectacular woman standing before me--this woman who had been by my side throughout my whole life, as my friend, my companion, my confidant, and now, my bride.

Her smile shifted to a smirk, and she gestured toward the officiant with her eyes. I could almost hear her voice in my head: *Pay attention, Deon.*

I did my best.

We had selected new readings last night, hurriedly combing through old books and reminding each other of poems we had loved over the years. One of Lilian's ladies recited a verse from a book of flower poems, and Reed delivered a passage from a novel Lilian had read to me once while I'd worked in the gardens. The words cascaded over me like water.

And then, Reed stepped forward with our rings. We'd picked these last night, too, in a last-minute dash to make this ceremony our own. King Alder had taken us to the royal treasury and showed us cases upon cases of jewelry that had been in the family for centuries. We'd chosen them together. Lilian's gold ring was shaped like a flowering lily, with a sparkling diamond in the center of the bloom, and mine was a strand of leafy vines twining eternally around one another into a perfect circle.

The officiant asked if anyone had just cause why we couldn't marry. The room stayed blessedly silent. And then, following his directions, we said our vows.

"I, Deon Gilding, take thee, Lilian Acacia Calanthe, for my wedded wife," I repeated. My heart pounded, and I felt as if I was about to stumble over the words, but Lilian's gaze on mine kept me steady. "From this day forward, I promise to be there for you always as a strength in need, a comfort in sorrow, a counselor in difficulty, and a companion in joy. Through all the seasons of our lives, in good weather and in bad, I vow to tend to our marriage with the love and care of a gardener blessed by the gods."

My voice caught. I'd forgotten those words were in the traditional Florian vows. Impulsively, Lilian reached forward and grabbed my hand.

The officiant smiled at us. I took Lilian's ring and placed it carefully on her finger.

She repeated the vows, her voice clear and strong. "I vow to tend to our marriage," she finished slowly, placing a gentle weight on each word. "With the love and care of a *gardener* blessed by the gods."

She raised my hand and slid the leafy band onto my finger.

"By the power vested in me by the Throne of Floris," the officiant declared, "and in the sight of all the world, I now pronounce you man and wife."

He took a moment to glance at each of us and let the tension hang in the air. Lilian shifted impatiently from foot to foot, and a dimple appeared at the corner of her mouth.

The officiant cleared his throat. "You may seal your union with a kiss."

Lilian's mouth claimed mine. Somewhere beyond the soft embrace of her lips, the room erupted in cheers. There was joy out there--the kind of joy that hadn't been seen in Floris since the flowers began to die. Lilian pulled back, and the light from the lilies whirled across her face and sparkled in her eyes.

Far above us, from the highest towers of the palace, bells pealed the news out to the kingdom. Our guests rose, still applauding, and we walked back down the aisle hand-in-hand, the scent of flowers all around us.

~

The wedding ceremony was followed by a luncheon, which was followed by a late-afternoon reception that was open to the public. Lilian and I stood together, shaking hands and accepting the congratulations of what seemed like every person in Floris. It was exhausting, but Lilian stood up straight and smiled for everyone. She had a knack for greeting complete strangers as if they were old friends, and seemed to have no trouble keeping the line moving without ever making our guests feel rushed. I just tried to keep something like a pleasant expression on my face and not keel over.

By the time the last person had gone through the line and the guards had closed the doors before anyone new could arrive, I felt like I could sleep for a week and still not have it be enough.

"How do you do that?" I muttered to Lilian, who was still looking fresh as a daisy.

She winked up at me. "Why do you think I take my dance lessons so seriously?" she asked. "Diplomacy requires *stamina*." She tilted her head. "You're new to this, poor boy. We've got a couple of hours before we have to dress for the ball. Come with me."

I groaned. "I forgot there was still a ball."

She laughed and took my hand. We escaped through one of the ballroom's side doors, and Lilian led me up to her quarters. She left me on her sofa and disappeared into her dressing room with one of her maids. By the time she came back, I had already kicked off my shoes and curled up on the couch.

"Sit up," she ordered.

I obeyed, bleary-eyed, and then abruptly noticed that she was no longer in her wedding gown. Instead, she was dressed only in a chemise and stockings.

I'd seen her in light summer dresses and bathing gowns before, and this chemise covered far more of her than those had.

But that had been Lilian, my friend.

This was Lilian, my *wife*.

She giggled, and my face grew hot.

"Stars, you're adorable." She sat on the couch next to me, then patted her lap. "Come here, my love. You deserve a few moments to rest. It's been a long month."

Obediently, I rested my head in her lap. She played with my hair and traced her fingertips along my forehead and cheekbones, smiling down at me with that cloud of golden hair surrounding her like a halo.

"How'd I get so lucky, Lils?"

"You were kind to me." She traced a line down the side of my jaw. "And you trusted me." Her fingers paused, and I opened my eyes to see her frowning. "Always. Even when I was running headfirst into the worst mistake of my life."

"I should have tried to stop you."

She shook her head. "That would have made you like him. He tried to tell me what to do all the time. You never have, even when we were little." She shifted, and her fingers started moving again, this time wandering down my neck. "You've never tried to diminish me or control me or turn me into something I'm not."

The thought was horrifying. "That's because I *like* who you are."

"I know," she said, smiling gently down at me. "Isn't that remarkable?"

Her fingertips drifted down to the skin between my collarbones, dipping just beneath the neckline of my shirt. My breath caught.

"I'm not going to tell you what to do," I said cautiously. "But I'm going to *advise* you, as your friend, that maybe you should stop doing that if we want to make it to the ball."

She turned bright red and laughed. She bent down awkwardly to kiss me, and I pushed myself up to make it easier for her.

"Your lips are the best thing in the whole world," I said.

"Better than strawberries?"

I snuggled back down onto her lap, and she returned to raking her fingers through my hair and scratching them along my scalp. "Better than strawberries."

I drifted into a blissful sleep and was woken all too soon by Lilian gently shaking my shoulder. We went our separate ways, and, for the second time today, I had the uncomfortable experience of being dressed by a valet.

"You can relax, sir," the man finally observed, suppressing a smile.

I shifted and gave it my best effort. It didn't take me very far.

"Sorry," I said. "I'm used to being a servant, not having one. I'm not sure what I'm supposed to do here."

The valet, Avens, whom I'd seen around the palace but never really spoken to, stopped buttoning my shirt for me and stepped back with a polite half-bow.

"How about you dress yourself, sir, and I'll make sure the back looks all right when you're through?"

I shot him a grateful look. "I think you and I are going to get along just fine," I said.

He allowed himself a tiny smirk. "I believe we are."

Once dressed, I met Lilian outside the ballroom. She had traded her chemise for a stunning evening gown of rose silk, with the skirt pinned up by clusters of live flowers from the wedding earlier. A ribbon of blossoming sweet peas wove its way through her hair.

I had timed them exactly right. The flowers had unfurled at the perfect moment. I touched one gently. "I'm going to keep growing you flowers, Lils," I promised.

"Of course, you are." She stood on tiptoes and gave me a quick peck on the lips. "Why would I marry the kingdom's best gardener if not to always have flowers in my hair?"

"Sure it wasn't my roguishly good looks?"

She giggled. "Those golden rings in your eyes might have had something to do with it."

I leaned down and kissed her forehead. "Me with the golden eyes," I murmured. "You with the golden hair."

Lilian wrapped her arms around me and buried her face in my chest. The embrace crumpled the front of her gown, but she didn't seem to care, and I couldn't bring myself to, either.

And then the doors opened wide.

"Their Royal Highnesses, Princess Lilian and Prince Deon," the announcer boomed.

I froze and glanced at Lilian. She smirked up at me.

"Yes, darling, you're a prince now," she said. "That's how we do things in Floris, remember?"

It didn't feel right.

But having Lilian on my arm did, and that was all

that mattered.

The ball slipped by in a haze of music and drink and light conversation. I didn't recognize most of the people here, although I took comfort in the fact that some of our guests looked as awkward as I did. Most of the young nobles seemed at home in the ballroom, but at least a few lingered near the wall and contented themselves with watching the goings-on rather than participating.

I caught the eye of one young woman with stern features and dark blonde hair pulled tightly back in a braid. She examined me from across the room, then gave me a respectful nod of what I assumed was congratulations and said something to the pretty red-haired woman next to her.

I rather wished I could be over there with them, sitting and observing the dancers. But it appeared I was a prince now, and I was determined to do as good of a job as Lilian--or, at least, to not completely embarrass myself.

So I danced, and I smiled, and I complimented elderly noblewomen on their jewels. I met King Alder's friends and pretended I knew anything about hunting, and accepted the congratulations of what felt like everyone in the room.

"I'm proud of you," Lilian whispered, as the clock crept toward midnight and sleep began to gather like sand in the corners of my eyes.

It was all I needed to hear. The fatigue cleared, and I was able to throw myself with real enthusiasm into a conversation with the Duchess of Clover about the sibling rivalries that were beginning to emerge among her fourteen cats.

And then, finally, the queen made her way to us

across the crowded dance floor. Her wig was bound back in a jeweled net, either to keep it from getting caught or to shield it from closer inspection. She touched my arm and leaned up to whisper in my ear.

"People are beginning to retire for the night," she said. "It's a good time to slip away."

I didn't need telling twice. I found Lilian, who had been cornered by a talkative baron. I only needed to give her the slightest nod for her to catch my message. She politely disentangled herself from the conversation and guided me to a side door. We slipped through it and into the luxurious quiet of the corridor outside.

The instant we were back in her quarters, Lilian kicked off her shoes and dropped onto her sofa with a sigh. A cloud of rose silk billowed around her.

"Is your life always like this?" I said, not sure I wanted the answer.

She laughed. "This was a wedding," she said. "Luncheons and balls are rarely like this, and even more rarely all on the same day." She leaned back and closed her eyes. "My feet are killing me."

I took off my shoes, too, and set them neatly next to the sofa. My room was usually neat enough, but I always made a special effort to avoid making a mess in Lilian's quarters.

I glanced around, realizing for the first time with a jolt that these were *my* quarters now.

That would take some getting used to. I had a feeling I wasn't going to miss my manure bed.

"Give 'em here," I said, settling onto the sofa.

Lilian instantly groaned in what I assumed was relief

and stuck both her feet in my lap. I laughed and began to massage one of them, rolling my thumb up underneath the ball of her foot and scraping my knuckle down the delicate arch.

"Deon," she murmured, closing her eyes and leaning against the arm of the couch. "I very well might marry you."

I let the words sink in. They were like rain after a drought.

"Lils?" I said.

"Yeah?"

"We're married."

Her eyes flew open, and she grinned at me with a smile so wide I was worried she was going to hurt herself.

"I know," she said.

"Like, *married,* married."

"I know," she said again, and her smile, if it were possible, got wider. "And I'm married to *you,* not some idiot ogre from Thornton."

"You married the gardener."

She threw her hands in the air and beamed up at the ceiling like it had done something to make this miracle happen. "I married the gardener!" she shouted.

I cracked up, and she nestled back down into the cough and grinned at me. I grinned back, and we stared at each other like a couple of happy owls as we soaked in the reality of our new life.

She winced suddenly. "Ooh, right there."

I focused on the spot high in the arch of her foot, and she made a face and then relaxed with a sigh.

"What are we going to do now?" I said.

Every thought I'd had about my life and my future had changed, transforming in an instant like the world under a sudden sunrise. I didn't have to leave Floris now. I didn't even have to leave the palace. I could stay here, and... and what? Would I continue to work as the head gardener? I didn't mind the thought, but I couldn't begin to imagine what the rest of the kingdom would think about it. Would I forget about gardening entirely and begin studying in earnest to one day be king? That didn't feel right, either.

I thought back to how Queen Rapunzel might have felt on her first night as King Alder's wife. She had been new to this royalty thing, too, as a bride, but she'd made a brilliant go of it.

"Maybe someone will show up with a baby," I mused.

"Stars, I hope not," Lilian said. She widened her eyes. "We've had quite enough surprises for one week. Not that I'm complaining." She nudged me with her free foot. "This has been an awfully good week."

"As surprises go, the duke's pre-existing marriage was a good one."

"I think we should start with the mushrooms," Lilian said dreamily. "The blight's the biggest problem facing the kingdom right now. Hedley and Reed and the magicians seem to have the enchanted glass approach well in hand, and it sounds like Hedley's going to stay for a while."

"I don't think we could pay him to leave," I said. "He'd never admit it, but I think this blight is the most interesting gardening challenge he's faced in a decade or three."

"And that leaves us free to begin researching the mushrooms," she said. "I don't even know where to start. We need to figure out all their properties and submit them for study by both magicians and botanists, and of course, we need to figure out if we can grow them on the palace grounds outside of your garden. That would be much easier than running back and forth to the woods all the time. We should determine if they're edible, too. If they are, they could be an excellent food source for people who can't get the enchanted glass right away for whatever reason."

"I wonder if they'd work as goat feed?" I said. "Even if they're only part of the goats' diet, that would lessen the amount we have to import from other kingdoms, so people could keep producing cheese and meat."

"Of course, if we can figure out how to cross-breed the mushrooms with other plants, we might be able to grow all sorts of blight-resistant crops," Lilian mused. "Maybe even some flowers. The geneticists in Tulis are getting quite good at isolating plant traits and introducing them into new species."

"It would be wonderful if we could keep growing tulips," I said. "I've been worried about what's going to happen to the economy now that our flower exports have all but stopped."

"It'll take time," Lilian said. "We're going to have a rough couple of years, I think. But I hope we can rebuild. We're resilient."

"Florians are the mint of the world," I said. "It might look like we've died back, but we're just about impossible to actually kill."

"You're a poet, Deon," Lilian said, laughing.

"I'm a gardener."

Her eyes softened. "That you are. Once a gardener of the palace grounds. Now a gardener of a kingdom."

The weight of that responsibility settled on my shoulders. It was heavy, but it wasn't a bad weight. If anything, it felt like something I was helping Lilian to carry, like my presence might somehow make her burdens lighter.

I began to work on her other foot. She closed her eyes and slid further down onto the arm of the sofa.

"Lils?"

"Yeah?"

"You're going to sink between the cushions and be lost forever."

"Don't care," she said, eyes still closed.

"Don't you want to take off that dress, at least? It doesn't look comfortable."

"It's not," she said.

I glanced around. "Where are your maids? Or your ladies?"

She opened one eye. "I told them they could take the night off since I'd be getting back so late," she said. "I figured you could just help me with the gown tonight. If you're willing."

"If I'm *willing,*" I repeated.

"You might not be," she said lightly. "You might think I'm a disgusting monster. You never know."

"A monster."

"Mmhm, a vile one."

I set her foot down and crawled over her, smashing her beautiful gown and pushing her further into the cushions. "I have an idea," I said. "Let's go get you out of that dress. You can snuggle up in bed where it's comfortable. I'll finish rubbing your feet." I kissed her and then drew back, keeping my lips close enough to her face that I could feel her breath. "And then I'll show you *exactly* what I think of you."

Her eyes sparkled beneath her long lashes. She wriggled, and I pulled back to help her up. She stood and gazed up at me for a long moment.

Then she bit her lip, turned toward her bedroom,

and held out her hand.

I took it, ready to follow her anywhere.

20TH APRIL

We didn't emerge from our bedroom until early the next afternoon. Finally, we were wrested from the dreamy cocoon of our chambers by a note from the queen, inviting us to a late luncheon.

"I'm not entirely sure I want to see my parents just now," Lilian admitted, cheeks flushed, and a mischievous sparkle in her eyes.

I knew the feeling. They'd only just gotten used to the notion that Lilian and I cared for one another as something other than brother and sister. The thought of them having any idea what we'd been up to all morning was enough to heat my face by several degrees.

"Still, they are the monarchs of the realm," I said.

Lilian snorted. "I guess that's one argument."

We made it to luncheon only a few minutes late, and I thought we both looked reasonably presentable. Something like a smirk passed over the queen's face when we arrived at her chambers, but it was gone so quickly I thought I might have imagined it.

Servants brought up sandwiches and scones with cream and a pitcher of the cook's orange-mint lemonade. Daisy followed them, bearing a tray of jams and mustards in elegant little pots. She caught my eye and then looked away, clearly unsure how to navigate the new space between us.

"Good afternoon, Daisy," I said.

She flushed, surprised to be acknowledged. It might not have been the ordinary way of things. But I wasn't going to be an ordinary royal.

"This is Daisy," I added to the king and queen. "She's a friend of mine. She snuck food out to me several times when I was living outside."

The queen blinked. "Excuse me?" she said. "Living *outside?*"

"Did we not mention that before?" I said.

She scowled, an unusual expression for her. "You most certainly did not."

"I lived outside for a while," I said. "Remington."

"He didn't like Deon very much," Lilian said delicately.

Daisy's lips twitched, but she didn't say anything.

"It's lovely to know Deon has such good friends," Queen Rapunzel said to Daisy. "Thank you."

A surprised smile flashed across Daisy's face before she curtsied and left the room. I wondered if she'd ever spoken directly to the queen before. Gardener or not, I'd been privileged to grow up with the queen's attention on me. I had a lot to be grateful for. It made my head spin.

We ate and talked about yesterday's celebrations. The king recounted an entertaining story about his tipsy great-aunt trying to pick a fight with a suit of armor in the hallway, and the queen reported that her ladies had witnessed not one but three marriage proposals during the course of the ball, our guests no doubt moved by all the romance in the air.

"We wanted to talk to you about your honeymoon plans," the queen said as we were sipping tea after the meal. She looked tired, but in a way that might have just been a result of yesterday's late night. Still, the gray of her eyebrows was beginning to show. "Lilian and Duke Remington were originally going to spend a week at his manor in Thornton, followed by a boating tour around the coast. I suspect you two might want to do something different."

"I think you should absolutely honeymoon at the duke's manor," the king muttered darkly into his teacup. "I'm not averse to someone rubbing that man's poor decisions in his face."

Lilian's eyebrows shot up. "Papa!" she exclaimed.

The king was usually the epitome of diplomatic calm. It was almost funny to see him this annoyed.

"Tempting as that may be, I advise you go on your *own* honeymoon," the queen said.

Lilian glanced at me, and I gave her a small nod. She smiled and turned back to her parents.

"Deon and I talked this over already, actually," she said. "We don't want to go on a honeymoon. We'll have plenty of opportunities to travel together, but right now, we want to follow some leads that might help us solve the blight."

The king raised an eyebrow. "You want to spend

your honeymoon gardening?"

"Some of that," I said. "We also need to speak to botanists and geneticists and consult with some magicians."

"Can we take over one of the rooms on the ground floor as an office?" Lilian said. "It would be nice to have somewhere to hold meetings."

"You don't have to keep working as head gardener anymore," the king said, hesitantly, as if unsure whether I already knew this.

I laughed. "I'd like to, Your Majesty. At least for now." I took Lilian's hand. "We have some important work to do together."

Queen Rapunzel watched us, amused, and then leaned back in her seat.

"Well, it seems you two know exactly what you're about," the king said. He frowned. "And Deon, you can just call me Alder."

I wasn't so sure about that. I nodded anyway.

"And me, Rapunzel," the queen said. "Or Mama."

She winked, and I laughed. I had slipped up more than once as a little boy, calling her *Queen Punzel* and *Mama* and *Lilian's Mother* in equal measure.

"Let us know if we can help with these ambitious plans of yours, whatever they are," she added. "Although it rather seems you won't need us."

Lilian's hand tightened on mine. "I'll always need you, Mama."

There was weight behind the words, an awareness that whatever was happening in the kingdom was tied to the queen, and that we didn't yet know how this story would end.

"I'm not going anywhere," she said briskly. "In fact, now that I have this charming wig, I'm quite ready to get back into the world. Things have gone sideways while I've been hiding away, and I don't intend to let them keep sliding."

She tilted her head and considered me, her expression soft and full of love.

"I'm terribly proud to have you for a son, Deon," she said. "Thank you for everything you've done to help me and the kingdom."

"I only wish I could have done more," I said. "But I'm going to keep searching for the answers to everything that's happening in the kingdom. Lilian and I think we know where we want to start, but if that doesn't work out, we'll try something else."

"And we'll keep trying until this blight is gone for good," Lilian said.

"I know you will," the queen said. "I have tremendous faith in you both."

The kingdom was still covered in gray, but now I could see a world of shimmering possibilities. I had magic, and parents-in-law who loved me, and a wife so dazzling it blinded me just to look at her. Lilian and I would heal this land. The soil would recover. The color would return. It would take love and hard work, but we had both in spades.

Someone knocked at the door, and Lady Camellia, one of the queen's ladies-in-waiting stepped in, an irritated frown on her face.

"I'm sorry to interrupt, but some of our weddings guests are demanding to see you, Your Highnesses," she said.

It took me a second to realize she was talking to me.

"I've told them you're otherwise engaged, but they simply will not take no for an answer. And, well, one of them has a baby dragon, and it appears to be getting agitated."

I looked to Lilian, but she seemed just as confused as I was.

"I don't know anyone with a baby dragon," she said slowly. "That sounds dangerous."

"She claims it's tame," Lady Camellia said. "Only I don't think that's actually possible, and I'm getting worried it's going to damage the furniture."

"It's *inside?*" the queen said. I couldn't tell if she was curious or horrified.

Lilian stood. "Let's go see what this is about." She narrowed her eyes at me. "I'll admit, I have no idea who they could be--"

"But you want to see the baby dragon," I finished.

"It's like you know me."

Lady Camellia led us downstairs to one of the conservatories on the bottom floor of the palace. I saw in an instant why she'd had them wait here; there were chairs, but they were all bare wood devoid of the usual upholstered cushions, and the stone and glass walls were likely among the least flammable in the palace.

We stepped forward into the room, curiosity brightening Lilian's face. Lady Camellia sighed and left, but not before muttering to me that she'd post a guard outside the room, just in case.

The three visitors shot to their feet as we entered, and the taller of the two women stepped forward. It took me a moment to place her, and then I recognized her face and her tightly bound hair. She'd been at the ball last night, watching me from the side of the room.

"Your Highnesses," the woman said. I half-expected her to curtsy, but she offered us a refined bow instead. She was dressed in a fitted tunic and leather leggings, and the young dragon with gleaming purple scales slunk around her legs and hid behind her leather boots.

Lilian tensed beside me, and I knew it was taking everything she had not to drop to her knees and try to make friends with the beast.

"Do we know you?" I said cautiously.

"You do not," the woman said. "I'm terribly sorry for bothering you, it's just that we desperately needed to see you before you left on your wedding trip."

"We're not going on one," I said.

The woman relaxed a little.

"Then I hope you have time to talk," she said. "Really talk. We're here because we know why your flowers are dying."

My heart jumped. Lilian took a tiny step forward.

"Why?" she demanded. "How? What do you know?"

"Have a seat," the woman said. She held out her hand. "I'm Azia."

Lilian shook the woman's hand, and so did I. Azia seemed to linger over our brief contact, her eyes fixed on my face.

I stared back. She had golden rings around her irises.

Just like mine.

"These are my travel companions," Azia said, gesturing behind her.

The woman with fiery hair I'd seen yesterday examined me intently. She was seated next to a young man with dark, shaggy hair and a rugged shadow that looked like it would become a proper beard if I only waited a few moments. They both had the same rings around their eyes.

"This is Blaise from Atlantice," Azia said, nodding at the red-haired woman. "And this is Castiel of Elder."

"Princess Blaise..." Lilian said.

She was a princess? And Lilian knew her?

Blaise brought her into a hug, and as I looked on, I realized I recognized her too. She had visited Floris a few years ago as part of a Royal Tour from Atlantice. I'd not paid much attention at the time, but it seemed that Lilian and she had kept up with each other. Lilian then turned to Castiel and offered her hand. Castiel kissed the back of it with a solemn expression.

We all sat. I stared at the visitors' faces. I couldn't help it. There was something of me in each of them. Our faces were distinct, and the shades of our hair and skin varied wildly, but their eyes--they stared back at me as if through a mirror.

The dragon began pawing at Azia's boot, and she frowned down at it. "You have wings," she said, in a tone that made me think she and the dragon had gone over this before. "You are perfectly capable of getting onto my lap on your own."

The dragon's tail whipped back and forth, and it stared up at her with its wide, jewel-like eyes. Azia rolled her eyes and bent to pick it up.

"May I?" Lilian said, leaning forward with her hand half-outstretched.

"Of course." A smile crept onto Azia's face. "This is Nyre, and she's a right little monster. Tell her *no* if she tries to nip at you."

The dragon blinked at Lilian as she carefully leaned forward. She let the creature sniff her hand, and then it butted her and shoved the top of its head under her fingernails. Lilian giggled, delighted, and scratched between the dragon's delicate little horns.

My wife's joy at making a new animal friend was utterly contagious. I loved watching her.

The dragon marched across Azia's lap and flapped

awkwardly over to Lilian. She leaned back to give it room, eyes enormous, and bit her lip in barely suppressed excitement.

"She likes you," Azia said approvingly.

The dragon curled up on Lilian's lap and started snorting like a contented cat trying to purr. A tiny tongue of fire emerged from its nose and disappeared into the air.

"I'm going to die," Lilian announced. "She's too cute."

"I'd like to learn more about our human guests, if I may," I said. "I'm sorry to be so blunt, but... Who *are* you? And what does it have to do with us?"

"We've been trying to figure that out," Azia said. "Now that we've met you, I think we might have found a clue."

They glanced between one another, but all their significant looks meant nothing to me. Finally, the redheaded woman leaned forward.

"We're here because something is wrong in our kingdoms," Blaise said. "It's been rough in Atlantice lately. I know people who are trying to make things better, but still, something isn't right. There's magic involved, but I don't actually know what's happening. Things are going wrong in Elder, too, but Castiel doesn't understand why."

"We decided to travel together in search of answers," Azia said. "My mother is dying. My adopted mother, anyway." She narrowed her strange eyes at me, and I felt like a sample under a microscope. "I'm adopted. We all are. We don't know if that's important."

"Given your eyes, I'd say it is," Lilian said mildly. She raised her eyebrows at me as if to say, *Well, isn't it obvious?*

"We're trying to find Azia's birth mother," Blaise

said. "And we're trying to find the woman who gave me to my parents. She had eyes like mine. Like ours."

I glanced again between their faces. Their eyes were uncanny.

"We think she has magic," Azia said.

I sat up straighter. "What kind of magic?"

Azia shrugged. "Who knows? Magic that might help the situation back in Draconis. And Atlantice. And Elder."

"And Floris," Castiel said, unsmiling. "My land is cursed. It appears yours might be, too."

Lilian and I exchanged glances. This was too much to be coincidence. I wished Hedley was in the room.

"They're all cursed," Blaise said. "My adopted mother was a mermaid once. She became human after she won her legs from a sea witch." Her lips curled in distaste. "But she's lost her legs. I need to figure out how to get them back. The woman that left me as a baby said I was a good luck charm," she added and pursed her lips. "Seems my luck's worn off."

"What else is happening in your kingdoms?" I said. A horrible thought struck me, and my stomach turned over. "The blight hasn't spread, has it?"

"No blight," Castiel said. "My kingdom was struck with a terrible disease. A madness that turned wolf shifters savage. I'm searching for a cure."

Azia let out a heavy sigh. "Something strange is happening to the magic in the world," she said, watching her dragon as Lilian scratched its nose. "Wicked witches seem to be gaining power if Blaise's recent experiences are anything to go by. Meanwhile, ordinary practitioners of magic seem powerless to stop whatever's happening."

My head spun. *Wicked witches.* Dame Gothel.

“We think our problems might have come from a witch, too,” I said.

These people were complete strangers. Caution battled with curiosity inside me; I couldn’t figure out how much I should tell them.

But we needed answers. These strangers might have them.

“Of course, they did,” Azia said dryly. “I’m not surprised.”

“Nothing would surprise me right now.” Blaise nodded at me. “Whatever’s happening, you’re part of it.”

I looked between the strangers, aware of our differences--and our glaring similarities.

“That’s why you came to talk to me,” I said. “My eyes. And my adoption.”

“We didn’t come for you, actually,” Azia said. She nodded at Lilian, who was still scratching the dragon’s head. The creature had fallen asleep, and the gentle sounds of its snoring provided a calm rhythm beneath our conversation. “We thought it might have something to do with you.”

“We had no idea we were arriving in the middle of your wedding,” Blaise added. “That was a strange surprise.”

“What were you hoping to find?” I said.

Azia and Castiel exchanged glances. Blaise shrugged.

“We didn’t know,” she said. “To be perfectly honest, none of us have any idea what we’re doing or why we’ve been drawn together.”

“We’re all on different missions.” Azia seemed to be the leader of this small group, inasmuch as it had a leader. “I’m attempting to find the woman who birthed me, whom I suspect might be able to help the situation in Draconis and heal my mother. Blaise is searching for someone who can restore the charm that gave her mermaid mother legs. And Castiel is trying to learn more about the curse that's plaguing his people."

"Or the person who cast it," Castiel said, a hint of threat running through his voice. "I'd settle for getting my hands on them."

Azia frowned but otherwise ignored the comment. "The three of us have problems, all related to magic. It made sense that we should travel together. Different problems, but the same problem. None of us know where we came from. We think our history...your history has something to do with everything. We just don't know what."

"There's safety in numbers," Castiel said. "Sometimes."

"You're ignoring the eyes thing," Blaise pointed out. "Doesn't anyone else think it's strange that we've all spent our lives thinking we have the most unique eyes of anyone we've ever met, and now, all of a sudden, there are *four* of us? And the woman who dropped me off as a baby had them, too?"

The sleeping baby dragon shoved its head deeper into Lilian's lap and stretched out one leg before relaxing again.

"I've had thoughts about this," I said slowly. "About what's happening in Floris and how it relates to me. My mentor--the man who all but raised me--said that something happened in Floris around the time I was left at the palace as a baby. He said the flowers grew like they'd never grown before, and it was like the whole kingdom was... blessed."

It sounded arrogant, phrased like that, but I pushed on anyway.

"I wonder if I maybe *did* bless the kingdom somehow. If we all did. Maybe the person who left us--maybe we were all adopted out by the same woman who gave Blaise to her parents." I looked around, but I didn't know these people well enough to read their expressions. "Am I crazy?"

Blaise's fiery eyebrows shot up. She pointed at Azia. "I told you. I said that."

"We can't jump to conclusions," Azia said more calmly. "I don't know anything about my birth family. Neither does Castiel."

"I usually try not to jump to conclusions," Lilian said.

Azia nodded. "Exactly."

"*However,*" Lilian continued, "there's jumping to conclusions, and then there's ignoring the evidence. Blaise is right; I've never seen eyes like yours on anyone else. It's possible you all came from somewhere else. There are undiscovered lands out beyond the edges of the sea; for all we know, they could be full of some golden-eyed race. But it also seems very possible--very *probable,* even--that you look like this because you have some kind of magic in common."

She gave me a significant look, and I knew she was silently urging me to tell them about the abilities I'd recently discovered.

I couldn't. Not yet. My magic was new and delicate, and telling them would almost be too personal.

Beyond that, it might force me into a decision I wasn't ready to make.

"Are you all in a hurry to move on?" I said.

Azia narrowed her eyes, clearly trying to interpret my words.

I waved a hand. "I'm not saying you need to go. I'm

just thinking that it sounds like we have a lot to talk about."

Lilian read my mind and jumped in. "You'd all be very welcome to stay at the palace for a few days. It sounds as if you could all use some rest and a few good meals, and we can provide both." She checked in with me, her blue eyes sharp and reading into every flicker of expression across my face. "Then perhaps we can continue this discussion."

Azia glanced at the other two. Blaise widened her eyes, urging Azia to agree, and Castiel rested his elbows on his knees and gave her one tense nod.

"We'd appreciate that," Azia said.

Lilian nudged the drowsing dragon on her lap, and it opened one eye as if it rather resented the interruption.

A tiny smile tugged at the corner of Azia's lips. "I can stay outdoors with her," she said.

"Nonsense," Lilian said. "We've got at least one chamber with tapestries I absolutely hate. I'll be thrilled if she burns them up."

"Thank you," Azia said. She was talking to Lilian, but her attention had caught on me.

I looked back at her, and my skin prickled at the familiarity of her gaze.

"But we can't stay long," Azia added. "Whatever this curse is, it seems to be spreading fast. I'd like to stay one step ahead if we can."

~

Once our guests were settled in their chambers, Lilian took my hand.

"I think we should go for a walk." She made it sound like an invitation, but I knew my wife. This was an order.

We wandered through the barren gardens as the sky darkened to dusk. A moon rose, a waning crescent as thin as the narrow side of a leaf. Lilian clutched my hand tightly in hers as we wandered in silence.

Neither of us seemed to choose a direction, but after a while, we found ourselves in front of the door to my private garden. I slipped the key from my pocket.

"You came prepared," Lilian observed.

I slid the key into the lock. "I always keep this key on me. I even had it in my pocket at the ceremony yesterday."

The door creaked open, and I guided Lilian inside with my hand on the small of her back.

"Never sure when you'll need to come tend your plants?" she asked.

"It's more of a talisman by now," I said. "When Remington was here, it became a reminder that I belonged here, whatever he said."

She turned and took my hand again. "I'm so sorry you had to go through all of that. I should have sent him packing the day he arrived."

I shook my head. "You didn't know."

"I knew soon enough."

I caught her up in a hug. "You can't blame yourself for him."

"I do, though," she said. "I should have known better. But I didn't, and you suffered."

"There's a metaphor here," I said. "Something about roses and thorns."

Lilian pulled back far enough to fix me with a stern frown. "Don't you dare bring up that stupid poem."

"What?" I said. "You don't want to have to memorize the entire epic Parable of Suffering? You don't *agree* with our dear tutor Barringtonia about how utterly *moving* those passages are?"

"I will murder you," she promised. "Just watch me."

"Yet joy cannot exist in life without its mirrors, pain, and strife," I began.

Lilian clamped a hand over my mouth. I continued reciting, though the words came out as a series of muffled hums.

"Deon," she said. "I will divorce you. I will divorce you, and then I will murder you, and *then* I will track down a necromancer to bring you back just so I can kill you again."

I fell silent, and she glared up at me. Her eyes betrayed her. They crinkled at the corners, and I knew she was half a breath away from dissolving into giggles.

She took her hand away and waited, eyebrows raised. I opened my mouth, and she tilted her head, warning me.

I couldn't help myself. "The rose that blooms without a thorn--"

Lilian threw herself at me, and I caught her and wrestled her back until I had her pinned against the wall. Her shriek of outrage immediately melted into laughter, and then into silence as my lips silenced hers. She kissed me back, her breath sweet and the heat of her body a shield against the slight evening chill.

"Divorce," she promised, voice soft with all the kisses. "Murder."

"I look forward to it."

She giggled, and her hand settled against my chest. The garden around us lay silent and empty, and it didn't matter, because it already held as much beauty as I'd ever hoped to coax from it.

"I don't want you to leave," she said suddenly. She wrapped her arms around my torso and buried her face in my chest.

I drew back, trying to see her face, but it was too dark to make out her features. "What do you mean, Lils? I'm not going anywhere."

She was silent for a long moment, then let out a heavy sigh. "You have to," she said. "Those people who showed up today. They want you to come with them."

"They didn't say that."

"They will."

I didn't want her to be right. But the thought had already started tugging at the edges of my mind while I tried fervently to ignore the pull.

"I just got you," I said. "I'm not going."

"You are. We have to save the kingdom."

"We can do that here," I said. "We're already making progress with the enchanted glass, and you and I have the mushrooms to study."

Lilian wouldn't look at me. She kept her cheek pressed up against my chest.

Gently, I touched her chin and nudged her face upward.

"I'm not going anywhere, Lils."

She swallowed. Tears shimmered in her eyes, but she fought to keep them from falling. "You have to go," she said. "This blight is bigger than us. It has something to do with those people, and that means it has something to do with you."

"There's no proof of that."

"There's *evidence,*" she said firmly.

A soft breeze floated through the garden. It didn't smell like Floris: not like flowers, or freshly cut grass, or herbs with their sharp medicinal notes. Its fragrance was of dull dirt and the sickly sweet aroma of decay.

"We *just* got married, Lils," I said.

"I know."

I wrapped my arms around her, trying to enclose her like I was a blanket thick and warm enough to shield her from the world.

She held on to me, too, tightly, as if, in spite of her words, she never planned to let me go.

21ST APRIL

"I had an idea," I said.

Lilian rolled over to face me. I'd known she was awake; she'd been staring out the window at the blue sky. Still, sleep clung to her features, softening her skin and weighing on her eyelids.

"Good morning to you, too," she said.

I kissed her. "Good morning, my love."

Off in the distance, in the corner of that patch of perfect blue, a hawk descended in a slow, gliding spiral. I watched it for a moment, then looked back at her.

"I had an idea," I said again. "About the mushrooms. I think we should try to grow two sets of them, one under enchanted glass and one without. They might end up coming out the same either way, but there might be subtle differences worth studying. And we should hire a specialist to help us propagate them. I've never grown mushrooms before. Hedley mentioned once that they can be finicky."

She blinked dreamily up at me. "I thought the palace grew all its own produce except for some grain."

"We buy our mushrooms from a man just outside Tulis," I said. "He's got a pretty big operation."

"Sounds like we should hire him." She wiggled under the blankets until she was nuzzled up against me, then closed her eyes and let out a contented sigh. "You should work on your magic, too."

I curled up next to her, spooning her body with mine. It was such a simple pleasure, being with her like this. I'd thought I belonged at the palace, but this--*this* was home.

"I'll keep at it," I promised. "Although I doubt it'll help much. Even magicians like Hemlock and Cypress haven't been able to heal blighted plants, and they've been studying since before I was born."

Lilian nudged her feet slightly backward so they tangled up with mine. "I don't mean for the blight," she said. "Having magic might be useful when you're traveling."

I didn't answer. Her words from last night still rang in my mind--not just her words, but the truth of them.

I nuzzled against the back of her head. Her soft golden hair floated around my face, smelling of magnolias and warmth. I could have stayed here forever with my nose buried in her hair.

"I don't want to leave you," I said.

She sighed softly. Then I realized the sigh hadn't been her at all, but one of her fluffy white puppies, which must have come to sleep at the foot of our bed sometime in the night.

I hadn't noticed the creature, small and half-buried in the cushions as it was.

As soon as I met the dog's eyes, its tail started wagging frantically, and it trotted clumsily up our bodies. Lilian huffed as the dog's paw landed heavily on her side, then rolled back over to let the puppy lick her face.

"How does your paw weigh so much?" she asked, roughing up the dog's ears. "How does that work? You don't look that big, but you're heavy as a horse when you jump on me like that."

The dog wagged its tail, delighted by the sheer honor of having its mistress's attention.

I knew exactly how it felt.

"You have to go, Deon," Lilian said. Her eyes were sad, but she smiled anyway. "I don't like it. I'll never enjoy being away from you. But this isn't a coincidence. Something's happening, and I need you to go figure out what. It might save our kingdom."

Our kingdom. It was ours, now--not just the land I lived in and loved, but now the land I had agreed to bear responsibility for.

I had promised to love Lilian. But I had also promised to help her bear the weight of her responsibilities as a princess, and someday queen.

"Mama and Papa would never allow me to run off," Lilian said. "And anyway, I can't be away from Mama right now. But you can. Maybe you can figure out what's going on. You and those people who look just like you."

I laughed. "They don't look a thing like me."

"That's true," she said. "And yet, they do. It's not just the eyes. There's something, I don't know, the *same* about all of you. Even aside from the problem of the blight, you owe it to yourself to figure out the magic that connects you to them."

"I've never needed to know where I come from," I said. "Or, at least, I didn't until yesterday."

I couldn't forget the way my skin had prickled when Azia had met my eyes. There was something within us that resonated at the same frequency--something deep, like the thread of magic at the core of a flower's stem.

"Go learn whatever you can," she said. "And then come back and tell me everything, because I'm dying to know."

I scratched the top of the dog's head. It closed its eyes and collapsed on top of Lilian, overwhelmed at having two people loving it at once. Lilian raised her eyebrows at the pup, then glanced up at me and giggled.

"I'll write you every day," I said. "Plus, telegrams if I see something I can't wait to tell you about."

"Cute animals?" she suggested.

"Of course. And good food."

"Collect recipes for the cook," she said. "When you get home, we'll have a feast, and I'll taste your travels."

"I wish you could come with me."

"So do I. Maybe we'll meet somewhere along the road," she said. "I'm sure I can arrange short trips here and there."

"You'll have to because I can't stand the thought of being away from you."

I'd never been away from Lilian, aside from her occasional diplomatic visits and family trips to the coast. But I had a feeling this journey would take weeks, maybe months.

"Even five minutes away from you feels like a long time right now," I admitted.

“I know.” She sighed. “I missed you yesterday when you went to go change your clothes.”

“We’re pathetic.”

I leaned across the dog to kiss her. The pup wriggled its way between us, trying to join in on the affection. Lilian laughed, which only seemed to excite the creature more, and I watched as joy and amusement colored Lilian’s face with shades of rosy pink.

“I wouldn’t change it,” I said. “Not for the world.”

We’d arranged last night to have a late breakfast with our guests. I’d wanted to learn more about them, and I’d sent a last-minute invitation to Hedley and the king and queen. They’d been the ones to suspect everything in the kingdom was happening thanks to a witch, and I hoped they’d have some information to share that could somehow illuminate our guests’ various quests.

The king and queen had declined with apologies, although the queen had included a hastily scribbled note asking for Lilian and me to please stop by her chambers this afternoon to answer questions about our guests. Hedley, however, arrived early, bearing a newspaper under his arm.

“I’ll be glad to meet your new friends,” he said, as we walked into the small parlor together.

Lilian and the queen used this space sometimes for breakfasts and teas with nobles. Cushioned wicker furniture covered with bright floral cushions sat in a cluster, spaced to encourage friendly conversation. The room had once been filled with potted flowers and vines hanging from birdcages, giving it the air of a conservatory in springtime. Now the birdcages hung empty, and the only flowers were the ones on the patterned cushions. Still, the sunshine made the space pleasant, and the trays of hot food spread out buffet-style along the windows were inviting enough.

Lilian urged Hedley to fill his plate, and then she and I sat to await the rest of our guests. They arrived exactly on time, Azia in the lead looking as though she'd already been up for several hours, and Blaise trailing behind and visibly suppressing a yawn. Azia and Castiel had brought their animals, and Hedley observed the wolf and dragon with interest.

The guests returned his interest, giving him either sidelong glances or brazen stares, depending on their dispositions. When we were all seated with food on our laps, I made the introductions.

"This is Sheldon Hedley," I said. "He's a gardener who's been working on how to fight the blight. He was the first person to suggest to me that magic might be involved, and I thought he might be able to help us figure out what's going on and what our next move should be."

"*Our* next move?" Azia inquired, the coolness of her voice belying her clear interest.

I cleared my throat. Lilian put an encouraging hand on my knee and nodded at me to go ahead.

Sticks and stones, the world would be dark without her at my side. I said a silent prayer that whatever adventure I was about to embark on would be worth the sacrifice.

"You all seem to be on a mission to find information," I said. "We're working here in Floris to combat the blight, but I think we all agree it would be better not to have a blight to fight with in the first place. If you're willing, I'd like to join you for a while and see if we can track this thing to its source."

"If it's a curse that affects our kingdoms in different ways, it stands to reason that someone *cast* that curse," Lilian said.

"We agree," Castiel said. "I hoped we'd find that person in Floris, but it seems you're as lost as we are."

"We thought a woman named Dame Gothel might be to blame," I said. "Maybe she is, and maybe she's not, but we could start there."

Hedley cleared his throat, and we all turned to look at him. I furrowed my eyebrows in question.

He picked up the newspaper he'd brought along. I'd assumed it was this morning's edition, but as he unfurled it, the paper crinkled as if it had been sitting somewhere for a long time. The edges curled, tinged slightly with yellow.

He looked through the pages, muttering to himself, and then he pulled a sheaf out from the center.

"I put in a request with the Central Archives at Urbis." He glanced around. "I don't suppose Deon mentioned that the world changed when he arrived?" he said. "Only for the better."

Blaise speared a rogue grape with her fork, and the tines scraped against the plate. "My parents said something like that about me. Called me a good luck charm."

Azia didn't say anything, and Castiel's jaw seemed to tighten slightly.

"I did some research into Deon's birth," Hedley said. "I thought it might provide us with clues."

I froze, waiting to hear that he'd learned about my birth parents, or that he knew where I'd come from originally.

"I didn't find anything," Hedley said.

Something deep inside me, a sense of curiosity that had lived buried and ignored for years, seemed to deflate. I'd told Lilian the truth: I hadn't cared that much about where I'd come from. Not until now.

"I did, however, discover evidence of yet another person around his age being adopted by a prominent family in Aboria," Hedley said. He held the newspaper out to the center of our little group. "By the king and queen, as it happens."

Castiel was the first to take the paper. He scanned the article, his gaze passing quickly over the text. His face betrayed very little, but at one point, his eyebrows twitched.

"Look at the bit about the eyes," he said, handing the paper to Azia.

She read, too, announcing the important bits aloud as she went. "The king and queen of Aboria adopted an infant. This must have been, what?" She glanced at the top of the newspaper. "Eighteen years ago."

Blaise leaned forward with interest.

"The child's origins were unknown," Azia continued, skimming down the page. "And members of the court have been 'astonished at the infant's unique eyes, which bear beautiful golden rings.'"

"That was the part that interested me," Hedley said. "I'd never seen eyes like Deon's. His note last night mentioned that you all have them, too. I see now it was no exaggeration."

"Where do you think they come from?" Azia said, observing him closely.

Hedley held out his hands, gesturing at emptiness. "I'd guess magic if I had to choose."

He leaned back and looped his thumb around his suspenders.

“Speaking of which,” he added, tone matter-of-fact. “How many of you have magical abilities?”

They all exchanged cautious looks.

No one else seemed eager to volunteer that information. But I’d given this some thought. If I was going to travel with these people, they deserved to know what I could do. I took a deep breath. “I have plant magic. I can control them a little bit, make them move, and things like that. I also seem to have the ability to grow plants even under difficult conditions.”

“He’s being modest,” Lilian said. “He maintained a beautiful private garden all through the blight, and if you saw the Gilded Lilies at our wedding ceremony, those were his. He bred them over a period of just a few years, and they’re magnificent.”

I shot her a grateful look. I didn’t so much care about the praise of the rest of the world, at least, now that my reputation had been rescued from Remington’s attempts to smear it. Hearing Lilian call anything I did “magnificent,” though, was everything.

“I can breathe underwater,” Blaise said, shifting in her seat. “I’m beginning to be able to control water too. It’s pretty new, but I’m working on it.”

“I’m a shifter,” Castiel said. “I can go from human to animal form, and I’ve got a lot of control when I do it.”

“Which animal does your shifter form take?” I asked. I’d heard of shifters. We didn’t have them in Floris, but his ability wasn’t as unique as Blaise’s or mine.

“All of them,” he shrugged. “I can turn into any animal I want.”

Well, that was different.

We all looked to Azia. She pressed her lips together and glanced down at the little creature curled up between her boots. “I can talk to dragons.”

Lilian leaned forward. "That's why she's so well-behaved!" she said delighted.

Azia permitted herself a grin. "She's a shifter too, but I'm not sure she is that well-behaved. She prefers her dragon form."

Hedley considered each of us in turn. Thoughts were forming in his head, and it wouldn't do to ask what they were until he was ready to share.

I looked around at the others, too. I'd thought I was special for having the fledgling powers I did. But I couldn't talk to *dragons*.

"My abilities are pretty new," I said, silently hoping Lilian hadn't oversold me. "I'm just learning to control them, and I definitely don't have what it takes to fight something like the blight."

Azia contemplated this. She set her empty plate on the table between us all and leaned forward, resting her elbows on her knees. "When did your powers show up?" she said.

"This year."

"Mine, too." She pursed her lips, eyes narrowed in thought. "After I turned eighteen."

"Same," Blaise said.

Castiel nodded.

That was another point of commonality, then. A thread tying us together, a strand that, combined with the others, had the beginnings of a powerful bond.

"This person in Aboria is eighteen, too," Azia said. "I'll bet they have abilities. Ones that manifested this year."

"That brings us to five," Blaise said. "There are four people out in the world who are just like me."

"More," Castiel said.

I frowned at him, but he was staring at the table in

front of him, his brooding face full of thought.

"There have to be more," he said. "We all ran into each other as a matter of chance. But if we were to start *looking,* as Mr. Hedley did, who's to say how many people are like us out there? People who don't even know they're like us, because maybe their powers haven't manifested."

"Maybe we're just a side effect of the curse," Blaise suggested. "Maybe something about it affected us, like how some people are allergic to food, and others aren't."

Azia shook her head. "I've had these eyes since I was born."

"Then maybe the eyes are just a way to let you know who's going to be allergic to curses," Blaise said, sounding a little impatient.

The entire concept sounded absurd, especially phrased like that. But if this past month had taught me anything, it was that something being wild or strange or impossible was no reason to dismiss it.

"I guess the only thing left to do is confirm our theory," I said.

Stinging nettles, I didn't want to be the one to suggest it. I didn't want to leave Lilian or the incredible miracle of our life together.

But she reached for my hand, and the warmth of her skin gave me strength.

"We need to go to Aboria and find this person," I said. "If our number five has powers that started this year, and if something terrible is happening in Aboria--well, that's a kind of answer, isn't it?"

"It's not *the* answer," Castiel said. "It doesn't tell us who's responsible for all this."

"But maybe the royal family of Aboria will know," Azia said. "And if not, we won't be any farther behind than we are now."

"We need to leave soon," Castiel said.

"Today," Azia agreed.

"We just got here!" Blaise said. "I'm not done appreciating that feather bed in my quarters."

"There will be time for feather beds after our mothers are whole," Azia said.

Blaise didn't seem to like it, but she sighed and nodded.

I couldn't go today. I couldn't leave Lilian behind this quickly. And what would happen to the gardens? To the greenhouses, and the mushrooms, and the solutions we were chasing together?

Lilian's hand tightened on mine, and she used one of her fingers to press my ring more firmly against my skin.

It was a clear reminder: We were married. We had found a happily ever after for ourselves. And now, we owed it to everyone else in the kingdom to try to find one for them, too.

"I'll arrange your train tickets," Lilian said. She cleared her throat. "Aboria is large, and there's no guarantee the royal family will be home when you arrive, so I'll reserve lodgings for you, too. There's a hotel I quite like near the capital city that should give you some privacy and allow you to go back and forth from the castle as you need." Her tone was brisk and polite, but her hand squeezed mine so tightly, the bones felt as if they might crunch together. "You'll enjoy yourselves if you haven't been to Aboria before. It's beautiful."

Nowhere on earth could be as beautiful as right here. I squeezed Lilian's hand back, and took a deep breath, steeling myself for the tasks that lay ahead.

~

The others stood on the driveway, shuffling around as they handed their belongings to the driver. Lilian and I stood some distance away, stealing the last few moments for ourselves.

She pressed an envelope into my hand. “It’s from Mama and Papa,” she said. “Money and a note wishing you luck. I promised to keep them updated, so if there’s anything you don’t want me to pass on, be sure to tell me.”

I leaned down until my lips grazed her ear. “There will absolutely be parts of my letters I don’t want you to share, but I trust you’ll be able to identify those passages on your own.”

Lilian flushed and grinned. “I can’t wait to read them.” Her smile faded, and she flung her arms around my neck and held on tight. “Stars, Deon, I’m going to miss you.”

“I’m going to miss you too, Lils.” I kissed every bit of her I could reach, from the warm hollows of her neck and the little dip behind her ear to the curve of her cheekbone. I saved up the kisses in my mind, hoping I’d have enough to pull one from my memory for each night we were apart. “I love you. I love you so much. I always have, and I always will, and I still can’t believe you’re my wife.”

“Make sure you eat,” she said, leaning back to look at me, but keeping her arms twined around my neck.

“Have I ever skipped a meal?”

She acknowledged this with a wry grin. “And make sure you *sleep.* And be sure to take care of yourself and write to me and be safe and don’t get into any trouble, and *please,* darling, if you find the person responsible for all this, *please* don't go chasing after them without backup. You're the Prince of Floris now. You can summon an army."

I glanced at the others. They were almost done arranging their things, and Azia was watching me.

"I think I might keep that bit quiet," I said. "At least some of the time."

"That might be best. You won't need to tell the king and queen of Aboria, though," she added. "They were literally here two days ago for our wedding."

I frowned. "Why didn't you say?"

Lilian shrugged. "No use, they left right after the ceremony. The king wasn't feeling well. That's part of why I arranged lodgings: I'm not sure they'll be up for visitors when you get there."

I kissed her forehead. "You're prepared for everything. How am I supposed to do this without you?"

"You won't be doing anything without me," she said. "We'll write each other. You can keep me in your pocket."

"I wish that was true," I said. "You'd be very cute pocket-sized."

She smirked. "I'm cute regular-sized, thank you."

I kissed her and then kissed her again. She clung to me, and the scent of strawberries and magnolias floated around me like a cloud. If there was a heaven, it felt like this.

Someone cleared their throat. I pulled away from Lilian. Azia stood not far away, politely not looking quite at us. "I'm sorry, we have to go," she said. "If we miss the train, we're stuck here another night."

"I'll be right over."

Azia left to take her place in the carriage. I bent to

engulf Lilian in an embrace. I wished I could be stuck here another night. And then another, and another.

From his seat on the palace steps, Hedley watched us. He gave me a nod, full of promises: to take care of the palace grounds until I returned, to create as much enchanted glass as he could manage, and to help Lilian learn everything she could about the mushrooms that seemed immune to the disease that had ravaged the rest of the country.

He always believed in me, from the first time I'd toddled after him in the garden to the moment a few hours ago when he'd pulled me aside and told me that he knew I would figure out what was happening in Floris and fix it. He trusted me, he'd said, and I carried his faith with me like a talisman.

"We're going to be fine," Lilian promised. Her voice caught. We both did our best to pretend it hadn't.

"Of course, we will," I said. "We've survived a blight and Remington. What's a few weeks apart?"

"Exactly. Write to me."

"I will. I love you."

"I love you, too."

"Lils?" I glanced down. Our arms were still around one another. "I can't let go."

"You have to," she said. "Because I can't."

I grinned. "Married two days and you're already making me do the dirty jobs."

"I've always made you do the dirty jobs, garden boy," she said.

Slowly, feeling as if I was tearing myself in two by doing it, I stepped back. She closed her eyes and took a deep, shaky breath, then opened them again and pasted on a broad smile. It was the most ridiculously fake expression I'd ever seen on her face, and I loved her for the effort and loved her even more for the failure.

I climbed into the carriage with the others. Blaise offered me a sympathetic smile. "I know it's hard," she said. "I left someone in Atlantice, too."

I smiled back. She was virtually a stranger. They all were. But somehow, being in this carriage with them felt right.

Azia knocked on the roof of the carriage. The driver called something to the horses, and the wheels creaked as they leapt into motion.

"What time is the train?" I inquired.

"We aren't going by train," Azia said. "I just didn't want to tell you in case you changed your mind."

"We've been traveling by foot mostly." Blaise rolled her eyes. "Incognito, you know."

"We'll take this carriage to the local town, and I'll try and arrange some other, less conspicuous form of transport. We are all royalty, and I have a dragon in tow. We can't travel by public transport."

"It's not so bad now that the weather is warming up," Castiel said.

I leaned out the window. A sliver of a moon was rising over the castle towers. In front of them, Lilian stood, her shoulders thrown back, and her head held high. She blew a kiss, and I waved, and I watched her until I'd passed through the castle gates and into the first moments of my next adventure.

ELIANA

DAUGHTER OF THE PRINCESS WHO SPUN GOLD

GRAB THE NEXT BOXSET IN THE KINGDOM OF FAIRYTALES SERIES

MEET THE TEAM

The Kingdom of Fairytales Series was a team effort. Below are the people that made it possible:

EQP Management: Rhi Parkes & J.A. Armitage

Our authors: J.A. Armitage, Audrey Rich, B. Kristin McMichael, Emma Savant, Jennifer Ellision, Scarlett Kol, Rose Castro, Margo Ryerkerk, Zara Quentin, Laura Greenwood and Anne Stryker.

Our Editor
Rose Lipscomb

Our Beta Team
Nadine Peterse-Vrijhof
Diane Major
Kalli Bunch
Stephanie Woodwood

Our Proof Reader
Tina Merritt

And to all the wonderful people who loved the world we created and reviewed our stories.
Thank you

READING ORDER

SEASON ONE
SLEEPING BEAUTY
Queen of Dragons
Heiress of Embers
Throne of Fury
Goddess of Flames

SEASON TWO
LITTLE MERMAID
Queen of Mermaids
Heiress of the Sea
Throne of Change
Goddess of Water

SEASON THREE
RED RIDING HOOD
King of Wolves
Heir of the Curse
Throne of Night
God of Shifters

SEASON FOUR
RAPUNZEL
King of Devotion
Heir of Thorns
Throne of Enchantment
God of Loyalty

SEASON FIVE
RUMPELSTILTSKIN
Queen of Unicorns
Heiress of Gold
Throne of Sacrifice
Goddess of Loss

SEASON SIX
BEAUTY AND THE BEAST
King of Beasts
Heir of Beauty
Throne of Betrayal
God of Illusion

SEASON SEVEN
ALADDIN
Queen of the Sun
Heiress of Shadows
Throne of the Phoenix
Goddess of Fire

SEASON EIGHT
CINDERELLA
Queen of Song
Heiress of Melody
Throne of Symphony
Goddess of Harmony

SEASON NINE
ALICE IN WONDERLAND
Queen of Clockwork
Heiress of Delusion
Throne of Cards
Goddess of Hearts

SEASON TEN
WIZARD OF OZ
King of Traitors
Heir of Fugitives
Throne of Emeralds
God of Storms

SEASON ELEVEN
SNOW WHITE
Queen of Reflections
Heiress of Mirrors
Throne of Wands
Goddess of Magic

SEASON TWELVE
PETER PAN
Queen of Skies
Heiress of Stars
Throne of Feathers
Goddess of Air

SEASON THIRTEEN
URBIS

Kingdom of Royalty
Kingdom of Power
Kingdom of Fairytales
Kingdom of Ever After

BOXSETS

AZIA
BLAISE
CASTIEL
DEON
ELIANA
FALLON
GAIA
HALIA
IVY
JAKON
KELIS
LYRIC
URBIS

www.ingramcontent.com/pod-product-compliance
Lightning Source LLC
Chambersburg PA
CBHW020354310726
48979CB00015B/2589/J